A HOUSE DIVIDED

A HOUSE DIVIDED

A NOVEL BY
FREDRICK BARTON

UNIVERSITY OF
NEW ORLEANS
PRESS

Library of Congress Cataloguing-in-Publication data
Barton, Fredrick,
A House Divided
p. cm.
ISBN 0-9728143-0-2 (hardback)

FIRST PRINTING

Jacket design, text design and cover photograph by Mark R. Bacon
Printed in the United States of America on acid-free paper.

University of New Orleans Publishing
2000 Lakeshore Drive
New Orleans, LA 70148

Acknowledgments

I am indebted to the William Faulkner Society, its founders Rosemary James and Joseph DeSalvo, and novel category judge Carol Dawson for awarding this book their coveted prize. Selections from *A House Divided* were earlier published in slightly different form in *The Double Dealer Redux, Cultural Vistas* and *The Louisiana English Journal*. My thanks to those publications for giving this material its first exposure. My thanks also to that fine writer Greg Garrett and Baylor University's Art and Soul Literary Conference for the several occasions to read from this work as it was being written and revised.

I also want to thank my friends and family for their assistance, direct and indirect. Specifically, I am grateful to Ed Uehling, Arlin Meyer, John Cooke, Jim Knudsen, Elizabeth Leblanc, Joeddie Harris, Lee Harris, Dana Barton, Tim Colenback and Liv Blumer, all of whom read this book in manuscript and provided me much in the way of insight, advice and encouragement.

I must also acknowledge the support of my colleagues in the University of New Orleans College of Liberal Arts office, Susan Krantz, Merrill Johnson, Charlotte Cannon, Mandy Meyers, Bobby Palfrey and Libby Arceneaux for their day-to-day camaraderie and fellowship.

Especial thanks to my writer friends Richard Ford, Bob Butler, Betsy Cox, Hal Crowther, Connie May Fowler, Curtis Wilkie, Lynne Barrett, Laurie O'Brien, and Jim White for their example. Others deserving my gratitude include my UNO writing colleagues John Gery, Joanna Leake, Randy Bates, Kay Murphy and Carol Gelderman and my many students, too numerous to name, for all of you, more than you know.

Thanks also to my Valparaiso University classmates Mark Schwehn, Peter Lutze, David Nord and Mel Piehl for the incredible gift of their lifelong friendship and to Valparaiso faculty members John Feaster, Meredith "Buzz" Berg, Al Meyer, Renu Juneja, John Ruff, Gail Eifrig, John Paul and Margaret Franson, fellow family members in my spiritual home.

And thanks to my UNO brothers and sisters, Bob Cashner, Jim Meza, Joe King, Tim Ryan, John Crisp, Russ Trahan, Bobby Dupont, Alan Artibise, Sharon Mader, Greg O'Brien, Lou Paradise, Don Pekarek, Bob Brown, Norma Grace, Linda Robison, Florence Andre, Sharon Gruber, Rachel Kincaid, Bobby Eason, Dennis McSeveney, Jack McLean, fellow soldiers in the field.

Especial thanks to Elizabeth Williams for her imagination and daring and to Mark Bacon, Florence Jumonville, Jennifer Spence, Kerri Barton and Gabrielle Gautreaux for their invaluable assistance with this book.

And, as ever, my humble gratitude to the great Will Campbell for his inspiration and treasured embrace. Most of all, and as always, thanks to Joyce Markrid Dombourian without whom little that I might be said to have accomplished would have ever been dared.

The end of man is knowledge, but there is one thing he can't know. He can't know whether knowledge will save him or kill him. He will be killed, all right, but he can't know whether he is killed because of the knowledge which he has got or because of the knowledge which he hasn't got and which if he had it, would save him.

ROBERT PENN WARREN

All The King's Men

For all have sinned and come short of the glory of God.

Romans 3:23

prologue

I F BENJAMIN WATSON HAD BEEN A STRANGER, he could never have gotten close enough. But he was hardly a stranger. He had been a staff member in one capacity or another since the summer of the Louisiana voter-registration drive, since the summer of 1963. He had been with them, if not earlier than all the others, then with few exceptions, longer. And he had been with them for the purest of reasons. Ben was a true believer, an instinctive self-sacrificer. He flocked to their light on the wings of genuine goodness. He answered their call with a heart full of decency and hope. He became a soldier in their movement, motivated solely by the dictates of his conscience.

I had been with them always, of course, from the days of the bus boycott and even earlier, when the movement was but a dream, a shared conspiracy of faith. But unlike Ben, who came to them out of personal calling, I came as a matter of family. I came as a child before I understood. I came as a teenager when the allure was primarily one of excitement. Later, when I was old enough to understand more truly, I did come, like so many others, in awe and with devotion, gladly and even bravely. But even then, I came as a matter of expectation. Denied an opportunity for real choice, I came as a matter of blood.

My father was Paul Jefferson Caldwell, the man the press often designated as "George Washington Brown's white right arm." In the 1950s my father and Dr. Brown kept a strategic distance in public. "It gives me more leverage," my father explained at the time, "a moment longer before I'm dismissed as being a 'nigger lover.'" My father's close friend and longtime movement ally, Edward James "Preacher" Martin, added in his own inimitable fashion: "And it keeps the good Reverend Dr. Brown from having to defend his resident whitey to every loud mouth who imagines himself a Mau Mau warrior." But by the 1960s my father's activities in Dr. Brown's organization were widely known.

My father was part of the beginning, of course. He tried to rally support among his fellow white ministers during the Baton Rouge bus boycott. Eventually my father and Dr. Brown evolved from mere allies into true friends. Together they fought Jim Crow in the dusty hamlets and nascent cities of the South and later fought economic and housing discrimination in the crowded ghettos of the North. My father bolstered Dr. Brown's determination to risk his organization's momentum with a denunciation of America's involvement in Indochina. Our collective memory of Dr. Brown's magnificent oratory is so vivid, it is often forgotten what a gifted speaker my father was, as well. In the early and mid-sixties he was in charge of college recruiting. And during those heady years he piqued the consciences of ten thousand Northern college students in a hundred different speeches as he organized volunteers for the summer voter-registration drives.

And through it all I was there with them. I was there before it began, with my mother Billye, in her veiled black straw hat. Surrounded by a multitude of moist black faces, I was there, short-legged on the rough-hewn, slatted back pew of that revival meeting in the rural church Dr. Brown pastored in north central Louisiana near the tiny town of Liberty Hill. I was there with the horseflies flitting against the lights and the mosquitoes buzzing against all the shining faces. I was there, squirming and slapping at my bare legs and neck, watching the adults fan themselves with pictures of a beatific, long-haired white Jesus glued to wooden sticks like those the doctor used to check my sore throat. Of course I was there, a little brown-haired boy in a nice, short-pantsed, blue suit and faithfully polished Buster Brown shoes, stirring a whirl of air through the sawdust that covered the packed dirt floor by incessantly kicking legs too short to reach the ground. That's when my father and Dr. Brown met, that Sunday of hymns and prayers and amens and the strange sound of clapping hands in church, that warm, sunny afternoon of dinner on the grounds, of fried chicken, potato salad, cold buttermilk, banana cream pie and homemade ice cream. That's when the conspiracy began. And I was there.

I was there, too, a year later, with Dr. Brown's son Robert, sharing my fire truck and his toy soldiers, playing on the waxed wooden floor in my family's apartment in New Orleans' Desire Project back when white people actually lived there. Like Robert, I was too small to be concerned with, and I was very young, but I was still somehow attuned to the novelty of Negroes in our living room. I listened with wide eyes as the big-voiced black man complimented my mother's coffee before my father banished her to the kitchen along with Dr. Brown's wife Annette; I listened while the two preachers shared their jokes and hatched their plans before the intent incomprehension of their preschool sons.

When I was finally old enough to be of some use, I was still with them, recruiting high school friends to help with banners or join in a march. As a badge of loyalty, I wanted to take a year off college to be with them all the time, but only my 2-S deferment protected me from the draft, so it was imperative that I stay in school. Such a confrontation was never necessary, but it is unlikely that my mother would have allowed me to interrupt my college years no matter what I desired. And I don't know what would have happened to my scholarship, because only my abilities as a basketball player enabled me to attend Tulane, which my family couldn't have afforded. So it was no doubt best that I stayed in school. But always I was with them in the summers. And I was with them whenever my school schedule allowed. And that was my privilege.

I finished college in that awful year of 1968, in the bloody spring when both Martin Luther King and Robert Kennedy were murdered and a brightness went out of the world. But Dr. Brown and my father soldiered on, as indeed they were called to do. And so I soldiered with them, a conscientious-objector volunteer with their organization, a full corporal in the movement they headed. I was a gofer, a typist, a telephone operator, an apprentice organizer. I was proud that my father had turned over to me the job of mustering the marshals for the march on the draft-induction center that night. And I had spent all day going over every step of our preparations, first with my ten lieutenants, then with the hundred volunteers whose job it was to lead in hymns, lobby for calm and offer their bodies as buffers should trouble arise with police or counter-demonstrators.

When I finished my meetings, I hurried by our apartment in a shotgun double on Dante Street to pick up my wife Glenda, who was still suffering from morning sickness and had spent the day in bed. She wasn't quite ready. I found her at the bathroom sink putting on lipstick. She had her marvelous mane of thick brown hair pulled back with a big black elastic headband, and as I watched her mash her lips together and then blot them on a square of tissue, I felt the same surge of desire for her that I had felt the first day I met her more than four years earlier.

Fueled by nightmares of her being crushed in the crowd or jabbed in her rounding stomach by the nightstick of a berserk cop, I had encouraged her to sit out this demonstration. But she'd have none of it, naturally, so I arrived late at the big church where the speeches were being given. As we'd anticipated, the crowd was much too large to fit inside and spilled over into the vestibule, out onto the veranda, down the paired exterior staircases and onto the lawn and sidewalk in front of the church building.

Anxious to hear my father's speech, I shouldered a path for Glenda through the throng of demonstrators listening to the loudspeakers we had fastened above the church doors. We worked our way to the rear of the building, went up the back stairs from the Sunday School rooms and entered the sanctuary to the right of the rostrum. We were stopped at the doorway by a security guard who'd been hired for just this purpose, but he recognized me and let us in. We had expected no place to sit and found none, but our friend Preacher Martin, dressed as usual in cowboy boots, jeans, T-shirt and buckskin jacket, was holding standing space for us against the wall along the outside aisle. The huge throng of people inside the church had defeated the air-conditioning system, and Preacher's bald pate shone with perspiration.

My father was just being introduced. I could see him sitting on a folding chair behind the speaker at the microphone. Next to him, in the ornate mahogany, vault-backed pulpit chair, sat George Washington Brown. The two of them had their heads together, sharing a comment before my father rose to speak. Dr. Brown, his close-cropped black Afro glinting a little in the light, was wearing his usual conservative charcoal-gray suit, starched shirt and solid red tie. My father, influenced somewhat by Preacher, had turned more casual in recent years. He wore pressed jeans, a white Oxford-cloth shirt, open at the neck, and a blue seersucker blazer. It was said that he looked a little like Gregory Peck, though he wasn't as tall. His hair had turned a steel gray now, but it was full, and he had let it grow. It fell over his horn-rimmed glasses as he turned his head to catch a last word from his friend. Then there was a thunder of applause from both inside the auditorium and out, and my father squeezed Dr. Brown's shoulder and strode to the pulpit, arms raised and with a beaming face, his slight limp all but unnoticeable.

I first noticed Ben at the door as my father began to thank his introducer, the members of the church in which we were meeting and those in attendance for their crucial support. The same security guard who had stopped me had stopped Ben, too. I could hear the muffled ejaculations of their discussion and briskly moved to inform the guard that it was okay to let Ben in.

"Where's Faye?" I whispered to Ben, referring to his wife.

"Sick," Ben grunted. He stayed near the front as I rejoined Preacher and Glenda.

Ben Watson resembled many young whites who had come early to the movement, volunteers my father dubbed "Hemingways" because they were all so earnest. Ben himself was an especially intense and pious fellow from America's fertile heartland. He had graduated from Northwestern in 1964 with a bachelor's degree in comparative religion. Ultimately planning to attend a Presbyterian seminary, Ben had first worked with the movement's voter-registration drive in Louisiana the summer after his junior year in college. When he finished school and was excused from the draft because of poor eyesight, he signed up full time, arriving at movement headquarters in New Orleans after a trip to visit, briefly and unhappily, with Faye Robinson's parents. Ben and Faye were the first interracial couple I knew.

I had a special spot in my heart for Ben. He'd once been my canvass captain. And he'd never shown the slightest resentment in later days as I'd been admitted to the strategy sessions of the inner sanctum and drawn assignments of responsibility that might have gone to him. Unlike me, I think, Ben undertook his movement work with such ideological purity that his ego never insisted upon the kind of insider's role that mine surely did. I admired Ben for that. And I trusted his goodness the way I did that of few men on earth.

Because Faye was Glenda's best friend in New Orleans, the four of us socialized on a regular basis; still, I can't say I actually liked Ben. I never really felt comfortable with him, no matter how much I admired his sincerity and devotion. I shared my father's assessment of him as "Un-Ben-Dable." My father and Dr. Brown teased all of us with deliberately deflationary nicknames. Dr. Brown's son, Robert, was derided as "Rules" because of his imperious manner. I was called "Gunner" after my fondness for shooting in basketball. Though I preferred the moniker "Mr. Automatic," which I'd gotten in my junior year of high school when I made seventy-eight consecutive free throws, the movement crowd called me "Gunner" or "Tommy Gun" precisely because they knew I didn't like it.

Ben was called "Un-Ben-Dable" behind his back and "Clock" or "Tick Tock" to his face. My father said he was as dependable as a Timex, which also became one of his nicknames. But he was so damned dogged and so humorless. And he was so unable to change with the times. His commitment never waned, but he never adjusted as the mid-sixties gave way to the tumult of '67 and '68. His abstinence and his early bedtime were incessant reproaches to the various debauches of the younger staff. He'd sit around drinking 7-Up while the rest of us sucked on quarts of Jax. And later when Robert had introduced us to grass, Ben would set his face in an attitude of ignored pain, as if he were about to get a shot at the doctor's office. Before long he would briskly excuse himself, his disapproval, though silent, nonetheless very clear. We snorted about Ben's unvoiced reproof, but many of us, myself included, worried semi-consciously that his purity was a model we ought to consider more seriously.

But on the whole, and this is what I want to communicate most, Ben was one of us. He'd been in the movement far longer than many whose personal fear of the draft had driven them there by the summer of '68. The credentials of his commitment were unassailable. He was a "Hemingway," he was too "stiff," and he was too "serious." But he was one of us. And none of us questioned his loyalty for a fleeting second.

When I'd wedged myself back against the wall between Glenda and Preacher, I glanced again at Ben. The late sixties had swept in without notifying him. A jock all my life, I'd worn my hair in a flattop until my junior year in college, but now my hair was shoulder-length and pulled into a ponytail. Ben still wore a crew cut and the same black plastic glasses he'd owned when I first met him. His trousers were always either blue or gray and never jeans.

He had a fondness for plaid shirts buttoned at the neck.

Ben was staring up at my father with the rapt attention he always focused on the movement speakers. He had confided in me once that he thought my father was almost as powerful a speaker as Dr. Brown, which was the equivalent of saying someone was almost as good a basketball player as Bill Russell. My father was working the crowd in his own special, ironic style, entertaining them with his drawled wit, but always leading them toward a place of enhanced commitment to our merged goals of Brotherhood and Peace.

"We've been chanting, 'Hey, hey, LBJ, how many kids did you kill today,'" my father proclaimed. "And I've got no problems with that. But while we're vilifying him, which he deserves, we might ought to pause to thank him too. Yessir, Lyndon, you didn't mean to, but maybe you've brought us together faster than we might have gotten together otherwise. All of you here tonight look about yourselves, black and white sitting together in this Southern city and nobody thinking a thing about it. I'm not saying we don't have plenty of enemies in this and every other town in this land. Hell, they're telling us to go back to Russia from every street corner and crossroads in the whole nation. But you'll notice that they hate us now because we won't fight their war. And they hate us so much for refusing to fight their war that they've lost notice of the fact we're black and we're white and we're going to the same church and we're staying in the same motels and we're holding hands when we tell 'em 'hell no we won't go.'"

Standing with my arm around Glenda's swelling middle, I felt her stomach jump as my father reached his climax, and the crowd burst into a cheering ovation as he concluded, with his arms raised, "So thank you, Lyndon, thank you for the silver lining to your cloud of destruction. Thank you, Lyndon, for making it easier to come together, to stand together, to march together with the man who has shown us the way for so long, the Reverend Dr. George Washington Brown."

The crowd was on its feet now, clapping and yelling as Dr. Brown came to the pulpit to raise his hands with my father in a gesture of solidarity. I disengaged from Glenda and began clapping, too. I'd heard this particular speech so often I could have delivered it myself, word for word, pause for pause, but the enthusiasm of the crowd made it as effective and as infectious as if I were hearing it for the first time. As Glenda and I applauded with the throng, Ben pushed himself away from the wall up front and started toward the rostrum. I noticed his movement out of the corner of my eye, I think, although perhaps I have just imagined that I did.

In his initial effort to quiet the crowd and get them reseated, Dr. Brown bent his head low to the microphone and in his rich, melodious voice said, "I'd like to thank the

Reverend Caldwell for his kind remarks." But the crowd only cheered louder at the mention of my father's name. Dr. Brown seized my father's hand again and raised it once more in a clasp of unity. In the wide aisle that separated the front pews from the rostrum, Ben Watson, his hands thrust into the pockets of his pants, paused a moment, head bowed as if in prayer. Dr. Brown smiled broadly, brought his lips low to the microphone and said, "God bless you, Reverend Caldwell." On cue, then, beaming, my father raised his hands to the crowd, alone, and stepped away from the pulpit.

What followed instantly was chaos. I remember it, I think, although I can't be sure how much my memory has been enhanced by the countless descriptions I have since read. But I certainly saw it all, or could have seen it all. I was there, too far away, but within fifty feet. As my father backed toward the rear of the rostrum and Dr. Brown adjusted the mike to his liking and waited for the crowd to quiet, Ben Watson stalked stiffly toward them, his left hand repositioning his glasses snug to his face. In his right hand, as if it were a magic wand, he waved a small-caliber, snub-barreled, dull-blue pistol. I saw him, I'm sure, before either my father or Dr. Brown did. I don't know why I noticed him. Perhaps I had been mystified by his movement away from his position along the wall, but if so, I was only mystified the way we are about a thousand instances of our fellows' behavior that are either barren of meaning or yield to the simplest explanations. But whether I had any conscious thoughts when Ben moved toward the rostrum, I can't say for sure. I certainly *did* nothing. I didn't do anything until I heard Ben scream out in a wail that seemed to come from the top of his head instead of his mouth, "I know what you did; I know what you did."

My father and Dr. Brown responded to Ben's cry in the same instant and in similar ways. They moved toward one another. My father edged back across the podium toward his friend as Dr. Brown stepped away from the protection of the pulpit. I shoved Glenda aside and ran toward the front of the church only to crash into the security guard at just about the moment Ben moaned out once more, "I *know* what you did," and began firing. His gun popped like a series of champagne bottles being opened one after another, five times in quick succession. Two of the bullets, we learned later, missed altogether. But three found human flesh. My father, who was closer to Ben, bent over double and sank to one knee. Behind my father, Dr. Brown fell on his back as if struck with a blackjack.

I scrambled up from where I'd tangled with the security guard and dived at Ben's calves, rolling him into a tackle that banged his face off the offering table and bounced his glasses clattering across the polished tile floor. Spinning out from under him, I reached out for his gun hand as he brought it around toward me.

"For God's sake, it's Tommy, Ben!" I cried.

Squinting, he shook the gun toward the sound of my voice and explained, "I *know* what he did." Then he raised the pistol to his mouth and splattered the altar with the back of his head.

2

My father was born in the winter of 1924. The Great Depression would not seize the rest of the country in its merciless jaws for five and a half years. But the rural Louisiana world into which my father was born had always been depressed. The people of Sherman Parish, Louisiana, had never known anything but toil, poverty, ignorance, pointless disease and early death. Roads were mud ruts. Water was pumped from the ground by hand or dipped from shallow wells in oaken buckets. Food was smothered in spices to disguise the fact that often it was spoiled. Clothes were passed from sibling to sibling to cousin and worn until they shredded or crumbled into powder. Education was an iffy commodity which spread as much darkness as it did light and seldom lasted beyond the age of twelve.

The unincorporated area in which my father was born was called New Peterstown, a curiosity since there never seems to have been a Peterstown that the lost namers of *New* Peterstown would have been referencing. The year my father was born, a relatively obscure state railroad commissioner named Huey Long, whose district included Sherman Parish, ran for governor with a concerted appeal to Louisiana's dispossessed rural voters. Long didn't win in 1924—he blamed a rainy election day and impassable roads for keeping his voters at home—but he would win in 1928, and in so doing he would change the nature of Louisiana politics forever. Growing up in a world dominated by Longs, first Huey and then his brother Earl, my father was influenced by their populism and by their relatively benign attitudes about race. His desire to stand before crowds and speak, he always said, began the day his mother took him to a political rally for Franklin Roosevelt during the 1932 presidential campaign. Huey Long was the featured speaker, and at age eight, my father couldn't understand why Huey himself couldn't become the president. Afterwards, my father said, he went into the woods behind his parents' house and climbed on a tree stump from which station he aped Long's thrusting gestures and regaled a stand of pine trees and wisteria vines with his thoughts on the issues of the day, most of which had to do with his desire to possess a far greater number of the items he coveted from the Sears and Roebuck catalogue.

In his teens, my father shifted his ambitions from the political arena to the ministry. Save for his one experience at the Roosevelt rally and that seductive glimpse of Huey Long, my father had little contact with the political world. There was no TV, of course. My father's family didn't even own a radio and lacked the electricity to run it if they had. But like most all the people in their rural community, the Caldwell family were faithful members of the local Baptist congregation, attending services at the New Peterstown Baptist Church three times a week, Sunday morning, Sunday and Wednesday nights.

In his teens my father felt the hand of God upon him. He felt the call of the Holy Spirit. And this feeling was genuine and absolutely sincere. To the end of his life, my father was a man of faith, and I want in no way to diminish his truly religious nature. But viewed from a purely sociological perspective, his decision to enter the ministry is hardly surprising. Each in the series of preachers who served New Peterstown as pastor was indisputably the area's most prominent citizen. Three times a week the pastor held center stage before the whole community. Even in the other activities that brought all the area residents together, the local minister was the central figure. There was the pastor standing between the bride and groom at every wedding. And there was the pastor standing over the casket at every funeral. In the days after a funeral, the talk of the town was as likely to be about the pastor's eulogy as it was directly about the deceased. So it's little wonder that a bright young rural boy, especially one with the gift of gab like Jeff Caldwell, would make plans to become the pastor some day so as to shift the spotlight of adulation to himself.

And there was another reason, as well, why my father decided that his professional ambitions lay in the ministry. During his childhood, from age four until age seventeen, New Peterstown Baptist Church had no fewer than five pastors. After several years' service at New Peterstown, each moved on to a larger, more prosperous church somewhere else. And as best they could, usually through letters written by the departed pastor's wife, the members of the local community continued to follow the progress of each of their pastors as he left his subsequent pastorate for a third and his third for a fourth. Like the fans of a Class D minor-league baseball team keeping track of a former player, yearning to share his glory should he ever make the majors, the New Peterstown church members followed the relocations of all their former pastors, assessed the size of their congregations and the appointments of their new parsonages. A perennial topic of local debate was which pastor would go the farthest, which would finally alight at the biggest church in the biggest city. A pastor's mobility spawned in my father a hope even greater than that of someday pastoring the New Peterstown Baptist Church; it represented a course by which he might actually escape from New Peterstown altogether.

This is my father's story. George Washington Brown's story has been told repeatedly, has become an indelible component of America's story during his lifetime. Dr. Brown's vision and courage helped make our country a different and better place. Of course, my father was at Dr. Brown's side for most of the things that he achieved; thus, my father is included, to greater and lesser degrees, in any story that is told about George Washington Brown. But my father's story, his as opposed to Dr. Brown's, his as opposed to his role in Dr. Brown's story, has not previously been told. And now I am telling it. In this story, because it is Jeff Caldwell's, Dr. Brown is a supporting player and not the central figure. We see Dr. Brown as he shaped events in my father's life, not the reverse.

My father's story has been assembled through the established procedures of contemporary historical and biographical research. I have read the thousands of accounts of my father's public activities, most of which are analyses of George Washington Brown's career and only tangentially address my father's role. I have interviewed those of his friends, associates and family members who are still living. I anticipate objections that many of the details included here cannot be known to me in quite the way I present them. But the fact that I have made up some of these details does not make them any less true. The details I have imagined are every bit as true as any incident I have simply recorded from memory. They are truer, I believe, than many "facts" which I report from my published sources, and at least as true as the accounts I have gathered from the testimony of those who knew my father, whose memories, like my own, are enhanced by their own imaginations.

For the purpose of objectivity, I have chosen to tell this story in the third person, and in so doing, I have tried to stand apart from myself, to reflect on myself and to render critical judgment about myself as I have about the individuals who people the pages of this book. So perhaps it's not quite accurate to say that this is my father's story. It is not the story he would tell about himself. Perhaps, it is more accurate to say that this is *my* story about my father. About this I should be forthright: however much my father is the focus of this story, this is, of course, my story, too, for I am the one telling it. And a story, even a true one like this one about the life of my father, finally belongs to and reveals the one who tells it.

THOMAS PETER CALDWELL, PH.D.
VALPARAISO, 2003

chapter one

A THICK WINTER FOG DRAPED the unpainted clapboard house on the cold February night Paul Jefferson Caldwell was born in the Sherman Parish community known as New Peterstown. His mother Osby Caldwell lay in the double bed in one of the house's two bedrooms, her face illuminated by a kerosene lamp. Osby was a gaunt woman, long-limbed and bony-hipped. Her drawn face was framed by once black hair that had turned ash gray, though she was only thirty-two. Her features were angular and marked by a sharp slash of a nose. Her lips were thin and stretched in a grimace now over slightly buck teeth. Osby was attended by her sister, Virginia Davis, and by the colored woman, Ivie Mapes, who functioned as the New Peterstown midwife. Virginia and Ivie had helped Osby with the birth of her first two children, who now lay side by side, awake and staring into the dark, in the house's other bedroom.

Pine logs burned in the fireplace but the warmth reached only about halfway to the exterior wall, against which the bed was placed. Over Osby's head, a rectangular quilting rack hung from the ceiling by twined strands of wire. Tufts of cotton batting still clung to the tacking posts. A low dresser stood against the wall, its top scarred by years of use, knobs missing from two of its drawers. The mirror over the dresser was yellowed and gave back a distorted image. Under the bed was a tin slop jar filled with urine. Either Ivie or Virginia would have to take it out soon and fling its contents from the porch lest they risk kicking it over. They had spread rags under Osby's hips to try to protect sheets already stained from her first two births, sheets that had been boiled and would be boiled again, sheets too costly to replace.

In the living room, Osby's husband Pruitt sat before the fire and passed around a jar of clear homemade with his brother Ralph and his brother-in-law Marlon Davis. All of the men were clad in denim overalls and shirts without collars. Pruitt had a red bandana tied around his neck. Each sat in an unpainted, straight-backed wooden chair. Behind them was a squat, cloth-covered rocker and two old sofas, one with wide wooden arms and the other with a back that could be levered flat to create a bed for visitors. The three men were not strangers to alcohol, but they did not drink regularly, and the strong spirits had made their cheeks flush crimson.

"Damn, but I hate this waiting," Pruitt said. At age thirty-three, Pruitt was a man of average height and slightly above-average weight. He was thick-chested and well-muscled, even though he'd begun to sag around the middle. His dark brown hair, flecked with gray, was dirty and hung long past his eyebrows. His repeated attempts to sweep it out of his eyes made his forehead shine as if polished.

"First the waiting, then the screaming," Ralph agreed.

"The screaming and then the mess," Pruitt added. He took a swig from the jar and handed it to his brother. "The screaming, the mess, and then the stink. The stink won't go away for days."

"And then another mouth to feed," Ralph said. He offered the jar to Marlon who waved it away.

"I love my little ones," Pruitt said. "I love 'em. I do. But this process of getting them into the world. It makes you wonder."

Ralph laughed. "Don't make you wonder about the whole process, I reckon." Nobody acknowledged the implications of Ralph's remark, and he took another swallow from the jar before handing it to Pruitt.

Ralph and Pruitt and Marlon had all been born in Sherman Parish. Pruitt and Marlon had both gone to France in the Great War where Pruitt had taken a piece of shrapnel just below his right knee. In the winter, when the weather was damp, as it so often was in central Louisiana, the knee ached and felt like it was clogged with gravel. Pruitt had been trying to get benefits from the Secretary of War since he'd returned home. In his letters to Washington he claimed to be disabled. But, in fact, he worked in the paper mill unloading trucks and feeding logs into the chipper. He could make more money in the field felling trees, but his knee swelled up when he worked out in the cold, so he'd had to take employment in the mill. He felt the nation owed him. He'd risked his life and suffered a serious wound. Now he wanted compensation.

And that night when his second son was born, he indeed had another mouth to feed.

Osby and Pruitt compromised in naming their new son Paul Jefferson. Pruitt preferred the name Paul and Osby preferred Jeff. When he was a baby, his mother and father addressed him by different names. But mothers normally prevail in matters such as these, and after a time he was called Jeff by all the members of the family. Perhaps as a result of losing this particular battle of wills with his wife, Pruitt took a disliking to Jeff that never really lessened. Eventually, Pruitt and Osby would have six children. Among them Jeff became far and away the most accomplished adult and a devoted, generous son. But until the day he died, Pruitt refused to show Jeff any warmth.

Jeff came into the world a small baby, barely five pounds, and Osby feared that he wouldn't survive the winter of his first year. He was sickly growing up, always suffering from coughing fits and a runny nose. But he had big green eyes and a way of staring at his mother that made him her favorite. Jeff also became the favorite of his sister Vivien, the Caldwells' firstborn. Vivien was five when Jeff was born, enough older that she was eventually able to provide some help to Osby in rearing her younger brother. When Jeff was a baby, Vivien liked to hoist him around on her hip and to feed him his bottle and to hold the tattered handkerchief with a little piece of sugar cane tied in a corner that the Caldwells used as both a treat and a teether. For the little girl, her baby brother was the doll her parents couldn't afford to buy her.

As an adult, Jeff loved to talk about his family's poverty. One of his favorite stories recounted his family's meager Christmas the year he was seven. Each child was to get a single present. Vivien would get a brassiere, an item of underclothing she'd needed for at least a year. All the boys were to receive new pairs of rubber-soled shoes, footwear they wore everywhere except to church. But Jeff had his heart set on a little red hatchet he'd spotted in the Sears and Roebuck catalogue. The hatchet cost the exact same amount as the shoes, and Jeff told his mother he wanted to have the hatchet instead. Osby should certainly have known better than to be swayed by Jeff's pleadings. But the boy touched her heart. Too smart to whine and wheedle, he made arguments about the logic and fairness of his getting the hatchet instead of the new shoes. Amused at his intellectual industry, and, as always, rueful that their lifestyle permitted them so little beyond necessities, she relented.

Jeff argued that he could wear the shoes his older brother Wayne had outgrown, and that's what Osby finally decreed. On Christmas morning the children got stockings full of pecans and one present apiece. Inside newspaper wrapping were the brassiere for Vivien, four pairs of canvas tennis shoes and a red pig-iron hatchet for Jeff. "What's Jeff going to wear for shoes?" Jeff's immediately younger brother James wanted to know.

"He's probably talked Mama into letting him wear his church shoes every day," Wayne said sullenly.

"He has not," Osby explained. "Jeff will wear your old tennis shoes, Wayne."

"Why's Jeff the only one to get a toy?" Franklin, the youngest, demanded.

"I'd wear old shoes, too," Monroe, the fourth son, said.

"He ain't wearing my shoes," Wayne said.

"Of course, he is," Osby said. "And don't say 'ain't.' We may be poor, but we are not ignorant."

"Jeff's ignorant," Franklin said.

"Jeff's not ignorant," Vivien interjected. "He's made a sacrifice and gotten a reward for it. That's intelligence, not ignorance."

"What's more," Osby added, "all you boys will benefit. I don't allow selfishness in this house. The hatchet is Jeff's Christmas present, but I will expect him to share it with all of you, and I'm sure he will do so gladly."

This business of sharing his hatchet came as shocking news to Jeff. But once the proclamation of sharing was out of his mother's mouth, Jeff knew he'd have no choice but to let his brothers use his new possession on any occasion when he wasn't actually chopping something with it himself. Doing so happily was another matter altogether, although he knew better than to show Osby any of the resentment he felt. Actually, he felt like he'd been tricked. Not by Osby but by fate.

When, as an adult Jeff Caldwell told this story of his little red hatchet, he never related his brothers' jealousy or his mother's dictum to share. In fact, in Jeff's direct accounts, his brothers played little role whatsoever, and often he made their tennis shoe presents seem joint acts of good sense whereas his own desire for the hatchet was a little unwise. That's because, as Jeff told the story, he leapt up from the Christmas tree after tearing the newspaper from his hatchet, dashed straight outside, across the porch, down the steps, through the yard and up to the grand old live oak which stood just inside the front fence. There, wanting to test the bite of his hatchet, he took one mighty swing and broke the hatchet off at the neck.

Telling this story as an adult enabled Jeff to illustrate the extent of his family poverty and to contrast the circumstances of his adult accomplishment with the deprivation of his rearing. It was a very subtle and effective way of emphasizing just how far he'd come. But as with most all storytelling, Jeff didn't relate events as they actually happened. He didn't tell the whole truth, and in that regard didn't actually tell the truth at all.

Pruitt quickly grew irritated at all the griping about Jeff's having gotten a hatchet instead of tennis shoes. And when the boys wouldn't stop yammering about it, he said testily to Osby, "You see what I tell you about treating Jeff that way. I'm dern sick of listening to all this guff." Then to the children he growled, "I'm going to walk out onto the back porch for a dipper of water, and when I get back I'm going to box the ears of any of you brats who are still here." The boys looked at their father wide-eyed and cautiously. "You understand what I'm telling y'all?" The boys muttered a chorus of yeses. "You understand what I'm telling you, Wayne?"

"Yes," Wayne said.

"Come here, son." The nine-year-old stood and walked over to his father who sat on a tattered sofa. "See this," Pruitt said, holding up his fist. Wayne flinched and stepped back, but Pruitt reached out, grabbed his arm and pulled the boy close. Then he held his fist in front of Wayne's face. "Know what this is, boy?" Wayne didn't answer. "This is the enforcer. This is the message sender." He bumped his fist off Wayne's nose. Just a bump, not remotely a punch, nothing that could hurt. But it startled Wayne, whose eyes started to water.

"Now you stop that, Pruitt Caldwell," Osby said.

"I'll send you a message if you don't shut up," Pruitt replied. He looked at Wayne again. "Here's my message, son. I want y'all out of here right now." Then he punched Wayne just below his collarbone, not hard, not hard enough to cause pain, but hard enough to knock the boy back a step. "Message delivered," Pruitt said.

Osby got up and threw into the fire all the newspaper that had been stripped from the presents. "Vivien, come help me start dinner," she said as she started out of the room. At the door she stopped and looked at her husband. "Merry Christmas, Pruitt," she said in a tone that was absolutely flat.

He looked at her and grinned as he reached into his pocket for a packet of cigarette papers. "Why, merry Christmas to you, too. Now that I'm getting you all out of here, I can sit here in peace and have myself a smoke."

Outside on the porch, the boys began a debate about sharing Jeff's hatchet. Jeff was quietly resentful that the hatchet no longer seemed to belong to him but to the group as a whole. He quickly resigned himself to this irreversible reality, however, and suggested that they each in turn use the blunt side of the hatchet to crack open their Christmas pecans. This activity occupied the brothers for a few minutes, but when it was Wayne's turn to hammer a shell, he declared, "This here ain't no nut cracker. It's for chopping stuff. And that's what I intend to use it for now it's my turn."

"We better not go chopping something without asking," Jeff said, remembering his school lesson about George Washington and the cherry tree.

"Girly Jeff," Wayne replied, "I don't know why you don't just get your hand-me-downs from Vivien instead of me."

"I'm just saying—," Jeff protested.

"You're just saying you're a yellow belly about every last thing," Wayne interrupted.

"I am not," Jeff said.

"You am not nuthin," Wayne said. "Come on guys, let's go chop something."

As the boys made their way down the porch steps, Jeff said, "Well, at least don't chop anything down."

"Oh shut up, you whiny baby," Wayne responded.

"Well, it's my hatchet," Jeff said. "I ought to at least get to decide what we chop."

That got Wayne's full attention. He stopped and turned an angry face on Jeff. "Who says it's yours, whiny baby. I'm the one holding it, and possession is nine tenths of the law."

"It's my Christmas present," Jeff said. "Mama gave it to me. She told me I had to share, and that's what I'm doing. But it's still mine."

"Not the way I figure it," Wayne said, waving the hatchet in Jeff's face. "Way I figure it, this hatchet is mine."

"Nuh uh," Jeff said.

"Yeh huh," Wayne responded.

Jeff tried to grab the hatchet out of Wayne's hand, and Wayne grabbed him by the shirt collar with his left hand and held the hatchet away, back over his head. "Gimme it," Jeff screeched.

"Take it," Wayne taunted. "Take it if you can, Mama's boy."

Jeff knew that it was fruitless trying to take the hatchet away from his older, stronger brother, so he quit struggling, and Wayne pushed him away contemptuously.

"You know it's mine," Jeff said.

"Was yours," Wayne said.

"It's still mine. It was my Christmas present. It was in the present to me. You know that, Wayne."

"I know that Mama gave it to you. And then she traded you my shoes for it, so now the hatchet belongs to me."

"You cain't even wear those shoes," Jeff said.

"Don't matter. They're my shoes. Then Mama traded them to you for this hatchet, which is now mine. And right now I'm going to walk over to that oak and chop a chunk out of it with my hatchet. You can watch if you want. And by the way, since Mama said for us to share this hatchet, after I chop a chunk, I'm gonna let James chop a chunk. And then Monroe, and then Franklin." Jeff didn't even bother to respond. Nor did he try to appeal to parental authorities inside. His father had banished them all to the yard, and Jeff knew better than to try to go back inside until his mother called them for dinner. So he trailed along with his brothers as Wayne strode up to the oak tree. "Watch this," Wayne said as he reared back for a mighty swing, "I'm gonna drop this sapsucker like Paul Bunyan." Wayne swung the hatchet into the tree as hard as he could and snapped the brittle pig iron in two at the neck.

Jeff couldn't believe what he'd seen. "You bastard," he screamed as he went flying across the yard and drove his shoulder into the small of Wayne's back, knocking his brother to the ground. But, as always, Jeff wasn't strong enough to defeat a brother two years older, twenty pounds heavier and natively stronger. Within seconds, Wayne had Jeff pinned to the ground and was kneeling on his chest.

"Say uncle," Wayne demanded.

"Go to the devil," Jeff responded.

Wayne snuffled and hawked. "Say uncle right now, and I won't drool this cob right on your mouth."

"Oh what's the use," Jeff said. "Uncle. Now let me up."

Wayne got off him and Jeff picked up the two pieces of his broken hatchet.

"You could have at least let me chop with it once, Wayne," Jeff said.

"What for?" Wayne replied. "It waddn't no good."

"It was mine, though," Jeff said.

"So what?" Wayne replied. "Now it ain't nobody's."

Wayne took the two pieces of the hatchet from Jeff's limp hands and sailed first one and then the other as far as he could into the woods on the other side of the fence.

"I didn't want no hatchet, anyway," Wayne said. "I'm gonna get me a real axe some day." Though he bitterly tried not to, Jeff started to cry, not hard, but hard enough for tears to run down his cheeks and add to his disappointment and humiliation. "Oh Jessums, Jeff," Wayne said. "Don't be a cry baby. I'm gonna let you keep my tennis shoes."

Jeff screeched and attacked his brother again. With exactly the same result. This time Jeff didn't wait for the threat of being spit on to relent. The three younger brothers watched their two older brothers fight without trying to interfere. When Jeff had surrendered a second time, James said to him, "Jessums, Jeff, you let him make you say uncle twice in one day."

"I wouldn't never say uncle even once," Monroe said.

The violence raged on between Wayne and Jeff for as long as they lived at home together, until Wayne left home to join the service. It got so bad by the summer Jeff was nine and Wayne was eleven that the two boys fought almost nightly. Cramped together in the tiny room where two double beds were placed with almost no room in between them against the wall across from the fireplace, the Caldwell boys had no escape from each other. And given that their personalities were so different, Wayne and Jeff argued constantly. One warm August night, just before Jeff climbed into the bed he shared with Monroe and Franklin, he lit the lantern on his side of the bed and tried to adjust it to a level where it wouldn't start the standard argument with Wayne about light falling in the older boy's eyes. Then Jeff reached under his thin feather pillow for the book he always kept there. Most recently he'd been reading a book called *Joe's Luck,* about a poor boy like himself who studied so hard in school he got a scholarship to college. His aunt Virginia knew how much Jeff liked to read and frequently brought him back books from the library in Alexandria. *Joe's Luck* was one of them. But now the book was missing.

"Where's my book?" Jeff asked his brothers. No one answered. And when he asked again, more impatiently, he was met with choked giggles from his two youngest brothers.

"Okay," Jeff said to his two bedmates, "What did y'all do with my book?"

"We didn't do nothing with it," Monroe said, and Franklin giggled again.

"Well then who did?" Jeff demanded.

"Ain't telling," Monroe said.

"Franklin, who took my book?" Jeff asked.

"Franklin ain't telling neither," Monroe said.

"All right, Wayne," Jeff said. "Give me my book."

"Who says I've got it?" Wayne responded.

"Just give it to me," Jeff said.

"I ain't got it," Wayne said.

"Well what did you do with it?"

"I borrowed it," Wayne said.

"Yeah, well unborrow it. Now give it to me."

"That'd be kinda hard," Wayne said, and the other three boys snickered.

"What did you do with it, you rat?"

"I took it to the outhouse."

"For what?" Jeff demanded. "You don't read anything that isn't assigned in school."

"The Sears and Roebuck catalogue was all used up."

"So?" Jeff asked. Surely the implications of what Wayne was telling him couldn't be true. Along with corn cobs, torn-up newspaper and old copies of the Sears and Roebuck catalogue were used in the outhouse as toilet paper.

"So the cob basket was empty, and I didn't feel like going over to the barn for another bushel."

Jeff couldn't believe what he was hearing. "So, so you're telling me you wiped your butt with my book?" Monroe and Franklin and James all burst out laughing.

From the living room Pruitt yelled out, "Y'all better hush up that racket in there, or I'm going to tan some fannies."

Jeff walked to the foot of his brother's bed where Wayne lay back on the sheets with his hands clasped behind his head. "Tell me you didn't wipe your butt with my book."

"Not all of it," Wayne said. "I'm not as full of shit as you." Vulgar language was a rarity in the Caldwell household, severely punished by Osby when she heard it. Hearing it now from Wayne, the three youngest brothers began to cackle again.

"I'm warning you," Pruitt yelled out. "If I have to come in there, every one of you is going to be sorry."

"I just tore out a few pages," Wayne said smirking. "And to show how considerate I am, I tore them out from the front; that way you can still finish your little story."

Jeff could feel his fists forming themselves into balls. "That was a library book," he said. "You're gonna get in trouble."

"I ain't gonna get in any trouble," Wayne replied. "Ain't my library book."

"You really did it, Wayne? You really tore up a library book?"

"Just a couple of pages. I've checked out library books before. They don't look at the front when you turn them in, just the little card pocket in the back. So just forget about it. Turn it in and don't say nothing."

"You rotten bastard," Jeff said in a whisper. "YOU ROTTEN STINKING BASTARD." Jeff threw himself on top of Wayne and began flailing at his brother's face with punch after punch. And for once, for a blow or two anyway, Jeff got the better of it.

But then Pruitt was in the room. "I told you brats to shut the devil up," Pruitt bellowed as he stormed across the bedroom. Pruitt grabbed Jeff by the nape of his neck and pulled him off Wayne. Pruitt's angry grip left a bruise across Jeff's back and right shoulder that didn't disappear for three weeks. In pulling Jeff away, Pruitt freed Wayne from the onslaught of his brother's attack and let Wayne push himself upright in bed, from which position he tried to deliver one last blow. Unfortunately, Pruitt had just started to swing Jeff backwards off the bed when Wayne threw a punch that came nowhere near his brother but instead glanced off his father's chin. Furious, Pruitt slung Jeff away. Tossed like a rag doll, Jeff landed on the small of his back and slid across the floor and banged his head against the wall, just as Osby came into the room.

"Stop it, Pruitt!" Osby screamed. "What are you doing? You're gonna break somebody's neck." Bedside, Pruitt slapped Wayne in the face with a full swing, snapping Wayne's head back against the iron bars of the headboard. Wayne's lip split and his nose started to bleed; he would still bear the imprint of his father's hand when school started four weeks later. "Stop that, Pruitt Caldwell, this instant," Osby screamed as she stooped to Jeff.

"Since when do you ever hit me, you little piece of pig slop?" Pruitt said to Wayne.

"I didn't—" Wayne wailed, tasting blood in his mouth.

Pruitt slapped him with his left hand, this time, deliberately not in the face but on the side of the boy's head, just above his ear. "Shut up you—"

"I said stop that, Pruitt."

Pruitt turned and looked at his wife. "Unless you want some of this, too, you'll be another one shutting up. If it's what's needed to get some peace and quiet around here, I'm ready to slap the whole lot of you silly." Pruitt looked back at Wayne and said, "Were you about to say something?"

"I didn't mean—" Wayne started.

But Pruitt slapped him above the ear with his right hand. "I told you to shut up, didn't I?" Pruitt slapped the back of his oldest son's head with his left hand and then his right again, and Wayne curled into a ball and tried to protect himself by covering his head with his arms.

"STOP IT!" Osby screamed, but Pruitt ignored her.

"Did I tell you to shut up?" Pruitt said to Wayne.

"Yes," Wayne said.

Pruitt slapped him again. "Then shut the devil up. You understand me? You understand me, son? Look at me. Look at me when I'm talking to you." Wayne peeked out between his arms. "You understand me when I tell you to shut the devil up?"

Terrified, Wayne nodded. Pruitt drew back as if to slap the boy again, and Wayne tried to curl himself into invisibility. Pruitt reached out and turned the boy on his back. "Look up at me now, boy." Wayne peeked out again. "You see this?" Pruitt showed his hand, poised as if to hit again. "I'm talking to you, boy. You see this?" Wayne moved his head in a jerk of fear. Pruitt feinted as if to slap him again, and Wayne flinched. "That's good," Pruitt said. He feinted still again, and once more Wayne flinched. "That's real good. Now we're getting somewhere. I think you're learning something."

Pruitt looked around the room now. James, Monroe and Franklin had retreated as far as they could from harm's way. On the floor with the two double beds in between them and Wayne and Pruitt, they watched the action in terror, ready to dive for cover. "You three see what I'm trying to teach Wayne here?" Pruitt asked. The three boys nodded without speaking. "Good," Pruitt observed. "Because if you want, I can come around there and teach the lesson to each of you personally. How would you like that?" The three boys shook their heads. "Now we're getting somewhere," Pruitt said.

He turned to look at Jeff, who was lying now with his head in his mother's lap, Osby stroking his face. "I'm glad to see you favoring him as always," Pruitt said. "You got a son up here with a cut lip and bloody nose, and you're cuddling that one."

"You could have broken Jeff's neck," Osby said, running her hand through the boy's hair.

"Only if I was lucky," Pruitt said.

"You don't even mean that," Osby said quietly, crying, but letting no emotion register in her voice.

"You think I don't mean it," Pruitt said. "One less mouth to feed, one less trap to yap."

chapter two

I N THE CHAOS FOLLOWING the shootings of George Washington Brown and Jeff Caldwell, Jeff's son Tommy found himself covered in blood and Ben Watson's brain matter. Tommy's arms were still tangled in Ben's feet as he lay slumped against the altar, his mouth slack and leaking blood, his eyes open and rolled back in his head. Later, Tommy was told that he began screaming, not words but a long, high-pitched wail. He never remembered this. But he did remember scrambling out from his entanglement with Ben and trying to climb up on the rostrum toward his father and Dr. Brown when he was tackled from behind, spun around and thrown back to the floor by two men in gray suits. Tommy was wrestled onto his back and pinned to the floor, one man holding down his arms while the other knelt on his chest and searched his pockets.

"What in the hell are you doing?" Tommy demanded. "Who are you guys?"

"That's the man," a voice said. "He's the one told me to let the other one in, to let the one in who did the shooting." Tommy swiveled his head to the left to see the uniformed guard with whom he had spoken earlier in the evening. "He's the one," the guard said. "No doubt about it."

"I'm Tommy Caldwell. Ben just shot my father and Dr. Brown. What are you doing?"

About that time, the man on Tommy's chest managed to yank Tommy's wallet out of the rear pocket of his jeans and fish out Tommy's driver's license. "Thomas Caldwell?" he said as if Tommy hadn't just told him that.

"Yes. Thomas Caldwell. Who are you guys? Let me up."

"FBI," the man on Tommy's chest said. "Special agent Mallory."

The man holding Tommy's arms said nothing.

"Why are you on top of me? I've got to help my father and Dr. Brown."

"Your father one of the victims?" the man holding Tommy's arms said.

"Yes. We've got to get them to a hospital."

"Help is on the way," Agent Mallory said. Without using his hands for leverage, he stood up from Tommy's chest, adjusting horn-rimmed spectacles as he did so. He looked like a marine, chiseled features and a crew cut. "Let's get him up," Mallory said to the man holding Tommy's arms. Then to Tommy he said, "Okay, we're gonna get you up. Slowly. Don't make any sudden moves."

"I'm Jeff Caldwell's son," Tommy said.

The agents helped Tommy up, the unidentified one still gripping Tommy's arms behind his back. Mallory explained that they wanted Tommy to accompany them out of the sanctuary to "a place where we can talk."

As Tommy was being steered away, he looked back at the rostrum. Robert was stalking back and forth between his father and Jeff. Robert's white shirt was stained with blood. Dr. Brown lay unmoving on his back, surrounded by Preacher Martin and several other aides on their knees, some of whom were wailing, others obviously praying. Someone had taken his suit coat off and wrapped it around Dr. Brown's head. Glenda had gotten onto the rostrum as well and sat on the floor with Jeff's head in her lap. Jeff's glasses were off, and though he was only forty-four, he looked like an old man. His jacket and shirt were soaked in blood, but Tommy saw him move his head so knew he was still alive. As Tommy was escorted through the double doors he had entered a short time earlier, he could hear the wail of sirens over the cries of anguished movement followers. Then the doors were closed behind him, and he was alone with the FBI.

The agents found an empty Sunday School room and sat Tommy down at a small table. They told him to keep his hands on the table. They did not sit down but walked back and forth in front of him.

What had made Tommy run toward the front of the auditorium, they wanted to know.

He had seen the gun in Ben's hand.

Had Tommy known Ben was carrying it?

Of course not.

Had Tommy encouraged Ben to shoot Dr. Brown?

Of course not. Why would they ask such an insane question?

How long had Tommy known Ben Watson? What reason might he have for wanting to shoot Dr. Brown? Had Tommy conspired with Ben to do it?

"What's wrong with you two guys?" Tommy demanded. "You must have been in the auditorium. Didn't you see that I knocked Ben down, that I was trying to stop him?"

"Are you a member of the Communist Party?" the man who had been holding Tommy's arms asked. He looked sort of like Buddy Holly, tall and thin with black, Barry-Goldwater–style glasses.

"What's your name?" Tommy asked him. "Are you FBI, too, like Agent Mallory?"

"This is Agent William Hinton," Mallory said.

"Do you deny being a member of the Communist Party?" Hinton said.

"Yes, I deny it, you morons. Dr. Brown and my father may be dying out there, and you're asking me these stupid questions. What's wrong with you?"

"Are you angry with your father? Do you have reason to be angry with your father?"

Tommy put his head in his hands.

Other people occasionally came into the room and conferred briefly with one of the FBI agents. Uniformed New Orleans policemen. State troopers. A nicely dressed woman smelling strongly of Chanel No. 5. Occasionally, one of the agents stepped out of the room for a while, but at least one of them kept badgering Tommy with questions—many times repeated questions—for nearly three hours. What was Tommy's role in Dr. Brown's organization? Why had he arrived at the church late? What was his draft status? Had he ever committed an act of violence against the United States government? Had he ever desecrated the flag?

"What does any of this have to do with the fact that Ben Watson just shot Dr. Brown and my father?"

"Why did you authorize Ben Watson's access to the auditorium?" Hinton demanded. "We have testimony from the guard posted at the door that it was you who insisted he be let into the front of the sanctuary."

"I didn't have to insist," Tommy said. "I just told the guard that Ben was staff, that's all. I was head parade marshal, so I went up to the guard and said Ben was okay."

"Did you consider Ben Watson your friend?" Mallory wanted to know.

"Yes, I did."

"Did you know him to be a violent man?"

"No, I didn't. He wanted to become a minister. And he talked of doing missionary work in Africa. Or at least he used to. Until people started saying that foreign missionaries were just the stooges of American imperialism. And then Ben started feeling guilty that he ever wanted to do that in the first place. Only he still wanted to. And he wondered what that meant about himself. He said that after this summer he was going to start his seminary work, and when he finished maybe he'd try to get a parish somewhere in Appalachia. He was a very sincere and devoted person. I can't fathom what happened to him. He practically worshiped Dr. Brown."

Eventually, Agents Mallory and Hinton took down Tommy's address and warned him to make himself available to them should they need to interview him further. They told Tommy that Dr. Brown and his father had been taken to Charity Hospital and were in surgery. Things did not look good for Dr. Brown, they said.

Dr. Brown was shot once in the neck, a very serious wound, but one from which he might have recovered. The fatal bullet, fired upward from Ben Watson's position on the church floor as his victim stood just to the side of the raised pulpit, hit Dr. Brown just below the left eyebrow and exited at the crown of his head, one and three-quarter inches above his right ear. He was dead at the scene although this fact was not announced publicly for several days. Though they knew the effort was completely hopeless, the doctors at Charity, specialists in bullet wounds, spent more than an hour trying to revive him.

Even at this late date in American history, in a city renowned for the cultural influence of its black citizens—a city that would shortly become majority black—there was, of course, no black physician on the hospital staff. The young emergency-room surgeons were as skilled at their craft as any in the nation. But they were not a particularly enlightened lot. Most of the gunshot victims on whom they labored were black, and they routinely performed their duties amid flippantly racist banter. Victims were routinely called "Tyrone" and their assailants "Leroy."

But no such sacrilege escaped the cynical lips of these young doctors as they labored fruitlessly over George Washington Brown. They were hardly fans of Dr. Brown. One of them had earlier wished him dead, declaring him a "communist nigger." The other physician was less vocal but no less certain that, left unchecked, the likes of Dr. Brown could destroy the civilized world. Still, these doctors would have saved Dr. Brown if they could have, had his brain not been completely destroyed by the .22-caliber bullet that tumbled through it. They would have saved him because they regularly employed their medical expertise to save black lives. And they would have saved him because the immediate scrutiny under which they found themselves would not have allowed otherwise. They were surrounded by policemen and representatives of the mayor's office from the moment of the initial examination. They tried to get all nonmedical personnel to leave the room, but this request was denied.

Moreover, although they refused to identify themselves immediately to the doctors, FBI agents were also present throughout the procedures. FBI agents, such as the two who sequestered and interrogated Tommy, always attended Dr. Brown's rallies. And two actually rode to the hospital in the ambulance with the two victims.

The public did not know how genuinely venomous his hatred was at the time, but J. Edgar Hoover was a sworn enemy of Dr. Brown and therefore of Jeff Caldwell and all Dr. Brown's lieutenants. Hoover considered Dr. Brown and his staff to be communists because they had always refused to repudiate communist support for the civil-rights movement and subsequently merged the civil-rights movement with the antiwar movement. So the FBI agents were not present at the big church on St. Charles Avenue to provide additional security. They were there, as always, to keep track and take notes, to fatten the files with which Dr. Brown and Jeff Caldwell might someday be prosecuted for sedition.

By the time the doctors abandoned their efforts to restart Dr. Brown's heart, the FBI had seized control of the hospital. They were in the operating room, outside the OR door and posted at all entrances to the building. City policemen remained on the scene, but the mayor's representative was sent away, and an emissary of the governor was denied access to the operating room. Afterwards, the doctors were subjected to intimidating interrogation and fevered background checks, a terrifying experience for two young white Southerners who had spent seventy-five minutes cutting open and probing the body of a dead black man.

Though the drive from the church to the hospital would normally have taken only about fifteen minutes, it took Tommy more than an hour; he finally had to park many blocks away. Directly in front of the hospital a crowd like that on Bourbon Street on Mardi Gras day had gathered to stand vigil. The scene was eerie for its almost utter silence. People stood shoulder to shoulder, mostly black people but many whites among them, particularly young white people, the girls with long straight hair and the bearded young men with equally long hair fastened into ponytails or tied back with bandanas. Automobile traffic had come to a complete standstill in the area. Thousands of people stood under a low, moonless sky and waited for a word that would be like a bullet fired into their own hearts. You can hear a Mardi Gras crowd from blocks away, but it was so quiet in front of the hospital you could hear the stir of the summer wind in the oak trees. The only sound that came from the multitude was that of quiet weeping or anguished, mumbled prayer. The many Catholics whispered their rosaries and worried their beads.

Tommy shouldered his way though the throng, trying to reach the hospital's front door, but when he came to the sidewalk, he found an interlocked fence of police barricades, metal crowd-control devices resembling bicycle racks that New Orleans police normally deployed along parade routes during Mardi Gras. Behind the barricades stood a phalanx of cops in riot gear: blue shirts, black pants tucked into their boots, hard plastic helmets and black batons already unholstered. Inside the barricade, television stations' remote vans were parked on the concrete plaza between the hospital and the street. Pickup trucks with powerful light units had been placed to light the square. Halfway up the front steps, a battery of microphones had been erected. At some point, someone was going to make a statement.

Tommy leaned over one of the metal barricades and asked a policeman how he could get inside the hospital. "You can't," the policeman responded in a clipped, no-nonsense tone.

"But my father's inside," Tommy explained. "He's been shot."

"Try the side door," the policeman suggested.

It took Tommy another fifteen minutes to make his way there. As he was talking to another policeman, he heard the microphone system crackle to life and immediately recognized the voice of Everett Essex. Everett was the black Baton Rouge minister who had helped Dr. Brown organize the bus boycott and who had been at his side through every campaign since. If Jeff Caldwell was a kind of vice president in the organization, Everett Essex was the first vice president. He was as devoted to Dr. Brown as Robert Kennedy had been to his brother John.

"Ladies and gentleman," Everett said, his voice choked with emotion. "I have a statement for the press and for all our friends gathered here tonight. But if you would all indulge me, I would first like to pray." Everett prayed to understand that God's ways are sometimes mysterious, prayed to embrace the faith that all things were the product of a divine plan, prayed to accept what he could not fathom. And then he told them. First he told them that the shots which Ben Watson had fired that night had felled two great leaders. Then he told them that Jeff Caldwell was clinging to his life with a bullet wound in his chest. And then he told them that George Washington Brown was gone.

At first there was silence, a silence of shock and disbelief, a silence of refusing to believe, a silence of pushing back knowledge that was not wanted. The silence lasted several seconds only, several seconds, if that long. But it seemed to hang there between Everett's dolorous words and what followed as if the silence had stopped time, as if what Everett had said would not become true until the crowd reacted to it. And so there was silence, a mutual attempt to will back and erase that which had already become. But though knowledge can be denied, it cannot be unknown. And so began a long, low moan of anguish that seemed to rise from deep inside each person gathered there. And only then were there cries of "No."

"No!" the voices demanded. "No!"

Everett tried to speak to the crowd again, although he was crying. "It is important that we honor the leadership Dr. Brown has provided us so long," Everett choked out into the microphones. "It is important that in this hour of our misery, in this passage of our grief—it is important in this painful time to focus on the meaning of

Dr. Brown's life and not the fact of his death."

"Burn it down," someone in the crowd yelled.

"We must remain calm," Everett said. "We must remain mindful of what Dr. Brown always strove to teach us."

"Burn this fucking racist nation down."

"Burn it down," voices chanted in unison. "Burn it down. Burn this fucking racist nation down."

"I am going to ask you to join with me now," Everett said. "I am going to ask you to join with me in this time of profound sorrow and raise your voices with mine to sing the song that is our anthem. Dr. Brown has led us in singing it so many times, and now I'm going to ask you to sing it with me in his name. I am going to ask Dr. Brown's son Robert to lead us."

Robert stepped to the microphone, still wearing his bloodstained white shirt. In a quavering voice he began to sing: "We shall overcome. We shall overcome. We shall overcome some day. Oh-oh deep in my heart, I do believe that we shall overcome some day."

None of the younger staff had ever been given a public role. Their work was always in small groups or one on one. None had ever given a speech before a crowd like the one that filled the street in front of Charity Hospital. And Robert wasn't supposed to speak now. He was supposed to lead the singing and then turn things back over to Everett. But instead, when the hymn ended, Robert began to talk. "My father was murdered today. The man who pulled the trigger was named Benjamin Watson. But he wasn't the real murderer. The police will tell you that they haven't learned why Benjamin Watson committed this heinous crime. But I know why."

"Then tell us," a voice in the crowd demanded.

"He committed this heinous crime because he was the product of a racist country," Robert continued.

"Right on, brother," someone yelled.

"And it's that country who is the real murderer," Robert went on.

"Right on."

"That country made Benjamin Watson."

"Amen to that, brother."

"That country put a gun in Benjamin Watson's hand. And that country encouraged Benjamin Watson to kill my father."

"Right on!"

"Right on," Robert rejoined. "All his life my father taught us that we shall overcome some day. Well, I believe that. And I think that day is soon, and that day will be spawned by Benjamin Watson's bullets. My father tried one approach, the approach of brotherhood and peace. He had the courage of his convictions. And he died being true to them. Tonight we must take a new direction. Tonight we must begin to erect a new nation to replace the one that gave birth to Benjamin Watson and will continue to nurture Benjamin Watsons until it is swept from the face of the earth."

"Show us the way, brother."

"Tonight we begin a new work."

"Lead us, brother."

"Tonight we take the first crucial step."

"Tell it, brother. Tell it now."

Robert inched closer to the nest of microphones and said in a barely audible voice: "Burn it down."

chapter three

J EFF CALDWELL FIRST HEARD of George Washington Brown in 1951 when Brown was a graduate student at the National Baptist Seminary in Baton Rouge. Jeff had just graduated from the white Baptist seminary in New Orleans and taken his first full-time pastorate at Ezekiel Baptist in Gonzales, Louisiana, about twenty-five miles downriver from Baton Rouge. Friends who considered themselves liberals (the term embraced by those in Southern Baptist circles who felt that improving race relations was part of their call to the ministry) told Jeff of a charismatic young Negro preacher whose eloquent sermons were drawing waves of attention from the established black clergy.

George Washington Brown was the son of Ralph Waldo Brown, the legendary pastor of Dryades Avenue Baptist Church in New Orleans, the city's prestige black congregation. Ralph Waldo Brown was the unofficial spokesman for New Orleans Negroes. A confidante of the New Orleans mayor, the young and forthrightly progressive Chep Morrison, Ralph Waldo was a favorite source for journalists at the city's three newspapers and was often quoted on issues concerning the black population. His son graduated as valedictorian from Booker T. Washington High School and went on to earn straight A's at Dillard University in New Orleans, where he was a champion debater. After he announced his intention to attend the seminary, George Washington was widely presumed to be Ralph Waldo's heir apparent at Dryades Avenue Baptist Church, where the father had first invited his son to preach when George Washington was a Dillard sophomore. Now, as he was completing work on a doctorate in theology, Negro churches in New Orleans and in the Baton Rouge area were already extending him invitations to address their congregations.

America's racial divide had yet to cause the crisis it would later in the decade, but it was an obvious issue on the national agenda. Jackie Robinson had broken the color barrier in major-league baseball, and black and white soldiers were fighting side by side in Korea. But public schools and most other facilities remained segregated throughout the South. In the South's rural areas, life for the average Negro was little different than it had been a hundred years earlier, at the height of slavery. He owned little or nothing, enjoyed little or no education and was denied the right to vote. He was routinely treated with contempt by his white neighbors, and any resentment he might show over his circumstances was curbed by the omnipresent fact of physical intimidation, including lynching. So black men in the South had learned to express their grievances in a code fashioned and articulated by the black clergy.

George Washington Brown might have taken a different path. His father wanted him to go to Howard University and then Yale Divinity School, but Brown actively feared leaving the South. He was afraid that he'd become seduced by living somewhere else, somewhere where his skin color would matter, no, never not at all, but less, crucially, tantalizingly less. For even as a young man, George Washington Brown both benefited from and suffered from a profound sense of calling. From the time he could reason at all, he understood both aspects of his father's place in the world, foremost in the black world, foremost black in a white world. In imagining a place for himself, George Washington knew his own transcendent gifts and recognized the obligations those gifts placed upon him. This sense of destiny both made him special and gnawed at his humanity. At age eighteen, when he contemplated going to Howard and then Yale, he imagined the pleasures of becoming an intellectual and a scholar. He imagined writing books about Negro history and essays about the Negro experience in America. He imagined being quoted and admired. And he rejected this course, fearing that it would provide him a shallow happiness coupled with a deep dissatisfaction, fearing he'd go to his grave a public icon and a private failure, a role model and a self-condemned coward.

And so young George Washington Brown stayed home to put up with all the indignities of segregation. He stayed home because, however much New York and Chicago might seem different, he was confident that they were different only in degree, not in kind. He stayed home because it was home, because it was what he knew, and knowing it from growing up in it, like a Choctaw growing up in a swamp, knowing it that way, knowing to look overhead for the moccasins sunning themselves on cedar limbs, knowing to watch the surface of the water for an alligator snout, knowing what the dangers were and where they lay—knowing all that, he felt safer at home.

And, of course, he stayed home because he loved it. He loved the food his grandmother cooked, the hominy and the fatback and the fried chicken and the stewed liver with mustard greens. And he loved the smells of home, the ripeness after a thunderstorm, the rich promise of a baking yam soon to be swathed in melting butter, even the rich human sweat of his father's church choir which no amount of dry cleaning could remove from their brown and gold robes. And he loved the clapping of hands as the choir sang and the ecstatic look on their moist faces as they belted out their gospel numbers. And he loved that gospel music. Maybe that's what he loved the most. Certainly, when the choir sang, he felt surest of his calling by God—which was ironic because, save for hymns, he didn't sing himself. His gifts did not include that of singing. But when he heard the singing, he felt stirred by his own gift, by the knowledge that God had given him the gift of words and the gift of voice and the gift of rhythm with his words. And he felt called to marshal those gifts on behalf of all his people, who had no voice like his own.

So he stayed home, practiced his gifts and mastered the code. He learned to speak of the Children of Israel and knew that his listeners understood him to be speaking of Negroes in America. He learned to speak of wandering in the wilderness, and he knew his listeners understood him to be speaking of segregation. He learned to speak about looking for the promised land, and he knew his listeners understood him to be talking about the promised land of America's own hallowed documents, the promised land where all men were created equal and free equally to pursue happiness.

In the pulpit George Washington could sense the power of his words. People stared at him with uplifted faces, wide eyes and jaws almost slack. They believed what he told them about the Children of Israel finding the promised land in their own lifetimes. But he was frightened that they believed what he told them because he didn't believe it himself. He only wanted to believe it, but he didn't, not really, no matter how much he wanted to. So he felt like a fraud before those who counted on him to tell them the truth. And he was frightened when, at the climax of his sermons, the faithful would call back to him, "Show us," "Lead us, brother," "Be with us, Moses." He felt like a fraud because he was twenty-four years old, and he didn't know the way to the promised land. He didn't know the first step. So he prayed intently for knowledge he didn't have so that he could cease being the fraud he felt himself to be. And his faith comforted him, because he did believe in God, and he did believe in his own calling, and he did believe that God would not abandon him. But he was frightened all the same because his faith wavered, and he wondered in the dead of night if he was a false prophet who would lead his people not to the promised land but to the abyss of destruction. So he prayed for divine guidance. And he waited for providential intervention, and his doubt wavered like a candle flame. And he kept on preaching because that was his gift.

Jeff Caldwell, like other white ministers without race hatred in their hearts, heard of George Washington Brown and wanted to experience the power of his preaching. So one week when Jeff and his friend Preacher Martin learned that the younger Reverend Brown was going to preach at a Dryades Avenue Church revival on Tuesday night, they decided to drive down to New Orleans to hear him.

Ed "Preacher" Martin, who had picked up his nickname as a theology major at Valmont College where he and Jeff first became friends before the war, had graduated from Union Theological Seminary in New York and now served as the Baptist chaplain at Louisiana State University in Baton Rouge. The two young clergymen shared their generation's sense that they were on the threshold of something transformational. They had survived both the Great Depression and World War II to live into an era of already astonishing prosperity. They literally felt that they could change the world. And to them the message and imperative of the gospel was clear. Jesus did not discriminate. The Negro would stand equal at the gates of heaven, and the true Christian must therefore afford the Negro equality on earth.

Time would show Jeff and Preacher to be prescient but foolish, because both thought that the Southern church would be the agent of dramatic social change. Though neither Jeff nor Preacher really had personal friends of color in the South, they liked to get together and speculate about the forces that would end segregation in their world. At the beginning of the 1950s, they imagined Jim Crow would be slain not by federal decree but by moral suasion, not by black-robed Supreme Court justices but by blue-suited Baptist preachers, not by rifle-toting national guardsmen but by Bible-quoting Christian churchmen, not by threats in the teeth of defiance, but by love in the name of brotherhood.

Thus, though Jeff and Preacher both imagined that organizations like the National Association for the Advancement of Colored People would be instrumental in leading the push for change, they felt the key leadership would come from an alliance of black and white clergymen who would together demand racial harmony in the name of Jesus. So Jeff and Preacher felt themselves already at work. Jeff organized a campaign for the purchase of new textbooks for the black schools in the Gonzales vicinity. He did not yet directly advocate racial integration from his pulpit—he thought it was still too early for that—but he did speak in only barely veiled terms about God's loving all his creatures equally. And he dared to believe that Jim Crow would be dead within the decade. Preacher organized a campaign to aid the poor of Baton Rouge and reflected in his sermons about the irony of Baptist mission work in Africa during an era of statutory segregation in America. With this as a topic, he organized a joint symposium with the chaplain at Southern University, the black school across town. Preacher's attitudes were tempered by his natural cynicism, and he regularly teased Jeff about thinking the world was going to change easily or soon. But he shared Jeff's sincere desire to make a difference, to play a part in the struggle that both saw coming.

Brown's power in the pulpit that Tuesday night proved electrifying. Afterwards, as Jeff and Preacher drove back to Gonzales along Airline Highway, they discussed Brown's charisma. "He's the one," Jeff said.

"The one what?" Preacher responded.

"Don't you think he's the one?" Jeff asked.

"I think he's the one who spoke tonight."

Jeff laughed. "You're a rounder, you are, Martin. And I say he's the one."

"Well, I agree he's *a* one," Preacher said. He was trying to break himself of chewing tobacco, a habit he loved but knew was absolutely disgusting, so he'd taken up smoking a pipe. And as he puffed, the car filled with the rich aroma of burning pipe tobacco.

"What?" Jeff said. "He's *a* one what?"

"He's a one Negro," Preacher said, his lips speaking around the stem of his pipe.

"You're a truculent bastard, you know that?"

"Truculent?" Preacher said, taking the pipe from his mouth and chuckling. "You been reading that dictionary again? Truculent's an awfully big word for a man who grew up pissing off his porch in some backwater even the Negroes wouldn't want to be equal in."

"He's the one," Jeff said.

"He might be the one," Preacher admitted, putting the pipe back between his teeth and puffing. "I worry that he ain't got a sense of humor, though."

"We don't know that."

"Naw, but I'm betting on it. Man can preach, but his eyes ain't got any twinkle."

"Maybe nothing looks all that funny from his point of view," Jeff said. "I sure wouldn't think being black was a barrel of laughs, and I'm just poor white trash myself."

"That's just what *is* funny," Preacher said. "Guy as smart and talented as George Washington Brown ends up being a Negro. And what becomes important then is not that he's smart and talented but that he's a Negro. That's funny. Think how funny it is that he's got two white boys he doesn't even know driving out through the Louisiana swamp saying, 'He's the one.' I'm laughing my rear end off."

In seeking to identify a black leader to whom they might attach themselves, Jeff and Preacher assumed that a civil-rights movement would emerge as a conscious plan. But the beginning came spontaneously out of everyday happenstance, and it ended in defeat. The beginning was like dry pine. It burned hot and bright, but fast. Still, it left embers from which the fires of resistance were ultimately kindled.

It began because Rufus Johnson refused to leave a discount-store lunch counter when it closed without serving him in February of 1952. Johnson was a sixty-year-old black man who made his living mowing the lawns and tending the gardens of the residents of one of Baton Rouge's exclusive neighborhoods. He was hard-working and friendly and natively deferential to whites in the way most Southern Negroes of his age were. Due to his willingness to work long hours and his careful courting of his affluent clients, he was more prosperous than most Southern Negroes who did physical labor for their livelihoods. Johnson's relative prosperity allowed him to indulge the luxury of purchasing midday meals at the lunch counter of the Wainwright Five and Dime. It began because Rufus Johnson stubbornly insisted on his right to do on February 22 what he had been successful at doing on February 20 and on practically every Monday and Wednesday and Friday for the previous five years.

Negro patrons were welcome at Wainwright where they provided the store half of its business. Negroes were even welcome at the Wainwright lunch counter, although, of course, they weren't allowed to eat at the counter itself or in the small area of tables across from the counter. All of these seats were reserved for white customers. Black customers could order food at a special section at the side of the counter and carry the food to a group of concrete tables and benches outside. Protocol required that white customers be served before black customers, so to avoid the wait which was sometimes required at noon, Rufus Johnson normally took his lunch at 1:30. The lunch counter closed at 2:00.

Two things conspired against Rufus Johnson the day it began. The first was that Daisy Martine, the lunch counter's efficient regular waitress, was home sick with a cold. Her place was taken by Joel Wagoner, Wainwright's assistant manager, who dourly resented being assigned such a lowly duty by store manager Richard Nelson—who, as was his usual habit, had gone home to eat his own lunch. The second was that on this particular day Miss Frances Bellingham brought her third-grade class from Sorrento to visit the Louisiana State Capitol and at 1:15 P.M. herded all twenty-three of her pupils into Wainwright for the midday meal. Miss Bellingham was an effective disciplinarian, and her young students were well behaved and reasonably quiet. But Mr. Wagoner was nonetheless almost completely undone by having to attend to them. He got orders mixed up and became frustrated when the children would not accept what he put before them. He managed to put a blue stripe from the collar down to the pocket of his white shirt when he jammed his pen back into his pocket. His forehead began to sweat. He smeared the right lens of his glasses with hamburger grease, and then he wasn't able to get it adequately clean with one of the lunch counter's damp dish towels.

This was the atmosphere that Rufus Johnson walked into at 1:30. He took his place at the "Colored Order Here" sign, the only Negro in line, and waited as Wagoner bristled back and forth between the tables and the grill where Marlene Jackson, the Negro cook, fried hamburgers and prepared ham and bacon sandwiches. For ten minutes Wagoner ignored Rufus completely while he tried to straighten out the confused lunch orders. As he waited, Rufus chatted amiably with Marlene, inquiring about Miss Daisy's absence and the unusual hubbub. When it became clear that all the white patrons had placed their orders, Rufus tried to place his.

"Good day to you, sir," Rufus said to Wagoner as the assistant manager walked past him with a hamburger on a small round plate.

Wagoner looked at Rufus but didn't speak. He set the plate on the work counter beside Marlene and said to her in a scolding tone, "Little girl don't want it with mayonnaise. She only wants it with ketchup."

"Yassir, Mr. Joel," Marlene said. She handed him an oval plate with a BLT and potato chips. "That for five," she said, indicating the table number. She picked up the rejected plate and said, "I'll fix this one right up."

Wagoner stalked away, ignoring Rufus. When the assistant manager returned to the grill, Rufus said, "I can give you my order, Mr. Joel, if you ready."

"Can't you see I've got white customers to wait on?" Wagoner snapped. Rufus looked down and did not reply. Wagoner picked up the burger that had gotten a new bun without mayonnaise and a plate with a ham sandwich on white with French fries.

"Seven," Marlene said.

"Which?" Wagoner said.

"The ham."

"What about the burger?"

"For the little girl who don't want mayonnaise."

Wagoner stood a moment glaring at Marlene. "And how the dickens was I supposed to know that?"

"Sorry, Mr. Joel," she said, her voice managing to register neither insolence nor contrition. The assistant manager spun away from her, and she thought of how Daisy would never have left the grill on a busy day like this one without enough dishes balanced on her arms to feed two tables of diners. With her back to Rufus and her hands busy making other sandwiches, Marlene asked, "You want your usual, Rufus?"

"Sho do," he replied, the knot of confused frustration above his eyebrows replaced by a spreading grin. In front of him Marlene slapped another hamburger patty on the griddle.

Wagoner made repeated trips back and forth to the tables, carrying a single plate in each hand, taking directions from Marlene as to what went where. He drew Cokes from the fountain and carried the glasses to the school children. Then he brought a hamburger back and set it beside Marlene saying, "This one don't want it with pickles." Marlene immediately lifted the top bun, picked the pickles off, replaced the bun and handed the plate back to her boss. "He'll probably say he can taste the pickle juice," Wagoner said.

"I'll make a fresh one if you want, Mr. Joel," Marlene replied.

Wagoner looked at his watch and made a sucking sound with his teeth and lips. "Just give it here," he said. As he turned away, he added, "Thank God this nonsense is almost over." Wagoner's eyes passed over Rufus as if Rufus were an inanimate object.

The assistant manager fixed more drinks and carried them to the tables, constantly having to ask the school children whether they had ordered Coke, ice tea or milk. Miss Bellingham handed him money, and he went to the cash register, totaled up the third graders' tab with pad and pencil, made change and returned behind the counter with a sigh that was one part exasperation, one part relief. He looked at his watch and said to Marlene, "Well, that's it. Finally. I presume Daisy will be back tomorrow."

Marlene didn't answer him. But Rufus Johnson said, "I best be settling my tab, I suspect, Mr. Joel."

Wagoner looked over at Johnson as if he had suddenly appeared from another dimension. "What?" he said.

"I should best be paying for my meal now, I reckon," Rufus said.

"What meal? We're closed. It's two o'clock."

Rufus looked at his watch and smiled. "Why yassir. Two minutes after, it is."

"We close at two," Wagoner said.

"Yassir," Rufus said. "So I best be settling up."

"For what?" Wagoner said. He walked closer to Rufus and stared at him as if he were an animal in a zoo. "You're not listening to me, boy. I told you already, and I ain't gonna tell you again. The lunch counter is closed."

"Yassir," Rufus said. "But I ain't got my burger yet."

"And you ain't getting it, neither," Wagoner said, raising his voice. "Are you deaf? I told you we were closed. Now you get on away from here before I call the police."

"But you don't understand," Rufus said. "I done ordered."

"No, you ain't," Wagoner said.

"I done got his hamburger cooked," Marlene said with her back to the two men.

Wagoner whirled around toward her. "You what?" he said.

"It's right here," Marlene said, indicating with a sweep of her hand the waiting hamburger on her work counter. "It's his usual. Rufus eats here every Monday, Wednesday and Friday." She stepped beside Wagoner and set the burger on the counter.

"Well, he don't eat here this Friday," Wagoner said. "We're closed and that's final. Now you throw that away. And you never take an order in this store again unless you plan on it being your last day."

"Now that ain't right, Mr. Joel," Rufus said. "I done waited my turn, and I'd like to just get my food and go on about my business like I always do."

Wagoner spun back around to Rufus, who could see the whites all around his brown eyes. "Nigger, don't you go telling me what's right and what ain't, not in my store you don't. I done told you to git. Now you git."

"Nawsir," Rufus said. "I waited my turn like I'm supposed to. Now I just want what's fair."

"Now you're telling me what's fair and what ain't in my own store. First what's right. Now what's fair. Now I'm telling you something. If you don't turn your black ass around and start walking out of here this minute, I'm going to see you in jail. That's what's right and what's fair."

This last speech, delivered in a very loud voice, succeeded in drawing attention throughout the store. Marlene turned around from her griddle and began wiping her hands on her apron. The two cashiers up front stopped checking out customers. Those who were still looking over merchandise began to move toward the lunch area, curious as to what was going on. Miss Bellingham stood up from the table where she had eaten three quarters of a bacon, lettuce and tomato sandwich. "Well, I never," she said. "Such language. And in front of children."

Rufus said, "You can put me in jail if you want, Mr. Joel. But I got a right to my food. I came on time, and I waited like I was supposed to."

Rufus Johnson was anything but a rabble-rouser. He was a man of average intelligence who had grown up in a Jim Crow world that he'd never really questioned. He recognized that his was a second-class citizenship, but he accepted it as his lot in life. His livelihood depended on good relations with white people, and he cultivated them with a pleasant manner and resolutely reliable service. If he was rained out one day, he started early and worked late the next to make up for it. He worked Saturdays and Sundays if he had to. And his efforts were appreciated. His customers recommended him to new arrivals in town and remembered him with gifts of cash at Christmas. He went to church. He was the father of three—including a son who had died in Germany during the war—and the grandfather of four. Insofar as he thought of an organization such as the NAACP at all, he worried that any push for more freedoms would result in fewer. So Rufus Johnson did not suddenly object to Joel Wagoner's refusing to serve him out of any abstract principle. Rather, he objected because Wagoner's actions were such a flagrant violation of established rules.

Livid, Joel Wagoner almost ran to Marlene's stove, where he roughly pushed her aside and grabbed the heavy iron skillet in which she cooked biscuits every morning. "I'll send you somewhere else, you goddamn nigger," Wagoner said as he came running back. He raised the skillet over his head. "I'll send you straight to hell."

Rufus did not back away, and the semicircle of people who gathered at the corner of the lunch counter did nothing to intervene. They just stood blinking, watching events unfold that they did not understand. "You can hit me with that skillet if you take a mind to, Mr. Joel," Rufus said. "But I ain't leaving here of my own will till I've eaten my hamburger."

"I'll kill you," Wagoner screamed. Up front a cashier rushed for the phone and called the police to report a race riot at Wainwright Five and Dime. "I'll kill you," Wagoner screamed again and smashed the skillet down on the hamburger Marlene had set on the counter in front of him. Shards of broken glass sprayed out, and the crowd leapt for cover as if gunshots had been fired. "I'll kill you," Wagoner screamed again and pounded on the hamburger till it was a flattened pulpy mush of meat and bread and glass. "Eat this, you dumbass nigger. Eat it and choke on it. Eat what a hog wouldn't be stupid enough to eat."

The police arrived shortly later and arrested Rufus for assault, felonious destruction of property, and violation of state separation-of-the-races statutes. Three other black men in the store and a black woman were arrested for inciting to riot. Each had tried to give testimony to police officers that the only violence that had been committed had been committed by the store's assistant manager.

He had murdered a hamburger.

But Rufus Johnson stood liable to going to prison for five to fifteen for the crime of trying to buy lunch.

The truth about this incident circulated immediately through the black community. Within hours a crowd began to gather in front of the city's central lockup. This gathering was utterly spontaneous and as peaceful as it was unorganized. People came for the same reason that Rufus Johnson had refused to leave the lunch counter when Joel Wagoner ordered him to. It was one thing to be subjected to legalized discrimination, quite another to have Jim Crow's own rules so flagrantly violated. White officials, predictably, overreacted. A cordon of police was quickly placed around the courthouse and jail, and the crowd was ordered to disperse. With a lot of grumbling, it did so. But that night a large number of black citizens gathered at the Four Gospels Baptist Church to discuss the situation.

The pastor of the church, the Reverend Zaccheus Greene, called the meeting to order. "We need to remain calm," he told them. "We need to make sure we have all the facts straight."

This remark led to indignant rejoinders by three women who had been in the Wainwright Five and Dime that afternoon. Each stated unequivocally that Rufus Johnson had done nothing more than order lunch. Each told the story in a slightly different way, however, and their incidental disagreement over insignificant details led to a brief squabble among the three.

"That's just what I mean when I say we need to get our facts straight," Reverend Greene said.

This was greeted by a round of grumbling. "It seems to me our facts are straight enough," one man said. "We need to decide what we're going to do."

"We need to elect a spokesman," another man said. "We should choose a leader, then set a course."

Someone nominated Reverend Greene, who vacillated between wanting the honor and not wanting the responsibility. Someone else nominated Moses Jones, a porter with the Illinois Southern Railroad and president of the local chapter of the NAACP. Reverend Greene rose at the front of the sanctuary. "Before we have all the facts of this case, I think we ought to be careful about involving the NAACP," he said. "We don't want to start ourselves a controversy."

"Ain't us that started this controversy," someone responded, and a general round of grumbling ensued again. Eventually the gathering could agree on only two things: to take up an immediate collection for Rufus Johnson's defense expenses and to meet again the next night.

Word of the incident at the Wainwright Five and Dime also circulated quickly through various contingents in the white community. Mayor Charles Bordelon met with the governor, who put the state's National Guard on ready alert. The governor also met with his cabinet to consider calling the legislature into immediate session—for what purpose was not clear, although there were obvious potential advantages to the governor's being seen as a man of action. The local Grand Kleagel of the Ku Klux Klan also put his forces on alert, and a platoon of good old boys in pickup trucks began to cruise the streets around the courthouse on the lookout for any "unlawful conclave of disrespectful niggers."

Among the liberal elements around LSU, another attitude held sway: how to defuse the situation as quickly as possible. To this end, historian H. Theodore Magnuson hosted an impromptu cocktail party on Friday evening while the Negroes were gathered at Four Gospels. As it happened, Teddy Magnuson was one of Rufus Johnson's employers, as were several other of his LSU colleagues. None of the people who sipped sherry and mint juleps at Magnuson's house could believe that Rufus Johnson was guilty of inciting to riot. They all knew Rufus too well as a quiet, responsible, respectful man. Magnuson proposed raising a defense fund among the gathered whites, but one of their number, Davis Patterson, an LSU law professor, responded with something even better. Patterson proposed organizing a *pro bono* legal defense among his law-school colleagues and other sympathetic members of the Baton Rouge legal community. Delighted with this approach, Magnuson also volunteered to lobby LSU president Francis Abadie to use his political influence to bring this matter to an early, peaceful and just resolution.

Elsewhere in the city, there were still other meetings going on. Among them was one at Preacher Martin's house that included Jeff Caldwell, a liberal lawyer named Hodding Morris, and several of Preacher's Negro acquaintances from Southern University. The conversation at this meeting evinced a mixture of altruism and opportunism. There was genuine concern for the plight of Rufus Johnson, but there was also a frank discussion of how this incident might be exploited for the purpose of achieving racial equality. It was thrilling to be in that room that night, thrilling for blacks and whites to sit together on what seemed a momentous occasion and actively plot to change the face of their country. This gathering lacked the undercurrent of acrimony that marked the meeting at the Four Gospels Baptist Church, but it was no more decisive. Those assembled could agree only to designate Southern University mathematics professor Taylor Carson as their spokesman. Early the next morning Taylor called Jeff and Preacher and the other members of their group and asked them to join him on Saturday night for the next meeting at Four Gospels.

While the involved black majority and the self-consciously conspiratorial black and white intelligentsia waited for Saturday night, Teddy Magnuson's group swung into action. Davis Patterson exploited his city-hall contacts to gain an audience with Rufus

Johnson. Meanwhile, LSU President Abadie contacted the governor, relayed the Magnuson group's character-witness testimony and urged him to resolve this matter as quickly as possible. The domino effect of that contact—from the governor to the mayor to the police chief—coupled with a meeting between Patterson and district attorney Bobby LeBlanc, resulted in an offer to reduce the charges against Rufus Johnson to criminal trespass, a misdemeanor carrying a maximum penalty of 180 days in jail and a $1,000 fine. Patterson agreed to take the offer to his client if the prosecutor would recommend the suspension of all jail time and a $500 fine. Coupled with Patterson's own promise to Johnson to raise the $500 for him, he felt certain he had a deal.

He was wrong. Rufus Johnson turned it down. "I ain't no criminal," Rufus Johnson said. "And I ain't guilty of nothing but being hungry. I done what I supposed to. I waited my turn." Patterson tried to explain how much progress had been made, how the serious charges had already been dropped. But Rufus didn't know the difference between a felony and a misdemeanor, and he adamantly refused to plead guilty to anything. "Bad enough I been arrested. Nobody in my family ever been arrested before. I sho ain't gonna say they was right to do it."

Patterson was worried about this response. And he was justifiably concerned that an angry prosecutor might reinstate the more serious charges if Rufus refused to accept the plea bargain. "Tell me what you want," Patterson asked his client. "Tell me what would satisfy you."

"Well, I think that man ought to apologize to me," Rufus said.

Patterson shook his head in dismay and said, "I doubt he'll agree to that."

"Well, I won't agree to saying I'm guilty of something I ain't."

"You tell that stupid nigger to go fuck himself," Bobby LeBlanc exploded when Patterson reported Rufus's response to the plea bargain. "I made him the sweetheart deal of the century."

"He doesn't want to plead guilty to something he didn't do," Patterson explained.

LeBlanc responded, "You tell him he's got his head so far up his ass, it's gonna take him five years to pull it out."

"That's if you win this thing," Patterson said, rising to the challenge. "I've got a store full of witnesses who'll say my client didn't do anything but stand at a counter and wait to be served."

"You got a bunch of nigger witnesses who'll start out stating that, and by the time I get finished with them they'll be saying they saw Moses part the Red Sea. Meanwhile I got Miss Frances Bellingham, an upstanding white school teacher who'll say she heard your nigger curse a white man, threaten him, and break property in his store. Who do you think a jury of nervous white folks is gonna believe?"

"Sometimes they do the right thing," Patterson said.

"Oh bullshit, Davis," LeBlanc replied. "You know as well as I do that if the Virgin Mary was a nigger, I could convict her of being the whore of Babylon."

Jeff Caldwell, Preacher Martin, Taylor Carson, and the other members of their organization knew nothing of these negotiations, but the impasse gave them the opportunity they needed to try to build a coalition around the larger issues of segregation. Jeff and Preacher and Taylor huddled with their associates in front of Four Gospels Baptist Church before the meeting began that night. They had learned that Rufus was still in jail and would be arraigned on Monday, the earliest he could be released. They could not agree, even among themselves, on what course to take inside the church, save to support Taylor as a spokesman. The crowd inside Four Gospels was larger than the night before. People sat in the aisles and stood in the back and along the walls. It was angrier and even more divided. And this night it was populated with a smattering of white faces—Jeff's and Preacher's and a half dozen others as well.

Reverend Greene called the meeting to order at 7:30, and a young Southern University student got the meeting off to a fractious start by inquiring why Greene was presiding. A speaker defended Greene's right to preside at a meeting in his own church. Someone else reminded the crowd that they had been in the process of choosing a leader the night before and said, "And again, I nominate the president of the Baton Rouge NAACP, the honorable Mr. Moses Jones."

Jones rose immediately to say, "I am proud to accept this nomination on behalf of the National Association for the Advancement of Colored People, whose local chapter I have served as president since nineteen and thirty-seven." He then went on at uncomfortable and only tangentially relevant length to extol the accomplishments of the NAACP.

A faint ripple of applause greeted the end of Jones's speech, but someone muttered audibly, "Round here NAACP stands for Noisy Ass Active Crap Purveyor," and those who heard laughed raucously.

One of Reverend Greene's church members again rose to nominate him for leader. Then Jeff stood up and nominated Taylor Carson, extolling his virtues as an educator and a man of broad vision. In addition, Jeff spoke of marching to the courthouse and picketing Wainwright, thereby proposing a course of action broader than his own group of conspirators had ever agreed to and saddling Taylor Carson with an agenda he hadn't endorsed. Preacher would castigate Jeff about his presumption with bouts of sarcasm and mimicry for days. ("Now that it's 10:30," he might say in a meeting, "the rest of us would like to take a break for coffee, but Reverend Caldwell, as I understand it, would like to propose we all drive down to New Orleans for a five-course meal at Antoine's.")

Jeff's nominating speech also brought him to the interested attention of the Negro community. In that regard it was a good speech, devoid of the kind of paternalistic condescension with which even the most well-meaning white people habitually related to Negroes. None of the black people in the church that night could recall ever hearing a white man speak so eloquently in favor of a leadership role for a Negro, and for these reasons, Jeff Caldwell would be a man the members of that largely black gathering would remember and talk about. But Jeff's nominating speech for Taylor Carson also ensured Taylor's defeat. It introduced issues not directly related to the unjust incarceration of Rufus Johnson. And it was, of course, a speech by a white man, so, however impressive, it was still suspect.

Taylor Carson's brief remarks accepting his nomination were notable for their lack of eloquence. He was a good mathematician, a kind, earnest teacher and a decent, admirable man. But numbers, not words, were his medium. His performance in the church that night was less than impressive. Someone demanded a vote, and Reverend Greene was elected spokesman, although without much enthusiasm.

At that point the gathering turned its attention to a course of action. After a whispered strategy session with Preacher, Jeff advocated picketing Wainwright and other downtown lunch counters starting Monday. Some spoke in favor of this idea. But others warned that the black cooks at the lunch counters and the black janitorial staff would lose their jobs. As the debate volleyed back and forth without much progress, it appeared that the crowd in Four Gospels might not be able to agree on anything at all. That's when George Washington Brown rose to speak at the front left side of the sanctuary.

Jeff and Preacher had not even realized that Brown was present. At five feet, seven inches tall, George Washington Brown was not a physically imposing man. He was thick-chested but otherwise slight of build. His dark suit was well-tailored, though, and he held himself with confidence. But it was his great, rich, resonant voice that gave him his command, his rhythmic cadences drawing listeners in the way a distinctive drum beat draws the ear to a song.

"Brothers and sisters," Reverend Brown began. "For nigh two hours now we have sought to choose a path through the forest. The forest is thick with growth, thick with high trees that keep us from seeing what is on the other side, high trees that hide from us the forest's depth, high trees that may cast upon us the dark and chilling shade of evil and hide from us the warming light of God's grace. The forest before us, moreover, is thick with undergrowth, thick with the razor thorns of prejudice, thick with the poisonous berries of sundry temptations, thick with the ensnarling vines of pride and personal ambition. Our brother Rufus Johnson stands somewhere in the forest, and our first task is to reach him. But as we reach him we must take him on, take him on and ourselves with him. Take him beyond the forest to the valley of righteousness which lies beyond. From where we stand tonight, we can see several paths before us. All paths lead in, lead in where dangers lie. All paths may lead out, and all paths may not lead out. Some paths lead more directly to our brother Rufus. That is the one I think we should take. But let any who stands before us tonight and points out a path, let any who dares say follow me, let him first bathe himself in the waters of humility, for though Jesus is surely here with us in the Holy Spirit which joins us together, for though Jesus through the Holy Spirit certainly walks with us, Jesus in his own flesh does not walk among us, not Jesus and not Moses—"

Brown paused now and a wry smile played across his lips. "Not Moses save for the honorable Mr. Moses Jones, of course." And a wave of laughter swept across the auditorium.

When the laughter died down, Brown continued, "Together we choose a path. Together we march closely down that path. We must acknowledge together how the path we choose will not be straight, no matter how it appears from here. It will wind closely by the myriad dangers which forests always harbor. In hindsight we may later see that another path would have been shorter and straighter. But I say this unto you all, and as I say it I feel myself filled with the Holy Spirit. It is better that we walk down a longer path together than that we walk down a shorter path alone. Tomorrow, brothers and sisters, let us attend worship, here in Four Gospels and at the other churches where we are members. And when service is over, let us gather here at Four Gospels in all our multitudes, and let us walk together to the courthouse, twenty blocks hence, and let us by our presence there say to the authorities as Moses said to Pharaoh, that they must let our brother go. Let us tomorrow, in the light of God Almighty, follow our elected leader Reverend Greene. Let this be our path. Let us walk it together in righteousness. And let us walk it together in the name of brotherhood. And let us walk it together in Jesus' name."

Reverend Brown sat down and a hush fell over the gathering. No one else rose immediately to speak. Finally, Jeff stood up and said, "So moved."

And the Reverend Greene rose after a moment and said, "All in favor, say Aye."

There was no dissent. And so it began.

It would seem from what followed that it did not really begin that night, but it did.

Two of the whites in the crowd that night were not, like Jeff and Preacher, fresh volunteers for a movement only now being born. Two of these faces were employees of the mayor, and they reported to their boss that a march was planned for the next afternoon. The mayor called Bobby LeBlanc and wanted to know where in the dickens the D.A. was in his negotiations with Davis Patterson.

"We're nowhere," LeBlanc said. "Stubborn nigger nitwit is too stupid to know the difference between not going to jail at all and going to jail for a very long time."

The mayor told LeBlanc that was not acceptable. "Now we got ourselves a situation on our hands, and I don't want it. We got a city full of niggers planning themselves a demonstration, and I want to take the wind out of their sails before they think they can go force us to do something. You understand me. I want a deal. And I want it two hours ago."

"Well, Jesus Christ," LeBlanc said. "We can't just let him walk."

"Plead him guilty to jaywalking," the mayor said. "Plead him guilty to ignoring a Don't Walk on the Grass sign. I don't care. Just fix it. Fast."

So Bobby LeBlanc called Davis Patterson at home. But Patterson told the D.A. that he didn't think Rufus Johnson would ever agree to any deal requiring him to plead guilty. "Well, why don't you try paying him?" LeBlanc suggested, only half joking. He told Patterson about the next day's planned march. "You and your liberal friends don't want that any more than troglodytes like me and the mayor," LeBlanc said. "Bad business. Fucking Kluxers liable to go crazy and kill folks. You gotta find a way to get Uncle Rufus to let us let him out of jail."

"You could drop all charges," Patterson suggested.

"Shit," LeBlanc said. "Now you know damned well, Davis, we can't do that. We gotta convict him of something. Nigger gets arrested is a guilty nigger. You gotta nice cushy job at the law school. I gotta run for reelection every four years."

"I'll talk to Rufus first thing in the morning," Patterson promised, but he wasn't hopeful that Rufus Johnson was about to budge.

When LeBlanc informed the mayor of the continuing impasse, the mayor responded with a series of oaths. Finally, he said, "Well, Bobby, I'd like to help these niggers out. I'm sure the assistant manager of the Wainwright Five and Dime is a pinhead. Meanwhile, though this Uncle Rufus's obviously got his head about one mile up his asshole, he's supposed to be a decent enough fellow. What I hear from his uppity LSU friends anyway. Still, ain't no niggers gonna embarrass me with no fucking demonstration march. Nosirree they ain't. And you can take that and put it in Chase Manhattan Bank and draw top-dollar interest."

Mayor Bordelon was actually a man of above-average intelligence. He'd regularly made the dean's list as an LSU undergraduate, and he'd graduated in the top ten percent of his LSU law class. But he had long ago adopted a good-old-boy public persona that led him always to break known grammar rules when he was expressing irritation. Bordelon's obsession with not being publicly embarrassed by Negro demonstrators was typical of politicians of his era. In part, it was born of his own entrenched racism. It infuriated him to think that a Negro or group of Negroes might ever try to coerce him into doing anything. But his concern was also purely political. Any white politician who could be depicted as anything less than a diehard supporter of Jim Crow was a politician looking toward early retirement.

So when he got off the phone with LeBlanc, Bordelon called his police chief to discuss handling the demonstration which now looked almost inevitable. The police chief pointed out immediately that the Negroes couldn't legally march from Four Gospels to the courthouse without a parade permit, which they hadn't even applied for. "Well, that's that then," Bordelon concluded. "They ain't having no demonstration march. End of discussion."

"Where do you want us to stop them?" the police chief inquired.

"I want you to stop their black asses before they start," the mayor snapped.

"Just what's that supposed to mean, Charlie?" the chief responded, irritated himself now. It was going to be his job to disrupt the march, and he wanted to have a real discussion, not an exchange of pointless posturing.

"I mean it," the mayor said. "I want them stopped before they get started. I don't want anybody to be able to say they even had a demonstration march."

"That's a whole lot easier to say than to pull off," the chief replied.

"Well, why in the hell is that?" the mayor wanted to know.

"Because, Charlie," the chief said with exaggerated patience, "they got a right to go to church. Once they get in the church we can't refuse to let them out. They got a right to go in; they got a right to come out."

"Well, stop 'em as soon they goddamn come out."

"They got a right to go home, too. We can't hold 'em prisoner in their church yard."

"Okay, wiseass, what's your idea?" the mayor demanded, really agitated by this point.

"Frankly, Charlie," the chief said, not even attempting to hide his exasperation, "I don't have an idea. They don't have the right to stage a march without a parade permit. But we can't stop them from doing it until they start doing it. I could set up barriers a block away, I guess. But looks to me like that isn't gonna satisfy your idea that they didn't have a march. I could make it a short march. But the newspapers are still gonna write it up that they had a march, and I don't see there's a thing we can do about it."

"Shitfire!" the mayor said. "Goddamn shitfire." He slammed the phone down.

But then he picked it back up and called the police chief right back. Without identifying himself or making any other kind of introduction, he said, "Pompous spade named Zaccheus Greene is the pastor of that Four Gospels Baptist Church, am I right?"

"What of it?" the police chief said.

"He's the man the niggers elected their leader."

"Okay?"

"You call up his black ass," the mayor directed, "and tell him if he so much as crosses the street tomorrow after church, we're gone slap him in jail for inciting to riot and throw away the key. You see what I'm aiming at? You explain to him all about needing a permit to parade and how he ain't got one and how we're going to hold his sorry ass responsible if he sets out to encourage his folks to break the law."

"Hmmm," the police chief responded. "Might work."

"Better work," the mayor said and hung up again without signing off.

And it did work. Police Chief Anderson woke Zaccheus Greene out of a fitful sleep. Greene was nervous enough about having been selected the leader of the next day's demonstration. After the chief got through with him, he was scared silly. He didn't know Rufus Johnson. And he didn't have any respect for colored folks so stupid as to get themselves in the kind of jam Johnson was in. Moreover, Greene sure as heck wasn't going to jail on behalf of a yard man who wasn't even a member of his own church. It took Reverend Greene most of the rest of the night to come up with a plan for getting out of this fix.

During Sunday services Reverend Greene stated that he'd received a vision from Jesus during the night and Jesus had told him that the Negro people must abide by the law. This perturbed him some because it had been called to his attention that their planned march would be in violation of the law requiring a parade permit. But Greene's words did not go down well. And for the first time in his own church he heard mutterings of "Shame, shame," directed at his own person.

By one o'clock, the square of lawn in front of the church and the sidewalks all around were crowded with black and a few white faces, the faithful who had come from other churches to join the demonstration. The police had thrown up barricades directly across the street, so the march wasn't going to get far before resulting in a confrontation. But confrontation, of course, is a central element in the theater of a demonstration.

When Greene did not emerge to lead the throng as agreed upon the night before, people began to crowd into Four Gospels church, where a debate among the members of Greene's own congregation was in full swing. Greene argued again and again that their hands were tied, that the police were prepared to arrest anyone who attempted to march to the courthouse today and that sending more people to jail was a foolish way of protesting Rufus Johnson's arrest and incarceration. Those who supported Greene, and many did, maintained that the gathering was obliged to heed the wisdom of their elected leader. But many, naturally, were frustrated that for the third straight day they were crowded into a church arguing about what to do rather than out in the streets actually doing something. Someone made a motion that Greene be stripped of his leadership, but the motion never came to a vote.

Eventually, the meeting broke down. People argued in small groups among themselves, creating a clamor in the church so loud that those who stood and addressed the whole crowd could scarcely be heard. There were frequent shouts for quiet, but after it became clear that Greene had altered the course that George Washington Brown had convinced them to follow the night before, the whole group could seem to agree on nothing. Gradually, people became disgusted and trickled out of the sanctuary. By 2:30, only half the crowd remained. By three o'clock fewer than one hundred people were still there. Finally, Greene declared that he would have his personal lawyer investigate a proper permit first thing Monday morning and then declared, "This meeting is adjourned." Some in attendance actually booed.

The next morning Davis Patterson proposed that Bobby LeBlanc reduce the charges against Rufus Johnson to loitering. LeBlanc hesitated, but finally said, "You get that mulehead to agree, and I'll do it. But this offer is on the table for exactly one hour and not one second longer." Patterson went to Rufus's cell to communicate the reduced charge of loitering. "I warn't neither," Rufus said. "Loitrin is for layabouts. I'm a working man. I was trying to buy my dinner. And I won't plead guilty to loitrin any more than I'd plead guilty to any of those other charges."

"I'm not going to ask you to say anything at all," Patterson responded. "I will do all the talking. You just stand when you're told to stand and leave the rest up to me."

"You're not going to say I'm guilty," Rufus asserted. "I'll get me another lawyer."

"No, I'm not. I promise that I'm not going to say you're guilty."

"All right then," Rufus said.

"Thank the Lord," LeBlanc responded when Patterson called to say they had a deal. "Let's put this thing out to pasture and get back to doing something important. Like golf Wednesday."

"Golf Wednesday," Patterson agreed.

In the courtroom later that morning, the bailiff read the charge against Rufus.

"How do you plead?" Judge James McElroy asked. The judge plucked half-lensed reading glasses, which he wore dangling against his chest from a black cord around his neck, and pinched them on his nose to study the case file open on the bench in front of him.

"The defendant pleads *nolo contendere*," Davis Patterson announced. At his side Rufus showed no emotion.

The judge looked up slowly, first at Patterson and then over at Bobby LeBlanc who spun toward Patterson like an LSU defensive back grasping after an elusive runner. "What?" LeBlanc demanded. "What are you up to, Davis? This wasn't part of—"

"May we approach, your honor?" Patterson interrupted.

At the bench, Patterson said under his breath to LeBlanc, "Now don't blow the deal, Bobby. It's like you said this morning, let's put this thing out to pasture."

"The deal was for him to plead guilty," LeBlanc whispered through gritted teeth.

"Come on, Bobby," Patterson said, keeping his voice low, letting an edge of pleading creep into his tone. "You know as well as I do that a plea of *nolo contendere* has the same effect as a plea of guilty."

"Well then why didn't you plead the bastard guilty?" LeBlanc whispered back.

"Because he wouldn't agree to it."

"Jesus," LeBlanc said and turned around to stare at Rufus. He turned back to Patterson. "Why didn't you tell me about this before we came in here?"

"Because it would have pissed you off."

"It does piss me off."

"And you wouldn't have agreed to it," Patterson added.

"I still don't agree to it."

"But we've come this far," Patterson said. "And everybody wants this thing to go away. Y'all got that demonstration march stopped over at Four Gospels Baptist yesterday afternoon. But you won't be able to stop it forever. Not if you keep this man in jail."

"I might keep him in jail for loitering," Judge McElroy said, smiling nastily.

"Now come on, Jimmy," Patterson said.

"Remember where you are, Davis," the judge said, seemingly without rancor.

"Please, your honor," Patterson said. "Now we all want to get this thing done. Including the court, I'm certain."

"Bobby ain't said he's agreed yet," McElroy said. "I cain't do a thing about it if Bobby decides not to accept a plea of *nolo contendere* and opts to bring more serious charges." McElroy looked at LeBlanc over his half-lensed reading glasses. "Course I might confide to Bobby that I'd look favorably on his accepting this plea. So's we could all get ourselves off to an early lunch."

"Oh, all right," LeBlanc said. He looked the judge full in the face a long moment and then over at Patterson. "But only if Jimmy—"

"Remember where you are," the judge interrupted in a tone of exaggerated patience.

LeBlanc started again, "But only if Judge McElroy gives a statement to the press immediately afterwards stating that *nolo contendere* is a guilty plea."

"You going to have to make mention of it in the courtroom while the defendant is still present?" Patterson wanted to know.

"I guess we can keep it secret till he's a free man," the judge said.

"Done," Patterson said.

The lawyers returned to their tables and faced the judge, who said, "Mr. LeBlanc, the defendant has pleaded *nolo contendere* to the charge of loitering. I presume you accept this plea."

"The people do, your honor," LeBlanc responded.

"Mr. Johnson," the judge said, addressing Rufus, "I find you guilty of loitering and fine you twenty-five dollars. Please pay the bailiff; then you are free to go." He raised the gavel and clicked it down lightly. "This court stands adjourned until 1 P.M."

"What?" Rufus said, trying to figure out what had happened as the judge rose from the bench and disappeared into his chambers. Rufus turned to Patterson. "What done happened?"

"I'm sorry," Patterson said. "The judge examined your case and found you guilty of loitering. But that's good news really, don't you see, because the prosecutor agreed to drop all the serious charges against you."

"I can see that second part," Rufus said. "But how can the judge find me guilty when I didn't get no trial?"

"But that's what we just had," Patterson said.

"When?" Rufus asked.

"When the district attorney and I approached the bench. We discussed the case—I did the best I could for you—and the judge made his ruling. You're free to go home. That's the most important thing."

"But I have to pay twenty-five dollars," Rufus protested. "And I'm found guilty of loitrin. I wasn't loitrin."

"You and I know you weren't loitering," Patterson said. "And you're free to continue to maintain your innocence. Meanwhile, your fine is being taken care of."

"Taken care of?" Rufus said.

"It's being paid for you," Patterson explained. "You don't have to worry about it."

"Paid for by who?"

"I'm not at liberty to reveal that," Patterson said. "But you have friends who didn't want to see you suffer a financial reversal because of this incident. So everything is being taken care of."

"Being taken care of?" Rufus said, as he walked with Patterson. "I shorely don't understand a mess of this."

At the bailiff's desk, Patterson took two ten dollar bills and five ones out of his wallet to pay Rufus Johnson's fine. Then they walked outside to the courthouse steps where Davis Patterson shook his client's hand firmly and wished him all the best. They parted there and headed in different directions.

At about that moment Judge McElroy admitted several journalists to his chambers and explained to them that a plea of *nolo contendere*, or no contest, was tantamount under the law to a guilty plea. Subsequent to their conversation with the judge, the writers interviewed Bobby LeBlanc. The result of these interviews ran the next day on the front page of the *Morning Advocate* under the headline: NEGRO ACCEPTS RESPONSIBILITY FOR INCIDENT AT FIVE AND DIME. In the article, the paper quoted LeBlanc as saying, "The verdict in the case of *The People v. Rufus Johnson* is a victory for the standards of law, order and civilized behavior. This case threatened to stir up a controversy and to open unfortunate wounds between the races where there historically have been none and need be none at this time. The verdict in the case negates that possibility and proves beyond any doubt that our policemen acted appropriately. There was an incident. And now, Mr. Rufus Johnson in his plea before the court has taken responsibility for the incident. He has been found guilty. He has been fined and has paid his fine. And I am sure he goes back to his daily pursuits a chastened man. The people are satisfied. Justice has been done."

Rufus Johnson was not quoted in the article. Neither was he interviewed. The journalists sought a statement from Davis Patterson, but he was unavailable to give one.

Rufus Johnson did not learn of the meaning of his lawyer's *nolo contendere* plea until he read about it in the paper. He made repeated attempts in the days following to reach Davis Patterson, but Patterson never returned his calls. Zaccheus Greene read Tuesday's newspaper with a profound sense of relief and a feeling of righteous confirmation. He had been right to refuse to lead the march on Sunday. The march wasn't necessary. The imprisoned man, Rufus Johnson, was now out of jail. And he had admitted to causing the trouble that landed him in jail in the first place. The idea of the demonstration was unwise to begin with, fostered by that imperious demagogue from New Orleans, George Washington Brown. Let Brown lead his own demonstrations. Zaccheus Greene had the Lord's work to do.

Preacher Martin learned of Rufus Johnson's release on Monday afternoon when the faculty rumor circuit that started among Davis Patterson's colleagues at the law school delivered the information to the chaplain's offices. Preacher called Jeff immediately, and the two spent an hour's worth of long-distance telephone money bemoaning what had happened. But they agreed that they had learned a great deal. Next time, they determined, the person arrested had to be one who was committed to a frontal attack on Jim Crow. That person had to be carefully chosen and had to be willing to serve extended jail time in pursuit of principle. Those who would lead the demonstrations on behalf of the incarcerated individual would have to be chosen, as well, chosen in advance. A cadre of organizers, loyal to the leader, would also have to be assembled in advance. Rufus Johnson had not meant to spark an incident. The next person arrested would have to do it on purpose. And all those who were joined with him would have to be prepared to swing into action immediately. It could be done. That was what the two white preachers felt they had learned. It could be done.

But they still had no idea how hard it would be. Their first move was to set up a meeting with George Washington Brown. Along with several other young black ministers, Brown met with Jeff, Preacher, Taylor Carson and several other faculty members of Southern University. Jeff and Preacher were dismayed at how formal the Negro clergymen were and how noncommittal Brown remained throughout. The exchanges were perfectly cordial but always reserved. Brown thanked the members of Jeff's group for the faith they expressed in his leadership potential, but he would not commit to any planned confrontation with the state's segregation laws. The meeting lasted two hours, and nothing concrete was accomplished.

At the end, Jeff felt frustrated and thwarted, but Preacher remained stubbornly optimistic. "Why should old George Washington want to be anointed by the likes of us?" Preacher pointed out to his friend. "Why should he want to be anointed king of this contest anyway? We don't have an army. And he's taken plenty notice of the fact that we're white."

"But we need him," Jeff said.

"Ah," Preacher responded. "But does he need us?"

chapter four

T HE 1934-35 CENTRAL LOUISIANA school year huffed towards its close in fetid classrooms full of damp children wearing clothes laundered too seldom. Jeff Caldwell was finishing fifth grade. About two weeks before the end of school on a Wednesday evening in early June, Jeff and his brothers went swimming as they did almost every day after finishing their chores.

The swimming hole on Black Creek lay three-quarters of a mile from the Caldwell homestead down New Peterstown Road, the rutted dirt roadway that wound through the area's piney woods and over which Huey Long's highway department had finally spread a layer of gravel. The swimming hole was one of only two summer gathering spots for the young boys of New Peterstown, the other being a weed-infested baseball diamond the boys had hacked out of a cow pasture. Over the years at the swimming hole, the boys had nailed wooden slats into the side of a water oak that towered over the lower of the two banks. Using the slats, they could climb the thick trunk and out onto a sturdy limb which hung over the creek to provide a perfect diving platform. From the limb of a white elm on the creek's opposite side, the boys had hung a truck-tire inner tube by a long strand of rope and made a swing they could use to propel themselves from the steep bank out to the center of the water.

Remarkable as it might seem, the boys practiced all these activities, as was the long-established local custom, stark naked. They might scratch themselves on the tree limb or abrade their backsides swinging out and flinging themselves from the inner tube. But the sheer joy of their recreation made these wounds inconsequential. Bathing suits would have provided them little protection in such a rough place anyway. Life was hard for boys in such circumstances, chores were dirty and often dangerous, and few went through a week without injuring themselves in some minor way or other. So suffering a little at their play seemed the natural price of pleasure.

Furthermore, the general poverty of the New Peterstown populace accounted in substantial part for the youngsters' swimming-hole nudity. A bathing suit was a luxury no family in the area could afford. Still, the boys might have swum in their underwear, of course. So the habit of skinny dipping derived at least as much from established tradition as from meager finances. The boys of the town swam naked because boys in the community had always swum naked.

There was nothing salacious about the boys' nudity, certainly nothing remotely homoerotic. While they were swimming, the boys were completely unconcerned with their nakedness, the way men are in the open shower rooms of a dormitory, army barracks or club. All the fathers had swum at the hole naked in their own youth. And mothers warned their daughters about never going to the boys' swimming hole.

The girls swam in a part of the creek a mile downstream and accessible from Back Road, a routeway perpendicular to New Peterstown Road, so named locally because it led back to State Highway 1. The few adults who still took time for swimming swam where their daughters did, and they all wore some sort of bathing costume. Miles upstream, outside that part of the parish considered to be New Peterstown (the area was not incorporated and had no precise boundaries), there were two other creek-bed holes used for swimming. The black people of the area swam in those two places, adults and female children in one, naked boys in the other.

The fact that the boys swam naked, though largely unremarkable in the community, was nonetheless a subject of enduring fascination to the girls of New Peterstown. They whispered about it at school recess every spring when the days grew warm enough and long enough for the swimming holes to provide the community a source of recreation once again. The boys always returned to swimming sooner than the girls, daring each other to be the first to dive back into water that remained cool in the tree-shaded creek all through the summer and could be freezing cold in the early spring. Those girls who had reached puberty inevitably claimed to have done the forbidden: to have snuck through the woods late some afternoon to spy on the boys sporting about in their birthday suits. Most never actually did it, but most claimed they had. Claiming it was required even though actually doing it wasn't. But some girls, feeling the pressure of this rite of passage, actually did make the trek to the boys' swimming hole. Three of them did so one June evening the year that Jeff was eleven.

The boys' swimming hole lay not far at all from New Peterstown Road. A rickety wood bridge stretched over Black Creek, and several hundred yards downstream, the creek bent sharply to the south. Just beyond this bend, where the land rose up on the eastern bank, the wash had created the swimming hole, deep enough throughout the summer for diving from the oak tree limb. The hole was out of sight of the road, of course, but it wasn't out of earshot. Anyone traveling along the road on a summer evening could hear the howl of the boys as they splashed and roughhoused in the water.

Unable to see where the noise was coming from, a newcomer might be startled by the shrieks and howls and laughter that seemed to emanate from a thick stand of pine, might think the woods an eerie devil's playground.

The girls who snuck up to see the boys at their play could not simply walk across the Black Creek bed and follow the footpath that was the most direct route. In fact, they couldn't be seen on the footpath at all. There was no reason for a girl to be in the neighborhood of Black Creek Bridge unless she had to cross it to visit some place on the other side; thus the entire area of the bridge was best avoided lest one's presence in the vicinity raise the curiosity of a passing adult or some boy on the way to or from the swimming hole.

So the three girls who set out to see the boys swimming in the buff left New Peterstown Road a half mile north of Black Creek Bridge and made their way through the woods. The last part of their spy's journey required that they cross a tiny stream the locals called Sludge Creek, which emptied into Black Creek just above the boys' swimming hole. Sludge Creek wasn't five yards across and wasn't more than a foot and half deep. But it was too wide to be jumped, so the girls had to sit down, remove their socks and shoes and wade across. On the other side, they dried their feet with leaves, put their shoes and socks back on and climbed the rise of the far bank. From there they made their way quickly to a spot on the east bank of Black Creek, from which they could see the boys cavorting in the stream.

The three girls who snuck up on the boys that day were fourteen-year-old Becky Price and her eighth-grade classmate Donna Holt and Donna's thirteen-year-old sister Peggy. Though the youngest of the three, Peggy was the biggest and was in many ways the group's leader. She had proposed undertaking the spy mission and pestered the two other girls until they agreed to accompany her. And she refused to let Becky and Donna turn back when they met the obstacle of Sludge Creek.

It was also Peggy who wanted to remain the longest once the girls had accomplished their mission. The three of them found a position in deep shadow under the dragging branches of a weeping willow from which they were able to watch the boys without being detected. After ten minutes or so, Becky and Donna had seen enough. Shriveled by the cold water, all the skinny young boys' penises looked to the two older girls like the curled pink tails on a pig. The girls weren't close enough to see more intimate details and weren't about to risk detection by venturing any closer. Donna and Becky knew they should feel more titillation than they actually felt and than they would claim they did feel when they recounted their adventure in the future. But, in fact, they felt a series of unpleasant sensations. They were being feasted upon by mosquitoes. They felt uncomfortable squatting on their haunches inside the willow branches. And they were afraid of being caught by the boys and subjected to unknown tortures.

After a very short time, Donna and Becky felt a little boredom and a considerable distaste. The boys were naked, and the two older girls discovered that they didn't find that fact attractive in the least. To Donna and Becky the boys looked like plucked chickens. They were all arms and legs and long necks. And their behinds were often smeared with mud from the creek bank. Rather than alluring, the dark creases in the boys backsides were disgusting. The two older girls felt that they had accomplished their mission, and they were eager to retreat and begin to savor the promise of bragging about their accomplishment as soon as possible.

But Peggy found in the experience a sensation that Donna and Becky didn't. Although she wouldn't have known the words to express it, she felt sexual arousal. Crucially, though, the sexual nature of Peggy's response to spying on the boys did not come from the direct fact of their nudity. She wasn't aroused by seeing their penises. Her mind brimmed with no fantasy of sexual contact with any of the boys, not even Wayne Caldwell upon whom she had a crush. Peggy Holt was both as knowledgeable and as ignorant about sex as any New Peterstown girl. She knew that sex consisted of a coupling between penis and vagina. But she did not now and in fact never had fantasized about having such contact between herself and Wayne or any other boy.

What turned Peggy Holt on that day as she squatted in the willow branches and spied on a dozen of her male schoolmates swimming in the nude, what made her indifferent to the mosquitoes swarming around her ankles, what made her determined to extend her adventure, was a sense of power over the boys that she had never known before. She had something on them now. And the pleasure of having it was stirring her in a way she had never before felt.

Peggy Holt was actually a rather pretty thirteen-year-old, although she had never been encouraged to think herself so. She had always been big for her age. At five feet, six inches, she was the tallest student in her grade, boy or girl. And she was big-boned. Until the last year she had always been a little chunky, as well. But since entering puberty, Peggy had shed all her baby fat. Like those of lots of girls her age, her features were undergoing a disproportionate transformation. Her nose seemed to have grown faster than the rest of her face, and she didn't like the look of her ears when she wore her hair pulled back. Moreover, like lots of girls her age, she occasionally suffered a spray of acne. But she had thick brown hair and a light splash of freckles across her cheekbones. Had she been born into a middle-class world two decades later, in the era of Marilyn Monroe, people would have asked her if she wanted to grow up to be a photographer's model or an actress. But in the rural world of New Peterstown in 1935, Peggy Holt was too big to be considered even adequately attractive. Her own father talked about her as if she were a draft animal, praising her size and strength the way he would a cart ox, openly referring to her wide pelvic girdle as indicative that she was going to make a good breeder.

At school her classmates treated her in comparable ways. The girls always picked her first in any game they might organize because she was well-coordinated, agile and fast. The other girls liked and respected Peggy, but they did not think of her as feminine in the way most of them regarded themselves. The boys, in contrast, treated Peggy with routine cruelty. A few months earlier, Miss Lubelle Perkins, the lower-grades teacher in New Peterstown's two-room schoolhouse, had asked the students to state what they'd like to do if they could do anything they wanted. Peggy had stated that she wanted to be a movie star, a response that the boys in the room greeted with hoots despite the fact that some of these children had never been to a movie and few of them had been more than a handful of times. Hoping to quiet the boys' ugliness by forging ahead with her questions, Miss Perkins asked Peggy what kind of movie she would like to play a role in, and Peggy responded by naming the only movie she had ever seen.

"Tarzan," she said, thinking of herself as the glamorous Jane, running about the jungle in her tattered outfits, swinging from vines, swimming bravely through swift rivers, sometimes needing Tarzan's help to get out of dangerous situations but sometimes, too, being the one who saved the day and Tarzan's life all on her own.

"Tarzan?" one of the boys in the back of the room hooted.

"And you would like to play the part of Jane," the teacher rushed on.

"She'd be better as Cheetah," one of the boys said, grunting in imitation of a chimp and scratching under his arms with inwardly curled fingers.

"The only part she could get," another boy said, "would be as one of those nigger women who carry things on their heads and don't wear no clothes except like a diaper."

"That'll be enough boys," the teacher warned.

"Big as she is," Wayne Caldwell said, "she'd probably have to play the elephant."

Peggy's cheeks burned as the boys made such sport of her innocently stated ambitions. She was particularly hurt by Wayne's chiming in against her. Wayne had never been mean to her before, and she had always liked his looks, his coal black hair and angular face. She especially liked his sinewy arms and the thick blue vein that throbbed just under the skin of his flexed bicep. Many of the boys had teased her about her size before, but Wayne never had, and no one had ever turned her own dreams against her as he did that day. From that moment forward, she burned with a desire to somehow even the score, somehow gain leverage on the boys that would erase the humiliation they had made her feel that day.

That's why she relished watching the boys running naked about the swimming hole. Now they were innocently exposed, and she was their master because she was taking something from them that they would never have given her. And that's why she didn't want to listen to Becky and Donna as the older girls began insistently whispering that it was time to leave. That tingle in her loins was too delicious. She would lose it if she left. And perhaps she'd never have it again.

"Peggy, let's go," Donna hissed through gritted teeth. Donna and Becky were already standing upright and had moved to the back of the cage of willow branches. When Peggy ignored them, Donna stepped back to her and said again, "Let's go. I mean it."

Peggy said nothing and Donna reached out and tried to tug her sister to a standing position. Peggy brushed Donna's hands away. Donna grabbed a piece of skin on Peggy's arm and said as their mother did when she was angry with the girls, "I'm gonna pinch a plug out of you if you don't come on."

Peggy didn't even turn around as she replied, "You pinch me and I'm gonna yelp like a fox in a leg trap, and all those boys down yonder will be up here before you can let go my arm. No telling what they'd do, too."

"We ain't staying any longer," Becky said.

"No, we ain't," Donna added. "Mosquitoes are eating us alive. And anyway, it's starting to get dark."

"Go on then," Peggy said. "I ain't holding you."

"You better come," Donna said.

"I ain't done looking," Peggy said.

"Well, they ain't gonna grow 'em any longer," Donna said.

"Oh, just leave her," Becky said to Donna and then added to Peggy, "They catch you, you better never tell them we was here."

Peggy was looking through the willow branches again and didn't respond. The two older girls looked at each other, shrugged in exasperation and made their way out of the hiding place and back toward New Peterstown Road. Neither said this to the other, but both wished they'd never bothered with this undertaking in the first place. It would have been a lot easier just to lie and say they'd done it.

Once they were gone, Peggy did what she wanted to do in the first place; she let her dress hem fall back into her lap so that she could touch herself. Like other rural Southern girls, she wore no underwear in the hot summer months. With her dress around her waist, she was completely bare. Touching herself at this moment was the thing she wanted to do more than any other thing in the world.

Afterwards, Peggy found herself immediately hungry again for the sensation that had made her need to touch herself. She resuscitated it by devising a daring plan. She made her way out of the back of her place in the willows and walked backwards away from the swimming hole until she was safely hidden in the woods. But then, instead of continuing on a northwest path across Sludge Creek and back to New Peterstown Road, she headed due west on a course parallel to Black Creek. As a result, she came to Sludge Creek this time much closer to the boys' swimming hole. As she took off her shoes and waded across the water, she felt that delicious tingling start between her legs again. Once she had dried her feet with handfuls of brown leaves and put her socks and shoes back on, instead of making her way on to the road, she crept fifty yards downstream. Darting from tree to tree, she crept down Sludge Creek until she could hear the boys splashing in the water of the swimming hole. Then from behind the protection of a sixty-foot sycamore, she held her nose to disguise her voice and began to yell the names of the boys she had watched from her hiding place on the hill.

"I saw you, Bobby Sawyer," she screamed as loud as she could. "I saw you, Johnny Davis." One by one she named the eleven boys she had spied on. At the swimming hole, the boys stopped all motion. Echoing off a thousand trees, dampened by the gurgle of Sludge Creek emptying into Black Creek, the voice seemed to come from the sky. "I saw you, Charles Blackforde and you, too, Danny Rains." And after she had named all the boys but one, she yelled, "And every one of you looks like a dumb sheared sheep." And then she paused for a second, hoping that the boys would think she had finished. But when she had waited five seconds, she yelled out one more time, "And I saw you, too, Wayne Caldwell, and your little pink-worm dinger is the most pathetic of all."

And then Peggy fled back up Sludge Creek. Before she made her way back onto New Peterstown Road to walk home, though, she leaned back against a live oak whose majestic branches dangled almost to the ground. And she lifted her skirt and touched herself again, more slowly than the first time, holding on to her excitement for seconds longer.

That night as she lay in bed next to Donna, Peggy played back the events of the afternoon and touched herself again, stirring her sister into semiconsciousness. "Quit jiggling around," Donna admonished. But Peggy simply slowed her motions until Donna drifted back into sleep.

Peggy Holt's triumph over the boys of New Peterstown might have been total had she not doodled the words "sheared sheep" in her school notebook one daydreamy school afternoon during a geography lesson. In the woefully underfinanced Louisiana schools of the 1930s, each child was issued a single black and white, thread-bound, lined notebook per term, and in it, using both sides of each page, the students wrote down their assignments, did their class work and their homework. The notebooks were not supposed to be used for doodling. But Peggy Holt had long had the habit of drawing pictures and writing down odd scraps of language on the margins of pages that Miss Perkins had already corrected. Why this doodling on used pages of the notebook bothered the teacher, Peggy could not understand, but Miss Perkins had reprimanded her about it in the past, and Peggy had tried to develop the habit of going through her notebook on Thursday night to erase her random musings before the notebooks were turned over to the teacher on Friday to be examined and graded over the weekend. Still engorged with her sense of victory over the boys a day earlier, Peggy didn't bother to do her homework Thursday night. She didn't even remove any of her school materials from the draw-stringed feed sack she used as a school bag. And so she failed to clean the doodles from her notebook. Escaped to a new fantasy world where queens ruled the world and men were their slaves, Peggy had no thought for her school work whatsoever. And that's why she was so completely unprepared for her teacher's complaint about the doodles having reappeared to soil her notebook pages. Peggy didn't remember having written in her notebook at all and was unprepared for the teacher's irritation.

"Children," Miss Perkins said to the class on Monday morning shortly after ringing the second bell signaling that lessons were now to begin.

The teacher was still sitting at her desk, and the students knew that the day did not really begin until she began writing something on the blackboard they had to copy into their notebooks, which still sat on her desk in two large piles.

So no one in the room was paying much attention, but they all answered by rote and almost in unison, "Yes, Miz Perkins."

To make for easier heating during the damp winter months by the big wood-burning stove which stood in the very center of the room, the school room had a low plywood ceiling nailed to the rafters of the pitched roof. But as a result of the low ceiling, the classroom became insufferably hot during the last six weeks or so of the school year, which didn't begin until after the cotton harvest in September and lasted all the way to the middle of June. It was only 8:30 in the morning, but already the room was stifling. The windows were open, as was the door that led out into the school's center hall where the students hung their coats in the winter on a line of hooks along each wall. But there was no cross ventilation, and little breeze stirred inside. Miss Perkins already had a spray of sweat across her forehead at the hairline.

"How many times have I asked you to be careful with the pages of your school notebook?" Miss Perkins asked.

No one responded. In the front left corner of the room, Jeff Caldwell gazed at the teacher with curiosity, trying to figure out what had made her so agitated. As he studied her, she rose from her chair with one of the notebooks in her hand and walked around her desk to stand in front of the room.

"Cally Jenkins?" Miss Perkins said.

"Yes, ma'am," Cally said.

"Well?" Miss Perkins said.

Like most of her classmates, Cally had been paying little attention and didn't grasp how the teacher wanted her to respond. She looked around the room, hoping to find a clue on one of her classmates' faces. Miss Perkins waited a moment before saying, "I asked you, Cally, how many times I've told the class to be careful with the pages of your school notebook."

"I don't know, Miz Perkins," Cally responded.

Exasperated, Miss Perkins stamped her foot on the unvarnished, wide oak floor and stirred up a cloud of dust that swirled around her ankles. Part of each teacher's responsibilities was the cleaning of her classroom, and Miss Perkins did her duty by sweeping her room once a week. The old wood floor seemed to create dirt on its own, however, and the room retained the stubborn grittiness of a barn.

"Mary Frances Branson?" Miss Perkins said, measuring each syllable of the girl's name.

"Yes ma'am," Mary Frances said.

Again Miss Perkins waited a beat until it was clear Mary Frances wasn't going to say more. A radiant beam of sunlight shone through the window as it did every cloudless morning after the middle of March and struck Mary Frances in her right eye, leaving her, as always, blinking and faintly dazed.

"Mary Frances!" Miss Perkins said.

"I—I don't know, Miz Perkins."

Fearful that Miss Perkins was about to pitch one of her fits that would result in detentions for the entire class, Jeff slowly raised his hand.

"Yes, Jefferson," Miss Perkins said.

"You've told us lots of times," Jeff said. "I'll bet you've told us probably a thousand times."

"Thank you, Jefferson," Miss Perkins said, and everyone in the room felt a relief that this particular crisis was about to pass, mixed with a faint disgust that Jeff Caldwell was such a suck-up.

"But not everyone abides by my instructions, do they, Jefferson?"

Jeff wasn't as eager to answer this question. It was one thing to get his classmates off the hook and save them from detentions. It was another thing altogether to seem to take the teacher's side in condemning them. He delayed long enough that Miss Perkins began to scowl again. Finally, as if divinely inspired, he said, "I know that I'm not always as careful as I should be, Miz Perkins. I promise to try to be better in the future."

In the back of the room, Wayne Caldwell reflected quite consciously that his brother always made him want to vomit. Even when Jeff did the right thing, Wayne wanted to punch him.

"Well, Jefferson," Miss Perkins said, "it's seldom you I have in mind. And it certainly isn't you I have in mind this time. Isn't that correct, Peggy Holt?"

By now, Miss Perkins' irritation had captured everyone's attention, and even Peggy Holt was listening. But the teacher's whole manner was confusing her. She hated this kind of attention to be focused on her. Suddenly she felt that her dress sash had been tied too tightly around her waist. She knew from watching the behavior of the room's other children that the teacher expected her to say something now. But she didn't know what she was supposed to say, so she tried, "Yes, Miz Perkins."

"Yes, what, Peggy?"

"Yes, ma'am, Miz Perkins."

Miss Perkins shook her head at the density of her students. She was a New Peterstown girl herself, now thirty and bitterly resigned to the fact that she was an old maid. She had gone off to normal school and gotten her teaching certificate, hoping to land a husband in the process. But she hadn't, and she couldn't understand why. Maybe she was too skinny, as so many had told her all her life, but wasn't that better than the broad-beamed, ponderous-breasted women who never went to college, didn't have a brain in their heads and still managed to find husbands. The world was a cruel and indifferent place, of that Miss Perkins was certain. After normal school she had returned to the New Peterstown school determined to help her students go further in the world than she was ever going to go. But she had come almost instantly to see the hopelessness of such a proposition. Her students possessed the academic aptitude of dairy cattle and the concentration of hummingbirds. They grasped nothing of the discipline Miss Perkins knew was required to succeed in the world outside New Peterstown. Those of her students who weren't just plain stupid she found lazy and distracted. A prime example was horsey Peggy Holt. Peggy was such a dull child, sitting there slack-faced every day, never knowing the place in the reader, half the time copying her assignments down wrong. Peggy was exactly the kind of female Miss Perkins resented. She was a huge girl, wide-hipped and big-shouldered. She'd no doubt marry and bear the world a brood of draft-animal children while a refined person like Miss Perkins would remain barren.

"What does all this stuff mean?" Miss Perkins demanded of Peggy, holding her notebook open to a pair of pages on which Peggy had drawn pictures of farm animals.

Peggy said nothing. Her mouth was as dry as chalk.

"Please explain to the class what this means, Peggy."

"Nothing, Miz Perkins," Peggy said. "It don't mean nothing at all."

"Anything," Miz Perkins said, sighing. "It doesn't mean anything at all."

"Yes ma'am," Peggy said. "Nothing at all."

"I see," Miss Perkins said. She turned to another page and asked, "Why have you written the words 'sheared sheep' all over this part of your notebook?"

"What?" Peggy said, startled by the teacher's question. Peggy didn't remember having written such a thing. She flushed crimson and felt the eyes of everyone in the room turning toward her. At the same time, she strangely felt that same tingle between her legs that she had felt while watching the boys swim. Only now it was less delicious, somehow cold and invasive rather than warm and alluring.

"Sheared sheep," Miss Perkins said again. She walked to Peggy's desk with the notebook held open and placed it down in front of the girl. "See, sheared sheep. You've written it on sheet after sheet." Miss Perkins turned the notebook's pages to make her point. "Whatever goes on in that silly head of yours, young lady?"

"Pink worms," Johnny Davis said, and the other boys in the room burst out laughing. Jeff laughed with the rest. Only Wayne failed to laugh. He sat at his desk in the back right corner wide-eyed, waiting for the infuriating moment when the other boys in the room turned to look at him.

"Pink worms?" Miss Perkins said, turning to Johnny Davis. "What in the world do you mean by that?" Johnny didn't say anything. "I asked you a question, young man. What did you mean by saying 'pink worms'?"

"I don't know," Johnny said.

"Yeah, but Wayne knows," Bobby Sawyer said.

Now it was Wayne who flushed. "Hey, you shut up, Bobby," Wayne said.

Miss Perkins walked back to the front of the classroom. "What is all this business

about?" she said. Nobody responded, not even with another quip. Wayne glared at both
Johnny and Bobby, daring them to so much as grin. "Bobby?" Miss Perkins said. Bobby
looked away from Wayne, darted a glance at the teacher and then stared down at his desk.
"Wayne?" Wayne stuck his lower lip up inside the upper one and said nothing. "Johnny?
You started this. Now I asked you what it means?" Johnny scraped at his desktop with a
thumbnail. "I asked you a question, young man. And you will answer me. What does this
pink worm business mean?"

"It don't mean nothing, Miz Perkins," Johnny said. "It don't mean nothing at all."

The teacher sighed and opened an arithmetic book. They would never get it. What was
the point of trying to get them to explain themselves? Words came out of their mouths
almost at random. "It doesn't mean anything, Johnny. It doesn't mean anything."

But, of course, it did mean something. And it meant something most of all to Wayne
Caldwell. He'd been teased by all the other boys about his pink worm since the voice in
the woods had singled him out. Wayne was not used to this kind of derision. He wasn't a
particularly big boy for his age. But he was wiry and strong. And having taken plenty of
them at home from Pruitt, he wasn't afraid of enduring a lick. Moreover, the product of
his father's bullying, Wayne had a seething anger in him that manifested itself in an
uncommon fury when he felt himself crossed. This combination of quick resort to
violence and indifference to pain pretty much enabled him to dominate all the boys in his
age range. He knew how to single them out and make any dispute one that could only
be settled in a one-to-one confrontation. And in such a confrontation he usually prevailed
by getting the other boy to back down. Fighting Wayne wasn't worth it. He was too
willing to be hurt in order to hurt. It was easier just to let him have his way.

This pink worm business, however, had introduced a new dimension into the entire
social fabric of New Peterstown. A voice had cried out unseen and had singled Wayne
out. None of the other boys could be accused of having started this. So Wayne couldn't
get it stopped by singling someone out and either beating him up or otherwise
intimidating him. And since all the boys had begun teasing him almost immediately, and
not without a considerable measure of malicious pleasure, Wayne knew that for once they
would stand together if he tried to use the threat of force to shut someone up.

But now Wayne knew whose voice had cried out in the woods that day. And from the
moment he knew it, he was determined to exact an appropriate revenge, a revenge that
could only become appropriate through being observed by those who had first witnessed
his humiliation. By making Peggy Holt pay somehow for what she had done, Wayne could

take the words "pink worm" out of the mouths of all his peers who had wielded those words like knives to flay his dignity.

On Monday at recess there was lots more talk about Wayne's pink worm and Peggy's evident interest in it, during which time Wayne seethed but remained uncharacteristically silent. When Bobby Sawyer started up the ribbing again on Tuesday, however, Wayne took one short step forward and hit Bobby just under his collarbone with a punch so explosive that he knocked Bobby down on the seat of his pants. The other boys yelled out, "Hey," almost simultaneously and quickly surrounded Wayne.

Wayne spit on the ground between himself and Johnny Davis. "I'm tired of this shit," Wayne said. "So let's get on with it. I'll fight all of you all at once, and I'll get whupped, but you mark my words, I'm going to knock some teeth loose starting with yours, Johnny."

"Why me?" Johnny said.

" 'Cause I happen to be looking at you," Wayne responded, pivoting his hips away from Johnny and toward Charles, even as he kept his eyes riveted on Johnny. None of the boys wanted to tangle with Wayne, and Wayne knew it. But the two who might summon the courage were Johnny and Charles. If trouble started, Wayne figured he had to take at least one of them out of play immediately.

"We ain't got no reason to fight with you, Wayne," Johnny said. "But we will if you make us." That was exactly the kind of resistance Wayne feared.

"You didn't have to hit me, Wayne," Bobby said, coming back into the circle. He dusted at his pants and then rubbed his chest where Wayne had punched him. "Dang it, Wayne," Bobby added, "that dadblasted hurt. I didn't do nuthin and you're punching me. Peggy saw all of us. It's her we ought to get. What's the matter with you sometimes, anyway?"

"Ain't nothing the matter with me," Wayne said. "But there's gonna be something the matter with every one of you if I hear any more about any of this business."

"Just settle down, Wayne," Jeff said. Jeff was standing behind his brother and spoke to the back of his head. "You ought to learn to take a joke."

Wayne whirled around and took a step toward Jeff, who took a matching step backward. "Shut up, Jeff," Wayne said. "Or I'll give you a licking just for the pleasure of watching you whimper."

But even as Jeff retreated, the other boys closed in on Wayne, and he sucked in his fury in a strategic retreat of his own. So there was no more fighting that day. But all the boys felt raw, and Wayne felt certain that they would continue to make fun of him behind his back if not directly to his face. After Wayne punched Bobby without warning, the boys came to remember the whole "sheared sheep, pink worm" episode with an increasing sourness. Wayne was the one they really resented, but they were unable or unwilling to take it out on him, so they began to mutter dire threats toward Peggy Holt. Variously they formulated violent fantasies about cutting off all her hair, smearing her with cow manure and setting her dress on fire.

This particular chapter in the lives of the New Peterstown adolescents reached its climax that Saturday. Early in the afternoon, Peggy Holt, her sister Donna and Becky Price all went swimming at the girls' and adults' hole. Becky and Donna remained miffed at Peggy because of her behavior the week prior. They were not aware of Peggy's having taunted the boys at their swimming hole. Moreover, the two older girls were in the upper grades class at New Peterstown School and didn't even know about Miss Perkins' confronting Peggy over doodles in her notebook, much less what those doodles meant. But Becky and Donna did know that something was wrong with Peggy. She had always been the strong-headed one among them. But since their spying mission, she had been notably vacant, as if always thinking about something else. They presumed she thought herself superior to them because she had first organized the trip to the boys' hole and had then lingered there longer. So they now assumed that her seeming aloofness was a manifestation of arrogance. That's exactly why they conspired to sneak off and leave her at the swimming hole when the three of them had walked down to the creek together. After the three of them had been in the water for perhaps an hour, Donna announced that she needed to pee, and Becky immediately said she'd accompany her friend to the women's outhouse the adults had erected a hundred yards into the woods. But when the girls got out of sight, they simply kept on going, deliberately leaving Peggy behind.

Peggy's distraction was not the result of arrogance, of course, but rather of fear. She knew from the banter in the classroom occasioned by the teacher's inquiries about her doodling that the boys were onto her. And she knew from their stares all week that they wanted to do something to her to get even. She couldn't imagine what form their revenge might take. But she dreaded any confrontation with them.

Peggy splashed around with the others who were at the swimming hole that day, waiting for her sister and Becky to return. After a time, she took to craning her head repeatedly in the direction of the outhouse, expecting to see them coming back out of the woods momentarily. Finally, she went up to the outhouse to look for them. But they had long since headed on home.

Realizing that she had been abandoned and feeling hurt that she'd been the victim of a mean trick, Peggy set about to change her clothes. Like the others who swam there, she had worn her bathing suit to the creek under her dress, which she had then removed in order to swim. And also like the others, in order not to walk home wet, her bathing suit gradually soaking through her plaid gingham dress, she had stepped into an area of woods that the adults of the town had cultivated, creating an enclosed dressing area by planting a series of ligustrums in a box shape with one vacant rectangle to serve as a "door." In this outdoor changing space, for modesty purposes standing close to and facing the ligustrums, Peggy had stripped out of her swimsuit, toweled off quickly and pulled her dress over her head, arms raised skyward, letting it fall down around her body. Then she sat on one of the stones that had been placed inside the ligustrum enclosure and put on her socks and thick brown shoes. Bending forward at the waist, she pulled her thick rope of hair in front of her and wrung it out, rubbing the ends briskly with a towel to try to keep water from dripping down her back as she walked home. Finally, she rose, wrung out the towel and her bathing suit, rolled them up and stepped out of the dressing area to head home in the waning light.

As it happened, her path crossed that of six boys who were on their way home from the boys' swimming hole. God, it seems, sometimes pays poor attention to the circumstances of his most vulnerable creatures. The afternoon was waning. The sun sat atop the trees like a giant Christmas ornament, and shadows reached out from the tree line toward the road. Sauntering homeward, in no particular hurry, were Wayne and Jeff Caldwell and their pals Johnny Davis, Bobby Sawyer, Charles Blackforde and Danny Rains. They all saw Peggy when she came up on the road from the path that led down to the swimming hole. Jeff instantly said a prayer that she'd soon be followed by someone else, best of all by an adult. But no one followed her.

Grabbing the arm of Wayne who was walking along beside him, Johnny Davis said, "Dang if that ain't Peggy Holt acoming toward us. Let's get her."

"Yeah, let's get her," Bobby Sawyer said, rubbing his chest, which was still sore from where Wayne had punched him five days earlier.

Jeff would remember the next moments all his life. At first, for an instant, none of the boys moved, and Peggy Holt walked on toward them. Then, as if propelled by a tidal wave, they all began running toward her at once, yelling first in separate voices and then in unison, "Let's get her. Let's get her. Get her. Get her. Get. Her. Get. Her."

Jeff ran a pace behind the others, last in a phalanx, but he ran toward Peggy, too. And with them he chanted, "Let's get her. Get. Her."

When Peggy realized who the boys were and that they were running deliberately toward her, she stopped dead still in the middle of the road. She stood there, her bathing suit and towel damp in her hand, her shoes fixed in the dust of New Peterstown Road. As the boys' words reached her ears and she realized not only who they were but that they were coming for her, she didn't turn and run. She stood her ground and waited, knowing that they would capture her and exert their powers of physical strength and superior numbers over her. Though she was not a particularly religious girl, Peggy attended the New Peterstown Baptist Church like practically everybody in the community. She made no conscious appeal to God now for deliverance, but she did look heavenward, upward to a white smudge of moon that shone indifferently in the gathering gray of the afternoon sky.

The boys surrounded Peggy when they reached her, each still standing an arm's length from her, none yet closing in. They had her now, but none of them knew what they intended to do with her. Johnny Davis looked at Wayne, who had his head cocked to one side and stared at Peggy with lips twisted to one side. Then Johnny said to Peggy, "Hey, we know it was you in the woods last Wednesday." Peggy said nothing.

"Yeah, we know it was you," Charles Blackforde said. Peggy turned her head and then twisted a half step backwards in order to see the boys behind her.

"Don't try running away," Bobby Sawyer said.

"You can't get away from us," Danny Rains said. "We got you now."

Peggy turned back in the direction she had been walking and stepped forward, trying to pass between Danny and Johnny Davis. Wayne said, "Grab her," and Johnny seized her shoulder. Peggy shrugged, like a fullback trying to shake off a tackler.

"Stop it," Peggy said.

Johnny dropped his hand down to her wrist and quickly twisted Peggy's arm behind her back, forcing her to bend forward at the waist. Feeling the pain in her shoulder, she dropped her towel and bathing suit into the gravel and dirt of the road.

"Let go," Peggy said. "That hurts."

"I bet she's gonna cry," Danny said.

"Bring her this way," Wayne said and stepped off the road and down into the woods. Johnny eased the pressure on Peggy's arm enough so that she could stand up straight again, then put his hand between her shoulder blades and shoved her in the direction that Wayne took into the woods. The other boys trailed behind, Jeff included.

As Peggy moved from the high weeds through a stand of cattails, Johnny moved his hand up from the hollow of her back under her neck and grabbed hold of her hair, twisting his fist a half turn to secure his grip. Walking just ahead of Peggy, Wayne pushed aside a low cottonwood branch, and when he let it go, it slapped Peggy full in the face, scratching a red welt just under her right eye.

"Ow," Peggy said.

"Shut up," Johnny said and gave a tug to the knot of hair he gripped in his left fist.

"Stop it," Peggy said.

In front of her, Wayne stopped and turned to face her. "He told you to shut up," Wayne said. "You best do what he says."

Wayne walked on, deeper into the woods, until he came to a little clearing in the center of which stood a nest of wild ginger, its flowers poking into the dying afternoon like tropical birds on the verge of taking wing. Wayne pushed into the center of the ginger until he came to a spot of bare ground perhaps ten feet in diameter, the broad leaves of the ginger growing over the top to form a canopy all around. With first Peggy and Johnny and then the others behind them, it was as if they had entered a thatched hut. Even at noon, only sparse light filtered into this space.

Wayne turned now to Peggy and said, "You saw what all we got, now you show us."

Peggy didn't move. Wayne looked at Johnny and raised his eyebrows, and in response Johnny jerked Peggy's arm higher up her back, forcing her to bend forward from the waist again. But this time Johnny's fist in her hair held her head back and thrust her chin out.

"We can hurt you if we want," Wayne said. "You better do what I say."

Johnny eased off on her arm again so that she could stand straight.

"Take your left hand," Wayne ordered, "and pull your dress up around your waist."

Peggy did what she was told, gathering the skirt of her dress into a ball she held at her navel, exposing herself to all the boys but Johnny.

"She ain't even wearing no panties," Danny said.

"None of them do during the summer," Bobby said. "Don't you know nothing?"

"What's it look like?" Johnny demanded.

"It's just this puckered-slice-like thing," Bobby said. "Like somebody cut her with a knife and it ain't healed up right."

"She ain't barely got no hair on it," Danny said. "She's got some, but not much."

"Well, you ain't got no hair on yours at all," Johnny said.

"Neither does Jeff," Danny said. "I ain't the only one."

"Shut up, Danny," Wayne said.

"Charles, you come hold her, so I can look," Johnny said.

As Johnny transferred Peggy's twisted arm to Charles, Peggy let go of the ball of dress material in her left hand and the dress fell back around her knees. Johnny stepped around in front of her and said to Wayne, "Make her pull her dress back up. I ain't got to look yet."

Peggy didn't move. "Pull it back up," Wayne ordered. Peggy still didn't move. Wayne stepped very close to her and reached out with his right hand and touched the swell of Peggy's breast, squeezing down with his thumb and forefinger until he gripped her nipple. "Ain't nobody around to help you," Wayne said. "We can hurt you if we decide to. You better do what we say."

Peggy stared right into Wayne's eyes with a face Jeff thought all the more frightening because it showed so little emotion, no fear particularly, not even anger. But there was in her face a profound defiance, a declaration of being that told Wayne he could never reach her, he could hurt her if he chose, he could kill her, but she would still escape him because she was Peggy Holt and whatever he did to her, he could not make her something other than Peggy Holt.

Or at least that's the way Jeff understood that straightforward but seemingly blank look on Peggy's face. Wayne understood it as an infuriating challenge. Viciously he began to pinch down on Peggy's nipple until she twisted to her left side and yelped from the pain. "You gonna do what I tell you?" Wayne demanded. He eased his grip on her nipple, and she stood upright again. "Now you gonna do what I tell you?"

"I done showed you," Peggy said.

Wayne pinched her nipple again, causing her face to contort in pain. "I asked you a direct question," Wayne said, bringing his nose within inches of hers. "Are you gonna do what I tell you?"

That's when Peggy spit in his face. The amount of spittle she managed was negligible. It was mostly air and spray, but she hit Wayne full in the face, and he reeled back as if struck.

Wayne wiped a hand down his face and then stepped back to Peggy and wiped his hand on her face. "Now you're gonna get it," Wayne said. "Grab her arms over her head," Wayne said to Johnny. Turning to the others he said, "Two of you grab her legs and hold them apart."

"You gonna fuck her?" Johnny said, grabbing Peggy's left arm and bending her forward as Charles brought her right arm out to the side and Wayne moved behind her. "Gonna fuck her like a bull mounting a heifer?"

"Shut up and watch," Wayne said. Danny and Bobby knelt in the dirt to clasp each of Peggy's legs, each boy surrounding a leg up to the knee, hugging himself against it with his head laid sideways against her flank. Johnny seized a handful of Peggy's hair and used it to keep her head down. Behind her, Wayne unzipped and flipped her dress up on her back.

At age thirteen, Wayne Caldwell was so ignorant of the female anatomy, he did not know that there was a female sexual orifice. And so, with some difficulty, unaware what he was doing, looking not down at Peggy's body but upward at the thatch of ginger which seem to sprout from the top of Johnny's and Charles' heads, Wayne sodomized Peggy. In front of him, her head trapped by Johnny's grip on her hair, Peggy bit down on her lower lip, whimpering but otherwise successful in her determination not to cry out.

When Wayne had finished, Johnny declared, "Now I'm gonna do her too. Come hold her, Wayne."

Wayne zipped up his pants but made no move to exchange places with Johnny. So Johnny said to Charles, "Grab a hank of her hair here. She can't move when you do that." As Johnny moved behind Peggy, Wayne carefully tucked in his shirttails, and as Johnny unzipped his own trousers, Wayne turned and walked back into the thicket of ginger. "Boy, this is gonna be fine," Johnny said.

Johnny ejaculated before managing to gain penetration, grunting once and then howling as he did so. His entire contact with Peggy's body didn't last ten seconds. Afterwards he stepped back and said, "Anybody want to go next?"

Nobody said anything.

Then Charles said, "Wayne's done took off."

Johnny looked around the small space. "Yeah, well, we can catch up with him." Charles continued to hold Peggy's head down, but the other boys had released her legs and stood up. "Watch this," Johnny said, laughing uproariously. He put his foot on Peggy's exposed buttocks and then kicked forward sending her sprawling face first into the dirt.

"Let's go," Johnny said, and the boys moved to follow him after Wayne, all except Jeff.

Peggy Holt would never tell anyone that boys in her class raped her one Saturday just before school was out in 1935. Two years later, when she was fifteen, Peggy would steal $15.36 from her father's coveralls and run away from home. No one in New Peterstown would ever hear from her again. Eventually, almost miraculously, she would get a college degree and become a junior high art teacher. But she would take up smoking, and she would never marry, and she would die of breast cancer two weeks before her fortieth birthday.

Now Peggy twisted and pushed herself to a sitting position on the ground. Jeff didn't approach her, but he did say in a quiet voice, "I hope you're okay, Peggy. I don't think anybody meant to hurt you or anything."

"Go away," Peggy said, not looking at him.

"Okay," Jeff replied, but he didn't move.

Slowly, Peggy got to her feet and grasped a thick green ginger stalk to steady herself.

Then she began to cry. She made no sound, but the tears leaked down her cheeks with every blink. After a moment, she lifted the hem of her dress with her free hand and wiped roughly at both cheeks. As she did so Jeff stared intently between her legs.

"I'm sorry," he said. But he couldn't make himself look away and hoped she wouldn't notice that he had an erection.

Jeff's voice seemed to upset Peggy's balance. To regain her equilibrium as she looked at him and almost absently dropped her dress to cover herself, she shifted her grip on the ginger stalk, pulling down on it and in the process opening a gap in the vegetation for a shaft of blinding sunlight that bore like a laser into Jeff's soul.

"I'm sorry," Jeff explained. "But I didn't do anything."

"Didn't you?" she said.

chapter five

A S THE CROWD OUTSIDE Charity Hospital began to battle with police, Tommy finally managed to make his way into the hospital and up to the intensive-care unit where his father was being attended after surgery.

Glenda was in the ICU waiting room. She had come with Dr. Brown and Jeff in the ambulance. Her shoulder-length brown hair was pulled back into a ponytail. Her pink-and-white-flowered maternity dress was smeared with blood. She had a magazine open in her lap, but she wasn't reading. The TV was on, covering the civil disturbances across the city, including those in the street right outside the hospital building. There, the police had conceded one whole section of Tulane Avenue where the crowd had succeeded in flipping a squad car on its side. Glenda stood up as Tommy entered; he embraced her, and she began to sob. "I'm so sorry," she said.

"How is he?" Tommy asked.

"He hasn't regained consciousness yet," she said and went on to relate that they were allowed to see him for only ten minutes every three hours. The bullet had nicked the large intestine and had destroyed a kidney. The intestinal wound meant that the risk of infection was considerable. He remained in critical condition.

Tommy and Glenda sat together on the couch, and Tommy held her hand and told her about being interrogated by the FBI. The TV switched to Washington, where David Brinkley reported on disturbances in New Orleans and across the nation.

"I hate this world," Glenda said and began to cry again, this time biting her lower lip and trying to fight back her tears. "I'm so sorry," she said. "I just hate this fucking world so much."

"All hell's breaking loose outside," Tommy said. "I don't know if there will be a New Orleans tomorrow."

"Or an America," she said. "What has happened to us? We were trying to make things better. And this is what it's come to. What happened to Ben? He was screaming about something Dr. Brown did. What was he talking about? He loved Dr.

Brown. Did he just go crazy?"

"I don't know," Tommy said. And that just about captured Tommy's response to all of life. In an instant, everything was topsy turvy. And Tommy didn't know. He didn't know if his father was going to live or die. He didn't know if America could survive, if the country had crossed some turbulent Rubicon into a land where martial law and censorship and suspension of civil liberties would become the order of the day. He didn't know what had driven Ben Watson to commit such a destructive act of violence. And Tommy certainly didn't know what it was Ben thought Dr. Brown did. About everything that mattered to him, Tommy didn't know.

"Has anyone been in touch with Faye?" Glenda asked.

"I have no idea," Tommy responded.

"I ought to try to reach her," Glenda said. "She must be absolutely sick. Her husband's dead. He killed Dr. Brown. This is like a nightmare."

"Investigators have probably got her in custody," Tommy said. "Given the way they think, the fact that she wasn't at the church probably makes her a conspirator."

Glenda and Tommy talked about how crazy that idea was, but then they conceded that the idea of Ben Watson's shooting Dr. Brown and Jeff would have seemed just as crazy only hours earlier. "I called Danielle," Glenda said, referring to Tommy's younger sister, who was in Chicago just beginning her college work in theater at Northwestern. "To let her know where they'd brought your father. She asked you to call her when you have the chance."

"She's coming?" Tommy asked.

"First flight she can get tomorrow."

"Thank goodness," Tommy said.

"You thought she wouldn't?" Glenda said. "Not even now? Not even at a time like this?"

"I wasn't sure. She and Dad—well, you know. But I'm glad she's coming. I guess I knew she would. If only for me."

Tommy's mother Billye walked into the waiting room and immediately made her way to the nurse's station to inquire about Jeff's condition. "What is she doing here?" Tommy said to Glenda under his breath.

"She came as soon as she heard," Glenda said. "She went in with me to see him when they first brought him up to ICU." Glenda patted his arm. "You knew she'd come, Tommy. You couldn't have expected anything else.

Tommy studied his mother's profile as she rested her left hand on the counter and conversed with a nurse in a starched white uniform. Standing perfectly erect in her white high-heeled shoes and dressed in a fitted blue frock with a wide white sailor collar and a matching white straw purse hung by a long strap over her left shoulder, Billye looked as she always did when she stepped foot out of the house—as if she were on her way to church. Her attire was never flashy enough for a cocktail party but always too dressy for someone on the way to work. She never wore attire casual enough for running errands, even when she was merely out running errands. She always wore make-up and earrings, and as now, she always wore a short strand of pearls around her neck.

The one thing different about Billye's appearance was her hair. Her high school yearbook had full-face pictures of her as Homecoming Queen and as a school Beauty, and in both photos she wore her hair in shoulder-length brown waves. From the time Tommy was a child, though, she'd worn her hair short and teased into a round, curly bouffant. The hairstyle had been popular among suburban middle-class hausfraus during the fifties, and Billye had taken to it and somehow got stuck there. She had worn it that way until the day she divorced. Now, she had let it grow long again, lightened it to a golden blond and curled it into a pageboy. Tommy wouldn't admit this, not even to himself, but at forty-three, his mother remained a beautiful woman.

Billye finished her conversation with the nurse and turned toward the sofa where Glenda and Tommy sat, approaching them in measured steps, the metal tips on her high heels clicking audibly on the tile floor. Tommy stood up, and she marched straight up against him and hugged him, her purse falling from her shoulder to her elbow. Tommy's arms circled her involuntarily, and he patted her back three times but then stiffened in a way that made her let go of him. When she pulled away, Tommy could see that her lipstick and mascara were fresh but that her eyes were bloodshot.

Before she could speak, Tommy said, "Is Dennis here with you, Mother? I don't want him here. He hasn't any business here."

Billye didn't answer immediately, just stepped away from her son and sat in a chair perpendicular to the sofa on which Glenda was still sitting. When she had tucked her dress underneath her legs satisfactorily and positioned her purse in the middle of her lap, she sucked in a deep breath and said, "Dennis isn't here, Tommy. He would have come had I asked him, but he wouldn't have come unless I asked him."

"What did the nurse have to say?" Glenda asked.

Billye turned to Glenda, and her face softened as she said, "Nothing to report. He's restless, but he hasn't regained consciousness yet." Billye looked at Tommy and said, "Glenda told me that you were detained by FBI agents. What was that about?"

"Nothing," Tommy said. "Usual bullshit."

Billye's face wrinkled at the curse word, just a moment's tiniest reaction, a twitch around the eye, a slight flaring of her nostrils, a tightness around the mouth. She didn't like coarse language, and Tommy knew that. Tommy sat back down next to Glenda, who rustled a little in her seat as if making room for him.

Billye smoothed the topside of her purse with both hands. "They don't suspect you in this in any way, do they?" she asked. "Surely that's not the case."

"They suspect everybody. We're all just a bunch of commie insurrectionists to J. Edgar Hoover. They'd suspect Glenda except for the fact that her being married and knocked up means that she's doing what every woman ought to." Tommy turned his body slightly and said to Glenda, "Take off your shoes, babe. Get into it."

"Stop it, Tommy," Glenda responded. "Jeff is lying in there barely alive."

"They didn't arrest you," Billye said. "They just asked you questions and let you go?"

"I guess if they'd arrested me, I wouldn't be here now," Tommy said.

Billye crossed her legs. After a moment she asked, "How well did you know this boy, Benjamin Watson? The one they say did this."

"He's not a boy," Tommy said and felt himself about to choke. "Jesus Christ, he wasn't a boy. He was twenty-six years old. He was married. He was going to go to the seminary. And now he's gone crazy or something. He went crazy, and then he killed himself."

"He was a friend of yours?" Billye asked.

"Yes," Tommy said.

"But you have no idea why he did this?" Billye asked.

"What's this third degree from you, Mother?" Tommy said. "Did I miss the notice where you joined the FBI?"

"Tommy, I want you to stop this," Glenda said.

"I'm sorry, Tommy," Billye said. "I don't mean to be grilling you. I'm worried, and I'm just trying to understand what happened. I don't want you implicated in any of this."

"Why should I be?" Tommy responded.

"Well, of course, you shouldn't be," Billye said. "That's just my point."

"I tried to stop it," Tommy said. "Only, I was too late."

"Of course, you did, baby," Billye said. "Glenda told me what you did. You did everything you could. You were very, very brave."

"Don't say I was brave," Tommy said. "You weren't there. You don't know what I was. I wasn't anything. I just reacted. Only it was too late." Suddenly he began to cry.

Tommy was not a person who cried. He felt at times that there was something wrong with him that he couldn't cry. When his grandmother Osby died his junior year in high school, his many cousins wept openly at her funeral. Three of his cousins, sobbing hysterically, even stooped to kiss the corpse. Tommy could not fathom such grieving and wondered if he would ever be lucky enough to love so deeply as to grieve with such intensity. He thought he loved Glenda that much—and his sister and father and even his mother, at whom he'd remained angry for four years—but he feared there was something so hard in him that in fact he did not love anyone as much as he should.

Tommy wondered why he hadn't cried when his weeping parents told him they were going to divorce. Their divorce left him with a profound feeling of emptiness, and Tommy remembered actually trying to will himself to cry, to force tears out to assure both them and himself that he wasn't an uncaring son. He wondered then if his inability to cry meant that he actually was uncaring, but even in this terror of self-examination and self-recrimination, he could not will himself to cry. So he was completely unprepared for his crying now. He was as surprised by it as were both his wife and mother, one of whom had never seen him cry, the other of whom had not seen him cry since he was in grade school. Tommy's crying seized complete control of him. It shook and convulsed him and rendered him helpless. He couldn't stop it, couldn't staunch its flood. For long distressing minutes he simply cried and the crying became all.

Tommy's crying that night was like a descent into a dark isolation chamber. There was no sight or sound or touch, just blankness, just crying. He was oblivious to Glenda's pulling him against her breast, or to his mother's moving from her chair to sit beside him. Tommy knew these things had happened only because when finally he cried himself out, he found himself in this new posture and them moving their hands on his head and back and arms, trying with their caresses to console. And they were crying too.

Cried out, Tommy sat up from Glenda's embrace and wiped at his eyes with his hands. He had cried for so long and so hard that he had wet the entire front of her dress.

"I'm sorry," he said.

"Don't," Glenda said.

"Oh, baby," Billye said softly. She took a handkerchief from her purse and started to dab at his face but then let him take it from her to mop at the tears.

"I'm sorry," he said.

"Shhhhh," his mother said. And then there was silence.

Tommy got up and went to the water cooler in the hall just outside the door. He wet a corner of Billye's handkerchief and used it to wipe cold water across his eyes. When he returned to the room, his mother had moved back to her chair, and he sat on the couch again next to Glenda. She winced just slightly as he did so, and he presumed the baby had kicked. He laid his hand on her belly and moved it gently against the fabric of her dress until she stilled it by placing her own hand on top of his. Tommy looked at his mother and asked, "Why are you here?"

"Do you want me to go?" she responded.

"I just don't understand why you're here. You've put this part of your life behind you. Haven't you? Isn't that what divorcing Dad means?"

"I was married to your father for twenty-two years," Billye said.

"And you're not married to him any more."

"Tommy," Glenda said, rubbing her hand in a circle around the back of his.

"I'm not trying to be ugly," Tommy said to Glenda, though he knew this was far from entirely true. He did consciously try to drain any hint of anger or bitterness from his tone. And he didn't feel like fighting with his mother. But since his parents' divorce, he related to her with thinly veiled contempt. For some time, he had felt righteous in punishing her with iciness and sarcasm. All of those complex and unpleasant feelings were still somewhere inside of him, but they were dampened down now by the dam break of crying and by his feeling of helplessness over all that had happened this awful night.

It occurred to Tommy now that his mother and he, though they had seen each other often enough, had never really talked about what had happened, about how she saw things, about how she governed her actions, about how she saw her obligations. On those occasions when they had been in one another's presence, they had talked as if over a wall, a wall he felt she was always trying to climb and he was always trying to build ever higher. And whenever he saw her fingers reach the top of the wall and threaten to pull herself into a position that would make him see her, he hammered at her fingers until she lost her grip and fell away. Now, however, with his father in intensive care and his whole world changed even more drastically than it had changed when his parents divorced, he found himself wanting to engage his mother in a way that he had not before.

"Really, Mother," he said. "I'm not trying to be ugly. I'm just asking a question. Just trying to understand."

"You can't be asking me why I'm here, Tommy."

"But that's exactly what I'm asking."

"And I've told you already. I was married to your father for twenty-two years."

"So you still care about him."

"Of course, I still care about him."

"But you don't care enough about him to be married to him anymore."

"Tommy, please," Glenda said.

"This isn't the time or place, Tommy," Billye said softly, without rancor. "But I will talk to you about this some day, if you want."

"I don't see why this isn't the place," Tommy said. "And we certainly have the time. In fact, this may be the last time we will have. There's bedlam outside these walls. By the time we leave here, there may not be any New Orleans left. Maybe the mob that's rampaging through the streets will decide to burn down the hospital. So maybe this is the only place and the only time we'll ever have."

"Tommy," Glenda said.

"I'm just talking," he said. "Mother says she's here because she still cares about Dad. But she doesn't care *enough* about Dad to still be married to him. I was just trying to get my head around how that works."

"People change, Tommy. You're young enough that you probably don't see that just yet."

"So how did Dad change? He seems just the same to me. He's committed to something important. He's paid a price for his convictions; now he may pay with his life, too. That's the kind of man he's always been, isn't it? He went through a bad time after he lost the church. He drank too much for a while. He got down on himself. But that's just when he needed you most. Only that's when you left him."

No one responded immediately to this little outburst. Finally, Billye said, "I'm the one who changed, Tommy. Not your father. I think you're right that he's been the same all along."

"How did you change?" Tommy asked.

"I came to want different things."

"Like money," Tommy said. "Like all the things that a rich lawyer's money could buy you. Like that Continental you drive now instead of the Volkswagen you had when—"

Billye stood up. "I love you, Tommy," she said. "I'm so sorry I had to divorce your father. I had to. But I'm so sorry I had to. I hope you can forgive me some day." Her voice started to tremble, and she rolled both lips between her teeth. "I'm going to go now. I understand that you don't want me here. And I'm not going to irritate you by staying."

"You don't have to go, Billye," Glenda said. "We appreciate your coming. Really, we do."

Tommy didn't say anything, and Billye looked through the double doors of the waiting room out into the hall as if someone might be waiting for her. "No," she said. "I should go."

"Why don't you just wait until we can go in to see him again," Glenda said. "Shouldn't she wait, Tommy?"

Tommy shrugged.

"They'll let us in to see him in twenty minutes," Glenda said. "Wait until then before you go."

"I'm not sure you're gonna be able to get out of here anyway," Tommy said. "All hell's breaking loose out there. You're parked in the garage, I hope?"

Billye sat back down. "I'll go in to see him with y'all if you don't mind. Then I'll go on home." For a while the three of them sat and watched the television news coverage of the riots. A reporter stood on Canal Street with an upside-down car burning behind him on the concrete busway where the streetcar tracks used to be. Sirens screamed in the background. People rushed by. The reporter said that all fire units were currently at arson scenes and that there were two dozen unattended fires burning out of control with no hope of fire-department response. Another reporter spoke from in front of City Hall, and as they watched, Everett Essex pleaded for calm and for people to return to their homes. Then the mayor announced an absolute curfew until seven o'clock the next morning. Everyone was ordered off the streets. But then the reporter covering the mayor's statement wondered how many people would even get such a message and whether the city possessed the manpower to enforce it anyway.

A nurse came out and told them that Jeff had awakened and that they could see him, but she warned them not to tax his strength. As she ushered them into his room she said, "Reverend Caldwell, your family's here. They're very worried about you."

"Hiiii," Jeff said as they entered. He smiled weakly, obviously trying to appear more chipper than he felt. His thatch of gray hair was matted on one side and stuck out straight on the other. His face was pale, although splotched with red across his cheeks and the bridge of his nose. He didn't move a muscle below his neck, and Tommy got a flash of terror that he'd been paralyzed. Almost instantly Jeff closed his eyes again.

"The morphine drip will make him drift in and out of consciousness," the nurse said. "But he's actually awake now and that's a good sign." Tommy wanted to ask about his fears of paralysis but would wait until the visit was over. They would only be allowed to stay with him for ten minutes, if that long. "Reverend Caldwell," the nurse said, "do you recognize your family?"

"Of course," his father said without opening his eyes. He smiled dreamily again, almost as if remembering a joke.

Glenda and Tommy moved to one side of the bed; his mother stayed near the foot at the other. Glenda reached out and rubbed Jeff's shoulder.

"Hiiii," Jeff said in response. But still he did not open his eyes, and it wasn't clear if he knew who was touching him or who was in the room. He had not yet spoken any of their names.

"We love you, Jeff," Glenda said. She rubbed his shoulder again and then raised her hand to his face, letting the back of her fingers graze his cheek.

"Hiiii," Jeff said.

The Caldwell family did not touch each other much, particularly Jeff. Billye had hugged and kissed her children, especially when they were young, but Jeff never did. Tommy could not remember ever hugging his father. Even on those occasions when they'd been separated for a while, father and son greeted each other with handshakes, a ritual of "manhood" that began when Tommy was as young as seven years old. As Tommy grew older, an unusual sign of affection from Jeff would be a clap on the shoulder blade. Tommy envied the naturalness with which Glenda touched people, but he felt uncomfortable doing it himself, even at such a horrible time as this. He fought down that discomfort, at least a little, and placed a hand on his father's forearm, almost consciously reminding himself at intervals to stroke Jeff's arm with his fingers so that Jeff might know that he was there.

"Do you know who's here, Reverend Caldwell?" the nurse inquired. "Do you want to talk to your son and your daughter-in-law and your—your—" She didn't finish the sentence, presumably not knowing what to call Billye. Finally Jeff opened his eyes and grinned goofily. It wasn't clear that he recognized anybody because he still did not greet anyone by name.

"He needs his glasses," Billye said.

She stepped to the nightstand and stirred around in a drawer until she found his round, wire-rimmed spectacles with the question-mark-hooked temples.

"Jeff, can you turn your head around here so I can put on your glasses," Billye said. "I don't think he can see the end of his nose without them," she said to the nurse.

Jeff opened his eyes again and turned his head toward the sound of Billye's voice. She smiled at him, bent from the waist and put the glasses on his face, slipping the temples carefully around his ears.

"There," Billye said. "How's that?"

Jeff's eyes clearly followed her as she stepped back. "Billyeeeee," he said.

"Yes," she replied.

"Billye," Jeff said. "Where in the world have you been?"

chapter six

HUEY LONG BUILT THE FOUR-LANE STRETCH of concrete that connected Baton Rouge to New Orleans. Central Louisiana boy that he was, Huey liked to get downriver from the state capital as fast as possible, get away from staid, small-town Baton Rouge with its stink of oil refineries to that great old city with its classy hotels, exquisite restaurants, honky-tonk strip clubs and bars that never closed. Huey ran his political campaigns against the sin merchants and snotty intellectuals of New Orleans, but every chance he got he had his driver speed him there. Huey called his twin strips of pavement Airline Highway, and it seemed to run straight as an arrow for ninety miles through the soft soil of southeastern Louisiana, cutting through swamps much of the way. Near New Orleans it rose on tall pilings over the Bonnet Carré spillway which was built to divert water from the Mississippi River into Lake Pontchartrain and thereby save the city from inundation should the river threaten to top its vast earthen levees.

Starting in 1952, when Jeff decided to return to the seminary to pursue doctoral studies, he came to have a special regard for Airline Highway as he sped up and down its matching concrete ribbons once a week. He resigned from his church in Gonzales and took a smaller congregation just up Highway 1 from Baton Rouge at New Roads Baptist Church, which agreed to accept a so-called weekend pastorate. Jeff moved his wife Billye, his six-year-old son Tommy and his two-year-old daughter Danielle to New Orleans. To save money, which was always tight, Jeff settled his family in the Desire Housing Project, located not far from the seminary's new Gentilly campus.

Every Saturday morning, as early as he could drag himself out of bed, Jeff climbed into the cream and maroon Dodge sedan Billye's father had given the family and drove northwest along Airline Highway, then through Baton Rouge and on into New Roads. Planning his sermon for the next day, or cogitating on other pastoral duties he had to shoehorn into the two days of his "field residence," Jeff paid scant attention to the swamp that crowded the highway as he sped along. The swamp itself was an almost jade green, its pools of water completely opaque and vibrant with lily pads and algae, its islets of damp land promiscuous with life. Trees rose high and arced toward the stripe of light created by the swatch of highway. But every tree was roped with strangling vines as if the swamp was determined that nothing should escape its grip. And those trees that stood tallest no longer stood straight. Too tall for the soggy soil, they sagged against their neighbors and slowly tore at the limbs that supported them.

Jeff spent late Saturday morning and all Saturday afternoon making his pastoral rounds. The chairman of the deacons at the small church kept a list for Jeff of those church members who were ill or had suffered some setback, were encountering marital problems, had endured the death of a loved one, had seen a child or a spouse or a cousin sent to jail. Jeff drove first to the deacon's bayou-side home, where he was always treated to cups of dark-roast coffee mixed with hot milk. Once he had his list, he spent the rest of Saturday, all the way to dark, driving the swampy lanes of New Roads to visit with parishioners in need of pastoral care.

Many of his church members still lacked telephones, so Jeff didn't call first, but even for those who had phones a call wasn't necessary. He was expected. He parked his car in front yards made firm and dry with clam shells, walked up onto unpainted-wood front porches and took off his gray fedora before knocking. Inside, he was offered iced tea or milk or coffee, and he always accepted something. To refuse would have given offense, would have denied his church members the opportunity to exhibit their hospitality.

This visitation was an essential part of Jeff's job, and he performed it faithfully. But he didn't like it. It was torture to him. Jeff liked preaching. He found Bible study stimulating and theological issues truly fascinating. Writing sermons was hard work, especially for his rural congregations. The church members were farmers or fishermen or oil-field laborers; they knew little of the world and absolutely nothing of the kind of theological discussions Jeff savored. Writing sermons for them provided a constant challenge. Still, he liked it. He liked knowing that he was good in the pulpit. He liked knowing he could find the words that would make them listen to him. And he liked the praise he received afterward as he stood in the church-house doorway and shook hands with all the worshipers as they departed.

But visiting those in need was an agony because he never knew what to say. A young widow's husband had been crushed in an oil-field accident, and now her five-year-old daughter had drowned. A man's wife had run off with a salesman who had come through town selling kitchenware they couldn't afford. A ten-year-old boy had fallen off a horse and would walk with a limp the rest of his life. A young couple was having marital problems. The husband couldn't stop crying, and the wife stared ahead saying nothing, her right eye swollen shut and her lower lip puffed as purple as the skin of a plum. A deacon's beautiful twenty-one-year-old daughter, the homecoming queen of her graduating high-school class and a senior at LSU, had developed a stubborn cough at Christmas and died of lung cancer just after Easter, eight weeks before her wedding day. Their problems were all different, but they were all the same. Something horrible had happened to their lives, something they couldn't control and could seldom undo. Why had God let this awful fate befall them?

Jeff hadn't any idea. He had nothing to tell them, nothing to ease their pain, no wisdom to impart. Other ministers, he knew, told them how the ways of God were mysterious, assured them that their loved ones had gone to a better place, promised them that God had a plan that man couldn't fathom, warned them that blaming God for what had happened would endanger their souls. Jeff couldn't do any of that. He wasn't sure he believed any of it, and he was pretty certain that little of it provided any comfort. And so, mostly, he was mute. He came. He drank a cup of coffee or a glass of milk or iced tea. Sometimes he ate a piece of cornbread or a biscuit with jam. And he said almost nothing whatsoever. If he sensed that someone needed physical contact, he would change chairs or find a footstool to move close. He would take a hand and hold it in both of his. He would stroke his top hand up and down the person's wrist and forearm. If the parishioner began to cry, he would sometimes whisper the utter inanity, "There, there," for which he always felt ashamed afterwards.

But mostly he would just sit silent, just keep his head bowed and try to keep his breathing even and say nothing at all. He never volunteered to pray with them, and he certainly never offered to pray out loud for them. But they would often ask, and when they did, he inquired first if they would like him to pray with them silently, and if so he would close his eyes and count slowly to one hundred and then say, "In Jesus' name, amen." But usually they wanted him to pray aloud. He would offer to lead them in reciting the Lord's Prayer. But that made many of them uncomfortable, so he was often forced to pray for them. He always began, "Our Father, who art in heaven and who gave us your son Jesus as our redeemer, Father be here with us today, here with this family that is suffering." Then he would speak some of the specifics that had brought him to his visitation and would close, "Let us be confident in your grace. In Jesus' name, amen." He came to understand that it mattered less what he said on their behalf than that a clergyman had come to their house and addressed God in their presence. He took comfort in this understanding, but nonetheless, he always went away feeling like a fraud.

This is not to say that Jeff didn't believe in prayer. In fact, he believed in prayer with all his heart, and he prayed on a daily basis. He prayed as Jesus taught in the Lord's Prayer. First he praised God. Then he expressed his gratitude: for having survived the war, for having escaped the impoverished circumstances of his upbringing, for the blessings of his family and friends, for the brightness of his future. Next, he made his requests: that the world should live in peace, that men might learn to live as brothers, that the infamous institution of Jim Crow might soon be abolished. And then he made his personal requests: that he might be a vital player in the struggle for racial equality and that in the process he might get a large church with educated members and a salary that would allow him and his family to live more comfortably. Finally, he apologized to God for any part of his prayer that was unworthy.

Jeff didn't ruminate a great deal on this habit of praying. He didn't try to examine how much he believed or failed to believe that his praying actually influenced God. But he did occasionally ruminate on the sense he had of being called by God to do some significant work. He confided to God that he felt an exquisite readiness, like a track runner who had already heard the words "on your marks" and "set." And in his own prayers he never felt fraudulent.

During the three years that Jeff spent doing his doctoral work, he spent almost every weekend away from his wife and children, a separation he regarded as an unavoidable necessity. His livelihood depended on his weekend pastorate, and the disruption of packing all the things young children needed made little sense to him. He knew Billye would have preferred being with him, but since he was in visitation all day Saturday anyway, what point was there in taking his family along?

Moreover, although he never admitted such a thing to Billye, he gradually came to like the solitude his weekends alone afforded him. He loved his wife and children, but he felt resentful of the clutter the children caused and the noise they made that required he return to the library after supper to study. Thus, his drive up Airline Highway was a cherished respite of reverie. And his Saturday nights in the New Roads Baptist Church's tiny, musty, sparsely furnished parsonage were a luxurious time of solitude. He ended almost every Saturday night after his bath by lying naked on the creaking double bed in the larger of the parsonage's two bedrooms and masturbating. Why he needed, even craved, this kind of relief he couldn't quite say. Perhaps it was because he and Billye had decided not to have more children, so their intercourse was always performed with a condom. Mostly, his masturbating represented a freedom there in the New Roads woods that he never had when he was home with his family, in fact, had never had at any point in his entire life.

In the summer of 1953, Jeff found himself staying at New Roads for entire weeks at a time, returning home to New Orleans mostly for Billye to launder and iron his clothes. For that was the summer Jeff became involved with the cause of Maisy Drake, a forty-year-old Baton Rouge school teacher. Maisy had tan skin and was slightly built. Her parents were sharecroppers from central Louisiana, just one parish removed from where Jeff had grown up. Three of her grandparents had been slaves, the fourth was a white plantation master. She had worked as a domestic servant in Baton Rouge to put herself through Southern University. After college she had married her childhood sweetheart, Cecil Drake, who worked with local NAACP president Moses Jones as a porter for the Illinois Southern Railroad. In the late forties, Cecil and Maisy had joined the NAACP and thereafter spent many hours discussing methods by which the indignity of racial segregation might be contested in their area.

And yet, Maisy's central role in what occurred did not result from any active plan, but rather from a developed mindset and a catalytic set of circumstances. Maisy habitually stayed in her fifth-grade classroom at Wilson Elementary School nearly an hour and a half each day after the children went home at three o'clock. On the day of the incident, as always, she straightened her room, graded papers and made lesson plans for the next day. The day was warm and humid, as Louisiana June afternoons most often are, and the school owned no fans to create a breeze. So Maisy was hot and damp as usual. She was also particularly tired. The school year was almost over, and her pupils had sapped her energy with their restless anticipation of the upcoming summer vacation.

Maisy usually caught the 4:32 Evergreen bus and rode to the last stop, then walked a mile to the five-room shotgun house she and Cecil owned in a Negro neighborhood up against the river just beyond the Baton Rouge city limits. Most of the riders on the Evergreen line were Negroes, although the drivers on the route, as all over the city, were white. Today, as most always at this time, the bus was practically empty. There were only three other passengers aboard, all Negroes.

Maisy enjoyed a cordial relationship with Mr. Jameson, the driver on the 4:32, and they greeted each other as usual when she boarded. "Another hot one, Miz Maisy," Jameson said as he collected her fare. "Bet those younguns of yours are running you ragged in this weather."

"Can't one of them sit still for three minutes straight," she replied and took her normal seat right behind the driver, the wide flat seat parallel to the bus's center aisle.

"They ready for school to let out?"

"Can't wait," she replied. "'Bout to bust their britches they're so excited."

The trouble began two stops later when a thirty-four-year-old white man named Steve Robertson got on the bus dressed in a rumpled gray suit and carrying a thick valise. He paid his fare, and as the bus pulled away from the curb, said to Maisy, "I guess you'll have to move."

Robertson was a big freckled man with large hands and feet. His hair was dark red and his skin was flushed from the heat. Maisy looked at him for a long moment. White people seldom rode the Evergreen line this far out. He was no doubt a door-to-door salesman peddling his wares in the black community. Maisy deliberately rode farther back when she used other routes, and she had never before been asked to move by a white person. On the Evergreen route, white riders sometimes sat opposite her without comment or even chose to stand rather than demand that she move. On those occasions both simply looked away, as if they hadn't noticed each other.

The bus swayed, and Robertson grabbed the silver pole at the end of Maisy's seat to steady himself. " 'D'you hear what I said?" he asked Maisy.

"You can sit over there," Maisy responded without planning to, indicating with her chin the identical wide seat across from her.

"I can't sit there with you in this seat. You know that. Now you gotta move."

Maisy slid down to the end of the flat seat farthest away from the driver. "Now you can sit over there up by the door," she said. "I'll be behind you like I'm supposed to be."

"Naw, now that won't be adequate a'tall," Robertson said. "You gotta move on back. We can't both be in the same row, and you know that as well as I do."

Maisy picked her satchel up, set it on her lap, folded her arms across it and stared straight ahead.

"You gonna do what I'm telling you?" Robertson said, heat in his voice.

Maisy said nothing.

"Driver," Robertson said to Jameson, "you better tell this nigger woman she's gonna have to move back or she's gonna get herself in a pack of trouble."

Jameson looked over his shoulder nervously. He pulled over to a stop and picked up a Negro rider who paid her fare and moved past the confrontation in the front of the bus. Jameson closed the door but didn't pull away from the curb. "He's right, Miz Maisy," he said. "You gonna have to move back a seat." Maisy tightened her grip on her satchel and did not respond.

"She ain't listening to neither one of us," Robertson said. "We gonna have to call us some police to deal with this."

Jameson slipped the bus into neutral, set his emergency brake, twisted himself out of his seat and stepped between Robertson and Maisy to stand directly over her. "Miz Maisy, this gentleman is right," Jameson said. "If you won't move back a seat, I'm going to have to call a policeman. That's the law. I'm not allowed to operate this bus unless it's properly segregated."

"You do what you gotta do," Maisy replied, staring straight ahead, never bringing her eyes to Jameson's face.

"Don't make me get you in trouble like that," Jameson said. "I know you're a school teacher and all, and I'm sure you haven't ever had any run-in with the law before."

That was true. And Maisy was surprised to find herself so close to legal trouble now. This was not something she had planned. But now that this situation had been thrust at her, her mind was made up, more suddenly and certainly than she could ever have imagined. She wasn't moving. And that was it. They could arrest her if they wanted to, and they no doubt shortly would. But she wasn't moving. Her mind swirled, trying to imagine what would happen after that, but about her immediate course of action, her mind was completely settled.

"Think about the example you'll be setting for your little school children," Jameson pleaded.

Yes, she thought and allowed herself a silent snort of laugh. Think of the example, indeed.

Robertson and the driver both left the bus, but the four Negroes riding behind Maisy stayed put. Robertson stood just outside the bus door and smoked a cigarette while Jameson walked two blocks to a drugstore and called the police. A squad car arrived about five minutes later. The four white men—two police officers, Robertson and Jameson—conferred for a bit and then the driver and the two patrolmen entered the bus. The senior cop said to Maisy, "As an officer of the municipal law, I am ordering you to comply with ordinance 766 with regard to racial segregation of the city public-transit system. Please take a seat farther back."

Maisy neither said anything nor moved.

"I don't think she's intending to do it, officer," Jameson said, his voice infused with regret. Miller Jameson was a congenial family man of forty-two, a veteran and a church member. His belief that Negroes were inferior to whites as a race did not inhibit his courtesy to, nor negate his genuine liking for, the many hardworking people who rode his bus. He was sorry that Maisy Drake was making this trouble for herself and figured that no good was sure to come of it. On the other hand, he and the policemen had given her plenty of opportunity to change her mind. "That's what I explained to your sergeant on the phone."

"You give me no choice," the senior patrolman said to Maisy. "I hereby arrest you for violation of city ordinance and for disturbing the peace. Please stand now." Maisy did not respond. "If you do not comply with my order to stand," the policeman said, "I will have to add resisting arrest to the charges against you."

Maisy looked the police officer full in the face for the first time. Slowly, she stood up. They took her satchel and purse away from her, handcuffed her with her hands behind her back, and led her out of the bus to the squad car. Without saying anything, the four Negroes who had watched the proceedings rose and exited the bus by the rear door. The four of them stood on the sidewalk and watched as Maisy was placed in the back seat of the police car and driven away.

When the cruiser had turned a corner and disappeared from sight, Jameson stepped off the front of the bus and said to his patrons, "If you folks will get back on board, I'll get you on home."

One black man in overalls turned to look at the driver, but the others refused to make eye contact.

"Let's get going," Jameson said, smiling. "We're already behind schedule."

The black man in overalls said, "I reckon I can walk on home from here," and set off down the street in the direction the bus was heading. The others followed him.

So began the Baton Rouge bus boycott.

Maisy Drake used her phone call from city lockup to call her husband, who immediately contacted Moses Jones. Moses and Cecil hurried to the courthouse with the intention of bailing Maisy out, but she had already planned out her next move. She well remembered the Rufus Johnson lunch-counter incident from two years previously, and she thought it important to remain in jail. If she stayed in jail while the system creaked forward, people would rally to her support as they had almost done for Rufus Johnson. And if she insisted on a full jury trial, she could put the indignity of bus segregation itself on trial.

Cecil counseled his wife that this was not her fight, but she responded, "If it is not mine, whose is it?"

But Maisy could announce her plans more easily than Moses and Cecil could carry them out. Moses contacted national NAACP headquarters for legal funding, hoping that the national office might even dispatch one of its lawyers to spearhead the case. To his shock, he was advised to pay Maisy's bail and send her home. The national office could not divert attention to a wrangle over public-transit desegregation when at that moment it was devoting all its resources to its upcoming U.S. Supreme Court hearing on the Topeka, Kansas, public school desegregation case of *Brown v. the Board of Education*. Jones was astonished at this attitude and pled that the Negro community in Baton Rouge was poised to act decisively. But national officials had little regard for this railroad porter and brushed him off. Frustrated but undeterred, Jones contacted Everett Essex, the one Negro minister in town who was himself an NAACP member, and asked him to host a meeting at his church that night. Essex had succeeded Zaccheus Greene at Four Gospels Baptist. Moses then used his local chapter's ditto machine to crank out flyers announcing Maisy's arrest and the meeting that night.

Cecil, meanwhile, arranged legal representation. He first tried a contact at the Southern University Law School, who told him that as state employees Southern professors were too vulnerable to losing their jobs should they dare try to dismantle the state's racial segregation laws. The contact suggested Jeff's friend Hodding Morris, who immediately agreed to take the case *pro bono*. Hodding alerted Jeff to Maisy Drake's situation and Jeff instantly drove into Baton Rouge to confer with Peacher Martin.

Jeff hoped to persuade George Washington Brown to assume leadership of whatever organization would emerge from the meetings later that night. Reverend Brown now had a significantly larger profile in the Baton Rouge Negro community than he'd had just two years earlier. After a year's internship in the small upstate community of Liberty Hill, he'd recently returned to Baton Rouge as pastor of the prestigious Pritchard Place Baptist Church. Four Gospels was the largest Negro congregation, but Pritchard had the largest membership of black professionals. When Jeff called Brown's church, however, he was informed that Reverend Brown was unavailable; Brown was preparing for a three-o'clock meeting at Four Gospels with Everett Essex and other area ministers.

"We should go too," Jeff said to Preacher when he got off the phone.

"Well, I only see one problem with that, Brother Caldwell," Preacher drawled.

"Which might be?"

"They ain't invited us."

"We'll invite ourselves."

"They might not like that," Preacher said.

"Why?"

"Well, there's this thing about them being Negroes and us not."

"Nobody said the meeting was just for Negroes," Jeff said. "Way I look at it is we're all Christians and that's what's important."

Preacher squinted at Jeff and cocked his jaw. "You really believe that, Caldwell, or you just full of shit?"

Jeff wrinkled his brow. "Of course, I believe it. Don't you?"

Preacher licked his tongue in a circle over his gums. "Truth be known," he said, "I'm never quite sure what I believe. Though I try never to let that inhibit my acting on some principle I'm attracted to."

Jeff looked his friend hard in the face, not sure whether Preacher was putting him on or not. "You really don't think we ought to go?"

"Didn't say that. Said I thought our going might annoy them some. But now that I see how devoted to it you are, I think we ought to go for sure."

Jeff was relieved. He did believe they ought to go, but he wasn't sure he would have dared to go alone.

"There's lots of good things you can do on a sunny afternoon," Preacher said. "And pissing off a bunch of Negro preachers is about as good as any."

Since they weren't invited, Jeff and Preacher weren't informed when the meeting was moved to 2:30. It was already underway in a Sunday School room when Jeff and Preacher arrived at 3. Everett Essex was at a podium listening to someone else speak as Preacher and Jeff crept into the room and slid into chairs in the back. Essex stared at them, perplexed, and the look on his face, evidently, caused the speaker to stop and turn to look at the two white men, a gesture mimicked immediately by everyone else in the room.

"Can I help you gentlemen?" Essex said.

"We just came to participate," Jeff said.

"Participate?" Essex said.

"Yes. We understood this is an organization of Baptist ministers concerned with the arrest of Mrs. Drake. That's correct, isn't it? And we want to participate. We're Baptist preachers, too. The Reverend Martin here is chaplain at LSU, and I'm pastor of the church in New Roads."

"I am acquainted with the Reverends Martin and Caldwell," George Washington Brown said. "Reverend Caldwell worshiped with us when I was in Liberty Hill." The other ministers turned to look at Brown, but he said nothing further.

"We had thought of this as a meeting of National Baptist ministers," Essex said, referring to the organization of black churches.

Preacher whispered to Jeff out of the corner of his mouth, "I may have mentioned they might feel this way." Jeff didn't even turn to acknowledge his colleague.

"We were just getting to the point of structuring an organization," Essex said, clearly implying that Jeff and Preacher should depart so they could continue their business.

"An organization?" Jeff inquired. "I think that's excellent. Have you settled on a name?"

No one responded for a long moment. Finally Reverend Brown said, "We're thinking of calling ourselves the Christian Social Conscience League."

"I like that," Jeff said. "I like that very much."

"Yes, well, gentlemen," Essex said, "you will forgive me, I'm sure, if I sound rude, but since this is a National Baptist organization—"

"But your name doesn't say anything about its being a National Baptist or even a Baptist organization," Jeff protested. "Preacher and I are Christians. We're Baptists even."

One of the ministers abruptly stood up, his face quivering with anger. "This isn't your problem," he said, enunciating every word. "This is our problem."

"It's the problem of everyone who believes that we are all equal in God's sight," Preacher said quietly. The Negro man snapped around and sat down with such force his chair scooted backward, causing the metal legs to screech against the linoleum floor.

"Gentleman, once again," Everett Essex began.

But Jeff cut him off. "There's stuff we can do," he said. "We can begin by organizing the other white pastors, and we can work with our own parishioners. If y'all are going to call for a boycott—"

"Who said anything about a boycott," the angry minister said, twisting around in his chair toward the white men.

"I said *if* y'all are going to call for a boycott," Jeff argued. "I'm trying to give you an example. *If* y'all should call for a boycott, we could ask our own church members to honor it. White folks ride the bus, too. It's not just Negro riders. Tell them it's what Jesus would want."

"How many of your white church members out in New Roads ride a Baton Rouge bus?" one of the Negro ministers wanted to know.

George Washington Brown stood up. "Reverend Caldwell," he said, "Reverend Martin. We appreciate your coming here today even if you have taken us by surprise. Could we in Christian brotherhood prevail upon you to step into the hall for a moment so that those of us who have been here for the entire meeting might discuss together your application to join our number? For just a brief moment?"

"Of course," Preacher said and rose to leave. A beat later Jeff stood and joined him.

When they were gone, Reverend Brown reseated himself. Essex looked out to the gathering and raised his hands, palms up to the level of his shoulders. "Your wisdom, brothers?" he said.

"Spies," the angry man said. "I'm against letting them join."

"So am I," another said.

"It would be magnificent if they could indeed organize white support," one said.

"And I'm going to grow wings and fly directly to heaven," the angry man said.

Reverend Brown stood again. "I am of the most fervent opinion," he said, "that we have no choice but to let them join. Not no choice in a narrow political sense, for we could indeed hold a vote and deny them membership in our fledgling organization. But no choice in the moral sense. We can only fight this fight in the name of brotherhood, and we can hardly begin the struggle by arming ourselves with the deadly weapons of exclusion. If we want God on our side, then we must be careful always to be on God's side."

Reverend Brown sat down, and his remarks were followed by a period of silence. Finally, one of the ministers said, "So moved."

"What exactly have you moved?" Essex asked.

"I move that we accept the Caucasian ministers as members of the Christian Social Conscience League," the man repeated.

"Second," another said. When they voted, not even the angry minister voted nay. Thus Jeff Caldwell and Preacher Martin became, along with the nine Negro men in the room, founding members of the CSCL. That night at Four Gospels, hundreds of people, overwhelmingly black people, elected George Washington Brown as its president and spokesman and voted to boycott the Baton Rouge public-transit system until it was desegregated.

Jeff's and Preacher's first efforts in support of the boycott were a dismal failure. They sought to get the area's white pastors to sign a Declaration of Christian Principle endorsing the boycott, but fewer than one in five agreed; the highest number was among the Roman Catholic clergy, the lowest among Jeff's and Preacher's fellow Southern Baptists. Other of their endeavors were more successful, however, and they established their sincerity and commitment in the eyes of Reverend Brown and Essex and other members of the CSCL.

The boycott itself started off well, with black ridership practically eliminated. In addition, whites stayed off the buses at the beginning amid rumors that bombs had been placed aboard certain vehicles. But the absence of convenient and inexpensive public transportation worked a great hardship on the Negro community, most of whom lived in enclaves around the city's perimeter. Those who could walked to work, but that added a level of physical discomfort to a population that was mostly engaged in physical labor. Walking to and from work, moreover, was a misery in inclement weather. And it seemed to rain that summer even more than it usually does in south Louisiana.

Most black folks who owned automobiles lent their cars to a carpooling system. And initially, the eleven Negro-owned taxi companies cooperated by providing rides at reduced rates. City attorneys stopped that, however, by getting Judge James McElroy to issue an injunction. Taxi rates were set by the city council, and any driver not charging the established rates was subject to losing his license; his company could lose its operating permit. Jeff and Preacher organized white drivers to assist in the boycott, and a surprising number did. In addition, many white housewives not otherwise cooperating in the carpool drove their maids to and from work each day, sometimes allowing a husband, child or neighbor to pile in for a lift somewhere along her route.

But after about three weeks, white ridership returned to near normal, and an increasing number of Negroes began to return to public transportation as well, some announcing with obvious irritation that they'd rather ride on the back of the bus than continue to walk in the rain. Still, the boycott continued, and the attitudes of hard-line whites grew increasingly violent. Bricks were thrown through the windows of carpoolers. Whites participating in the carpool got phone calls harassing them as "nigger lovers." Everett Essex and George Washington Brown got death threats. At first, neither took the threats seriously, dismissing them as scare tactics. But then someone fired rifle shots through both their houses on the same night. The next night Reverend Brown received a midnight call claiming that a bomb would go off in his house in the next ten minutes.

Reverend Brown rushed his family out of the house, terrified that he was shepherding them from the safety of shelter to an ambush where gunmen could cruise by and shoot them down like paper targets on a firing range. But the Brown family—all barefoot, five year-old Robert and two-year-old Denise in pajamas, Annette in a nightgown, and Reverend Brown in just an undershirt and boxers—had been outside less than three minutes when two fire engines and three police cars roared up to the house, sirens screaming. Newspaper reporters were not far behind. The cops—all white, of course—rushed up to the family and led them off the lawn and into the street while firemen scurried under the house. Within minutes, as photographers' flashbulbs crackled, a fireman emerged from under the house holding an alarm clock strapped to what appeared to be a bundle of dynamite.

Reverend Brown was both astonished and relieved when the authorities arrived. But then it occurred to him that he hadn't called the police.

"How did you know to come here?" he asked a policeman. The officer shrugged, and Reverend Brown repeated his question.

"Just following orders," the policeman said without looking at the minister.

Reverend Brown laid a hand on the policeman's shoulder. "But I didn't take the time—"

The policeman spun around suddenly and snapped, "Get your hands off me, nigger. If it was up to me, I'd let them blow your black ass to kingdom come."

Reverend Brown stepped back, shocked and stung. As a Negro clergyman he was usually treated with at least grudging courtesy by white people. But, of course, he'd never before led an attempt to pull down a pillar of Jim Crow.

"Who is in command here?" Reverend Brown said, trembling, willing his voice to sound calm.

"Whassit to you?" the officer said, refusing once again to look at Reverend Brown.

"I have a right to speak to the commanding officer," Reverend Brown said.

At that moment, a tall, gray-haired policeman walked over from where he'd been speaking with the fire chief and introduced himself as Captain Reinecke. Reverend Brown introduced himself and extended his hand at almost the precise moment Reinecke took off his policeman's cap with his right hand and ran his left through his hair.

Reinecke nodded at Annette and said, "Evening, ma'am." Then he put his hat back on his head and looked at Reverend Brown, who still had his hand extended. He chuckled at something known only to himself, took Reverend Brown's hand and shook it. "Sorry about the trouble. But it looks like we got here just in time."

"How did you know to come?" Reverend Brown asked.

Captain Reinecke raised his shoulders. "Anonymous bomb threat came into the station house. We called the fire department bomb squad and got here as fast as possible."

Reverend Brown relaxed a little. That sounded reasonable enough, he guessed. "The bomb was real?" he asked.

Reinecke replied, "Looked real enough to me to have turned your house there into a pile of toothpicks."

A photographer walked up. "How about a picture of the survivors?" he asked, screwing a bulb into his flash pan.

Reverend Brown looked down at himself, dressed only in his underwear. "Please," he said, raising his hand just as the first bulb went off.

"How about you and the missus and the captain," the photographer said. A second walked up and took a photo as well.

"Make them stop," Reverend Brown said to Reinecke. "We don't have any clothes on."

Reinecke shrugged. "No can do, Reverend. Freedom of the press, you know."

"Then my wife and I must go into the house to dress."

"Afraid I can't let you do that," Reinecke said. "Found one bomb. Don't mean there ain't another one. We best give the place a thorough going over before we let you folks back in. Wouldn't want to be derelict in my duty and then be responsible for these two young children getting hurt in any way."

The police kept the Brown family standing in the street for more than an hour, during which time they were at the mercy of the swarming photographers. When Reinecke finally did rule an all clear, he walked up on the porch with Reverend Brown and held the screen door open for Annette and the children.

"You know, Reverend," Reinecke said to Reverend Brown after the others were inside, "we may have been lucky this time." He licked his lips. "Next time, we might not be so lucky. Next time, bomber might not call us. Might not even call you."

Reverend Brown studied the policeman's impassive face a moment before saying, "I understand."

In the living room Annette was crying. "They've turned the house upside down," she said.

The next morning's papers covered the bomb scare on their front pages, each featuring a series of photographs of the Brown family in their nightclothes. One even showed Reverend Brown holding the fly of his undershorts closed with a fist gripped at his crotch. He was greatly embarrassed, but he took solace in knowing that such was exactly what was intended. The membership of the Christian Social Conscience League met at eight the next morning at Reverend Brown's church, where he briefed his colleagues on what had happened the night before. Many were suspicious that the Baton Rouge authorities had conspired with the bombers or even planted the bomb themselves. Everyone wanted to know if anything was missing from the Brown house after the bomb squad had gone through it.

"As best we can tell," Reverend Brown informed them, "only my address book."

"In which all our names are listed," one of the pastors said.

"Along with a great many other people," Reverend Brown observed.

In the discussion that followed, many ideas were considered. Some felt that Reverend Brown should immediately depart the city and let others take up his position at the forefront. But, of course, then the same tactics would only be employed against whoever took Reverend Brown's place. Then perhaps he should retreat to New Orleans and take advantage of that city's relatively greater reputation for racial tolerance. Advocates of this position argued that he could still lead the Baton Rouge protest from that distance.

But Reverend Brown refused. "Driving our leadership into hiding is their top priority," he said. "If our leaders cannot stay in the field, how can we expect those whom we would lead to stay there?" Then perhaps he and his family should abandon the Pritchard Place parsonage for some undisclosed location where they would be safer. But Reverend Brown rejected this option for the same reasons he opposed flight to New Orleans.

"Well, then at least, for God's sake, let us take your wife and children away into safety," one of the pastors exclaimed.

"I have another idea," Jeff said, rising to speak. The men in the room, Preacher Martin included, were astonished at what he proposed.

That afternoon, the CSCL called a press conference to respond to the bomb threat of the night before. Everett Essex spoke first. "Last night," he said, "as has been prominently covered in the local press, villains unknown purportedly planted a bomb under the home of the Reverend George Washington Brown, pastor of the Pritchard Place Baptist Church and president of the Christian Social Conscience League. We deplore such an action. And we call upon the police authorities of our city to do their duty and provide protection to the citizens of this community, whatever their color of skin. We furthermore extend the hand of brotherhood to the perpetrators of this heinous act, and we offer all involved the cup of Christian forgiveness. Jesus said to those who walk in the paths of perfidy, 'Go and sin no more.' This we say also unto those who would have done harm to Reverend Brown and his family."

When Essex finished, Reverend Brown stepped to the podium. "Like sailors on a boundless sea beset by a howling tempest," he said, "we find ourselves in the midst of great controversy. Some of us on this great sailing vessel that is our fatherland have ridden in the staterooms of privilege. Some have ridden in the cramped quarters of steerage. Others of us have been confined below decks, asked to sweat and toil to maintain the great engines that drive us forward, never to be allowed to walk the deck of equality on the grand promenade. Now those who have toiled are humbly asking for a chance to feel the salt spray in our faces, to gaze upon the horizon of opportunity and prosperity which is our joint promised land. But some are so determined to deny all our citizens the equal chance to gaze upon the beauty of the sea that they resort to planting bombs, bombs which may kill the targets of their hatred most immediately, but bombs which will just as surely send all aboard to a watery demise. Jesus, while still in human form, took his disciples into the midst of the tempest on the Sea of Galilee, which he calmed by the raising of his divine hand. Thereafter, he dared to step out on the water where he trod as if upon solid ground. And his disciples were amazed. And Jesus beckoned to them to walk with him. But they were afraid. Like them, I am afraid. But I understand what Jesus asks. He asks us to venture out upon the water beside him. The sea of the controversy rocks beneath my feet, but I believe in Jesus. And I believe in what he has promised. I will step out and ask you to step out with me. For he will, he will, hold us up. He *will* hold us up."

When Reverend Brown had completed his remarks, Jeff Caldwell stepped forward to speak: "As a minister of the gospel, it is my duty to follow the teachings of Jesus in all things. And as those many of you who are my fellow Christians well know, Jesus told us that there are two great commandments, first that we love our Lord God with all our heart and all our soul and all our mind and all our strength. Second, that we love our neighbors as ourselves. As a minister of the gospel I do not find anywhere in holy scripture where Jesus provides exceptions for this second great commandment based on the color of a man's skin. And so this afternoon I am announcing my intention to accept the invitation of my neighbors Reverend George Washington Brown and his family who have been placed in harm's way by those who do not heed this second great commandment. On behalf of my family, I accept Reverend Brown's invitation to come for a visit to his home at the parsonage of the Pritchard Place Baptist Church."

Jeff stepped away from the podium, turned and picked up his three-year-old daughter and hoisted her onto his shoulder. He grasped his seven-year-old son by the hand and nodded at his wife who stepped forward to join her husband. The four of them faced the battery of cameras together.

"This is my beautiful wife Billye," Jeff said. Billye nodded and forced her face into a tight smile. "And this is my son Tommy." Jeff raised the little boy's hand until his arm was fully stretched out. "And this is my precious daughter Danielle." He bounced the toddler, who giggled and squirmed away from the crowd. "We have been invited to visit for a while with our neighbors George Washington and Annette Brown and their children Robert and Denise. We are filled with gratitude for such an invitation and will begin our visit with the Browns this very evening."

Little Danielle, her shoulder-length blond hair curled into a soft pageboy, had squirmed down onto Jeff's chest, her arms around his neck, her chin hooked over his shoulder. He wrestled her around until she was facing forward again and brought his hand up to cup her chin and caress her face. "We will be there every day and every night for some time," he said. "So let whoever might think to do harm to this household know that they will be doing harm to this lovely, innocent little girl."

Jeff's gesture was based on his presumption that the Klansmen and other madmen whose racial hate was great enough to justify murder could never justify the taking of a white life, particularly not the life of a white female child. And though Jeff's naiveté remained considerable, and though there would come a time when not even white females would be spared by the Klan, it was early enough in the struggle that his calculations were correct. The Caldwells did indeed move in with the Browns, and the Browns' home was spared another bomb threat for the duration of the boycott.

But eventually the boycott was broken. As the weeks went by, black ridership continued to increase, and the city's white leaders took several actions to inhibit the carpools. The suddenly formed White Citizens Council demanded that all whites cease participating in the carpool. This did not influence the truly committed, but it did have an impact on housewives who had been driving their maids to and from work. Warned that their business relations would be affected, husbands ordered their wives to require their maids to make other arrangements. The critical blow, though, was struck by a city council ordinance that ruled the carpools an unlicensed and therefore illegal taxi service; drivers were to be punished by five-hundred-dollar fines and up to thirty days in jail. Movement attorney Hodding Morris argued that such an ordinance was blatantly unconstitutional, as it was subsequently ruled in a suit brought by the American Civil Liberties Union. But that took two years. In the short term, after three drivers were arrested and fined, the carpools collapsed. With them the boycott collapsed as well.

There were many casualties of this failed action. Preacher Martin was relieved of his position as Baptist chaplain at LSU. He would never again hold a denominational position of any kind. A minister without a pulpit, he would never pastor a church. He would move to New Orleans and work as a journalist and ultimately write seminal books about the civil-rights movement. Jeff Caldwell resigned as pastor of the New Roads Baptist Church under pressure from his board of deacons. But national and even regional coverage of the boycott was limited enough that his role was not widely known outside the Baton Rouge area, and he was able to move to another so-called weekend pastorate while he finished his doctorate.

Maisy Drake was not so lucky. She was relieved of her position as a fifth-grade teacher at Wilson Elementary and was unable to find another teaching job anywhere in the area. The lost income and professional emptiness caused a deep wound. She refused to accept proceeds from a fund Everett Essex and George Washington Brown organized for her within their churches. Within a year she and Cecil relocated to Chicago. He continued to work for Illinois Southern but was killed in a train-yard accident two years later.

Maisy never remarried, but she did find a teaching job on Chicago's south side and continued to do volunteer work with the NAACP. Then in 1967, on a cold day in January, walking from her school to her apartment in the early darkness of late afternoon, she was robbed of her purse and school satchel and shot once in the chest. She died before an ambulance could reach her. A black youth was seen running away from the scene immediately after the gunfire. Her killer was never apprehended.

chapter seven

FROM THE DAYS OF HUEY LONG'S FIRST STATEWIDE campaigns in the mid–1920s, the New Peterstown, Louisiana, community had been promised funds to pave New Peterstown Road, which wound through its center. The year Jeff Caldwell was thirteen, in the aftermath of the massive 1937 flood, the state faced extensive road repairs just to regrade and retop the road with gravel. If the state was ever going to pave the road, now seemed the time, so the highway commission adopted plans to move road-building equipment into Sherman Parish. Like several of his neighbors, Jeff's father Pruitt considered inquiring about employment. Pruitt could handle a heavy truck, he figured. And he could wield a shovel as well as any man. But in the end he reckoned the paving project wouldn't last but a year. He might well make better money for a time with the highway department, but then the road would be paved, and the equipment would be moved elsewhere, and he'd wish he had his job back at the sawmill.

Others evaluated the situation differently, but none of the New Peterstown men managed to land a job on the project. Then two days after the arrival of the heavy equipment at the junction of New Peterstown Road and State Highway 1, Pruitt's brother Ralph and his cousin Marlon Davis came by with several other men—Curley Lewis, Ossie Preston and Lucian Nash. Marlon was one of the local men who had been turned down for a job on the road-building crew.

Like all of the houses in New Peterstown, the Caldwells' house was raised on square brick pillars about four and a half feet off the ground and stabilized in the center with two brick chimneys. Such construction, the house's surrounding porch, wide eaves and ten-foot ceilings, kept the interior decidedly cooler in the summer, a comfort paid for in the cold, damp winter months. The Caldwells' six-acre plot of red earth, house, barn, hen house and two outhouses lay atop a low ridge. A mud drive dropped through a swale off New Peterstown Road and across a crude log-and-plank bridge over a narrow creek before rising up to the Caldwell property.

The men came walking up out of the swale shortly after seven in the evening, three of them swinging unlit kerosene lanterns at their sides. All wore overalls and sweat-stained hats pulled low on their foreheads. The Caldwell family had already finished dinner, and Pruitt and his sons had retreated to the porch. Pruitt was in his rocker, a chaw of tobacco already in his cheek. One brown high-topped work shoe was positioned flat against the corner pole, and Pruitt's knee flexed in a slow rhythm as he pushed against the pole to rock himself. As the men made their greetings and came up on the porch, Pruitt scooted his chair back to provide more space, ordering Jeff and his older brother Wayne off two stools that were the only other places to sit save for the boards of the porch itself.

Two of the men took the stools Wayne and Jeff vacated; two others sat down on the porch, each dangling a leg over the edge. Tall and bony with a prominent chin and heavy eyebrows, Marlon Davis chose to stand and leaned his back up against the corner pole, steadying himself by propping a work boot against the pole. Before he began to talk, Marlon rolled himself a cigarette, wet it in his mouth, pulled it out through pursed lips like a fish bone and lit it with a match he struck against the denim fabric of his overalls on the back of his thigh. Then he told the story about his not getting a job on the highway project. The job would entail blasting around an area on the ridge where a granite outcropping narrowed the current road down to one lane. Marlon had figured he was a cinch for working on at least that part of the project because of his demolition training during the war.

Marlon had other news as well. Niggers, he reported, were getting hired for jobs that ought to go by right to men like him. The other men had already heard the story and, save to interject the occasional sneer, remained silent as Marlon talked. When Marlon finished his account, Pruitt spat into his spit can and said, "Now let me get this straight, they gonna pave this road—our road right out here in the middle of our community—with niggers?"

"What I say," Marlon responded and sucked on his cigarette.

"Nuthin but niggers?" Pruitt said.

"Don't know about that now," Marlon said, pausing to pull a bit of tobacco off his tongue. "Didn't say nuthin but niggers. Don't imagine that's right neither. Even those pinheads down in Baton Rouge wouldn't try to work a job with nuthin but niggers. Boss man I talked to was a white man. Coonass named Lebeau, but I guess that's white."

Pruitt said, "But you saw niggers down there?"

"Naw, now," Marlon said, showing a certain exasperation, "I didn't say that neither. I didn't see any niggers, and I ain't saying I did. They ain't doing any work down there yet. They're just setting up. All the men I saw was white. Counting the coonasses."

"Then how do you know they been hiring niggers?" Pruitt asked.

"Well, dang it, Pruitt," Marlon said, "you got some kind of problem with what I'm telling you here?"

Pruitt spit in his can and wiped the back of his hand across his mouth. "I ain't got a problem," he said mildly, staring at Marlon, who crushed out his cigarette on the porch under his work boot and reached into his shirt pocket for tobacco and papers to roll another one. "Can't imagine what kind of problem I might have. I'm just trying to get the facts about this thing."

"Well, the fact is," Marlon said, "that the highway department is hiring niggers to pave New Peterstown Road."

"Some of our niggers from around here?" Pruitt asked.

"Well how would I know that?" Marlon said, his voice heated.

"What difference does it make?" Ralph said. He was shorter and slighter than Pruitt, but they were unmistakably brothers. "Niggers is niggers, the way I look at it."

"Better not be one of our niggers," Ossie said, his round face florid and glistening. "If I can't get a job, I'd kill the nigger who took it."

"If you didn't see any niggers yourself," Pruitt said to Marlon, "how's it exactly you know that niggers gonna be taking our work?"

"Man I know told me," Marlon said evenly. "Said the highway commissioner is gonna back Earl Long next time for governor and figures Earl's gonna be needing the nigger vote if he wants to beat whoever the New Orleans machine decides to back. Give a nigger a job, he'll vote for you if you're the devil his own self."

"Niggers round here can't vote," Ralph said. He looked around at the other men on the porch. "Can they?"

"Naw, they know better than to try to vote around here," Curley Lewis said.

"One of our niggers tried to vote, he'd shortly be one of our dead niggers," Ossie said.

Marlon said, "Is exactly what I pointed out. But the man says he knows what he knows."

"Just cause the niggers don't vote around here," Pruitt said, "don't mean some niggers don't vote somewhere in this state."

"What the man says," Marlon agreed.

"They even got rich niggers in this state," Pruitt said. "Niggers that got a hell of a lot more than anybody on this here porch."

"Ought to be a law against that," Ossie said. "No white man ought to have less than some nigger."

"Go on into Alexandria some time," Pruitt said. "Drive by the fancy house where their preacher lives. Got a fancy car in the drive. Got a flush commode right inside the house,

I hear. Lawn looks like it's been worked on by a barber."

"Speaking of barbers," Curley said. "I hear they got nigger barbers with nice houses in Alexandria, too. Nicer than mine, for sure."

"Do," Pruitt said. "Nigger barbers and the nigger mortician. They even got a nigger lawyer in Alec now, I hear. And I bet they all vote. That's what happens when you get in the cities and the niggers get some money. Lord knows how many of 'em they let vote in New Orleans."

"But they don't vote around here," Jeff said. Everybody turned and looked at him because he was the first of the children to say anything. He brushed a lock of sandy brown hair out of his eyes. "Y'all just said that none of the niggers around here could vote."

"Your point being?" Marlon said to Jeff.

"Well," Jeff said. "I don't know. I guess."

"Git on inside," Pruitt said, glaring at Jeff. Then he looked at his other sons. "You younguns just go on inside. Or go sit on the back porch if you want to. But we're talking about grown-up stuff, and we don't need any of you butting in. Now git."

"Not me," Wayne said. "I didn't say nuthin."

"You too, buster," Pruitt said. Wayne got up with a scowl on his face; as he passed into the house behind Jeff, he punched his brother as hard as he could in the arm. A short scuffle followed, but neither boy raised a cry to avoid bringing Pruitt in behind them.

"Something I ain't got figured out about this business," Lucian said, wiping his jowly face with a red bandana and breathing shallowly in short gasps. "Niggers with money, the preachers and morticians and such. They ain't gonna want no highway job. So what difference does it make to give some other niggers jobs that white folks round here might want?"

"You just ain't got a hang of politics," Pruitt said. "Rich niggers don't want highway jobs. But they got cousins and nephews who do want highway jobs. Politicians, they understand that. Rich niggers without any family still want other niggers to get work. That's money they'll pay a nigger barber. See what I'm saying?" There was a chorus of grunting assent around the porch.

"So you figure they gonna hire some of the rich niggers' family who live around here?" Lucian said.

"Maybe," Pruitt said. "Maybe not. Maybe they'll set up something like those CCC camps they had a while ago. Only with niggers. Maybe niggers who are from somewhere else."

"Exactly what my friend told me," Marlon said. He looked at Pruitt and nodded.

"What we gonna do about this?" Ossie said. "We can't let our road get paved by no goldanged niggers. Not while I live and breathe."

"What I say," Marlon agreed.

"I say we ought to kill those niggers," Ossie said.

"What if there's too many of 'em for us to kill?" Lucian wondered. "Hanging a nigger for rape is one thing, but—"

"Lucian's right," Pruitt said. "Might be too many of them for us to kill."

"Well, we got to do something," Marlon said.

"Yup," Pruitt said. "We can agree on that. We got to do something."

Sitting in the living room around 10:30 that night, Jeff could hear the sound of Marlon and the other men preparing to depart. They had spoken in lowered voices for some time, but now they became louder. And whereas only one man at a time had spoken before, usually Marlon or Pruitt, now many spoke at once. Jeff could hear the creak of the porch boards as the men stood up and the scrape of hard-soled shoes on wood as they stamped blood back into cramped legs and made their way down the steps into the yard. Presuming that their banishment was over, the three older Caldwell children—Jeff and Wayne and their sister Vivien—went out onto the porch and watched as the men trudged down through the swale and up onto the road, lighting their way with swinging lanterns. Vivien asked what that was all about, but Pruitt told her it was men's business and therefore none of hers. Vivien shrugged and returned inside, followed by Wayne.

As Pruitt was stepping through the screen door, he said to Jeff, "You better get on in here. It's gotten late and the morning comes early."

"I'm coming," Jeff replied, though he made no move to follow. He wrapped an arm around a roof pole and leaned the weight of his upper body against it, oddly savoring the slight bite of the sharp wood into the flesh of his chest. He watched the men depart until the waving light of their lanterns shrank to yellow dots like fireflies blinking in the distance. It was a warm and humid night, the land still giving back the moisture of the flood. When Jeff went to bed, he took off his white T-shirt, rolled it into a tube and laid it across his eyes to block out the light of a full moon that shone like a silver spotlight onto the bed he shared with his two youngest brothers. He slept only in the striped pajama bottoms that had once belonged to Wayne. As the hour crept past midnight, and the evening air finally cooled a bit, Jeff woke briefly and drowsily pulled a sheet up over his chest.

To wake Jeff at 2 A.M., Pruitt tugged on that sheet. He was not a man who routinely concerned himself with the rest of others. But this night, he crept into the boys' bedroom on tiptoes and spoke to Jeff in the faintest whisper as he shook the sheet to rouse him. Jeff came only into the dimmest consciousness. Such a strange sight, he thought, his father leaning over him, gently shaking him. Pruitt's big face, stubbled with gray whiskers, bent down to bring his lips close to Jeff's ear; his breathy words beckoned Jeff to rise and dress. Jeff sat up, casting a shadow in the moonlight over James and Franklin. He rubbed his eyes with the back of loose fists and blinked and yawned and blinked again. "Come on, now," Pruitt whispered.

"Where we going," Jeff whispered. Drowsily he noticed that Wayne was up and pulling on his clothes.

"Just come on," Pruitt insisted. "Get your britches on. And wear a long-sleeve shirt."

Jeff rose, slipped off his pajama bottoms and pulled on a pair of boxer shorts and his dungarees. Still yawning, he got a long-sleeve shirt out of the armoire, which creaked as he opened and closed the door.

"Here are your shoes," Pruitt told Jeff, handing him a pair of canvas tennis shoes. Jeff accepted them sleepily, hugging them against his chest with folded arms. "Now let's go." In the living room Jeff and Wayne sat on the couch to tie the laces of their shoes in the light of the fireplace embers. Pruitt paced back and forth in front of the door to the porch.

Suddenly Jeff's mother Osby called out from the bedroom, "Pruitt? Are you up? You aren't sick, are you?"

"Dadgummit," Pruitt said to his sons who were barely awake. "Now you've gone and waken your mother. Now get your backsides up from there and let's go."

But before they could rise, Osby entered the living room, tying the sash of her robe. "What's going on in here?" Osby said.

"Nothing," Pruitt said. "Go back to bed. This is none of your affair."

"What are you talking about?" Osby said. "You've gotten up in the middle of the night. You've gotten Wayne and Jeff up. And it's none of my affair?" She walked over and stood by the boys. "Last time I looked, these were my sons. When I went to bed, this was my house."

"You better shut your trap, woman."

"What are you up to, Pruitt Caldwell? What are you doing out here in the middle of the night? What are you doing with these boys?"

"We got business to do."

"What kind of business?"

"Business that ain't none of your business."

"If you're taking my sons out somewhere in the middle of the night, it's my business."

Pruitt pointed at his sons and ordered, "You two get your rears up. It's time to go."

"You two sit right where you are," Osby countered, glowering at her husband.

Wayne got up and moved next to Pruitt, but Osby dropped her hand on Jeff's head, and he remained seated, her palm pressing down on him, her fingers gripping into his temples.

"This is about that highway business and the niggers, isn't it?" Osby demanded.

"I said get yourself up from there," Pruitt told Jeff. He took two long strides and grabbed Jeff by the arm. But as he tried to pull Jeff up, Osby began to slap at Pruitt's right shoulder with both hands. Pruitt shifted his grip on Jeff to his left hand and raised his arm to the level of his head, leaving Osby to flail away uselessly against his elbow.

"You stop that, Pruitt Caldwell," she screamed. "You leave this boy alone."

Twirling with cruel grace, Pruitt pulled Jeff to his feet and flung him across the room to the front door, turning so that Osby was now hammering against his back and then the back of his head. Then in a sweeping, continuous movement, Pruitt spun around and smacked Osby in the face with the back of his left hand and knocked her to the floor. She landed on her seat and her head whipped back with a thud against the fireplace.

Pruitt stood towering over her and licked at the back of his hand before running his fingers through his hair. "Now goldang it, woman," he said. "This is on you. I told you, and I told you that this was none of your affair. But you wouldn't let it be, and now I had to bust you. And right here in front of the kids. You know how I hate that. Now I'm going, same as I was before you caused this."

Pruitt turned away from her and said to Wayne and Jeff, "Outside, you two." Then he looked across the room to the doorway where James, Monroe and Franklin stood cowering. "You three better be back in bed before I reach the front door. If you ain't, I'm gonna keep right on coming in your direction and you'll goldarn sure wish you hadn't provoked me." The three youngest Caldwell boys disappeared from view immediately, closing the door soundlessly behind them.

Jeff and Wayne waited for their father by the front steps. When Pruitt came out, they followed him down to New Peterstown Road, where the three of them waited silently for a few minutes before Marlon Davis came along in his truck, followed by two other pickups. Ralph Caldwell slid to the middle of the cab to make room for Pruitt, who indicated with his thumb for the two boys to climb into the back. In a convoy, they drove south.

The spring night sky was high and bright; the moon and stars bathed the woods along the road in a luminescent silver. The temperature was mild, but the air was damp, and Jeff felt chilled as the wind whipped around the cab and buffeted him in the back of the truck.

After several miles, Marlon slowed the lead vehicle and shut off his lights; the trucks behind him followed suit. Marlon eased the pickup off the road, through the rain gully and up into the brush on the roadside.

Pruitt popped out of the truck and came back to speak to his sons in a whisper. "Come on down out of there and follow along with us and keep quiet. We tell you to do something, do it. Don't ask any questions. We don't need either one of you for this work, but I figured I ought to give you the chance to be men, so that's what I done. Now let's go. Try not to kick up any gravel while you're walking or otherwise make any kind of racket."

As Jeff and Wayne walked toward the front of the truck, their uncle Ralph handed their father a shotgun. The boys fell in behind their father and the other men, seven in all; all the adults were carrying shotguns or deer rifles.

When the men and boys had walked fifteen minutes down New Peterstown Road and had come near the junction of state Highway 1, Marlon Davis stopped and turned to the others, who gathered around him in a formation like a football huddle. They made a circle and all bent forward from the waist to bring their heads together, balancing themselves against the barrels of their firearms, which were anchored butt down against the road; those who weren't also carrying kerosene lanterns threw their free arms around each other's shoulders.

"Way I figure it," Marlon said, speaking in a voice little above a whisper, "is that they got the dynamite in the truck with its canvas top padlocked down to its sides and tailgate. So first we check that out. Then we go from there. Might be in the bossman's trailer, but I doubt it, not with him a pipe smoker."

"And you sure they ain't got no night watchman?" Lucian said.

"I ain't sure of nuthin," Marlon said, irritably. "I ain't been down here in the night time, now have I. That's why I said we go in quiet and watch ourselves."

"Ain't likely they'd post a night watchman clear out here," Pruitt said. "Probably got whatever crew ain't from around here lodged at that tourist court on 1 just out of Alec. Still, we do what we agreed. Ossie sets up in front of the trailer. If they got a night watchman, that's where he'd be. The rest of us check out the canvas top. Anybody comes out of the trailer, Ossie takes care of him."

"You gonna shoot him?" Jeff asked.

"I told you to keep your trap shut," Pruitt told his son.

"If it's a nigger night watchman, I'm gonna shoot him," Ossie said to Jeff.

"You could go to jail for murder, even if he's a nigger," Jeff said, and his father grabbed the flesh on the back of his upper arm in a withering pinch that Jeff endured with a grimace of pain but without uttering a sound.

"You done now?" Pruitt asked Jeff who was twisted in agony with his chin down on his chest and one leg off the ground.

"Yes, sir," Jeff said through gritted teeth.

"Good." He let the boy go, and Jeff backed off a step rubbing his arm. Pruitt turned to the others. "Ain't gonna need to be no shooting," Pruitt said. "Now let's quit the jawing and go get done what we come for before the sun comes up."

"I sure hope there ain't gonna be no shooting," Lucian said. "I ain't planning to get into any of that."

"Enough," Marlon said. "Now let's go. It's just around this next bend."

Marlon led off again and everybody followed, taking care to move as soundlessly as possible. As they came around a thick stand of pine trees, the roadside opened up to reveal what was now the headquarters for the New Peterstown Road paving project. Marlon stopped them and signaled with his hands that they were to approach through the woods.

The first thing the project officers had done was clear a space of trees and scrub in a circular shape, the road itself cutting off the bottom quarter of the circle. Then they had spread gravel over the whole area to facilitate the storage of vehicles and other equipment. The trailer where Marlon had sought employment sat at the top of the circle. A clear space in front of it led all the way to the road. To the right were parked two earthmovers, two rollers, four dump trucks, one long-bed lumber truck and the canvas top. Save for two crew trucks, the space to the left was empty, presumably to provide for daytime parking. The moon had fallen low enough in the sky now to cast long shadows of the pines that ringed the cleared area. But the sky was cloudless and full of stars, and the clearing was lit as if by silver neon.

The seven New Peterstown men and two teenagers circled right through the woods, keeping the road-building equipment and a line of trees between themselves and the trailer until they reached its rear. There Marlon stopped them again and signaled for the men to take up their positions. Two men moved to the right of the trailer, two to the left. Then Ossie wordlessly handed Wayne his deer rifle, pointed into the clearing and used his hands and arms to feign taking aim toward the trailer, pulling the trigger and having the rifle recoil straight up. Finishing this charade, he grinned broadly and curled his thumb and forefinger into the okay sign. He punched Wayne on the shoulder and for good measure punched Jeff, too. Marlon jerked his thumb toward New Peterstown Road, and Ossie gave him the okay sign as well. Then Ossie reached underneath his shirt, pulled a pistol out of his belt and strode off to the front of the trailer. Pruitt signaled that his sons were to retreat more deeply into the woods.

Ossie walked up to the door of the trailer, his pistol dangling behind his back in his right hand. With his left hand balled into a fist, he hammered on the door, shaking the whole structure as he did so. "Anybody in there?" Ossie bellowed, his sudden outburst echoing into the night and causing Jeff to jump. "Anybody in there might be of some assistance?" There was no answer, but after a second, Ossie continued. "I'm broke down back a ways up New Peterstown Road," he called out. "Ain't got a tool in my trunk. Not a wrench. Not even a screwdriver." He hammered on the trailer door again. "Anybody in there?" Ossie looked at his comrades stationed at the trailer's sides. They had crept forward now so as to be able to see the trailer door. Ossie shrugged at them. They heard no sound from inside the trailer. No light came on. "Anybody in there been giving out our jobs to any niggers?" Ossie called out and then laughed at his own question.

The men to the sides of the trailer lowered their firearms, and Ossie tucked his pistol back inside his pants. Marlon and Pruitt came rushing around from the back, Wayne trailing a step behind.

"All right," Marlon said, "Come on over to the canvas top. We got business to attend to." At the canvas top, Wayne tried to hand the deer rifle back to Ossie. But Ossie waved him off. "You can carry it if you want. I got my Colt."

Grumbling under his breath, Marlon used a knife to saw a hole down the side of the canvas. Lacking leverage, Marlon cursed the tough work as he shifted his knife from hand to hand. Finally, he got a hole big enough to crawl through and hoisted himself in, first kicking his legs against the truck sides and then slithering in like a worm being sucked down by a bass.

When Marlon had handed out everything he needed, he climbed back to the ground and directed the others to bundle the dynamite sticks and place them on each piece of equipment. He fixed each bundle with blasting caps and ran long lines of fuse back to the detonator. Neither Wayne nor Jeff was allowed to handle the explosives, so they did little other than try to stay out of the way. The work took the men more than an hour. Marlon supervised and inspected every detail, constantly reminding everybody of his knowledge and warning all the men of the danger involved. The only thing in the clearing they didn't prepare to blow up was the trailer. Pruitt argued and the other men concurred that the state might just abandon the trailer and they could come back later and haul it off.

When all the charges were set, Marlon wound a spool of fuse two hundred yards north into the woods parallel to New Peterstown Road. Underneath the sagging branches of a water oak, he fastened the connections onto the detonation box and looked around at his collaborators. "Who wants to do the honors?" he asked.

"Let Jeffy do it," Ossie said and punched Jeff in the arm once more. "Let Jeff do the honors and blow this road project to smithereens."

"Yeah, let the kid do it," Curley said. "Give him something to remember for a long time."

Jeff hesitated outside the ring of men. "Go on," Pruitt ordered. "Marlon'll show you what to do. Ain't nothing to it."

Still Jeff hesitated. Pruitt stepped over to Jeff and bent low to whisper in his ear. "Now don't you embarrass me, you little squirt. You been a mama's boy all your life. We're giving you a chance to be a man."

Without a word, Jeff stepped into the center of the ring, and Marlon instructed him that all he had to do was push in the plunger and look up in time to see all hell break loose. Jeff balanced himself over the detonation box, and the men peeled back behind him, squinting in the direction of the clearing. When Marlon signaled to him with a clenched fist, Jeff leaned forward, his arms stiff, letting the weight of his upper body force the plunger down. Instantly Jeff heard a crash of sound that left his ears ringing, and the world lit up in the New Peterstown night. A ball of flame jumped fifty feet into the air. For a long second afterwards, the men behind him were silent, and then, as if on cue, they all began to whoop. They screamed into the night like cowboys starting a cattle drive. Then the secondary explosions began as the equipment gas tanks ignited, and the men fell back, frightened by the fury they had let loose. They quieted and stared into one another's faces and saw the orange flame reflected in one another's eyes. Then they whooped some more, like fans celebrating victory in a long-awaited and hard-fought athletic contest.

Ossie was the first one to clap Jeff on the back, and all the men quickly followed suit, even Pruitt. Pruitt clapped Jeff on the back as the others had done, and then kneaded with thumb and fingers the thin strand of muscle that stretched away from Jeff's neck across the top of his shoulders. Finally, Pruitt relaxed his hand and stood for a moment with his arm around his son. For a second Jeff felt just as he did in school when he knew the right answer and was the only one who raised his hand.

Then Wayne fired Ossie's rifle into the air. Following his example the men began to fire their guns into the air. Pruitt fired two blasts of his shotgun into the woods in the direction of the flames in the clearing. Afterward he cracked the barrel open, let the spent shells slip to the mat of oak leaves and pine needles on the ground, slipped in two more rounds and handed it to Jeff, saying to him, "You done good, buddy. Go on now. Shoot off a couple. You earned it." Jeff's two shots clipped branches and brought down a rain of pine needles and two cones like a censure from above.

"Let's go check over what we done," Marlon directed. He led the men out of the woods onto the road and down to the clearing where everything was still aflame, the fire spitting into the night air and licking at the branches of surrounding pine trees. Needles glowed like sparklers against the black woods or rode the flame-stoked gusts away from the inferno and fell toward earth like tiny arrows of fire. Later that night Jeff discovered that one had fallen against his shirt and burned a small round hole in the fabric.

All the trucks and earthmovers were ruined. Even the trailer, which had not been dynamited, was severely damaged. All its windows were broken. The white paint on the front had been seared down to bare metal from the heat of the other explosions, and the whole structure seemed to curve from the sides inward to the door.

Sixty paces to the west of the trailer, in a clearing in the woods, a black man lay choking to death on his own blood. The night watchman had gone into the woods to relieve himself only moments before Marlon and his squad of raiders arrived at the trailer. He was armed with a pistol but elected to remain in hiding rather than confront so many men with rifles. His refuge of scrub bush and pine, however, proved scant protection when a piece of shrapnel torn from the fender of a truck hurtled through his neck like a spoon through warm pudding.

The state judged its losses as total and walked away from the whole project immediately and without looking back. The clearing where all the road-building equipment had been parked looked like a battleground and became for a brief time a shabby monument to New Peterstown's resistance to the most distant rudiments of racial equality. State policeman showed up to make inquiries with reference to the man who had died, but their investigation was undertaken with little fervor, their concern for the life of a Negro little greater than those who took it.

The raiders themselves never talked about what happened that night, not even to each other. They knew without pledging so that silence ensured their security. The police detectives were hardly surprised when they developed no leads in the case and soon directed their energies elsewhere. But the town buzzed, of course. For a time, people would pass the clearing with its jumble of twisted metal and point it out to each other. Without ever claiming so directly, some who were not there that night let on that they had been and accepted the approving nods and nudges of admiration they had not earned.

But this fascination with the event passed quickly, and within a year the people of New Peterstown passed the clearing without commenting on it at all. With astonishing speed, the whole area returned to the woods from which it had briefly emerged. The trailer and trucks and other pieces of equipment were overgrown with vines, and speculation about the identity of the heroes ceased to be the community's central topic of conversation.

Eventually, what was done there and why was recalled only vaguely. As the civil-rights movement began to dominate the news in the 1950s, the few from New Peterstown who any longer knew even the rumor of that night treated it as the fable of another generation determined to have its own war story, a tale of victory in America's hundred years war over civil rights. Meanwhile, the decades passed, and the New Peterstown Road remained a pot-holed, gully-washed, mud-and-gravel track until the administration of Governor Edwin Edwards finally paved it in 1974 with a road crew that was more than forty percent black.

For the rest of his life, Jeff Caldwell wore that night like a hair shirt. He would not confess his role in the sabotage and the murder until he lay on his own deathbed. But he would strive to make amends. He would risk his life in the company of brave black brethren on the Freedom Rides, and he would stand at their shoulder to face fire hoses and snapping dogs. He would enter the ministry, and he would become a soldier in the civil-rights movement because only in so doing, he believed, might he stand the chance to save his soul.

chapter eight

THE MORNING AFTER Ben Watson shot George Washington Brown and Jeff Caldwell, Tommy Caldwell was awakened after less than five hours sleep by a phone call at 7 A.M. from Hodding Morris, the movement's lead attorney. Hodding wanted Tommy to meet him at central lockup in order to accompany him to a meeting with Robert Brown. Tommy agreed, but he told Hodding he couldn't come until he'd gone to Charity to check on his father.

Tommy woke Glenda, and they threw on their jeans, T-shirts and tennis shoes and stumbled out to their black Volkswagen Beetle. During the night, Louisiana's governor had declared a state of emergency and had mobilized the National Guard. Aside from those providing essential public services, workplaces were ordered to shut down, and people were asked to remain in their homes except in cases of emergency. The drive down St. Charles Avenue was like a journey through a dreamscape. The world was eerily empty and perniciously changed. New Orleans looked like a central European city in the last days of World War II.

The air of the city choked with the thick smell of recent fire. Local television reported that all the blazes from the night before had been brought under control, but from the clearing at the corner of St. Charles and Napoleon, Tommy and Glenda could see puffs of thick black smoke rising into the summer sky from three different locations. St. Charles and Napoleon Avenues seemed cavernous with so little traffic, and Tommy thought of newsreels showing the huge Moscow squares where gigantic armaments looked like miniatures. It was as though something from the pen of George Orwell had sprung into existence. The grassy esplanades of the city endured, but a population had disappeared.

The day before had been so full of determination and hopes for changing the world. Tommy and Glenda had seen tragedy often enough that they should have known better than dare the dreams they did. Now, just like the bustle of people and the cars, their dreams had vanished in an eye blink.

Jeff was still in intensive care, and the doctors said his condition remained critical. He did not stir during their visit, and they did not try to wake him. On either side of him, Glenda and Tommy held his hands and stared into his ashen face. Tommy's concern was heightened by Jeff's wan and unkempt, stubble-bearded appearance. Jeff was always so fastidious; not even on weekends or during vacations could Tommy remember seeing him unshaven.

When the ten-minute visiting period was over, Tommy left Glenda at Charity and went to the city jail on the corner of Tulane and Broad to meet Hodding Morris. Tommy arrived first and took a seat in a hard-backed, straight wooden chair in a grungy waiting area. The stand-up ashtray next to him overflowed with reeking cigarette butts, and the floor under his feet was worn through to bare wood shredding in thin white strips like pulled pieces of string cheese. Tommy sat for fifteen depressing minutes until Hodding finally huffed through the doors, lugging his briefcase. Out of breath from hurrying up the building's exterior steps, Hodding ran a finger inside the collar of his white shirt and adjusted the jacket of his rumpled gray suit. He looked exhausted.

Like Jeff Caldwell and Everett Essex, Hodding Morris had been with Dr. Brown from the beginning. He was in his middle forties now, graying and starting to show a paunch. In the early days, Dr. Brown and Jeff and the others had been arrested repeatedly. Hodding had always been the man to negotiate their release and cajole the local law-enforcement officials into guaranteeing their safety.

As the movement broadened, gained strength and eventually drew the attention of the nation, Hodding had stayed on with ever more to do and no pause to reevaluate and perhaps move off in another direction. He was a normal man with normal appetites and ambitions. At first he thought he was just delaying his own dreams of one day becoming a rich man. He seldom thought of such things any more; he seldom had the time. He moved constantly from one crisis to the next. This was his life now, and the success of the movement meant as much to him as to anybody. He was surely as devastated by Dr. Brown's death as anybody on the staff, and yet here he was, attending to business, doing his job, trying to get another of his people released from jail.

"Christ," Hodding said to Tommy now, "it never ends, does it?" He shook his head and his brown plastic glasses slid down to the end of his nose; he shoved them back against his face.

"You get any sleep?" Tommy asked.

Hodding responded with a sharp breath of laugh, all in his mouth, no sign of ironic mirth brightening the fatigue in his eyes. "You wait here," he instructed, ignoring Tommy's question. He spoke quietly to the attending officer; the policeman slid some papers through the slot in the wire which Hodding signed. He turned, waved Tommy over and showed Tommy where to sign as well.

"You know the routine," the policeman said when he had the form back in his possession. Hodding put his hands on Tommy's shoulders and directed him inside a gate where Hodding surrendered his briefcase, which was opened and searched. Both he and Tommy were patted down.

Finally, they were shown into a small room where attorneys were allowed to meet with their clients. One wall was half-glass, lightly reinforced with mesh, as was the pane in the top half of the door. The side walls were plaster, marked with graffiti and smudged with grimy fingerprints. Two windows overlooked a gray-walled interior air space that dropped to a slab of concrete at ground level. Each window was padlocked shut with a rusted wire gate. The reinforced casement windows were cranked open half-way, but whatever fresh air came in didn't mask the smell of the place: a potent stench of stale cigarette smoke, human body odor and ammonia. The room was hot, and the air stirring in from the outside made it worse, not better. The air-conditioning was poor throughout the building, and someone using the room earlier in the day had no doubt opened the windows in hope of improving things.

"I'm going to need your help," Hodding said as they entered the room.

"Sure," Tommy agreed. "Anything you need."

They sat at the scarred brown wooden table that filled the center of the room. Hodding took some papers out of his briefcase and lay a fat, black, gold-trimmed fountain pen on top of them.

"It's sweltering in here," Tommy said. "Aren't you hot?"

Hodding shrugged.

"I'm gonna close the windows and give this shitty AC a chance," Tommy said.

"Whatever you like," Hodding replied, as Tommy got up to crank the windows closed. "Look, Tommy," he went on. "You gotta lend me a hand here. Robert's out of control."

"Still?" Tommy said, cranking the second of the four panels.

Hodding snorted in reply. "He doesn't know what he's doing, and he isn't listening to me. I need you here to calm him down. Whatever I tell him he needs to do, you back me up. Can I count on you for that?"

"Sure," Tommy said, his back still to the table. "I'm sure Robert's just completely—"

"Here he is now," Hodding said, scraping his chair legs on the dirty wooden floor as he stood up. A guard let Robert into the room, then released him from his handcuffs. Tommy closed the last window and turned to greet his friend of so many years. Robert looked like hell. Dark circles under his lusterless eyes contrasted with his cafe-au-lait complexion. His bushy Afro, usually picked to a shiny black nimbus, was dull and matted almost flat on the right side. His usual hip dashiki had been replaced by the bright-orange jumpsuit that was the official Orleans Parish Prison uniform.

The guard unshackled Robert and left. Tommy reached his hand out to Robert, and they shook hands in the counter-cultural style of the day, their thumbs intertwined and their fingers curling around the back of their hands at the wrist.

"Brother Brown," Tommy said softly, and they joined all four of their hands together.

"Brother Caldwell," Robert said after a moment, his words barely audible.

And then Tommy embraced him, his arms circling across his shoulder blades, pulling their chests together. "Good Brother Brown," Tommy said as he patted Robert on the back. Gradually Robert's arms came up from his sides and clapped Tommy on the back in return. Desperately wanting to say something that would lance the boil of depression they all felt, Tommy said, invoking Emerson, "So Robert, what are you doing in here?" The reference was inappropriate, of course, since Robert was in jail, not like Thoreau for civil disobedience, but for inciting to riot. Still, Tommy expected him to respond, "The question is, Thomas, what are you doing out there." Instead his eyes blazed up as if Tommy had issued him a challenge. But Robert said nothing, and Tommy's attempt at levity hung in the air like a foul odor.

Behind them, Hodding announced, "Fellas, we need to get to work. Y'all come sit down."

Hodding scooted a black plastic ashtray toward himself and lit a white-filtered cigarette with a silver Zippo. Exhaling, he placed the pack on the table and nestled the lighter on top. Tommy sat next to Hodding and Robert sat across from them. As Hodding stirred through his papers, Robert rubbed his eyes. Then, without asking, he picked up the pack of Kents and lit one. Tommy had seen Robert smoke tobacco before, but never when they weren't partying. Hodding pushed the ashtray to a position between them.

"As we talked about last night," Hodding said to Robert, "I would like to pursue a defense of diminished capacity. Given who you are and the circumstances of last night, I think we can get bail, and I think we can get the judge to accept our plea and grant a suspended sentence. You'll have to do some kind of community service, but that's what you do anyway."

"Fuck that," Robert said. He spoke softly, but his voice was full of rancor. "I told you last night, fuck that. What don't you understand about the words fuck that?"

Hodding licked his lips and darted a glance at Tommy as he tugged at his right earlobe. He reached to the ashtray for his cigarette and took a drag. "Robert," Hodding said carefully. "I'm not getting through to you. This town is still smoldering from—"

"If it's only smoldering," Robert interrupted, "then I didn't do my job well enough. It should still be in flames."

Hodding waited him out. "This town is still smoldering," Hodding said, "from fires you incited last night. What you did is exceedingly serious—"

"Right on," Robert said.

"It is exceedingly serious, and it can send you to jail for a very long time. Fifteen years." Hodding paused, presumably to let this sobering fact sink in.

"Shee-it," Robert snorted. He leaned back in his chair and took a deep drag off his cigarette. He held his right wrist in his left hand almost as if he were still cuffed.

"I don't want to mislead you in the slightest way," Hodding said. "Given what happened, I don't think there's any way you would do that much time. But you have got to understand this: the people of this city are plenty pissed off. An awful lot of property went up in smoke last night."

"Fuck their property," Robert said, leaning forward and tapping ash off his cigarette.

"Robert," Hodding said, "the prosecution will show film of you telling ten thousand people in front of the hospital and two hundred thousand watching on TV to burn the city down."

"Damn straight," Robert said.

"No, Robert," Hodding responded, "not damn straight. Not damn straight at all. What in the hell has gotten into you?"

Robert took another drag on his cigarette and blew two plumes of smoke out his flared nostrils. "What in the hell has gotten into *me*? What in the hell has gotten into the whole fucking country, man? My father spent his whole life preaching nothing but peace and brotherhood, and some Bible-spouting cracker put a bullet in his brain. And you ask what in the hell has gotten into *me*?"

"Hodding is just trying to get you out of jail, Robert," Tommy said.

Robert looked at Tommy, his eyes squinting in contempt. "Shut up, Tommy."

"What?" Tommy said, stunned.

"What in the fuck are you doing here anyway?" Robert said to Tommy. "You fill out some matchbook cover and get a law degree last week you failed to mention?"

"What's the matter with you, man?" Tommy said. "You're in some deep shit here, and Hodding is trying to get you out. So why don't you drop the attitude and start trying to help yourself."

"Shee-it," Robert said with a burst of breath. He shook his head and sucked air through his front teeth, then took another drag off his cigarette.

"Robert," Hodding said, "a plea of diminished capacity will allow—"

Robert slammed his open palm down on the table with a bang that echoed through the room like a gunshot and made the plastic ashtray dance over on its side.

Instantly, the guard came into the room.

"Please excuse us, officer, but there isn't any reason for you to be concerned," Hodding said.

"Better not be," the guard said. He hitched up his pants and stared at each man in turn.

"Thank you," Hodding said.

The guard closed the door and returned to his station in the hall. Hodding lit another cigarette and toyed with the pack a second before setting it and the lighter back on the table. He stood up and pushed his chair under the table. "Look," he said, "I need to go to the john. You two talk about whatever for a minute. I'll be back." Before leaving the room he took another cigarette out of his pack and slipped it into his shirt pocket.

Robert crushed out his first cigarette and lit another. "Well, well," he said. "You supposed to soften me up so that Mr. Hod-Ding Morris can take me out when he gets back from his alleged trip to the can?"

"I don't know what you're talking about," Tommy replied.

"Yeah, and Jackie Robinson was a white man."

"What's that supposed to mean?"

"What are you doing here, man?"

"I'm here because I'm your friend."

"Yeah, right."

"Why else would I be here, Robert? My father is in intensive care. I left him to come see you, to do whatever I can to help get you out of here."

"Your father is in intensive care. Mine's in the morgue." Robert stared up at the ceiling and took a drag on his cigarette. He snorted as he exhaled. "The white man always gets the better of it, doesn't he? Even when shots ring out, it's the black man who dies and the white man who ends up in intensive care. That way in Nam; that way in Crackerland, USA."

Tommy reached over to Hodding's pack of Kents and pulled out a cigarette. He placed it in his mouth and rolled it around between his lips before finally lighting it.

"What you doing there, brother?" Robert said, laughing. "I got you so uptight you gonna break your tobacco cherry?"

"I've smoked before," Tommy said, puffing out a thick cloud of gray smoke.

"Shee-it," Robert said, chortling way down in his throat. "What? You smoked when you were ten out behind my daddy's church in Baton Rouge?"

"Since then sometimes, too." Tommy smiled. "Once or twice. After a half-dozen or so too many beers. You were probably there those times, too. Only maybe there wasn't so much of you left behind your eyes on those occasions."

"My ass. You're the most health-conscious, body-as-temple guy I know. I've never seen you with a butt. I had to teach you how to inhale a joint."

"Let Hodding get you out of here, Robert. Please."

The mirth in Robert's face collapsed into a scowl. "Don't start up again," he said.

Tommy took another puff on his cigarette. "What's going on here? You can't possibly want to stay in jail."

"Of course, I don't want to stay in jail. But I'm not letting Hodding plead me out on any 'diminished capacity' shit. I'm not letting the press have it that I'm just another wild-ass nigger, ripping out his hair and keening about, screaming the first thing that comes into his head. I told 'em to burn the motherfucking place down, and what I meant was burn the motherfucking place down. White man don't want to give us a piece of the pie, piss on the whole pie. I knew exactly what I was saying, and I meant every word of it."

"You couldn't have meant it. Our fathers have spent their whole lives—"

"My father's whole life is over. Don't you get it? He's gone, and with him gone, his rules are gone, too."

"But his legacy—"

"Fuck his legacy. I'm his legacy. And I'm sick to death of white people killing every black man who sticks his head up out of the cotton patch and dares to point to his chest and say out loud for everybody to hear, 'I am a man, so treat me like a man.' White people can't bear for a black man to stand up. Medgar does it. Medgar is dead. Martin does it. Martin is dead. Malcolm does it. Malcolm is dead."

"Malcolm was killed by black people," Tommy said.

Robert's eyes widened until they showed white all around the brown iris. "Fuck you, Tommy."

"What'd I say? You're blaming white people for killing black leaders. Fine. But the gunmen who killed Malcolm were black. You know that as well as I do."

"Fuck you."

"Okay, fuck me. And fuck you, too." Tommy looked at the smoldering cigarette in his hand and crushed it out in the ashtray without taking another drag.

"You think white people weren't behind killing Malcolm, white people didn't want to shut him up?"

"What's this about? Of course, there were white people who wanted to shut Malcolm up. And there were plenty who probably would have killed him if they could. But no, I don't think white people were behind the men who actually shot him."

"Then you're just another duped little white boy. White people were the ones who benefited by Malcolm's being silenced. Obviously, white people had him killed."

"That's crazy conspiratorial bullshit, Robert. Your daddy didn't believe anything like that."

"Well, obviously he should have."

"Why?"

"Because he's dead. Shot dead by a white man," Robert said. Tommy put his head in his hands. "Shot dead by another motherfucking racist white son-of-a-bitch."

Tommy looked up at Robert. "I don't even think that's true," Tommy said. "And I don't believe you do either. Something is really fucked here. I don't know what the hell happened. Some kind of madness. But Ben Watson wasn't a racist. I knew him. You knew him."

Robert was on his feet. "Get the fuck out of here," he screamed.

"What?" Tommy asked, shocked by his reaction.

"You come in here, tell me you're my friend and then defend the man who killed my father."

"Sit down, Robert," Tommy said. "What's the matter with you? I'm not defending the man who killed your father. Are you crazy?"

"That's it," Robert said. "I'm out of here." He walked to the door and hammered on it three times in rapid succession before the guard came in, followed immediately by Hodding.

"What's going on?" the guard and Hodding said almost in unison, the guard looking at Robert and Hodding at Tommy.

"I'm tired of talking to these two white fucks," Robert said to the guard.

"I don't know," Tommy said to Hodding. "We were talking and then we were yelling at each other."

"This man is your attorney," the guard said to Robert. "You have the right to confer with him. If you are done conferring, I can return you to your cell."

"Robert, please calm down," Hodding said. "Please let's go sit back at the table and talk about your case."

"Fuck you," Robert said to Hodding.

"Stop this, Robert," Tommy said. "This isn't even you."

"I'm finished here," Robert said to the guard. "Take me back to my cell. And the next time you bring me in here to confer with a lawyer, make sure that lawyer has black skin."

Later that week, represented by a black attorney from Chicago who had long handled cases for the Nation of Islam, Robert Brown pleaded diminished capacity to the crime of inciting to riot. His sentence of three years at Angola was suspended, and he was ordered to do one thousand hours of community service. A year later Robert was among the leaders of the radical Weather Underground who staged the infamous Days of Rage. A warrant was issued for his arrest. After that, Robert disappeared.

Tommy would occasionally read in the press accounts of Robert's pursuit. One long piece in a publication called *Changing Times* speculated that Robert and several other radicals of the era had been identified and assassinated by a special hit squad of the FBI. In addition, *Changing Times* claimed that the FBI had brainwashed Ben Watson into assassinating Dr. Brown by convincing Ben that Dr. Brown was an establishment collaborator and an enemy of true racial equality. Meanwhile, a right-wing publication in Maine called *Sentry* magazine spun that claim in a different way. *Sentry* maintained that Robert Brown and Ben Watson were part of a radical group that had grown frustrated with the slowed pace of civil rights, had become enamored of figures like Huey Newton and had conspired to murder Dr. Brown to "hasten the revolution."

chapter nine

WHEN TOMMY CALDWELL WAS GROWING UP, he didn't realize what an important man his father was. Jeff Caldwell finished his doctor of theology degree in 1954 and immediately accepted a position as pastor of the Gentilly Boulevard Baptist Church, the city's third largest and most progressive. Located in a section of the city that had just started to develop before World War II and was home to many of the area's young professionals, Gentilly Boulevard was the perfect match for Jeff's professional and social ambitions. The church membership was educated and relatively open to the verities of a changing world. It was also large enough to afford an associate pastor.

During Jeff's tenure Gentilly Boulevard went through several associate pastors, most of them seminary graduate students working for their doctorates. The associate pastor conducted Wednesday-night prayer meeting and visited the congregation's ill and troubled. Jeff preached on Sunday mornings and Sunday nights, but his associate handled church business during the week, freeing Jeff to work with George Washington Brown and the Christian Social Conscience League.

Jeff and Dr. Brown were critically involved in a series of landmark civil-rights events. They were key consultants to Martin Luther King during the year-long Montgomery bus boycott in 1955 and 1956. And they were in Little Rock when Central High School was desegregated in 1957. During that violent time, Jeff and Preacher Martin were among the white ministers who held the hands of the Negro students and walked with them through the howling mobs that hurled invective and spit at them with every step. In the years leading up to the 1960 presidential election, Dr. Brown and Jeff kept up a hectic schedule of speaking engagements, mostly on college campuses and to political groups lobbying for the civil-rights vote, often to labor union gatherings and civic groups outside the South.

As a boy, Tommy was well aware of his father as pastor; he never missed a Sunday service. But he did not grasp the immense principle for which his father stood. Jeff was gone a lot of the time, and most of the children's rearing fell to Billye. It was she who read to them, took them to the park, prepared their meals and helped them with their homework. Far too busy for these domestic duties, Jeff was a remote figure to his son. He was someone to be admired but not known. As Tommy grew, it was Billye who went to his youth league baseball games and bragged to Jeff about what a good batter Tommy was. It was Billye who took her ten-year-old son to the school playground and taught him to shoot baskets.

During this time of dawning consciousness, Tommy saw his father as the taskmaster and the disciplinarian. The summer Tommy was eight, his father assigned him responsibility for mowing and trimming the lawn of the family's new house on St. Roch Avenue. Tommy didn't mind this duty, and he very much liked the twenty-five cents his father paid. What Tommy didn't like was what Jeff referred to as "inspection." After Tommy finished his lawn work, he was expected in Jeff's military phrase to "report in." Jeff seldom found much amiss, but on no occasion did he pronounce Tommy's work altogether satisfactory. There was always a place cut carelessly low over an outcropping of tree root, or a section along the flower bed that needed closer attention with the grass shears, or a stretch of sidewalk that needed another pass of the yard broom. Tommy resented these corrections, but he knew better than to protest. The one time he attempted to resist his father's complaints was the second Saturday of his lawn assignment. He "reported in" as "ordered," and he and Jeff walked the yard together, Jeff noting a short series of Tommy's failings as an eight-year-old gardener.

When they had toured the whole yard, front and back, Jeff said, "All right, here's the mop-up detail. You need to trim more closely around the oak tree in the back yard and the mimosa in the front. And don't pull the grass out with your hands. It's faster, but it doesn't look as good. You have shears, and I expect you to use them. Next week I want you to do a better job sweeping the driveway, but I'm going to let it go for now."

Tommy hung his head in exasperation. He had worked on the lawn for an hour and a half, and he was tired of it. There was a baseball game going on in the empty lot at St. Roch and Spain, and he was already late. Afterwards, he wanted to stop by McGregor's Drugstore for a nickel pack of baseball cards and a nectar soda. He wanted his father to give him his quarter and leave him alone.

"We clear on the mop-up?" Jeff asked.

"I'm late for baseball," Tommy said. "I'll do that trimming tomorrow."

"On a Sunday?" Jeff said.

"All right," Tommy said. "On Monday then."

"No indeed," Jeff said. "Work is meant to be finished, not postponed. I'll not have a procrastinator for a son. You understand me?"

"Yeah," Tommy said, his eyes downcast, his voice sullen.

"What did you say to me, young man?"

"Yes sir," Tommy said, looking away toward the front of the house.

"And look at me when you speak to me. I'm your father, and you will look at me when you address me."

Tommy stared his father hard in the eyes and repeated in a clipped tone, "Yes sir."

"That's not any impertinence I'm hearing, is it?"

"No sir," Tommy said, trying to inflect his voice with only as much insolence as he could fully deny.

"There better not be, son. I want this done right, and I want it done now." Tommy turned toward the back yard, his shoulders slumped. Under his breath he muttered, "Who but you would ever notice?"

"What did you say to me, young man?" Jeff demanded.

"Nothing," Tommy said and kept on walking away.

"Stop right there, buster." Tommy stopped but kept his back to his father. "Turn around and march yourself right back here," Jeff ordered. Tommy did as he was told, but he refused to look at his father. "Now repeat what you said to me," Jeff demanded.

Tommy looked up at Jeff, his eyes suddenly ablaze with defiance. "I said who but you would ever notice."

Instantly, Jeff slapped Tommy's face. Afterwards, Jeff told himself that the action had been so spontaneous it was like a hiccup. He consoled himself that he'd popped his hand away as soon as palm touched cheek.

Tommy's eyes watered when his father struck him. And his lip began to tremble. But strangely enough, he felt almost no pain, just shock and anger. He bit down on his lips trying to keep his teeth from chattering, and he blinked, trying to hold back tears. But when one rolled down his offended left cheek, he chose not to brush it away rather than raise a hand to acknowledge it.

"Now see what you've made me do?" Jeff said, his own lips trembling. "Now you see? I'll not tolerate this kind of disrespect, not in my own house, not on my own property, not by my own son. Now you see what you've done?"

Tommy didn't say anything, and Jeff didn't know what more to do. Tommy's cheek was red, though maybe that was from being out in the sun. Jeff prayed that the slap wouldn't leave fingerprints on his son's face and thanked God that it was summertime and that the boy wasn't in school. Jeff took a deep breath and mopped his forehead with the back of his wrist. "It's hot out here," he said, "and I don't want to argue with you about this anymore. Now you go on and do what I told you."

Though the "inspections" continued every time Tommy finished cutting the grass, they never again resulted in his being slapped. Father and son did, however, have another important confrontation over Tommy's lawn-care responsibilities. When Tommy was in the fourth grade, his teacher did a social-studies unit on the American Civil War and asked her students to memorize the names of various battles and the generals who were in command for either side. The class learned about the beginning of trench warfare and the valor of Robert E. Lee. Slavery as a cause of the war was not covered. Like most boys his age, Tommy thrilled to the stories of the cavalry charges and the brave men who gave their lives for their cause. And that's how he came to be rumbling his throat, "eh, eh, eh, eh, eh," in imitation of a Gatling gun as he mowed the front-yard grass one Saturday afternoon.

"What are you doing?" Jeff asked his son when he came out of the house.

"Playing," Tommy said, continuing to push the mower back and forth between the brick-bordered flower bed and the knobby hackberry tree.

"Playing what?" Jeff said. "You're supposed to be working."

"I *am* working," Tommy said, stopping now and looking at his father. "I make up games when I'm working. Mostly the same game, actually."

"Which is what?" Jeff wanted to know.

"I'm playing Civil War," Tommy said. "The lawnmower is my Gatling gun, and I'm shooting down Yankees. See." He began to push the mower back and forth again, saying, "Eh, eh, eh, eh, eh. Die, you blue coats. Eh, eh, eh, eh, eh!"

Jeff was horrified. "Stop that this instant," he demanded.

"Stop what?" Tommy said. He quit pushing the mower and looked at his father quizzically.

"Stop everything. Turn that mower off so I can talk to you."

Tommy stepped down on the metal flange over the sparkplug, and the mower sputtered to a stop.

"Don't you understand anything?" Jeff said. "Don't you know what I've been struggling for? Don't you ever listen to anything I tell you?"

"I don't know," Tommy said.

"You make me so ashamed," Jeff said. "Here I've been giving my heart and soul trying to achieve basic decency for our Negro neighbors, and I've got a son who thinks of himself as a machine gunner for the forces defending slavery. What have I been trying to teach you about Negroes, Tommy?"

Tommy didn't understand the connection his father was making between playing Civil War to relieve the boredom of mowing the grass and what his father had taught him about race relations. He wrinkled his face in confusion and said nothing.

"I asked you a question, son. What have I been trying to teach you about Negroes?"

"I don't know," Tommy replied, still trying to make the connection between sounding like a Gatling gun and his father's sudden irritation.

"How can you not know?" Jeff demanded. "How can a son of mine not know?"

"Negroes aren't niggers," Tommy said. He raised a knee and tapped it with his fingertips the way Jeff had when he'd taught his son this lesson. "Knee," Tommy said, and then he made a climbing motion with his fingers, gradually raising his hand above his leg. "Grow," Tommy said. "Knee Grow. Not nigger. Not nigra. Not even colored people. Nigger is a horrible word, and I never say it. Honest."

"Okay," Jeff said. "That's right. I'm glad you understand that."

"And Robert Brown is just as good as me," Tommy rushed on, "even though he's a Negro and can't go to my school because Negroes aren't allowed."

"Aren't allowed, *yet*," Jeff said.

"Aren't allowed, *yet*," Tommy said. "Someday they will be because that's what we're working for."

"Yes," Jeff said. "So why were you playing a game about killing Yankees? I'll not have that, you understand."

Tommy didn't understand. He was just playing. And he didn't understand why his father got so upset about things.

"I don't want you ever doing that again," Jeff said. "I want you to promise me that right now. Okay?"

"Okay," Tommy said, though he guessed that if he didn't make the sound of the Gatling gun out loud, his father would never know whether or not he was playing Civil War while he mowed the grass.

"Okay, what?" Jeff asked.

"Okay, sir," Tommy said.

Jeff shook his head. This time he hadn't meant to instill the lesson of proper respect for elders. He had wanted Tommy to repeat what he'd learned. But he let it go. "Go on back to your chores," Jeff said.

"Yes, sir," Tommy said.

"And don't sweep the grass clippings up onto the lawn," Jeff added. "Sweep them down the sidewalk and the driveway, and then pick them up with the dust pan."

In the winter of 1960, the year Tommy was in eighth grade, he led the public school junior high basketball league in scoring, and in the middle of the season, for the first time in his youthful athletic career, Jeff began to attend his games. In that period at the end of the fifties, between the passage of the first civil-rights legislation since Reconstruction and the furious segregationist counterattack that broke out after John Kennedy was elected president, Jeff had more time to be at home, and he turned his attention to his family in a way he hadn't before.

Jeff had never cared for sports, and he had always dismissed Tommy's trophies as questionable glorification of insignificant accomplishment. But when he finally went to one of Tommy's junior high basketball games, he discovered with amazed delight that his son was a genuinely gifted athlete. Tommy scored nineteen points that night, coming within two points of outscoring the entire opposition. Tommy could drive around the other boys as if their tennis shoes were glued to the court, and he had a way of leaping into the air (a jump shot, Tommy called it) and shooting the ball over the outstretched hands of his opponents. Where had he learned such things, Jeff wondered.

"You're some player," Jeff said in the car after the game.

"I've been telling you that," Billye said. "Why do you think he has all those trophies?"

"I thought maybe he robbed a trophy store," Jeff said with a laugh.

"That's not funny," Billye said.

"No?" Jeff said. "I thought it was funny. I meant it to be funny."

"It was pretty funny, Mom," Tommy said.

"You always score that many points?" Jeff asked.

"Yes, sir," Tommy replied. "I mean, not always. But I always score the most on the team."

"Why's that?" Jeff asked. "You're not hogging the ball, are you?"

"Jeff!" Billye said.

"Oh, come on, honey, I'm just teasing."

"Coach says I'm the best shooter," Tommy explained, "so the team runs plays for me."

"So you do hog the ball," Jeff said. "Only with the coach's permission."

"Stop it, Jeff," Billye said.

"Yeah, stop it, Daddy," Danielle said. "Tommy's the best. He's going to get a scholarship and play for Tulane."

"Well, if he wants to go to Tulane, he better get a scholarship," Jeff said laughing. "I sure don't have the money to send him."

"Tommy can go to Tulane or wherever else he wants to go," Billye said.

"I'll get a scholarship," Tommy said. "So you don't have to worry about it."

"I'm not worried," Jeff said. "Do I look worried?"

"Who can tell how you look, Daddy," Danielle said. "Don't you know it's dark, and we can't even see you?"

In the summer of 1960, as New Orleans prepared to take its first baby steps toward integrating its public schools, Jeff suggested to Billye that they try to arrange a transfer for Danielle from her school in Gentilly to one of the two elementary schools the school board had scheduled to desegregate in the middle of the term that fall.

About 10:30 one night in mid-July, after the children had gone to bed, Jeff went into the den where Billye was trying to fix an antique clock that was losing about ten minutes a day. She had the back off and was working on the clock mechanism with a screwdriver and tweezers.

When Jeff made his proposal to move Danielle, Billye looked up from her work, squinted at her husband and said, "Are you crazy?"

"Don't talk to me like that," Jeff said. "I'll not have it." He was wearing an undershirt and boxers, his habitual dress around the house in the hot summer months.

"You will too have it, Jefferson Caldwell," Billye said, "if you think you're going to put my daughter on the racial battle lines."

"She's my daughter, too," Jeff said.

"Then act like it," Billye said.

"Why should our children be exempt from this fight?" Jeff wondered. "This is probably the most important thing that will happen in their lifetimes."

"And this is the only time in their lifetimes they're going to be children. Why would Danielle want to go to another school? She has all her friends at Gentilly. She'd be miserable at another school where she doesn't know anybody."

"But it's something she'd remember all her life. She'd be right there, centrally involved in the struggle."

"She's not even ten years old yet," Billye said. "It's not her struggle. It's your struggle."

"You've never really stood with me on this, have you?" Jeff said.

Billye set her tools down inside the back of the clock. "How can you say that? We've been married for eighteen years. I've raised your children while you've been off with the movement. Have I ever told you don't go? Have I ever failed to be here when you got back?"

"But you're not really committed to the struggle. I don't think you'd be involved at all if you weren't married to me."

Billye snorted and moved the clock off her lap, setting it beside her on the sofa. "Who knows what I'd be if I hadn't married you, Jeff? If my father hadn't been a pharmacist with enough money to send me to college, maybe I'd be a telephone operator or even a stripper down on Bourbon Street."

"Don't talk nasty," Jeff said.

Billye ignored him and went on. "If I hadn't met you, maybe I'd have finished college and be an architect now or even a doctor."

"You're going back to school now," Jeff said. "I've encouraged you in that."

Billye responded with a dry burst of laugh. "The point is that I did marry you. No, I might not be involved in this movement otherwise. But because I married you, I am. And that's my life. It's not fair of you to question my commitment when you haven't any grounds to."

"But you've resented the things I've asked you to do."

"Like what?"

"Like living with the Browns during the bus boycott," Jeff said.

"I did resent that," Billye admitted. "I also resented the fact that except to bring me your laundry you hadn't been home for weeks. I resented that I was stuck without a car with two children in a public housing project. I resented that it was hot and lonely and I had to ask girlfriends for rides whenever I needed to go somewhere. I resented that you had this whole life apart from me and your children, one evidently more important to you than me and your children. I admit it. I resented all that."

"But that's just it," Jeff said. "I brought you and the kids up to Baton Rouge to be a part of it, to be right in the middle of it. Danielle was too little and won't remember. But Tommy will. It's something he can be proud of for the rest of his life. He was there. He was right there."

"He was right in a place where the night before someone had planted a bomb."

"But that's why we were there," Jeff said. Still standing, he moved now to take a seat in the low-back overstuffed chair next to the sofa. As he sat, the fly of his drawers gaped open, but he didn't notice.

"Yes, that's *why* we were there," Billye said. "And maybe we should have been there."

"Of course, we should have."

Billye looked down into the back of the clock beside her. "Yes," she said. "I think we should have been there. But I think you should have asked me. That's what I resented. That you decided to employ our family as a shield for the Browns, and you didn't ask me."

Jeff scooted around in his chair. "See," he said, "all this time you never said anything, but I knew you resented it."

"I resented it," Billye said. "But I stood by you, and I made the best of it. Just like I did when I was pregnant with Danielle and you told me you had black blood, and though Tommy was a white boy, the next child could turn out to be black. I've never been so shaken in my life. But I stood by you then, too, didn't I? I told you that if the child was black she would still be our child. And I meant it."

Jeff looked up toward the ceiling. "I shouldn't have done that," he said. "It was wrong, and it was mean, and I've said that before. I wish you could forgive me."

"I have forgiven you, Jeff. I'm just citing it as an example of my standing by you."

"It was my stupid way of testing you," Jeff said, pulling the skin of his forehead into a pinch hold over his right eyebrow. "I was young and full of it. I wanted to see how you'd react. Whether you would still love me if I was part black."

"I'm not bringing it up to punish you, Jeff. I'm bringing it up to defend myself."

Jeff took a deep breath. "Okay," he said. "But can we please discuss transferring Danielle?"

"No," Billye said.

As it happened, had the Caldwells decided to send their daughter to a desegregated school, she would have gone there practically alone. Afraid that Orleans Parish schools might close down as had happened in Virginia, many white parents placed their children in private schools that fall of 1960, including into the so-called "segregation academies" that opened specifically to take advantage of this first manifestation of white flight.

The white protest in New Orleans was smaller and less violent than that which took place in Little Rock High three years earlier. But it was ugly enough. The first day was like the two months of school days that followed. The crowd chanted "Two, four, six, eight, we don't want to integrate," and "What do we want? Niggers out! When do we want it? Now!" Police were supposed to keep the crowd across the street from the school, but when the little black girls showed up, the cops looked the other way as incensed adults, their faces masks of venomous hatred, crowded up to the sidewalk and screamed vulgarities at six- and seven-year-old children.

As he had done at Little Rock, Jeff escorted a black child through the crowd, holding her little hand in his. A step or so behind, Preacher Martin walked hand-in-hand with another child. Introduced to the parents of the Negro children by George Washington Brown himself, Jeff and Preacher had arranged to escort the children into the school building to spare their parents from exposure to the mob. Driving her own car and assuring everybody concerned that she considered this service a privilege, Jeff's church secretary, Naylynn Jensen, took Jeff and Preacher to pick up the children. The crowd began to scream as soon as they saw black children emerging from Naylynn's car, and she sped away as soon as her passengers got out.

Jeff and Preacher tried to maintain a brisk but dignified pace from the curbside down the sidewalk to the school's front door. They did not want to provoke the throng further by seeming to run from them. They did not speak to the people who screamed at them. They did not even make eye contact. Each shielded the child he escorted with his own body. The crowd had no idea who Jeff and Preacher were and thought they must be federal marshals. At the end of the walk both Jeff and Preacher were covered with spit. Jeff had been hit in the back of the neck with an egg which trickled down inside his shirt.

For an entire school year, Jeff and Preacher each walked a Negro child to her school. As the days passed, the size of the mob gradually dwindled to a hard core of bitter racists. The children were astonishingly brave. Neither one ever cried nor even flinched. They surrendered their hands to the two tall white men and marched through a stretch of hell just to sit in seats that white children had abandoned. Jeff had the most profound respect and affection for these children, but for the first time in his life—a product of his age, he guessed—Jeff began to wonder if it was worth it.

Preacher saw things from a different angle. "We've been working with the wrong people," he told Jeff when it was clear that the white kids weren't coming back to school. "It's the screamers and the spitters we've got to change somehow. We need to convince them to love before the black folks surrender to hate."

The 1960 integration of Orleans Parish schools was a mere token, of course, just the lower grades in two elementary schools. The system still wouldn't be fully and truly integrated when Danielle graduated from high school in 1968, and it would remain integrated for only about seven years. The blacks came, and the whites went. The last class to have a sizable white student population graduated in 1976. After that, Orleans Parish schools were almost precisely as segregated as they had been in 1960.

Danielle didn't transfer schools as her father wanted. And so she wasn't "right there in the middle of it." In fact, for the fifth graders at her Gentilly school, integration day passed almost wholly without notice. The same was hardly true at Tommy's Capdau Junior High School, where a social historian could already detect what was to come over the next decade and a half. For days, Tommy heard the whispered plans for an integration-day protest walkout at Capdau. The big instigators, as far as Tommy could determine, were two brothers, Mike and Frank Eisley, big bluff guys who played on the football team that Tommy quarterbacked. Mike played defensive tackle, and Frank played beside him at end.

They weren't particularly well coordinated, but they were strong. Both had failed a grade, so they were just plain bigger than everybody else in school. They headed a loose-knit gang of school toughs who called themselves The Radiators "because they could really heat things up." Most of the more affluent kids in school called them "the hoods" or "the greasers," the latter a term carrying no ethnic baggage whatsoever but referring exclusively to the fact that they wore their hair long and greased back into duck tails.

Tommy had regarded the Eisley brothers as laughable dullards until they found their racist calling. He got along with them well enough; their mutual participation in football provided a connection. They could be funny in their crude way. But they could also be disgusting. They were the kinds of boys who thought spitting on other kids was a real knee-slapper. They liked to sneak up behind someone in the shower and urinate down his leg, howling with laughter when their prey discovered what they'd done to him. And they always bragged about doing something illegal in a pile-up—like pulling an opponent's leg hair or punching him in the groin. The Eisleys were tough customers, and most students at the school were afraid of them. When they began to spread the word that they were leading the walkout right after lunch on integration day, many students, including many of Tommy's friends, felt they had no choice but to go along.

This was the first real moral crisis in Tommy's life. By age fourteen he knew exactly the nature of his father's beliefs and the intensity with which Jeff held them. Tommy had never violated those ideals in his own life. He always said "Negro," never—for fear of being struck by lightning and transported directly to hell—"nigger." When his schoolmates and neighborhood chums announced that "Martin Luther King and George Washington Brown are communists who report directly to Khrushchev," he could say, "Aw, y'all don't know what you're talking about," and get away with it. They'd just respond, "Man, Tommy, you just have to say that because you're the preacher's kid." And he could even say, "You ought to think some time about what it's like being a Negro. You wouldn't like it, I can promise you that." To which they'd inevitably reply, "Man, if I was a nigger, I'd just have to kill myself."

But none of those exchanges ever had any purchase on Tommy or his pals. The Caldwells lived in the city's most thoroughly segregated section. There were no black residents for dozens of blocks in any direction. Tommy knew Robert Brown, of course, but not in the same way he knew his own friends who didn't know any Negroes their own age. The only black people any of them ever encountered were maids and janitors and shoe-shine men. Tommy believed the things his father had taught him to believe, and his friends believed the opposite things their fathers had taught them to believe, and until now it never had made any difference.

The basement lunchroom at Capdau Junior High usually sounded like an echo chamber. Naked galvanized water pipes striped the ceiling, the floor was linoleum laid over cement, and the walls were unadorned concrete block. At a normal lunch time, students sitting directly across from one another at the folding, fiber-board tables would have to scream just to be heard. But on integration day, the cafeteria sounded like a funeral parlor. Everybody spoke in low voices, barely above a whisper, and everybody talked about the same thing.

"Are you going to walk out?"

"I don't know. Are you?"

"Won't they suspend us?"

"How can they suspend us if the whole school walks out?"

"My parents would kill me no matter what the principal might do."

"Mike and Frank Eisley and the other greasers might kill you a lot sooner if you don't walk out."

This was the dilemma the Capdau students found themselves in. Most of them had no thirst for trouble and no direct involvement in the events taking place at a grade school in another part of town. They were Southern kids with predictable prejudices but no deeply ingrained bigotry. Left to their own devices, they would have gone to class and given the integration of elementary schools across town scarcely a thought. Challenged by the Eisley brothers to take a stand, however, they found themselves caught in a bind. They didn't want to get suspended for violating school rules, but they also didn't want to be called "nigger lovers."

Tommy Caldwell's dilemma was somewhat different. He gave no thought to walking out. He knew he *was* a "nigger lover," odd as that fact was, given that he knew so few Negroes. But a "nigger lover" was a white person who believed in racial equality, and he did. Still, he had no desire to turn this belief into a confrontation. He basically liked his life. He was captain of the football team and had led the basketball team in scoring as an eighth grader. He was on friendly terms with almost everyone. Most of the kids he knew felt that Negroes were innately inferior, and even though he disagreed with them, he didn't see that disagreeing with them was going to change their minds. So Tommy joined with the majority of his classmates in wishing that this whole business of a walkout would just go away.

Tommy sat at his table with his closest circle of friends: among them Earl Kardowski, the football team's shifty left halfback and star player; Sidney Detweiler, the fullback who would go on to be an outstanding running back at LSU; Mickey Stein, the right halfback and Tommy's favorite receiver; and Tommy's best friend Clint Carter, the football team's center and a bulky forward on the basketball team. At the table directly across from theirs, Tommy's girlfriend Tammy Bailey, an eighth-grade cheerleader, sat with her friends. The Eisleys had stopped by these tables earlier saying, "End of lunch: walkout," and then shooting everybody at the two tables four thumbs up.

The boys around Tommy chatted nervously about what was to come, but Tommy kept silent. The tuna sandwich he had fixed himself that morning tasted like sawdust, the potato chips like sandpaper. He drank a bottle of Barq's root beer and got up to buy himself another. He had just returned to his seat when Tammy came over. She leaned in between Clint and Tommy and said in a low voice, "Are you going to walk out with those Radiator jerks?"

The conversation at Tommy's table stopped, and everybody turned to look at him. He slipped his right arm around Tammy's waist and tipped the root-beer bottle to his mouth with his left hand. He drank half the bottle in three gulps, then set it back on the table and wiped his mouth with the back of hand. "No," he said, "I'm not."

"I didn't think so," Tammy said.

"You're not?" Earl said. "Why not? Those guys are gonna call you a nigger lover."

"What of it?" Tommy said, more casually than he actually felt.

"I ain't letting them call me no nigger lover," Earl said.

"How you gonna stop them?" Sidney wanted to know. "Both of 'em are about twice as big as you."

"I'm gonna walk out with them is how," Earl said. "Aren't you?"

Sidney looked at Clint. "You walking out?" Sidney asked.

Clint Carter was the one kid at Capdau who was as big as the Eisleys and probably stronger than either one. If there was trouble afoot, Sidney wanted to know where Clint stood. Clint shrugged. "I'm with the captain," he said, referring to Tommy. "Why should we get our butts busted for those assholes?" He glanced at Tammy. "Sorry," he added sheepishly. "For those jerks."

"For those assholes," Tammy said, reddening the ears of every boy at the table and endearing herself to all of them forever.

"What about you?" Clint asked Sidney.

"I'm with you guys," Sidney said. "Bell rings, we just go to class and that's it."

"I can't believe you all," Earl said. "Man, I'm walking out. You guys can be nigger lovers for the rest of your life, but not me."

The bell rang, and the Eisley brothers stepped up on chairs at either side of the main cafeteria doors and began to chant, "Walk out! Walk out!"

In various parts of the room, the other Radiators joined in, "Walk out! Walk out!" and began to herd students toward the central staircase doors.

After a moment, Tommy stood and walked slowly toward the north end of the room where doors opened to another staircase. Clint and Sidney and Mickey fell in behind him as did all the girls from Tammy's table.

As Tommy's group started past Mike Eisley, he yelled out, "Hey, where you guys going?" Students just about to pass out the center doors stopped, and those behind them began to bunch up into each other like sheep in a pen. At first Tommy and his group didn't respond. They just kept walking toward the north staircase. "Hey, I asked you a question, Caldwell," Mike said. "Where you going?"

"Yeah, where you going?" Frank Eisley echoed across the heads of students jammed in the doorway.

Tommy's entire group turned toward Mike, who hopped down off his chair and started in their direction. As he did so, Clint Carter stepped around two of the girls, putting himself between them and Mike, who immediately stopped. "What?" Mike said. "Are you guys a bunch of nigger lovers or what?"

"I told you," Earl said from the crush of students.

"Shut up, Earl," Sidney said.

Earl raised his arms in a protest of innocence. "I'm just saying what I told you."

The pack near the door had started to ease now as the students at the rear began to back up and circle around the tables along the wall across from the center doors.

"You the head nigger lover, Caldwell?" Mike said. "I hear your old man is a professional nigger lover, so I guess you're just his little amateur."

"Leave my father out of this," Tommy said.

"Shut up, Eisley," Clint said.

"Shut up yourself, Carter," Frank Eisley said. "Mike wasn't even talking to you. He was talking to nigger-loving Caldwell."

"Both you Eisleys can shut up," Clint said.

"Both us Eisleys may come over there and kick your ass, Carter," Mike said.

"Any time," Clint said. "Right now, tomorrow, next year. One at a time, both at once."

"Yeah, right," Frank said.

"Look, Eisley," Tommy said to Mike, "you and the Radiators are organizing a walkout. Well, we're not walking. We're supposed to go to class, and that's what we're going to do."

"And any of you who don't want to walk out don't have to," Tammy said to the throng of students. "We're going to class, and y'all can come with us."

Tommy turned around and started walking again toward the doors to the north staircase, and when he did, Mike Eisley took three running steps in his direction, only to be cut down by Clint Carter's chop block just above his left knee. Mike flipped over onto his back, and Clint, who never left his feet, came immediately up over him. Behind him Frank Eisley jumped off his chair and pushed his way through the crowd of students toward Clint, only to be intercepted by Sidney, who simply stood in his path and said, "Uh-uh."

And so it was over.

Tommy never related these events to his father because he knew Jeff would have found his behavior cowardly rather than heroic. That's how he found it himself. The walkout wasn't defeated in the name of desegregation. Tommy didn't even raise the issue. The walkout was defeated because the star athletes and the cheerleaders opposed it, and Tommy suspected that, as the "popular" kids in school, they could have led everybody outside if the Eisleys were trying to make them go to class. Tommy tried to comfort himself that his forthright advocacy of racial equality wouldn't have changed any minds anyway. But maybe it would have.

That night, as Tommy watched the TV news coverage of his father being screamed at and spit upon while walking a Negro child to school, he reflected on his own actions in comparison. It was absolutely clear where Jeff stood. And Jeff did what he did without the likes of Clint Carter and Sidney Detweiler to block for him. That's why Tommy always recalled his own integration-day confrontation with shame rather than pride.

chapter ten

J EFF CALDWELL WAS SLEEPY getting up at 4:30 to breakfast with his family on cold cornbread and coffee. But he felt good as he waited on New Peterstown Road in the gray summer dawn for the crew truck to pick them up. He had grown four inches in the last year, and at fourteen he was almost as tall as his brother Wayne, who was two years his senior. Pruitt had gotten the whole family jobs on a cotton-picking crew and had promised each child that if he worked hard, he could keep a portion of what he earned. The two youngest boys could have three cents a day for their very own. James could have a nickel. Wayne and Jeff could have seven cents. Or at least Jeff could have seven cents rather than five or six if, in Pruitt's opinion, he picked as much cotton as his older brother. Jeff was determined to match Wayne, even if he had to go without lunch to do it. So as Jeff stood in his white cotton shirt alongside his parents and brothers, he ignored the slight chill he felt and relished the thought of the money jingling in his pocket at the day's end.

As the Caldwell family rode standing up in the back of the truck, jostling as the truck bounced over each pothole, stumbling forward each time the truck stopped to pick up other families, lurching backwards when it jolted into motion again, Pruitt seethed that he'd been reduced to this. With the New Peterstown lumber mill closed, he had no choice but to do itinerant farm work. All the millable lumber in a forty-mile radius had been bought up, chopped down, sawed up, sold off and hauled away.

The lumber company had opened up a new mill in the Jonesboro area, but that was seventy miles away, and though Pruitt had been told he could get work there, such a thing wasn't feasible. He couldn't move his family there. The Caldwells had always lived in New Peterstown. He couldn't support his family on his six acres, but he could raise enough food to feed them. Or Osby could, anyway. It was she who planted and weeded and tended the garden, she who canned and made preserves, she who kept the hen house.

But that was fair. He worked in the mill, bought the feed for the chickens and kept clothes on all the kids' backs. Or he had, anyway, until the mill closed in the spring. But there weren't any buyers for his land. It wasn't bottom land and wasn't good for anything other than a garden. Even Osby's corn was always stunted, no matter how much manure she and Vivien and the boys spread around it. Pruitt couldn't sell the land, and he couldn't live without it, and he couldn't make it back and forth to Jonesboro every day. So he was out of the lumber business until the trees grew back. When would that be? When his grandkids were pointing out his grave to their children.

So now this. Picking cotton. Nigger work. He told the damn crew boss he'd do nigger work if he had to, but he wouldn't work alongside a nigger. He'd let his family starve before he'd reduce them to that. He'd pick and his wife and kids would pick until their hands were raw. But he'd walk in a second if they brought a nigger into the field beside him.

As the truck turned off New Peterstown Road onto State Highway 1, they passed the first of the stump fields that were everywhere now in central Louisiana. Where once had stood a forest of live oak, baldcypress and red maple, there was now only an ugly, snaggle-toothed wasteland, a devil's grin of blackened tree bottoms and a viperous protrusion of root intermingled with tangles of scrub brush and the occasional worthless scraggly pine, bowed and frail like an old man who'd lost his cane. The land on either side of New Peterstown Road was still verdant, with pine mostly, soft wood trees good only for firewood. Here along Highway 1, however, the hardwoods had grown to the roadside and over the last few years had fallen to the crosscut blades of the mill timber men. This early in the morning the stump field was shrouded in a veil of mist, which draped over the surviving vegetation like a spider web.

Another man gazing out upon this bog of destruction might have found it sad and hideous, even frightening. But the forest's devastation didn't bother Pruitt. He possessed no appreciation for natural splendor. Still, he stared at the field with resentment, bitter that what once was had disappeared—not because something beautiful was gone, but because the forest wasn't forever renewable, because it had been used up and wasn't there anymore to provide raw material for his livelihood. He resented the forest itself, not the lumber business that had made it disappear, because, as if a willful act on the part of the forest itself, by disappearing, the forest had chopped him down to the level of a nigger.

In resentment, Pruitt spit at the stump field over the high rail of the truck. But the velocity of his spittle was not great enough to carry it beyond the wind force of the truck, and it merely flew backwards, splattering against Wayne and James and Monroe. As each youngster mopped the wet from his face without raising a complaint, he wondered whether his father had spit on him purposely or purely by accident.

Jeff felt a keen sense of anticipation as the truck pulled off Highway 1, traveled a short distance down a gravel road, and turned through an opening in a waist-high, barbed-wire fence. The truck rumbled over the rails of a cattle grate and continued for a half mile along a private drive, two tire tracks on either side of a strip of tall grass that rustled against the truck's undercarriage. It was just after sunrise now. A stand of birch trees lined the narrow one-lane drive and blocked the sun, but Jeff could see yellow streaks of light arcing into the eastern sky. The predawn chill had evaporated with the morning light, and the day ahead promised to be seasonally hot. But Jeff was used to the heat. What he wasn't used to was getting paid for his labor. He was eager to get his day of toil under way.

The truck pulled to a stop on the edge of a vast open field that stretched away for a third of a mile in three directions. The Caldwells piled out and followed Pruitt to a black Chevrolet sedan parked next to a huge wooden wagon. Behind the wagon, four collared mules were tethered in the shade of a live oak. A man leaned against the wagon, one foot propped up on a wheel spoke. He wore khaki pants, dusty wing-tipped brown shoes, a white short-sleeve shirt, open at the neck, and a yellow straw hat with a black band. As the man waited in an attitude of faintly annoyed impatience, he smoked a cigarette. Jeff could see the dark red pack of Pall Malls through the material of the man's shirt pocket.

The day's workers gathered around the man in the white shirt. Like the Caldwells, they were people reduced to doing work that they felt shamed them. They were men like Pruitt Caldwell who had little to be proud of but who had taken pride in not having to put their children into the labor force. And they were the wives and children of these men, standing there in the bright morning light because they had no choice, because this was their lot. Standing before the man in the white shirt were children younger even than Franklin, who was nine, and elderly people who should have been easing away their last years in rocking chairs. One old couple, dressed identically in blue denim overalls and red neckerchiefs, appeared to be near seventy.

Most of the children were dressed either in dungarees or blue denim overalls. The women wore long, loose-weave cotton dresses. The smart men had long-sleeve muslin shirts, though many, like the Caldwell boys, wore plain white T-shirts. Pruitt had a white cotton shirt much like the man before them, only frayed at the collar and stained with large yellow circles under each arm. Everyone there had some sort of hat, including a man in a pith helmet. Pruitt wore a sweat-stained, striped engineer's cap, his sons tattered baseball caps. In addition to her wide-brimmed straw hat, Osby had a blue bandana knotted at the base of her throat and spread open over the back of her neck. She had equipped the men with white handkerchiefs to tuck under their caps and drape down their necks for added protection from the sun.

The man in the white shirt looked at his work force, seeming to take scowling note of each face. He took a last drag on his cigarette and crushed it out in the dust under his feet. Before speaking, the man ran his tongue under his top lip and made a whistling sound as he sucked air through his teeth. Then he picked a shred of tobacco off his tongue and said, "Once you got your bag filled—or for you younguns who can't handle a filled one, once you got the most you can still drag—you bring your sack over here and place it on the scale." He pointed with his thumb at the truck driver who had circled around the crowd of workers to stand beside him. "My man Morley here will write down your pick weight."

Morley was dressed like many of the pickers, a collarless, long-sleeve cotton shirt worn under the bib of blue overalls. His hat was a soiled fedora pulled down low on his forehead. He held up a clipboard now on which were fastened some dog-eared sheets of lined white paper. "I got the names of each of your families wrote down here," he said.

Morley looked at the man in the white shirt, who seemed oblivious that Morley had uttered a word. "Once your pick is registered," the man in the white shirt continued, "then you dump it in the wagon and get on back to work. Don't even think of such tricks as trying to weigh down your sack with clumps of dirt or a load of rocks. Morley will be right there. Anything but cotton comes out of that sack, you're off the crew. No pay for anything you may have picked before. No ride home. Get caught doing such monkeyshines, just start walking on out of here because you're through."

The man in the white shirt made a hissing sound as he spit through his teeth into the dirt. "We want you picking the boll clean," he continued after wiping his mouth with the back of his hand. "Don't go breaking the stalk and filling your bag up with a lot of stick and leaf. Morley will be right there when you dump. Too much stalk and debris in your pick, he's gonna deduct weight. And his word is final. I won't tolerate no arguments about a deduct. I hope everybody's clear on that. Just pick clean and keep moving. The more and cleaner you pick, the more you make. You get the picture?"

"We get the picture," Pruitt said, not loud but loud enough for the man in the white shirt to hear him. Under his breath, Pruitt said, "Ain't like we're a bunch of stupid coons."

"What's that?" the man in the white shirt said to Pruitt who looked around at the others, none of whom would meet his gaze. "Did you have something to add?"

"I said we ain't a bunch of niggers," Pruitt announced in a modulated but clear voice. "We know what to do."

"Dern straight you ain't a bunch of niggers," the man in the white shirt said. "A nigger'd know enough to keep his blame mouth shut. And I wouldn't have to pay him as much as I'm gonna be paying you to do it. Now do you have anything *more* to add?"

"I was just trying to say we're chomping to get started," Pruitt replied, smiling broadly. "Can't earn anything if we ain't picking."

The man in the white shirt stared at him, his jaw working as if he was chewing the skin on the inside of his mouth.

"Just anxious to get on out there and get after it," Pruitt added. "Didn't mean nothing but that."

For a long second, the man in the white shirt stared hard at Pruitt, who averted his gaze. "You'll get started a lot sooner if you keep your dern mouth shut," he said.

The people near Pruitt shuffled their feet and angled their bodies away, trying to disassociate themselves from any trouble he was about to get into. Pruitt cast his eyes down and lowered his head so that the brim of his cap kept him from making eye contact with the man in the white shirt.

"Okay," the man said. "Just one more thing. Mamas and daddies, you're responsible for all your younguns. Any mischief they cause, it's your deduct." He looked at Morley and said, "Give them their rows and get them going."

Jeff started down his row, determined to clean plant by plant and pick pound for pound alongside Wayne who was working the next row over. During the first hour, the canvas sack felt like a feather, and Jeff couldn't understand why his mother had reacted so somberly to the news that Pruitt had found all of them this work. Plucking the bolls on the first plants felt as easy as picking up a sock off the floor. Jeff moved quickly, sliding his fingers around the tuft of cotton and pulling it away from the plant with single twist of his wrist. Within minutes, it was clear that he was working faster than Wayne.

After two hours, however, the continual twisting action of the pick made Jeff's wrist sore, and the weight of the sack made his back ache. To drag it from plant to plant, he had to bend forward at the waist and put all his weight into the effort, the strap biting into his sweat-soaked shoulder. By late morning, his right hand was so raw he began to pick with his left, an awkward process that slowed him down and increased his overall fatigue.

At noon, Morley honked the horn of the truck to signal a lunch break. The pickers dropped their sacks exactly where they lay and moved to the far end of the field, where a row of water oaks grew along the banks of a creek. The man in the white shirt provided no provisions for any of the workers; the only food available was what they had brought from home. Osby gave each of the Caldwell males a square of cornbread she had wrapped in a piece of wax paper and kept in the large pockets of her skirt. As she dispensed the food, she retrieved the sheets of wax paper and folded them back into her pockets to be used again tomorrow. Jeff and his brothers sat with their backs against oak trunks, savoring the shade.

The cornbread was moist enough, but Jeff was so parched he got up twice to drink from the stream. When he returned, Wayne said to him, keeping his voice low and speaking almost without moving his lips, "What you busting your hump about? Daddy ain't gonna give you no more than seven cents even if you pick twice as much as me."

Jeff took another bite of cornbread before answering. "We're not having a contest," he said. "This is about how much cotton all of us pick, not whether I pick more than you or the other way around."

"Yeah," Wayne said. "Sure. Just remember, all we get is seven cents."

Jeff shrugged and the two brothers sat without talking until Morley honked his truck horn again, and they got up and went back to the field. If Pruitt took any note of the fact that Jeff had picked more plants than Wayne, he didn't say so, and in the afternoon, Jeff noticed, Wayne filled his sack as fast as Jeff. At four o'clock, they walked to the truck together, and when Wayne's bag was dumped, Jeff noted with a certain satisfaction that Wayne was filling his bag with a great deal of husk and stalk, evidently keeping up with Jeff only by ripping the cotton away from the plant carelessly. There was so much debris in Wayne's pick, Jeff expected to hear some comment from Morley, but Morley said nothing. Perhaps he didn't notice. More likely, Jeff suddenly realized, Morley just didn't care.

The day dragged on toward sunset, but the heat in the shelterless, unshaded field was unrelenting. The bags became steadily more cumbersome and the work more tedious. Jeff had never before known work so brutal, but he labored on, spurred to each new boll and each fresh plant by the jingle of coins dancing in his head. How, he wondered, did slaves ever manage to do this work with no incentive in it for themselves. Finally, just after seven, Morley sounded the horn, and all the pickers struggled toward the wagon to weigh and dump their cotton one last time. After a numbingly long day, in heat that fell on exposed skin like the prick of a thousand needles and rose again in waves off the baked red soil, their tired feet felt as if they were being cooked inside their shoes. The pickers formed a quiet line and waited as Morley weighed their bags and entered the figures on his ledger. Because they were all in it together, all relying on Morley to drive them home, no one could leave until all were finished.

The trouble started at 7:30 when the man in the white shirt returned in his black Chevy sedan. He got out of his car carrying a brown, quarter-inch-thick yardstick and took over supervision of the dump. As the pickers lugged their sacks from the scale to the wagon, he would bark out at them impatiently, "Come on. Come on. Ain't got all night here," or goad them needlessly, "Lordy, lordy, this one looks like he never did an honest day's work before in his life," or pick at them heartlessly, "Look at this one now, so tired the seat of his pants is dragging his tracks out," all the while beating insistently with his hard stick against the tailgate of the wagon.

Then, when each sack was dumped, he stirred around in the pick suspiciously with his yardstick before ordering Morley to enter a debris deduction on practically every sack that now went into the wagon. The pickers were tired enough that the boss man's mean hassling fell on largely indifferent ears. But the pickers, bone tired, dirty and hungry, were frustrated and angered at having their weight credit cut. Many thought of pointing out to the man in the white shirt that they had been picking the same way all day and Morley had not once ordered a deduct. But all knew that the man in the white shirt would only use such an argument against them, would only then insist that Morley enter a deduct next to each weight with which they had already been credited. In addition, since there was more cotton to pick the next day in this field and more yet in the days to come in other fields supervised by Morley and the man in the white shirt, no one wanted to jeopardize future employment. Better not enough than nothing at all.

Those who made their way forward in line ahead of Jeff accepted the cruelties of the man in the white shirt with no more comment than a slump of resigned fatigue. But behind them, Jeff presumed himself exempt. He had listened carefully to directions, and he had taken special care to get a clean pick all day long. When the man in the white shirt ordered a deduct on his pick, Jeff objected more from surprise than indignation. "Now that's not right," he said, as much to himself as to the man in the white shirt.

The man in the white shirt looked up, not sure he'd heard what Jeff said. "You say something to me, boy?" he inquired.

"Yes sir," Jeff said, blinking, stung by the idea that he hadn't done what he was told.

"He didn't say a dern thing," Pruitt said to the man in the white shirt. Pruitt reached out to Jeff and grabbed him by the back of his upper arm, pinching hard on the piece of flesh he squeezed between thumb and forefinger. "Get over here, boy," Pruitt said to Jeff.

"Owwww," Jeff responded.

"What'd that boy say to me?" the man in the white shirt asked Pruitt.

"I warned him about getting debris in his pick," Pruitt said. "He was hoping you wouldn't catch him."

"Yeah," the man in the white shirt said.

"But I guess you got all of us," Pruitt said, nervously aware that he'd now called this man's attention to him a second time. The man in the white shirt did not respond, and Pruitt jerked Jeff away in the direction of the crew truck, telling Jeff in a hushed voice as he pushed the boy in front of him, "You are as dumb as cow flop, and I'm gonna kick your rear end up around your neck. Now get over by the truck and button your stupid lip."

As Pruitt gave Jeff a dressing down out of earshot of the dump wagon, the man in the white shirt faced another picker, the man in the pith helmet, a tall, swarthy man with prominent cheekbones and jet black hair, who looked as if he almost certainly had Indian blood. "What's your name?" the man in the white shirt asked.

"Smith," the man in the pith helmet said. "George Smith."

"One pound deduct, George Smith," the man in the white shirt called over to Morley.

"What for?" Smith wanted to know.

"Debris," the man in the white shirt said.

"Wasn't no debris in my pick," Smith said.

"Looky here," the man in the white shirt said. "He stirred around in the cotton with the yardstick he was holding in his right hand. Husk. Stalk. Warned you about that this morning."

"Wasn't no husk or stalk in my pick." Smith said. He squared his shoulders and spread his legs slightly.

"I just showed it to you," the man in the white shirt said. "Now move on along."

"You didn't show me nuthin," Smith said. "Nuthin that come out of my bag. What you're pointing at come out of somebody else's bag. Ain't so much anyhow, that I can see."

"You like this job?" the man in the white shirt said.

"No," Smith said. The man in the white shirt reared up at that, his head and neck moving back on the line of his shoulders. "Don't like it at all," Smith said. He looked at the man in the white shirt evenly. "It's hot, dirty, hard work. What man would like it?"

The man in the white shirt laid the yardstick down on the wagon flap and slid his right hand into his pants pocket. With the fingers of his left hand cupped over his crotch, he worked at a knot in his underwear. "I know a man might like this work," the man in the white shirt said after a moment, cocking his head to one side and appraising the man in the pith helmet through squinted eyes. "Man ain't got no other work, he might like it."

The pickers had been talking tiredly as they waited in line, sat on the bumpers or leaned against the sides of the crew truck. Now they became completely silent. Even Morley stopped weighing and writing in his ledger to watch this scene unfold.

"It's what I'm saying," Smith stated plainly. "Ain't no man likes this work. He does it if he has to. But he don't ever like it."

"Where you from, Smith?" the man in the white shirt wanted to know. "I bet you ain't from around here."

"I'm stopping with family in Dry Prong," Smith replied. "I'm from Alabama originally. Over by Montevallo. You know it? South of Birmingham 'bout forty miles or so. Heard they had oil field work around here, pay a decent wage, but I ain't found none."

"You look kind of Eye-talian, Smith," the man in the white shirt said. "You sure you ain't got some Dago name like, what, Hernandez or Rodriguez?"

The man in the pith helmet didn't say anything to that at first. Finally, he said, "I already told you. My name is Smith. George Smith."

"And where'd you get that stupid-looking hat?" the man in the white shirt asked.

"My daddy," Smith said. "Brought it back with him from the Great War. Traded his own overseas cap with some British fellow."

"It's stupid looking," the man in the white shirt said. "I don't like it."

"It's cooler than other hats," Smith responded. "That's why I wear it."

"I don't like it," the man in the white shirt repeated.

"Well, then I guess I won't buy you one come next Christmas," Smith said.

The man in the white shirt took a sudden half-step forward but, noting Smith's size and sinewy arms, stopped himself and just pawed at the dusty ground with his foot. He spit in the dirt and used his shoe to stir the wet spot into paste. "You a right smart aleck, now ain't you, Smith?" the man in the white shirt said.

"I been told I can tell a joke as well as the next man," Smith said.

"Well, I'm gonna tell you something you ain't been told evidently," the man in the white shirt said, biting off each word. "I don't like no Eye-talian arguing with me about a deduct when I done warned him that I wouldn't put up with it. So now I'm gonna tell you something else you're too dumb to have figured out for your own self. You're done around here. So you just turn your sorry tail around and start walking on out of here."

"I'll be glad to go once you pay me what you owe," Smith said. "I don't want to be working for no cheat, that's for sure."

"You calling me a cheat?" the man in the white shirt said. His eyes opened wide, showing white all the way around the irises.

"You try to deduct off my weight," Smith said, "then you're cheating me out of what I earned. That's what a cheat does. So I guess I'm calling you a cheat."

"I can have you arrested for that," the man in the white shirt said. "That's libel. And you've gone and done it in front of a whole bunch of witnesses."

"What's true ain't libel," Smith said. "And anyway, you don't arrest somebody for libel. Any fool knows that."

"So now I'm a fool, is it?" the man in the white shirt said. "Well, here, I got something to fool you with." From his pants pocket, he pulled a black snub-nosed revolver and pointed it at Smith. "Now I already told you to git. You better do it before I make you wish you had."

"I want my pay," Smith said.

"You ain't listening, boy," the man in the white shirt said. "You done messed up. I warned you about that this morning. You ain't got no pay coming, and you better git before I have to commit a justifiable homicide."

"I picked your cotton," Smith said. "I expect to be paid for it."

The man in the white shirt cocked his pistol. "I'm giving you to five to turn your sorry backside around and start walking off this land."

Smith did not move.

"One."

"You ain't gonna shoot me in cold blood in front of all these witnesses," Smith said.

"Two," the man in the white shirt said.

"I'm calling your dern bluff, Mr. Boss Man. You won't do it 'cause you got too much to lose. Not with everybody here watching you."

"My employees," the man in the white shirt said. "Folks that need the work I give them. Now your time is just about run out." He raised the gun to the height of his shoulder and stretched his arm out. The barrel was now less than three feet from Smith's chest. "Three."

Smith did not move. Behind him the crowd shuffled, now genuinely afraid they were about to witness bloodshed. The people standing behind Smith circled away in case the man in the white shirt fired and somehow missed.

"Four."

"For God's sake, man," Jeff Caldwell called out, "it isn't worth dying for. Even if he cheated you."

"Shut up, you," Pruitt said to Jeff and slapped his face so hard he knocked Jeff down.

At the sound of the slap, the man in the white shirt blurted out, "Everybody just stay exactly where you are," and jerked his gun in the direction of Pruitt. This motion required the man in the white shirt to twist his hips slightly to the left. When the gun moved away from Smith's chest, Smith stepped immediately to the side, taking himself farther out of the line of fire. And as he moved, he reached out with his right hand and then his left and grabbed the gun wrist of the man in the white shirt. A shot rang out, and all assembled, Morley included, hit the dirt as Smith forced the gun skyward. There was a cracking sound and a shriek of pain, and when the pickers pulled their faces out of the dust to see what had happened, Smith was holding the gun in his left hand, and the man in the white shirt was on his knees with his arm twisted behind his back, his face red and contorted in agony.

"Where's the money?" Smith asked him, his voice strong but no louder than he would use in normal conversation.

"Let go, you stinking bastard," the man in the white shirt replied, his words coming out in grunts. "You're a dead man. You just ain't been killed yet."

"I ain't feeling so dead just at the moment," Smith said. He thrust the pistol into a back pocket of his coveralls.

"I'm going to kill you," the man in the white shirt promised.

"Not just at the moment," Smith said. He squeezed on the broken wrist of the man in the white shirt and eased his arm an inch higher up his back until he yelped. "Now where is the money?" Smith demanded.

"Give him the goddamn money, Morley," the man in the white shirt ordered. "Give him the money, you idiot, before he tears my arm off."

Morley stuck the pencil he'd been chewing on behind his ear, went over to the Chevy sedan, opened the passenger-side door and fetched a metal lock box off the front seat. He brought it back to the spot where Smith still held the man in the white shirt by the arm. The boss man was bent over in the dirt, his head down. Beads of sweat dripped off his brow into his hat, which had fallen off directly under him. "Here it is," Morley said.

The man in the white shirt winced as he looked up and quickly lowered his head again. "Give it to him, you stupid idiot," he ordered.

Morley held the cash box out toward Smith. "All I want is what's coming to me," Smith said. "I want pay for my exact pick without no deduct penalty."

Morley set the box down in front of the man in the white shirt, stood up, took the pencil from behind his ear and began scratching calculations onto his ledger. "One dollar, thirty-eight cents," he announced.

"Lotta sweat for so little, ain't it," Smith said, smiling. He looked to the crowd of somber people in a circle around him, many of whom nodded in agreement.

"Give him two dollars," the man in the white shirt ordered, bringing his head up for the briefest second. "Goddammit, give him five dollars. Just give him."

"One dollar thirty-eight cents," Smith said. "Ain't near enough, but it's what I agreed to." Morley counted out the change, wrapped it in the bill and handed it to Smith who took it and put it in the front pocket of his coveralls. "Now pay the rest of them," Smith told Morley. "No deducts for any of them either."

"What's that to you," the man in the white shirt snarled. "You think you're Robin Hood now?"

Smith chuckled at that. "If I was Robin Hood, I would just divide out all this money among everybody here. That would be robbing. But I ain't doing that. I'm just keeping you from robbing us. I'm just doing what's fair. So I guess I'm Fair Doin Hood." Smith laughed again at his own joke.

"I should have shot you," the man in the white shirt said. "If I could still get away with using niggers in these times, I wouldn't have to put up with the likes of you. And I wouldn't have given a nigger no five count, you can bet on that."

"Another time I'm glad I ain't a nigger," Smith said and laughed again. He looked over at Morley, who stood transfixed in front of him. "Let's go man," Smith said. "We got to get these people home before midnight. Get that last cotton weighed and dumped and pay these folks."

"You do nothing of the sort," the man in the white shirt said to Morley. "These other pickers are none of his affair. You pay them what's in the ledger and not one red cent more."

Smith jerked his arm ever so slightly and the man in the white shirt yelped. "No, for the time being Boss Man, you ain't in the position to give no orders. Morley takes notice that I've got the gun, so that don't give him no leeway but to do what I say."

Morley went back to the scale, weighed out the last sack and sat on the front bumper of the crew truck. With the cash box perched on the bumper beside him, he scratched out his calculations, then counted out the day's pay for each family. The Caldwells had earned $7.23.

Smith continued to hold the boss man bent over in the dirt. He eased the tension on the man's arm but kept a firm grip on his wrist, ready to reassert control should if he had to. When Morley finished, he closed the cash box, stood up and looked over at Smith, waiting for his next set of instructions.

"How much you got left in there?" Smith asked, indicating the cash box with his chin.

"Money?" Morley asked, and then answered his own question. "We still got some thirty dollars or thereabouts. You gonna take it?"

"Naw, I ain't gonna take it," Smith said. "You go put it back in the boss man's car. And everybody take note that we coulda taken his money but we didn't." Morley did as he was told. Smith tapped the man in the white shirt on the head. "You got that, Boss Man?" When he got no answer he tapped a little harder and repeated, "Say, you got that, Boss Man?"

"Yeah, yeah," the man in the white shirt said.

"And now everybody take note," Smith said, "that the boss man has acknowledged we didn't take anything we hadn't a right to." Morley returned from the Chevy sedan and Smith said, "Okay, let's everybody load up the crew truck so we can get on home." When the pick crew was packed into the back of the truck and Morley had gotten behind the wheel, Smith said to the man in the white shirt, "Now I'm about to let you go. I hope you got sense enough not to struggle any. I ain't looking to hurt you any more than I already have."

The man in the white shirt made no response, which Smith took as a sign of cooperation. Smith eased off his grip and stepped quickly back from the man who fell forward, then squirmed to a sitting position. Smith backed toward the truck, keeping a wary eye on the man in the white shirt all the while. Holding his injured wrist, the boss man followed Smith's movements without saying anything. Rigid, he stared at Smith with an icy hatred as Smith hauled himself up into the truck.

"I ain't sorry I won't be coming back here tomorrow," Smith said to the man in the white shirt. "I am sorry about hurting your arm. I wish it wasn't, but I think it may be broke." The boss man saw that Smith was no longer holding the gun, perhaps hadn't been holding it for some time. He saw that Smith stood watching him with his back to a truck-load of pickers, and not one of them tried to seize Smith and hold him to account for what he had done.

Smith yelled at Morley to get rolling toward home. Morley turned the key, stomped on the ignition button, eased the truck into gear and pulled away. Smith watched the man in the white shirt, whose head dropped down to his chest. As the truck leapt forward, its tires ground and sent a cloud of dust wafting over the man in the white shirt, who did not even wave a hand in front of his face in protest of this last indignity.

Nobody said a word as the truck rolled along in the gathering twilight. When the truck crossed the Highway 1 bridge over Black Creek, Smith reached into his back pocket for the snub-nosed pistol and flung it in a high arc over the bridge rail. It glinted in the dying light as it fell down into the water. Shortly later, on a dark stretch of road somewhere north of New Peterstown Road, Smith called out to Morley to stop the truck. Some of the pickers had already been dropped off by then, but more than half were still aboard, including the Caldwells. When the truck stopped, Smith pointed at Pruitt and Jeff and asked them to get out. Jeff immediately jumped down from the truck, but Pruitt objected, "I ain't got no reason to get down out of here. Why should I?"

"Only 'cause I asked you to," Smith said.

Pruitt hesitated as all eyes watched to see what he was going to do. Finally, he climbed down, and Smith led Pruitt and Jeff a few steps away out of earshot of the others.

Looking at Jeff, Smith said, "I want you to know I only stood up to that man back there because you did first. If you hadn't, I wouldn't have either. You believed in your pick, so I believed in mine. You remember that."

Then Smith said to Pruitt, "I reckon the fact that you slapped this boy for standing up was what saved me back there. Maybe saved my life. So I got to be grateful to you. But you oughtn't be hitting on this boy. Not long from now you *won't* be hitting on him 'cause he can whip you. You want to be stopping before that. You want to make that lick you give him this evening the last one. You remember that."

Pruitt didn't respond, and Smith didn't press him to. He put his hands on the backs of each of their necks, walked with them to the truck and told them to get back in. When they were aboard, he slapped the truck bumper and yelled to Morley to take on off.

As the truck crunched through the gravel and eased back onto the blacktop, Jeff kept his eyes on Smith. The sun was down and darkness was rising fast out of the languid land. As they were losing sight of each other in the gathering dusk, Smith took off his pith helmet and waved it high over his head. Not sure if he could be seen, Jeff took off his own cap and waved back.

Aside from church, the only social gathering spot in New Peterstown was Rufus Caine's Grocery and Feeds, the general store. After buying their supplies, area wives lingered to talk while the younger children played games like kick-the-can in the dirt parking lot and the older children engaged in adolescent boasting and flirting with the opposite sex.

The summer the Caldwells picked cotton, the trip to the store on Sunday afternoons was a special treat because they had money to spend. Osby bought such staples as flour, lard and sugar, but her children spent their earnings on gum, sweets and soft drinks. Wayne liked candied apples; James preferred Baby Ruth candy bars; Monroe and Franklin bought a thick twist of black licorice for each day of the week.

Jeff contented himself with lemon gum drops, five for a penny, and otherwise mostly saved his money. The only other extravagance he allowed himself was a bottle of orange soda, which he didn't particularly care for but which he knew was the favorite of Mary Frances Branson. Jeff had developed a crush on brown-haired, blue-eyed Mary Frances, and he liked to curry her favor by offering to share his drink with her. On those Sundays when Mary Frances was at the store, he would pluck his soft drink from the galvanized wash tub filled with ice and water and toss his nickel into the cash basket. Then he would saunter out onto the porch as if his every move were not calculated. He would lean up against the porch rail on whichever side of the front steps Mary Frances had chosen to sit that day, take a swallow of the sweet orange drink and casually, as if he'd just thought of it, look over at Mary Frances and offer her a swallow, too. When she accepted, which she always did, he'd wipe the mouth of the bottle with his shirt tail and pass the drink to her. And she'd wipe the mouth of the bottle again on the hem of her dress before taking a sip. He wondered if she noticed that he never wiped the bottle when she passed it back to him.

Aside from the lemon drops and orange drink, Jeff saved his money assiduously. He turned his collection of pennies and nickels into dimes and quarters and eventually into dollar bills, all of which he kept rolled in a sock and hidden in a hole on the underside of his mattress. He did all this because he had a plan. When school started, and his work in the cotton fields had ended, he wanted to take Mary Frances Branson to a Saturday-night movie in Alexandria, buy her some popcorn and a Coca-Cola and afterwards buy her a malt at the Rexall.

Jeff fantasized about every detail of his date. Since he wasn't old enough yet to drive legally, he would have to persuade Wayne to double-date with him. It would be crowded, the four of them in the cab together. But that was part of Jeff's plan, too. Mary Frances would have to ride in his lap, his arms wrapped securely around her waist so the jouncing of the truck over the rutted gravel road would not send her flying against the window or into the dash. Thus existed the exquisite possibility that an awaiting pothole would bounce her so violently that his hands, unavoidably and guiltlessly, would slide across her breasts. In pursuit of this plan, Jeff judiciously sought rapprochement with his older brother and tried to avoid their usual run-ins.

Meanwhile, Wayne had a plan of his own. He began to fine-tune it when he located Jeff's hiding place and discovered that Jeff had amassed an astonishing treasure of more than three dollars. Later, when Jeff broached the subject of a double date, Wayne agreed immediately and without his usual expression of surly suspicion. Instead, Wayne smiled lewdly and punched Jeff lightly on the arm. "I know what you're looking forward to, little brother. Four of us together in the cab, you get to squirm all the way to Alec with Mary

Frances Branson on your lap. I wouldn't mind that treat myself. Specially if she don't wear panties 'cause it's too hot. Maybe I'll just drive down the road apiece and then let you get behind the wheel once we're out of sight of the house."

"I'm the one taking Mary Frances Branson, you understand," Jeff said, alarmed. "You gotta take somebody else. That's what a double date means. Two girls. One for each of us."

"You mean the two of us wouldn't be doubling up on Mary Frances?" Wayne said.

"No!" Jeff replied.

Wayne laughed out loud and punched Jeff again, still not hard. "You are so easy to rile. I'll take Becky Price. We'll have ourselves a good old time."

The whole plan seemed to be falling into place so effortlessly that Jeff didn't realize for a day or so after school began that he hadn't actually asked Mary Frances for a date. When he finally did so at afternoon recess during the second week of school, Mary Frances's reaction was so blasé that Jeff found it unsettling. "Oh, sure," she said without additional comment. Jeff stated the exact time two Saturday nights later, and Mary Frances responded, "That's fine." She didn't ask what movie he wanted to take her to or any other details, and in the absence of any stated interest on her part, Jeff quickly broke away from her and subsequently decided to avoid her at school until after they'd gone out.

On the Friday eight days before Jeff's date with Mary Frances, after school and after all the Caldwell boys had finished their chores, Jeff was sitting on the back porch steps reading a library copy of *Oliver Twist* when Wayne came to sit beside him. The sky was yellow and fading, and a blue-black line of thunderheads could be seen thumb-smudged on the horizon over the trees to the southwest. Jeff was still in work clothes, overalls and a T-shirt. He had removed his shoes and scratched absently at the tops of his feet as he read. Wayne was barefooted, too, and shirtless as well; his jeans were buttoned but he hadn't buckled his belt. He had just come out from the washing shed where he'd cleaned up after working under Osby's direction in her vegetable garden. He mopped at himself with a towel as he sat down next to his brother.

"You planning on just playing bookworm all night?" Wayne asked Jeff.

Jeff shrugged and kept on reading. He was practically immune to Wayne's relentless verbal harassment. So Wayne draped his towel over Jeff's book.

"Stop that, dang it," Jeff said.

"I want to ask you something," Wayne said.

"What?" Jeff replied, handing the towel back to Wayne.

"Want to go out riding with us tonight?" Wayne said. "Bobby's got his daddy's truck. Me and Johnny are going with him over to Dry Prong. Their high school's got a sock hop in the gym this evening."

"I don't know," Jeff said. He was surprised to be included on such an outing and did not really want to go. Bobby and Johnny were Wayne's friends, not Jeff's. Johnny Davis was crazy as far as Jeff was concerned. And Bobby Sawyer would let Johnny egg him on into just about anything. The last thing Jeff wanted to do was have to break up some scrape Bobby and Johnny might get into with the Dry Prong boys. But he didn't want to say no straight out because he didn't want to queer his arrangement with Wayne for the next weekend. So he said, "I don't know anybody at Dry Prong."

"Aw, come on," Wayne implored. "Who's it gonna hurt. Maybe we'll just ride around awhile. But if we end up over at Dry Prong, maybe you'll meet you a girl you like even better than Mary Frances Branson."

Such a notion was preposterous, but Jeff finally agreed to go with them. "You better go on and wash up then," Wayne said. "Bobby will be by here in twenty minutes."

Every Saturday night Osby insisted that each of the Caldwells take a full hot bath in the galvanized tub in which she scrubbed the family laundry against a metal washboard. Saturday baths involved taking the wash tub into the kitchen where water was heated in a huge iron kettle on the stove. Bathing took almost the entire evening as the tub had to be emptied and refilled after the first three boys soaked and scrubbed. The women always bathed after the men, and when Vivien was still at home, Osby always let her go first.

On the days other than Saturday, washing was done in the shed and didn't involve either a bath or hot water. This kind of washing was practiced every other day in the warmer months, less often in winter. Following his usual routine, Jeff undressed and dipped a tin pail into the wash tub. He set the pail on a warped wooden table where a bar of soap lay still tacky from being used by Wayne. Jeff studied the soap suspiciously, always concerned that Wayne might have done something foul with it which Wayne would later reveal for the purposes of humiliating Jeff. Jeff wet his hands in the pail and rubbed the soap briskly into a lather. Holding the soap in one hand and grasping the pail with the other, he stepped over to the hole in the middle of the floor that allowed the water to drain to the ground below. He rinsed both his hands and the soap bar itself, then soaped up the communal wash cloth, rubbed it vigorously against itself and rinsed it over the drain. Only then, with what he considered a clean bar of soap and a clean cloth, did he begin to wash himself, lathering with his hands and using the wet cloth to wipe away the soap. Afterwards, he dressed in clean clothes and went to wait with Wayne on the front porch.

Johnny was already in the truck when Bobby arrived, and Wayne immediately climbed into the cab, thumbing Jeff into the gritty bed in the back. Jeff was used to this common snub and barely took notice. It would have been crowded and uncomfortable had he tried to squeeze into the cab, and he wouldn't have had anything to say if either Johnny or Wayne rode with him in the back. So he was content to ride along with only his thoughts for company. The moon was just coming up, a huge orange disk that shone through the trees. The wind was cool and pleasant whipping through his wet hair, and life seemed delectably worthwhile as Jeff mused about bouncing along this same route a week hence with Mary Frances Branson perched on his lap. The moon would not be so large that night, he knew. But it would be exquisitely lovely; he was sure of it.

At State Highway 1, Bobby turned north. Jeff disliked this stretch of highway with its cutover land on either side. Stripped of its trees, the land absorbed more heat, and even though Bobby picked up speed on the pavement, Jeff could feel the temperature ratchet upwards, draining some of the pleasantness out of the night. When they reached the parish road into Dry Prong, Bobby passed it by; Jeff was thoroughly perplexed when Bobby eventually turned east off the highway rather than west. As the truck rattled out onto still another local gravel road, Jeff hammered on the rear window of the cab and yelled out, "Where we going?" The boys inside responded only with laughter, and Jeff pounded on the window and yelled out a second time, "I said where we going?"

Wayne stuck his head out the window and yelled back, "You'll find out when we get there, won't you?"

Jeff shook his head in resignation and twisted around to sit again with his back against the cab, his right arm thrown up across the rail to steady himself as the truck bounced along. He knew he should have stayed at home. He might have finished his book. He made no more inquiries, denying Wayne and the others the pleasure of refusing to tell him what they were up to. He watched the central Louisiana landscape slide by on either side of the truck. The night was bright, and as they passed out of the ugly expanse of cutover, he could make out the star-shaped leaves of a row of sweet gums growing in the sluicy area just past the roadside ditch.

After fifteen minutes of riding through an area of scrub pine growing back from an earlier cut, Bobby turned onto a rutted drive that had never been graded. The truck slowed to less than ten miles per hour as the vegetation canopied over this dark lane. Through the night, carried on a breeze smelling of damp earth, night-blooming jasmine and muscadine, Jeff could suddenly hear the sound of music, the tinkling of piano keys and the low wailing notes of a saxophone. He stood up in the back of the truck to look over the top of the cab, almost losing his balance as a wheel slammed through a washout hole. "Where in the devil are we?" Jeff called out.

Wayne stuck his head out the window and said, "Sit down and shut up, or we're gonna make you get out and wait here for us in the dark until we get back."

Jeff spread his legs wide for balance and continued to peer over the top of the cab, which Bobby steered left and right along the twisting, downhill track. Jeff squinted in a vain effort to see beyond the reach of the truck's headlights whose reflection off leaves and branches had the odd effect of making the truck seem enveloped in a closed green cave of vegetation. Jeff could smell slow-moving water; they were coming down to a bayou somewhere, or a lake perhaps. The music grew louder, and now Jeff could hear the murmur of voices.

Finally, the truck eased into a clearing, and its lights flashed across a building awash in the glow of a hundred kerosene lamps. A dozen vehicles of various kinds—a lumber truck, a milk truck, and a hearse, along with several pick-ups and black sedans—were parked haphazardly in front of an unpainted two-story wood building erected on pilings out over the water of a bayou. Steps from the front porch came down on land. At the foot of the steps someone had spread fresh wood shavings over a bed of gravel.

"What is this place?" Jeff asked as he climbed out of the bed and the other boys got out of the cab.

"Come on and find out," Bobby said, and they all started for the building. As they drew closer, Jeff could see in the flickering light people standing on the porch in small groups, mostly couples, some with their arms around one another. Inside, the music started up again, fast music with a hard beat, and some of the couples moved inside. It wasn't until Jeff started up the steps that he realized everybody on the porch was black. Some of the people were dressed like most every Negro he had ever seen, the men in loose cotton shirts and coveralls and the women in shapeless, loose-weave shifts. But many of them were dressed like no Negro he had ever seen, not even those prosperous, black-suited Negro preachers and funeral directors he had seen a time or two in Alexandria. Here many of the men wore shiny, striped suits and bright shirts with colorful ties. Most of the women wore clingy, satin dresses with plunging necklines. This was a place from outside Louisiana, from outside any world that Jeff had ever encountered.

Perhaps it was just the loud music that drowned out the sound, but Jeff felt as if all conversation had stopped and all eyes were following the four white boys. Tobacco smoke hung heavy in the air, and Jeff felt disoriented. No one had said a word to them, but Jeff felt distinctly alien. As the boys reached the level of the porch, a full-figured, red-haired black woman of forty or so came out from inside on the arm of a tall, thin black man wearing a wide-brimmed hat and smoking a cigarette in a long white holder. The woman wore a red lace dress with a flared bottom, trimmed in black satin, black, ribbed nylons and open-toed shoes with very high heels. On her head she had a small black hat, like a skull cap with four points. Its veil reached down toward the arch of her eyebrows, which were plucked to the width of a pencil lead.

"Oh, honey, now ain't that the truth," Jeff heard her say, and she laughed and patted her companion's arm. Then she noticed the four white boys and said to the man at her side after sizing them up, "Now looky what we got here." None of the boys made a response, and the lady in the red dress stepped over to them, leaving the thin man standing in the doorway. "You boys know where you are, now do you?" she asked, walking down the line of them, looking each one frankly in the face. Jeff had never known a black person to relate to a white person, even a white child, with such brazenness. Unable to meet her gaze, he looked down at his shoes.

"Red Ruby's," Johnny Davis said, and the lady in the red dress turned her eyes to him.

"Why, I do believe some people use that name," she said, licking her lips and smiling.

"If this is Red Ruby's," Bobby Sawyer said, "then I guess we come to the right place."

"Oh, have you now, honey?" she said.

"I guess we have," Bobby replied.

"And what would be bringing you out to this dark place?" the lady in the red dress asked, and the man in the doorway behind her snickered and turned to say something to someone behind him.

Almost immediately, he was joined by another Negro man, also dressed in a fancy suit. Both men stared at the line-up of white boys with unconcealed amusement.

"What would be bringing you white boys out in this black night?" the lady in red asked, and both the men in the doorway guffawed. Not one of the boys had any idea what they were laughing about.

"We heard we could get some action here," Wayne said, and Jeff heard the slight quaver in his voice.

The lady in the red dress turned on her heel and moved directly in front of Wayne, who stood at the end of the line. She cocked her weight onto one leg and rested her hand on her hip, lifting her opposite leg to brush against Wayne's ankle with her toes. "Now are you the leader of these boys?" she asked Wayne. "Are you the one they followed into this inky holler?"

"I guess," Wayne said. "It was my idea. But they all wanted to come."

Not me, Jeff thought. He had no idea what was going on.

"So you want some *ac*tion for all these boys," she said, emphasizing the first syllable of action. "Is that what you want, leader man?"

"I guess," Wayne said. "Yes."

The lady in the red dress turned again and walked down to where Jeff was standing. "Even for this baby?" she said to Wayne. "Even for this baby who probably ain't even got any hair…" She reached out and rubbed Jeff's face along his jaw line. "…on his chin?" The men behind her laughed loudly again.

"I'm fourteen," Jeff said, somewhat indignantly. "I shave sometimes. Over my lip."

"I'm sure you do, honey," the lady in red said, continuing to caress Jeff's face. Then she turned away and walked back to Wayne. "Action ain't free, leader man; I'm sure you understand that."

"I got money," Wayne said.

"Good," the lady in red said. "And what about your fellas and my baby boy? Do they have money, too. For their *ac*tion?"

"I got money for all of us," Wayne said.

"Why, you all want to follow me then," the lady in red said, smiling broadly. She turned and moved toward the doorway, the boys falling in behind her single file. Jeff brought up the rear, perplexed about what was going on. He suspected Wayne was going to buy moonshine, and if so, Wayne had another think coming if he thought Jeff was going to drink any of it.

As the lady in red swept through the doorway, she said to the two men in the doorway, "These fine young white boys have come to Red Ruby's for some *ac*tion." The two black men seemed to think that was the funniest thing she had said all night.

The downstairs room at Red Ruby's was a dark sea of ripe humanity. The room was thick with cigarette smoke under which hung a smell of perfume and body odor and another smoky smell, sweet and green, that Jeff could not identify. It was very warm. The top-hinged shutters to all the windows were propped open with wooden slats, but little of the heavy outside air stirred inside. Showers of yellow light fell from kerosene lamps standing on every window ledge and splashed across the wooden tables set up around the edge of the room. Pools of red shimmered about the flickering candle in the center of each table and illuminated the litter of beer and liquor bottles and overflowing ashtrays. In the far corner of the room, four musicians, a pianist, a bass player, a drummer and a saxophonist, played their narcotic music as if in a trance.

The lady in red led them through a gyrating throng of dancers and up a staircase to the second floor. As they walked down a hall, the lady in red closed a door through which Jeff could hear a buzz of voices, men and women together. At the end of the hall, the lady in red showed them into a room with two sofas facing each other and two hard-backed chairs closing off the square. Here she told them to wait. She directed that Bobby, Johnny and Jeff sit down on one of the sofas and that Wayne accompany her back into the hall. Jeff could hear them talking in the hall, but he could not hear what they were saying. A few minutes later, Wayne returned and sat with the others.

"Y'all ever gonna tell me what the devil's going on?" Jeff inquired.

Bobby and Johnny snickered.

Wayne said, "You ain't gonna have to wait no time at all to find out, little brother. So just hold your horses."

"Somebody else is about to hold his horse," Bobby said and laughed.

"If he's got himself a horse, that is," Johnny replied and socked Bobby in the arm.

Bobby winced and said, "Ow, Johnny, that hurt." He rubbed the spot where he'd been punched.

"Oh, don't be such a baby," Johnny responded, scowling, "or we won't let you have none neither. Will we, Wayne?"

"Shut up, the both of you," Wayne said.

The lady in red opened the door and came back in. Trailing behind her were four young Negro women. All were older than the four white boys, but none was older than her early twenties; the two youngest appeared to be seventeen or eighteen. Each was dressed in a long, white cotton smock that hung just below her knees. The lady in red lined them up opposite the boys.

"Okay, girls," the lady in red ordered. "Show them what you got."

The girls lifted their smocks up around their necks. Underneath they were completely naked. Jeff was offended in a way. It was so indecent making the girls display themselves like this. But he couldn't take his eyes away. He looked at each of the girls in turn, at their breasts and at the tufts of black hair between their legs. Jeff knew exactly what was happening now. He had heard Wayne and the other boys talk about whorehouses, and he'd even imagined going to one, although never to one with Negro girls. But even when he'd imagined it, he'd never imagined this. He thought of just him and the whore in a room all alone. And the two of them getting undressed and her not minding that he touched her. His fantasies about visiting a whorehouse had always had a core element of romance. He would be nice, and she would find him special. But this was so raw he felt ashamed even as he became utterly aroused. He wondered if the girls could see that his pecker was standing up like a twenty-year-old pine.

"Turn around, girls," the lady in red ordered. "In case one of these boys is a rear-end man." She laughed. "Just remember, reverse action costs twice as much."

Jeff had no idea what she was talking about. The girls dropped their hands to gather the backs of the smocks and then turned around to face away from the boys.

After a moment, the lady in red said, "Okay, y'all can turn around again. But keep your dresses up until you're chosen."

The girls faced forward, and Wayne said, "I'll take the yellow one."

He pointed out the lightest skinned of the four women. Her hair was a reddish brown, and she had freckles all over her body. When Wayne pointed to her she looked briefly at the lady in red who nodded slightly and then she let her smock drop.

"I want the one with those big titties," Johnny said. She was the tallest and had the second darkest skin, and Jeff was glad Johnny picked her because Jeff wasn't really attracted to her thick-waisted, heavy-breasted body. She looked almost bored by the proceedings and dropped her dress immediately when Johnny pointed to her.

"Your turn now, Bobby," Wayne said.

"I don't know," Bobby said.

"Well ain't but two left," Johnny said. "Pick one of 'em and let's get on with it."

The two girls left were barely older than the boys. Both were slightly built. One had brown skin and medium-size breasts. Jeff liked her looks. She kept her eyes on the floor, and Jeff liked that about her. His heart went out to her. The other girl had the prettier face of the two, Jeff thought, and the pigtails into which she had braided her dark hair made her seem younger than she presumably was. But she hadn't any breasts at all to speak of, just a little puffiness on either side of her chest and two long puckerings of nipple. Her skin was so dark it was almost blue. She didn't meet anyone's gaze either, but she kept her eyes lifted and stared straight ahead of herself, and Jeff found himself somewhat intimidated by the fire in her eyes.

"You don't pick one right this second," Wayne said, "I ain't gonna pay for it."

"Okay," Bobby said. "I'll take that one." He pointed at the dark-skinned girl. Johnny snickered for some reason, and Bobby instantly said, "No, no, I guess I'll take that one," pointing out the other girl.

"Jeesum Petes," Wayne said.

"Well, I don't know which one to pick," Bobby said to Wayne. "You pick one for me."

"I don't give a dern which one you pick, Bobby. I ain't gonna do it to her; you are."

Bobby finally, uncertainly and unhappily, settled on the lighter-skinned girl, and the woman in red showed them to separate rooms. "You boys got yourselves thirty minutes of *action*," she said, laughing. "Not that it should take any of you nearly that long."

The room Jeff entered with the dark-skinned girl was tiny and bare, painted white to capture and hold the light. There was a lamp on the window ledge that held out the night and lit the room in flickering gold rings. Underneath the window was a hard-backed wooden chair and next to that an iron single bed with open springs and a thin cotton mattress. There was no top sheet, and the bottom sheet was stained with gray and faintly yellowish splotches. On the chair, a tin bowl full of water sat next to a bar of soap and a folded yellow hand towel. There was nothing else in the room.

"What's your name?" Jeff asked the dark-skinned girl. With her smock down and her pigtails bouncing against her neck she looked about twelve.

"Leila," she said. She sat at the head of the bed with her legs next to the chair.

"I'm Jeff." He sat at the foot of the bed. He did not know how to begin and wasn't sure he really wanted to. His erection had disappeared.

"I got to wash you," Leila said. "That's Miss Ruby's first rule."

"You don't have to," Jeff responded. "I already washed before I left home."

"I still got to wash you," Leila said. "Like I said, it's Miss Ruby's first rule."

"You don't even have a towel," he said. "That yellow thing there isn't barely bigger than a wash rag. And there isn't near enough water in that little bowl."

"I ain't got to wash nothing but your peter," Leila said. "But I got to wash that or we can't do nothing else." Jeff was astonished but said nothing. "Some mens likes the washing part."

"Well, what do you want me to do?" Jeff said. She still hadn't looked at him. "You know. About the washing."

"Well, you can just unbutton and poke it out if you want," Leila said.

"I guess I can wash it myself," Jeff said. "Maybe I ought to just do that."

"I don't know," Leila said. "I'm supposed to. Miss Ruby showed us the right way and all." Jeff was thoroughly uncomfortable, but he stood up and started to unbutton his fly. "You can take your britches all the way off, if you want," Leila said. "Some mens does that." Jeff stopped unbuttoning himself and looked at the girl. She was staring at the wall across from the bed. "I likes it better if you takes your britches all the way off."

Jeff continued to stare at her, but she refused to meet his gaze. "Why's that?" he asked, not sure he wanted to pull his pants off.

"I just likes it better," Leila said. "You can leave your drawers on if you want."

"What difference does it make?" Jeff said. Leila didn't answer. "I'll do it however you want, I guess, but I don't know what difference it makes." He sat back on the bed and started unlacing his shoes.

"If you just poke it out your pants," Leila said finally, "then I get hurt up some by the buttons." Jeff finished untying his shoes and took off his pants. "Those buttons feels mighty hard, when the mens gets to pounding."

"I won't hurt you," Jeff said.

"Yeah," Leila said.

"I promise," Jeff said. "If I start hurting you, you just tell me, and I'll stop."

"Yeah," Leila said. Jeff laid his pants across the bed's iron foot rail and sat back down. He was wearing just undershorts, his T-shirt and a dingy pair of white cotton socks. "Well," Leila said, "I guess you better come on. Miss Ruby don't like it taking longer than it should."

"We don't have to, I guess," Jeff said, surprising himself because, in fact, he did want to.

Finally, Leila looked at him, her face immobile but her eyes wide pools of black fire. "What you mean, you don't want to do it now? I ain't done nuthin. I just told you to come and let's get started. That's all."

"I just thought maybe you didn't want to," Jeff said. "If it hurts you sometimes and all."

"I didn't say it hurt. Don't you go telling Miss Ruby I said that."

"Don't get riled up," Jeff said. "I'm not gonna tell Miss Ruby anything."

"I'm not riled up," Leila said. "Don't be saying *that* neither." Her eyes were glistening now, and she turned her face away from him back toward the wall across from the bed. "Now just come on down here and poke your thing out so I can wash it and we can get started."

Jeff got up and walked to the head of the bed. He stood in front of her and pulled himself through the fly in his boxers, and she washed him with the bar of soap, rinsed him with wet hands and then used the little towel to pat him dry. He was hard by the time she finished. Then she pulled her smock over her tiny breasts and up under her arms and lay down on her back in the middle of the bed. Jeff got on his knees between her legs, and she took him in her hand and guided him inside her. He looked into her face, but though her eyes were open, her gaze would not interlock with his. And so he began, rocking himself in and out of her. And she lay still beneath him, save once to open her legs wider. And he was determined to remain mindful of her concern about pounding, and he tried to go slow, but then he closed his eyes and lost himself. And he shuddered uncontrollably and disappeared into a vast blackness.

When Jeff opened his eyes, Leila was staring at him with hot black eyes that were no longer wet. He lowered his face to hers, meaning to kiss her lips, but she turned her head away and offered only her jaw which bulged and relaxed, bulged and relaxed as if she was chewing something. Jeff eased out of this waif-like Negro girl and fixed himself back in his drawers. He sat back on the end of the bed, saying nothing, and she lay as he had lain upon her, her head still turned to the side staring at the wall, immobile except for the pulsing bulge of muscle in her jaw.

After a few minutes, there was a knock on the door, and Jeff could hear Miss Ruby's voice from the hall. "Time's up in there, baby." And then she laughed.

Jeff pulled his pants back on and laced up his shoes. He looked one last time at Leila, who still lay unmoving on the bed. He wanted to say something to her, but he had no words. So he rose and left the room and closed the door gently behind him as if he were leaving her sleeping and taking care not to disturb her. He would carry her burning black eyes with him for the rest of his life.

On the way home, Jeff rode again in the back of the truck, the three older boys up front. The moon was high in the sky now, and a canopy of stars had popped out, dimming only where the moon's glow washed away the competing twinkles of light. As Jeff stared at the arcing night sky, the truck seemed to come to a standstill, and all the motion of the world concentrated into diaphanous wisps of cloud that glided across the silver lunar disk like sailboats bound for the edge of the earth on an endless black sea. He could hear Bobby and Johnny and Wayne laughing inside the cab, but he couldn't hear what they were saying and didn't care. Just after they turned off of State Highway 1 onto New Peterstown Road, Bobby steered the truck to the side of the road, pulled up with his right front wheel in the weeds, and stopped, leaving the motor running and the lights on.

"Piss stop!" Johnny announced. All three of the older boys piled out and stood side by side in the glare of the headlights, ghostly figures bathed in a swirling mist of illuminated dust. They stood together and urinated into the cattails and sawgrass that grew in the roadside ditch.

"You better get down here and drain your water snake," Wayne yelled to Jeff over his shoulder. "Something may have crawled off that black bitch and up your pee hole."

Bobby laughed wildly at this remark, and Johnny threw back his head and howled like a wolf. The arc of his urine stream raised in the glare of the headlights and Johnny yelled out, "I'm pissing so hard, I'm gonna pee out the moon," and then he howled like a wolf again.

When Bobby turned the truck off New Peterstown Road at the Caldwells', he raced down through the swale and gunned the engine as he climbed back up toward the house, then slammed on the brakes and whipped the wheel to raise a clatter of gravel as he sent the old pickup into a sideways slide just outside the front gate.

"Yahoo!" Johnny yelled.

As Jeff climbed out of the truck bed, Johnny said, "Hey, Jeff, you know what they say?" Jeff stopped and turned to the cab where Johnny poked his head out the window, crossed his eyes, stuck out his tongue and panted like a dog. "Take heed, little brother. 'Cause once you go black, you cain't never go back." Johnny looked around at Bobby and then back at Jeff before adding, "And so that means your sorry little pecker won't never plow no white girl's furrow."

Bobby cackled with laughter and Johnny joined in, pounding on the rooftop with the flat of his hand in appreciation of his own wit.

"Know what else they say, Jeffie, my man?" Johnny asked.

Jeff made no reply.

"They say, Yahoooooooo!"

After his Saturday bath a week later, while Wayne was bathing, Jeff slid under his bed and pulled out the sock in which he kept his money. But when he dumped it out, he found not dollar bills and coins, but folded scraps of notebook paper and a fistful of metal washers. He wasn't shocked. He wasn't even as angry as he would have suspected, and the actions he took next were more those of icy resolve than those of hot reaction.

Once during the week, Wayne had smirked and said to Jeff that they ought to forget about Becky Price and Mary Frances Branson and just go back to Red Ruby's. "Probably wouldn't cost us a dime more," Wayne said, "and we'd stand a damn straight better chance of getting our peters wet."

But otherwise, Wayne had kept up the pretense that they were double-dating that night. Faced with what was now so obvious, Jeff walked into the kitchen where Wayne was sitting in the metal tub with his soapy knees up around his chest. Jeff was carrying his sock in his hand, swinging it back and forth like a clock pendulum, propelled by the weight of the washers in the toe. When Wayne saw Jeff come bursting in through the door off the porch, Wayne leapt to a standing position, sloshing water onto the unvarnished pine floor. Monroe and Franklin, who were keeping Wayne supplied with hot water from the kettle simmering on the stove, were waiting at the table in their underwear, and they leapt up too.

Wayne managed to get one foot out of the tub before Jeff swung the sock at him. Thankfully, Jeff missed because he swung with enough force that had he caught Wayne full in the temple, he might have killed him. But in ducking under Jeff's weapon, Wayne lost traction on the wet floor and went careening backwards, banging his face on the edge of the table and dazing himself. Jeff stepped around the tub, put his sock on the table, rolled Wayne flat on his back and kneeled down on Wayne's chest, in the process pinning down Wayne's left arm. Wayne's right eye was already beginning to swell, and Jeff chose it as a target, hammering at it with two quick punches that landed flush and bounced Wayne's head off the floor. And then Jeff heard something come out of Wayne's mouth that Jeff had never heard before.

"Uncle," Wayne said with a thick tongue.

Jeff had already reared back for another punch when he heard his brother's surrender. He stopped himself from swinging, for just an instant letting the tension out of his arm. Then he thought about all his summer's toil in the broiling sun of central Louisiana cotton fields, and he immediately reared back again.

"Uncle," Wayne said, getting the hand that wasn't pinned up in front of his face. "I said, 'uncle,' goddogit."

"You took my money, you piece of hog slop," Jeff said, his fist still raised to strike. "Admit it. You stole my blame money, and you spent it on whores." Wayne kept his hand in front of his face and turned his head to the side. "You admit it, or I'm going to pound your thieving face into jelly and break your hand bones into baby powder."

"All right," Wayne said finally

"All right, what?" Jeff said.

"All right, I admit it," Wayne said. "You can stop waling on me."

"You're lower than cow flop," Jeff said, and he spit in his brother's face. He jerked his hand as if to strike once more, but then he stood up, and the battle was over.

"I done said 'uncle' more than once," Wayne said, wiping the spit from his face. "Don't see you got the right to spit on me, too." Jeff stepped over Wayne and turned toward the door. "Least ways you could help me up. I still got to take my bath." Watching his brother walk away, Wayne propped himself up on an elbow and called after him, "Least I spent some of the money on you, too. That one you had wasn't free or nothing." Jeff hit the wooden cross slat on the screen door with the heels of his hands and slammed it open so hard it bounced off the exterior wall of the house and almost hit him in the face. "And I sure didn't hear you say you didn't want none. You're all steamed now, but I know dern well you wouldn't give back your part of it."

With exaggerated calm, ignoring his brother, Jeff slowly opened the screen door a second time and stepped out of the kitchen onto the porch. Closing the door behind him, he turned right, walked across the porch back through the living room and out the front. And he kept walking, briskly at first, until he had half run down into the swale and marched back up to New Peterstown Road. He kept on at a hard clip until he was completely out of sight of the house. He slowed then, but he kept on walking until he neared Mary Frances' house. He paused at the foot of the drive off New Peterstown Road up to her parents' unpainted wood frame house, waiting to cool a bit before walking on up the lane. He was damp, and he fetched a handkerchief from his rear pocket to mop away beads of sweat on his forehead and the back of his neck.

Finally, he continued on. The Branson dogs picked up his scent when he was halfway down the drive and came howling out from under the house to bark at him. They ran circles around his feet until he stepped up on the porch and only then retreated to their cool resting places on the packed gray clay under the steps. There were three straight-backed wooden chairs and one tattered sofa on the porch. The main door to the house was open, though a screen door covered the entrance.

Before Jeff could knock, Mrs. Branson called out loudly enough for Jeff to hear, "Mary Frances, your young man is here." Jeff squinted in an attempt to see through the screen, but he could see only a few feet into the living room. "Mary Frances ain't quite ready, I don't think," Mrs. Branson said to Jeff through the screen. "You can set out there or come in here and talk with me a spell, about the good Lord only knows what. Whichever you like."

"I guess I'll just rest out here," Jeff said. "I'm kind of sweaty from walking over."

"Suit yourself, honey," Mrs. Branson said. Then she called deeper into the house again, "Mary Frances, Jeff's outside waiting on you. You hurry up now."

About ten minutes later, Mary Frances came out wearing a long plaid gingham dress that hung below her knees and had a scooped neck trimmed in white lace. Jeff could smell the soap on her. Her shoulder-length, wavy brown hair was still damp from washing. Jeff couldn't help wondering if she'd put on any panties on a warm September night like this. Mary Frances stared into the packed-dirt front yard and squinted down the long drive toward New Peterstown Road. "How'd you come over?" she asked.

"I walked."

"Isn't Wayne bringing your daddy's truck like you said?"

"Well, that's what I came over to tell you," Jeff said.

"Tell me what?"

Jeff suddenly reflected that he might have played his hand a different way, if he'd kept his head and not lit into Wayne. If Wayne had any of Jeff's money left, maybe Jeff could have gotten it back and even gotten Wayne to drive. There wouldn't have been enough money for movies and popcorn and all that. But maybe there was enough for gas and a shared malt or something, and maybe Mary Frances would have been satisfied with just that. But it was too late now.

"I'm afraid we're not going to be able to go to the show tonight after all," Jeff said. He couldn't look at her. "I'm sorry," he added.

Mary Frances moved in front of him and sat on one of the hard wooden chairs perpendicular to the sofa. Jeff sneaked a glance at her. She had her head turned to the right, out toward the gathering night.

"I'm awfully sorry," Jeff said again.

She didn't look in his direction. But after a second, she said, "This is my new dress. Momma sewed it for my birthday. I ain't worn it but once before. To the revival meeting."

"I remember," Jeff said. "It's a nice dress. You sure look pretty in it." Mary Frances didn't respond to his compliment. After a few moments of excruciating silence, Jeff said, "I guess you probably want to know what happened."

"It don't matter," Mary Frances said.

"Well, I want you to know that I really did want to take you. I saved my money from picking cotton this summer, but—"

"I heard you done gone with a nigger whore up on Bleed Bayou," Mary Frances said.

"Why, that's a dern lie," Jeff said immediately.

"Ain't what Johnny Davis says," Mary Frances replied. She was still looking away from him out at the yard. "Not what Bobby Sawyer says neither."

"Wayne stole all my money," Jeff said. "He found the place I hid it, and he stole every last penny. I busted him a shiner for it. You'll see in school on Monday. I saved that money, and he stole it. That's why I can't take you to the show."

"It don't matter," Mary Frances said. "I ain't mad or nothing."

"Well, I'm glad you're not mad," Jeff said. "I sure hate to disappoint you, though."

"Naw," Mary Frances said. "I never really thought you was going to take me to the show anyhow."

chapter eleven

AFTER GETTING NO ANSWER on several occasions, Glenda managed to get a phone call through to Faye Watson two days after her husband Ben shot George Washington Brown and Jeff Caldwell and then turned his gun on himself. As soon as she recognized Glenda's voice, Faye began crying.

"Oh, Glenda," Faye said, sobbing. "I'm so glad you called. I didn't think anybody would. I should have called you. But, well, I don't know. I just couldn't somehow. I just couldn't. It didn't seem like I should."

"It's me who should have gotten through to you at a time like this," Glenda said.

"Oh, no," Faye replied and broke down again, managing to choke out the words, "No you shouldn't. Not with what you and Tommy are going through."

"Do you have somebody to be with you?" Glenda asked. She heard a male voice in the background and then Faye's voice no longer speaking into the phone. "Faye?" Glenda said.

"I'm sorry," Faye said, sounding fragile and distracted as she returned to the phone. "They're here now, and I guess I have to go."

"Who's there?" Glenda said.

"The police. The FBI, I guess. They say I have to go."

"Go where?"

"Back to the motel."

"What motel?"

"You know. On Tulane."

"No, I don't, Faye. A motel on Tulane Avenue? What motel?"

"You know. The Fontainebleau."

"You're staying at the Fontainebleau? Why?"

Glenda could hear Faye talking to someone else again. When she came back on the line, she said, "It means so much to me that you called. The paper this morning said that Jeff's condition hasn't worsened in the last twenty-four hours. Tell him I am praying for him."

Before Glenda could respond, she could hear the male voice again and then Faye answering. "They say I have to go now," Faye said into the phone.

"Are you under arrest?" Glenda asked.

"No," Faye replied. "Why would you say that?"

"The police seem to be telling you what to do. Have they been questioning you?"

"Well, of course, they've been questioning me. I'm Ben Watson's wife."

Three days after his murder, George Washington Brown was remembered in a huge memorial service on the steps of the state capitol in Baton Rouge. More than a million mourners crowded onto the capitol grounds. Countless others tried to get there but were unable to, blocked by a mammoth traffic jam that brought the city to a standstill. Many who had journeyed from all across the country to pay their last respects listened to the service on their car radios. President Johnson spoke, as did Democratic presidential candidate Hubert Humphrey, Massachusetts Senator Edward Kennedy, New Orleans Congressman Hale Boggs, Reverend Andrew Young and Everett Essex. Jeff would have been among the speakers, but he remained in intensive care in New Orleans.

Robert Brown was escorted to the service by two New Orleans policemen who stood with their hands on him the entire time. They did have the decency to unshackle him and let him wear a suit. But he was not allowed to speak, and he was returned to central lockup in New Orleans immediately after the service.

Tommy saw Robert standing with the policemen across the podium from his own position. They nodded at each other, and Tommy tried to indicate with his hands that he intended to visit Robert. But if Robert understood what Tommy was trying to communicate, his face didn't show it.

The service organizers had erected a canopy to shade those on the podium from the blistering August sun, and in their relative comfort, the speakers talked too long. A service that was supposed to last for an hour continued from 1 P.M. until nearly 3:30. The crowd, many in Sunday dress clothes, sweltered in the pitiless heat. But they never broke rank. And when they joined together at the end to sing the benedictory hymn "Just as I am/ Without one plea/ But that thy blood/ Was shed for me," Tommy felt as if a flood might rise up from his heart to drown him.

Afterwards, Dr. Brown's body lay in state in the capitol rotunda, and the crowd passed the coffin four abreast until after midnight. Most of the mourners were black, but there were a great many white faces in the throng. A smaller, predominantly black service was held the next day at the University Baptist Church near Southern University in north Baton Rouge. Dr. Brown was buried the day after that in a memorial park dedicated for him on the campus at Dillard University in New Orleans.

Tommy kept busy assisting with all these events. Glenda, who no longer had a formal staff position in the organization, had no direct responsibilities. Her pregnancy taxed her energy, and she opted not to go up to the University Baptist Church service. Instead, she vowed to get back in touch with Faye Watson, about whom Glenda was increasingly worried.

When no one answered the phone at Faye's apartment, Glenda tried her at the Fontainebleau. But the desk clerk said that no Faye Watson was registered. Frustrated, Glenda hung up, then called back to ask when Faye had checked out. The clerk said she could find no record of a recent guest by that name.

After a meeting to plan the burial ceremony, Tommy told Preacher Martin that he and Glenda could not find Faye and were worried about her.

"I think I better make a phone a call or two," Preacher responded.

"To whom?" Tommy inquired. He was always amazed at Preacher's vast network of contacts. "Who do you know that you can just call up and find out the whereabouts of somebody the FBI might have made off with?"

"Maybe I'll just call J. Edgar himself," Preacher said, exaggerating his North Louisiana accent for maximum cornpone. He plucked the blue Cubs baseball cap off his head and smoothed down a few wisps of hair. "It don't bother me one whit that he's a fairy. It's the fact he's a Nazi that I don't like."

"You really telling me that son-of-a-bitch J. Edgar Hoover is a fairy?"

"I wouldn't say that too loudly if I was you," Preacher warned.

"Why?"

"Place might be bugged."

"I'm not the one who said J. Edgar Hoover was a fairy."

"Oh no? Sounds to me like exactly what you just said."

"How can you say something that scandalous and then warn me not to say it?"

"I can do lots of things you can't," Preacher asserted. "I'm older than you."

"Gimme a straight answer," Tommy said.

"I got a friend," Preacher said. "Maybe could help. Maybe not. Won't hurt to call."

"You can sling more bullshit," Tommy said. "How did you ever get along with an organization freak like my father?"

"Whoever said I got along with your old man. I never got along with him. I don't even like him."

But that was a ridiculous lie, of course, the humor arising from its patent absurdity. Preacher and Jeff were like brothers or like army buddies who had forged a bond deeper than any of mere blood. They were both World War II veterans, but the real war they fought together was the war to topple Jim Crow. After Dr. Brown, Preacher had always exercised the greatest influence on Jeff, pushing Jeff out of his natural cautiousness. Although Preacher practically never put two serious sentences back to back, Jeff paid the most careful attention to whatever Preacher argued. It was Preacher who had urged Jeff to reach out to working-class and rural Southern whites, who had long been the most violent opponents of desegregation. At their worst, these people were the very lifeblood of the Klan. "But these are *our* people," Preacher maintained, meaning his and Jeff's. "We know where they come from because it's where we come from. These are the people we have to have."

Jeff took this counsel seriously and made the South's working poor whites a focus of his own ministry after 1965. But even as Jeff took Preacher seriously, he delighted in Preacher's incessant tomfoolery and enjoyed Preacher's company more than anybody else's. In the midst of a campaign, younger staffers regarded it a special treat to be invited to Jeff's motel room to listen to him and Preacher tell war stories, the wilder and crazier the better. Nobody else made Jeff laugh the way Preacher could, and no one else elicited funny stories from Jeff the way Preacher did. Observing their relationship had given Tommy his first glimpse of Jeff's humanity.

"Are you going to level with me?" Tommy implored Preacher now. "Do you know somebody at the FBI you can call?"

"I don't like leveling with you," Preacher said. "Given that I have to stoop down so low. But, yes, I know somebody at the FBI I can call. Maybe he can help; maybe he can't."

"How do you know you can trust him?" Tommy asked. "Hoover's boys haven't exactly been our friends."

"I can trust him till I can't," Preacher said. "Been able to trust him so far. Funny thing you gotta remember. Once upon a time we did regard the FBI as our friends. They were the lawmen that could put the fear of God into the local sheriffs, who'd just as soon beat us senseless and throw us down some abandoned well as treat us like 'we the people' our Constitution speaks of. Some of those G-men were proud of helping us out. Good old boys, some of them. Eggheads, some of them. In Little Rock and then in Norfolk, Birmingham, Montgomery, you kept running into the same guys. Some of them watched you like you had a disease they didn't want to catch. Others, you could tell, they believed what we believed. Or some of it, anyway. Enough of it. I used to hook up with a few of them. Drink a little whiskey. Swap some yarns. Just folks. Learn a name. Pass along some information. Ask a favor once in a while. Not as easy now with fucking Vietnam and all. But you got to do what you got to do. Seems like forever now what with Medgar and Martin and G.W. all gone. But it wasn't that long ago. Five, six years, a decade. Less. Lots of those guys still around and they don't buy J. Edgar's crap that we're all just a bunch of commies. I'm the only communist around, and even I'm not a fucking communist."

"Makes sense to me," Tommy said.

"And it's what I like about you, boy."

At the burial ceremonies, Preacher delivered his reflections on George Washington Brown with his usual wit, claiming that, all the way through Dillard and then National Baptist Seminary, Dr. Brown had been known as "Bookworm" Brown. Tommy had no idea whether there was even a shred of truth to this. But Preacher achieved something remarkable on such a somber occasion. He had the audience laughing through their tears, as he maintained that the name "Bookworm" referred not only to Dr. Brown's disciplined study habits but also his evidently uncontrollable tendency to writhe around in his chair when he was involved in scholarly debate.

"It was as if he was tormented by the illogical arguments of his opponents," Preacher told the crowd. Then, doing a dead-on impression of Dr. Brown's speaking voice, Preacher reenacted Dr. Brown's purported wiggling response at a religious conference in the early 1950s when Dr. Brown skewered a fundamentalist for believing everything in the Bible as literal truth except for the words of Jesus. "G.W. would twist one way like old Satchel Paige about to throw a screwball and then wind around the other way like Pancho Gonzales rearing back for his backhand. Old white peckerwood's eyes liked to bugged out of his head watching this act. Thought G.W. was doing the watusi when what he was actually doing was flinging out truth like arrows from the tautest archer's bow. Bookworm. Yes sir, that's what we called him. Couldn't answer nonsense without wiggling around like a worm. And Lordy, Lordy, did he know the book."

After the ceremonies, Preacher told Tommy that he had spoken with his friend in the FBI, his "movement mole," he called the man. Faye Watson was indeed under FBI supervision at the Fontainebleau. She hadn't been arrested or even declared a material witness, but she had been voluntarily relocated from her apartment to the motel room. Preacher proposed that they pay her a visit. If she wasn't being officially detained, then no one could object to her receiving visitors. They could check up on her, see how she was doing, make sure that her relocation really was voluntary.

"But we can't just go marching up to the Fontainebleau," Tommy said. "We can't expect to just walk through the lobby and go knocking on her door."

"Why's that?" Preacher wondered. "I think that's almost exactly what I had in mind."

"Because we don't know what room she's in," Tommy pointed out. "And the people at the Fontainebleau don't even admit she's there."

"Oh, I know what room she's in," Preacher said. "Don't do much good to have yourself a bona fide movement mole if you don't use him for all the information you need."

At 3:30 that afternoon, Tommy and Glenda pulled into the Fontainebleau parking lot and parked next to Preacher's faded red Ford pickup. Preacher was sitting behind the wheel of his truck smoking an unfiltered Lucky Strike and reading a tattered copy of the Bible. He folded down a page corner to mark his spot as they walked up.

"First Corinthians," he said, getting out of the truck with the black, hard-bound copy of the Bible still in his hand. He took a last drag on his cigarette, dropped it on the blacktop and crushed it with a high-topped work boot.

Preacher gestured at them with the Bible, and Tommy could see that it was embossed with "Placed by the Gideons" in gold letters across the bottom.

"Don't know that I altogether approve of old Apostle Paul," Preacher said, waving the Bible at arm's length. "Kind of a know-it-all. Always telling people how they were supposed to act in every situation. Don't fornicate. Don't hang around with fornicators. Hell, man, did he pay any attention to the kind of people Jesus hung around with?"

Glenda and Tommy looked at each other, neither of them knowing how they were expected to respond.

Preacher turned and tossed the Bible through the window and onto the flat seat of his truck. "Some theologians think Paul was a fruit," he continued. "I don't think so myself. Not that I consider myself a theologian and not that I care if Paul was a fruit if he was a fruit. What I think is, Paul was afraid of his pecker and spent altogether too much time thinking about it and making up rules for what other people were supposed to do with theirs. I mean, what's that got to do with Jesus? Now, it's true Jesus himself had some things to say about fornication in the Sermon on the Mount, lust in your heart and all that, but his point was that none of us was making it in the purity department. My basic position is that Jesus didn't worry about his pecker, and that's why there's nothing in the Bible about his banging Mary Magdalene, which I have every confidence he had the good sense to be doing. See my point?"

"No," Tommy said, laughing.

Preacher turned his gaze to Glenda and said, "Do *you* see my point?"

Glenda laughed, nodded her head up and down, but then said, "No."

Preacher smiled. "Good," he said. "I was worried there that I was starting to make sense and would have to start a cult or something." Preacher stuck his hand out toward Glenda. "How are you doing?" he said. Glenda shook his hand briskly. "I hope you didn't take offense at my use of the word *pecker.* It's just a crude euphemism I learned as a boy. I should have said something more polite like *Johnson* or perhaps *joint.*"

Glenda laughed again. "I normally prefer to say *dick*, although *cock* works for me, too."

Nodding at her swelling belly, Preacher declared, "Looks like *cock* worked for you just fine."

To Tommy's surprise, Glenda blushed.

Preacher saw that he'd succeeded in embarrassing her and said, "Honey, two rules you got to learn about hanging around with the likes of me. First rule: find something better to do with your time. Second rule: if you violate rule number one, absolutely never pay the first bit of attention to a single thing I might have to say."

Glenda laughed once more, covering for herself. Then she said, "Tommy says you might know which room they're holding Faye in."

"Down to business," Preacher said. "Probably the best plan, though there's much to recommend standing out here in the hot sun and embarrassing your friends. The girl's in room 234. Let's climb some stairs and knock her up—Britishly speaking, that is."

"You're incorrigible," Glenda said. She turned to Tommy. "He's incorrigible."

"Twelve letter word for *asshole*," Preacher said.

"What's that?" Glenda asked.

"*Incorrigible*," Preacher said.

"Christ, let's go," Tommy said.

"I warned you about that cult stuff," Preacher said. "I'm against it."

"Jesus," Tommy said, laughing. Preacher looked at Glenda, raised his eyebrows and shrugged his shoulders, and they all burst out laughing.

"Now we're having fun," Preacher said. "Let's go do some good works. Maybe even get ourselves arrested. Funny how often those two are related, isn't it?"

Preacher struck out across the parking lot, and Glenda and Tommy followed. He avoided the lobby and took an exterior staircase to a row of rooms that opened onto a balcony overlooking Carrollton Avenue. As they walked, Preacher offered a quick dissertation on the New Testament book of James. "James always made a lot more sense to me than pious old Paul. You know Paul, 'not by works but by faith are you saved' and all that. I think James knocks Paul right on his bowhind when he says in 2:14, 'What does it profit a man to say he has faith when he has no works?'" Preacher chortled at this. "I like that one," he added. "I like the hell out of that one."

"Do you wander around all day wrestling with stuff like this?" Tommy asked.

"Of course, I do," he responded. "That's my job, ain't it? That and getting enough works on my ledger to make up for whatever lapses of faith I might have."

A man with a crew-cut, wearing a charcoal gray suit, was leaning against the wall and smoking a cigarette on the second-floor landing. Preacher said, "Howdy," as they passed him, and he grunted in reply. When they reached the second-floor walkway, Tommy turned around and noticed that the man had come out behind them and was staring at them.

"Number 234 must be on around yonder on the side by the railroad tracks," Preacher said as he ambled along. They passed under the roofline through an open area with an ice machine, a candy dispenser and a soft-drink machine and knew they had found the right place as they approached the other side. A uniformed New Orleans policeman stood guard outside a door in the middle of the walkway. Across from him, two men in blue suits rested their haunches on the wrought-iron balcony rail.

"Can I help you?" a voice said from behind them. They turned, and the gray-suited man walked out into the sunlight beside them.

"Well, I don't know," Preacher said. "Do you want to help us?"

That was obviously not a response the man expected. "What?" he said.

"Do you want to help us?" Preacher repeated.

"Why?" the man said, the spark of irritation in his voice extinguished immediately with a chill of self-control. "Why would I want to help you?"

"Well, I don't rightly know," Preacher said, taking off his ball cap and mopping at his forehead with the back of his wrist. "That's what I asked myself when I thought I heard you volunteering to help us."

The gray-suited man looked at Preacher like an entomologist might, holding a specimen with tweezers and lifting it to study under a magnifying glass. "What do you want up here?" he demanded.

"Are you with the hotel?" Preacher asked. He smiled broadly and put his cap back on, snugging the bill down to his eyebrows. "If you are, you might indeed be able to help us."

"I don't work for any hotel," the man said. He pulled a wallet from his inside coat pocket and flipped it open to reveal a badge. "Agent Fred Mason. FBI."

"I might have suspected," Preacher said, slipping even more deeply into his cornpone act. "Y'all are probably providing protection for our friend Faye Watson, down here in room 234."

"How do you know what room Mrs. Watson is in?" Agent Mason asked, grim-faced. A knot of muscle in his right jaw bulged.

"Why, I think you told me, didn't you, Tommy?" Preacher said.

"Why, no, no, I didn't, no," Tommy stammered, wondering what in the world Preacher expected him to say.

Preacher smiled. "No?" he said to Tommy. "Well, somebody told me," he said to Agent Mason. "Does it matter? Room 234 is right down here. Let's just go knock."

"She's not receiving visitors."

"We really are her friends," Glenda said. "I talked to her on the phone a couple of days ago. We're worried about her."

"Yeah, well, as I said," Agent Mason snapped, "she's not receiving visitors."

"Oh, that can't be right," Preacher said. He looked at Glenda. "Didn't you say she asked you to stop by as soon as you had a chance?"

"Well—" Glenda said. "Yes. Yes, she did."

"When was this exactly?" Agent Mason asked.

"Why—when I talked to her on the phone," Glenda said.

"Well, she's still not receiving any visitors," Agent Mason said.

"Is she meeting with her lawyer now?" Preacher asked. "Is that why she's not receiving any visitors?"

"What lawyer?" Agent Mason said.

"Well, I don't know what lawyer," Preacher said. "But surely y'all aren't holding her without letting her consult one. Why that would be against the law and—"

"Who said we're holding her?" Agent Mason stared hard at Preacher and licked his lips.

"You aren't holding her?" Preacher said.

"No," Agent Mason said.

"Well, then, why don't me and my friends just walk on down to room 234 and give her a little knock. If she doesn't want to receive visitors now, why, we can arrange to come back some other time."

Preacher turned away from Agent Mason and started down the walkway. As Glenda and Tommy moved to follow, Agent Mason said, "Hold it right there, folks."

Preacher stopped and turned around but did not move back toward Agent Mason. After a moment's hesitation, Mason moved to where Preacher was standing. Tommy thought it was as if they were in a football game and had just gained ten yards for a first down. "I'm going to need to see some ID," Mason said.

Preacher responded, "Yes, why that's understandable. It's natural that you'd want to know who you're dealing with." He fished out his wallet and handed Mason his driver's license. While Mason was looking at it, Preacher took a business card out of his wallet as well. When Mason looked up, Preacher handed it to him and said, "Did I mention that I'm with the *States-Tribune*?"

Mason seemed to blanch at this announcement. He studied Preacher's card. "This says you're the religion editor."

"That's correct, yes, sir," Preacher said.

Mason returned Preacher's license and card. Glenda and Tommy extended their identification, but he waved them off. "What's this the business of the religion editor?"

"George Washington Brown and Jefferson Caldwell are Baptist ministers," Preacher said. "Faye's late husband Benjamin was planning to attend the seminary."

Preacher, of course, had no plans to write a story about Faye Watson. The religious section of the *States-Tribune* only ran stories directly connected with New Orleans area churches. But his implication that he had come here as a reporter was brilliant bullshit, and Agent Mason's resolve deflated like a punctured balloon. He said to the uniformed policeman, "See if she wants to talk to these people."

She did, of course, and after they were all patted down, they went in, followed by Agent Mason who closed the door. Faye sat on one of the two double beds with pillows propped behind her back, an open magazine face down on her lap, a box of Kleenex by her side and a half dozen wadded-up tissues strewn around her. She was an enormously attractive woman. Tall and thin with a spray of freckles across the cheekbones of her light-brown face, she looked like Lena Horne. But now she looked gaunt and worn out. Her shoulder-length brown hair was unwashed and frizzy. Her skin was almost gray, and she had dark circles of fatigue around her eyes.

Glenda sat down on the bed and put her arms around Faye, who began to sniffle and then to cry. She buried her face against Glenda's bosom, her whole body heaving with sobs.

Tommy turned to Mason with some irritation but managed to say quietly, "Don't we get to visit with our friend without you standing over us like a prison guard?"

Mason did not respond.

"Come on, man," Tommy said through gritted teeth, "Why can't you give us some privacy?"

"I don't know you," Mason said without looking at Tommy. He spread his feet a little, bounced once, ever so slightly on the balls of his feet, and folded his arms across his chest. "I thought you folks came here to do some sort of newspaper story."

"And I thought you said that Faye wasn't in any kind of custody," Preacher replied.

"We're protecting her," Mason said, his voice rising. "Don't you know there's a bunch of crazy Negroes in this town who would like to kill her because she was Ben Watson's wife?"

"No, I don't know that," Preacher said. "But we ain't crazy, and unless we dipped ourselves in vanilla ice cream, we ain't Negroes."

"I can run you right back out of here, you know," Mason snarled.

"I don't doubt you can," Preacher said. "But I bet you'd not want the fact you did to appear in tomorrow's newspaper. Why don't you just go stand outside with your men and let us talk to this girl? I can get a lawyer to make you do it, but that'd have to be in the story, too."

The knot of muscle in Agent Mason's jaw bulged again. Finally, he said to Faye, "Mrs. Watson, you feel all right me leaving you to visit with these people?" Faye nodded. "All right," Mason said to Preacher. "But you remember that I'm right outside."

When Mason was gone, Tommy sat on the other bed, his feet in the space between them. Preacher pulled out a chair from under the room's tiny desk and sat down in it. They asked how she was doing and if she felt comfortable with the "protection" she was receiving from the authorities. She really didn't feel harassed by the lawmen, she said, though she was weary of answering the same questions over and over. They had questioned her several times since the shootings, and each day brought a new interrogator. But the questions were always the same. Had she collaborated with Ben? Had she had known beforehand what he was going to do? She hadn't, of course. She was pretty sure they believed her about that. It still seemed incredible that Ben was a murderer.

"Did they ask if you were a member of the Communist Party?" Tommy inquired.

"That was one of the first questions they asked me," Faye said. "And whether or not I had ever desecrated the American flag."

"Did you ask them to let you see an attorney?" Preacher asked.

"No," Faye said. "I didn't do anything. Why would I need a lawyer?"

Preacher pursed his lips and nodded. "Just remember," he said, "you have the right to consult with an attorney if you want to. If you ever feel they are implying you had some involvement, you should demand a lawyer immediately. They have to let you see one, and they have to stop asking you questions until you have an attorney present."

"I could call Hodding Morris," Faye said. "I know him. He would help me."

"Yes," Preacher said, "I'm sure he would."

"Well," Tommy said, uncertainly and uncomfortably, "since Ben, you know, shot… Well, Hodding might feel a conflict of, you know."

"Oh, well, I wouldn't—" Faye said, blinking rapidly and shaking her head from side to side.

"Of course," Preacher said. "But Hodding would help you. Don't forget that. He would get somebody for you."

"Well, but I wouldn't—" Faye said.

"Or you could call me," Preacher said. "I could arrange legal assistance for you."

"Or me," Tommy added. "Or me and Glenda."

Faye took a deep breath. "I don't think any of that will be necessary," she said. "I don't think they suspect I had any part—" Her eyes welled up and she wiped them with a tissue.

When she could speak again, she explained that the FBI had wanted to search her apartment and had moved her to the motel so she wouldn't have to watch them going through her things. She considered that genuinely sensitive on their part. Preacher asked if she'd been able to contact any family to be with her during this time, but she explained, as Glenda and Tommy already knew, that she was completely estranged from her family. Faye's father could not abide the fact that she had married a white man. He had warned her that marrying Ben would bring her nothing but heartache, and now he was right.

Faye's father was now pastor of the largest Negro Baptist church in Pascagoula, Mississippi, but Faye had grown up in Mobile, Alabama, where her father had pastored the Mount Holly Baptist Church. He had built a comfortable middle-class lifestyle for himself and and his family. He chafed under the indignities of Jim Crow, but he was basically conservative, determined not to rock the boat for fear of losing what he had. Faye's marrying a white man was the kind of act that could bring him to the attention of the Klan, and he had ordered Faye and Ben never to come to Pascagoula to visit.

Faye's father berated himself for ever allowing Faye to go north to school in the first place. That's where she got all her disastrous ideas about race mixing. He had wanted her to go to Spelman in Atlanta, but she had gotten a scholarship to Northwestern, where she'd filled her head with beatnik politics. Faye's mother and father had begged her not to marry Ben, and when she did, they cut off all contact. Now Ben was dead, and she had no one.

Preacher had barely known Ben and Faye before the shootings. He didn't know any of their personal histories and asked how they met. Some of the things she related, even Glenda and Tommy did not know.

Ben and Faye met at a Northwestern ban-the-bomb rally just after the Cuban missile crisis, and they would talk when they saw each other on campus. Later, both volunteered to work at a soup kitchen on Chicago's south side. They'd started seeing each other after that. Their dates were formal affairs at first. Ben always wore a jacket and tie. They would go down to the Loop to see a movie they considered suitably highbrow or to the symphony or to a play at the Schubert. From the beginning, they went to church together on Sunday mornings.

Ben never proposed. But gradually they began to talk about what they were going to do after graduation and decided to enter the Peace Corps. But in the spring of their senior year, Jeff Caldwell came to campus to speak, and they ended up going to Mississippi to help in the voter-registration campaign. They never left the movement after that, moving from volunteer status to paid staff positions in the fall of 1964. That Chirstmas Dr. Brown presided at their wedding.

Ben's parents were dead. He had a brother, Rodney, fifteen years his senior, who sold insurance in Des Moines, but they were never close. Rodney had once called Ben a communist and told him he was obviously insane for marrying a "colored woman." Faye doubted that Rodney had tried to contact her since the shootings. Basically, all she and Ben had were each other and their commitment to the movement, loyalties so intertwined as to be inseparable.

Preacher asked Faye if she had any inkling what might have led Ben to do what he had done.

"No," she said, which was hardly surprising. What Ben had done was beyond anyone's comprehension.

"Or maybe I do," Faye whispered.

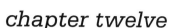

chapter twelve

J EFF CALDWELL FIRST BEGAN TO HEAR COMPLAINTS about his civil-rights work in the fall of 1960 during the local school integration crisis. Preaching sermons about brotherhood was one thing; so was participating in distant civil-rights activities in places like Little Rock, Arkansas. Such activity was not cherished by some of the parishioners at Gentilly Boulevard Baptist Church in New Orleans, but it seemed less threatening because it seemed far away. Seeing his face on the news night after night during the integration of Orleans Parish schools was something else again. Jeff was their pastor. Shouldn't he have been attending to pastoral duties instead of giving aid and comfort to trouble-making Negroes?

Disgruntled parishioners took three broad complaints to the chairman of Jeff's board of deacons: he was working to defy the law of the State of Louisiana, whose state's rights had been illegally abrogated by the United States Supreme Court; he was promoting miscegenation, which was abhorred by God; and he was denying the inferiority of the African race, which had been cursed by God in Genesis.

Jeff responded by addressing the complaints directly from the pulpit. First, he laid out the constitutional arguments that underpinned the federal court system's persistent attack on Jim Crow. But then, rather than simply accepting those arguments as indisputable matters of law, he quoted Jesus: "Render unto Caesar that which is Caesar's."

Jeff stepped out from behind the pulpit and over to the edge of the rostrum so that nothing stood between him and the members of his congregation. "If this is Caesar's concern," he said, reaching out toward the worshipers with cupped palms, "we should leave it to Caesar to attend to. That is the law. And as citizens we have an obligation to obey the law. But as Christians, we have an even greater obligation, the obligation to follow the example of Christ. Most often, that requires that we obey Caesar's law because Caesar's law reflects God's. But as those of us who served in World War II, or had husbands or sons or brothers who served in World War II, well know, sometimes Caesar's law is not God's at all but the very opposite. The law in Hitler's Nazi Germany required us to give up our neighbor to the gas chamber because he was a Jew. Could a true Christian do something so heinous? Of course not. And in that case, then, the example of Christ would require us to break the law."

That was Jeff's approach. In a series of sermons addressing the issue of desegregation, he repeated the refrain, "What would Jesus do?" And he closed each sermon with this directive: "Since that's what Jesus would do, how can we profess to be his followers and do something else?"

Those who disagreed most vehemently departed during the school-integration crisis and took up membership elsewhere in town. At first, this exodus was of little importance. The Gentilly Boulevard church was large and prosperous, and the loss of a few disgruntled members made little difference. The complaining got louder, however, in the spring and summer of 1961 when Jeff, Preacher Martin and Everett Essex joined the Freedom Riders, an integrated group of civil-rights activists who set out from Washington, D.C., determined to travel by bus all the way to New Orleans in defiance of local ordinances and state statutes that still required the buses to be racially segregated.

The Freedom Riders endured threats from South Carolina onward. In Alabama, the bus was attacked by a mob and burned, and everybody aboard was beaten. Jeff and Preacher ended up in the hospital with head and facial wounds. The *States-Tribune* ran a front-page picture of Jeff as he entered the hospital, blood soaking through first-aid bandages around his head. The caption read: "Local Minister Beaten on Freedom Ride."

Thereafter the Caldwells began to get harassing phone calls and letters. A sample letter was addressed to Billye: "Your husband has been having sexual intercourse with nigger women." Another letter to Billye proved more worrisome. "I feel it my Christian duty," it read, "to inform you that your husband has been having extra-marital relations with the secretary at his church, Miss Naylynn Jensen. Some nights when your husband tells you he's at a meeting, he's with her. He has relations with her right in his office." This letter had a disturbing specificity. The writer knew Naylynn's name and her position and had knowledge of Jeff's work habits. The segregationists were becoming more violent, and Billye didn't like the fact that their gaze had fallen on her husband.

Billye also detested this nasty letter because it made her confront the jealousy she felt toward Naylynn. Twenty-six years old and a graduate of Valmont College, where Billye had begun her own still uncompleted college training two decades earlier, Naylynn had been Gentilly Boulevard church secretary for two years. She had big, pretty brown eyes and thick, wavy brown hair. She was tall, slender-hipped and big-breasted. Preacher called her "the girl with the hello how are yas." But whatever her physical attributes, Naylynn was a hard worker and a valuable church employee. She had turned the church office into a professional operation for the first time, coordinating Jeff's busy schedule, keeping him free of routine church business responsibilities and helping with his civil-rights work. She was fiercely loyal to Jeff, whom she regarded (as she once said to Billye) as "the most brilliant man I have ever met."

Not long after Naylynn began working for Jeff, Billye asked her husband as they prepared for bed one night if he wished Billye had bigger breasts.

"Why?" he asked, folding his trousers over a hanger.

Billye pulled her dress up over her head and laid it across a chair. "Well, you men make such a big deal out of breasts. That *Playboy* guy has made a fortune off them."

Jeff laughed as he pulled off his shirt. "Nah. I like you just the way you are," he assured her. "You know what they say—more than a handful is wasted."

She touched herself on top of her brassiere. "I don't have a handful."

"What brought all this up?" Jeff inquired.

"Oh, Preacher making such a fuss over your new secretary's bosom, I guess."

"Preacher's just a boob man," Jeff said. "Not me, I'm a bowhind man."

Billye slapped herself on the rump. "Then I guess you married the right woman. I got your secretary beat in that department."

Later in life, Tommy Caldwell would remember the years 1963 and 1964 with distinctly mixed emotions. It was a grand and exciting time in many ways. His high school basketball team won the state championship his senior year, for instance, and he felt an elation he later worried he would never again experience. But those were also years in which Tommy first became extensively involved in his father's civil-rights work, and in that regard they were years of astonishing tumult and horrible violence. Medgar Evers was murdered by Klansman Byron de la Beckwith. Denise McNair, Carole Robertson, Addie Mae Collins and Cynthia Wesley were killed by a Klan bomb at their Birmingham church. Civil-rights workers Viola Liuzzo, James Chaney, Andrew Goodman and Mickey Schwerner were murdered for trying to register black voters in Mississippi.

In the summer of 1963, the summer after Tommy's junior year, the Christian Social Conscience League launched its Louisiana voter-registration drive, and Tommy went into the field with his father. The CSCL was quickly and overwhelmingly successful at getting Negroes to register to vote in Orleans Parish. But outside the city, they met with fierce resistance. Parish registrars would put up "Out to Lunch" signs whenever black citizens showed up to register. Voter rolls were purged on the flimsiest of pretexts, the names of Negroes eliminated for various imaginary failings. The process was like Sisyphus battling the vindictive gods. Nothing was ever finished. Everything had to be done and then done again.

Then the state legislature passed the purposely vague literacy-test law, which allowed white registrars throughout the state to rule that Negroes had failed to meet the standard. This law was wielded so ruthlessly by white officials that Negro schoolteachers, attorneys and ministers who had been voting for many years were actually thrown off the rolls. In response, George Washington Brown and his lieutenants organized a six-day march from New Orleans to Baton Rouge, where they planned a rally around the Huey Long statue in front of the capitol. The first day sixty thousand people marched from Jackson Square in the French Quarter to the airport in Kenner. The second day's goal was for the CSCL leadership and a cadre of one hundred or so supporters to continue on another fifteen miles to the little town of Laplace.

The day was sunny but mild, and the march moved out on schedule at eight o'clock. But the marchers barely made it a mile. As they left Jefferson Parish, the Jefferson sheriff's deputies lined up their vehicles across the road behind them. The deputies' cruisers cut off the march's two support buses and the two television vans that were right behind them. Tommy saw the bus and van drivers and the reporters climb out of their vehicles behind the wall of police cars and begin an animated discussion with several uniformed officers. He went back to find out what was going on. Robert, meanwhile, jogged to the front of the line to inform the march leaders of problems at the rear.

Tommy asked a deputy why the support buses had been stopped. "None of your goddamn business," he was told. "So your nigger-loving ass better catch on up with your coon friends before I arrest you for blocking the road." Tommy contemplated that information longer than the officer liked. The deputy abruptly unsnapped the nightstick from his belt and screamed, "Get," as he raised it above his head.

Tommy bolted away and sprinted to the front, where he found more trouble. The St. Charles Parish sheriff had lined up police vehicles door to door at the mouth of the causeway across the Bonnet Carré Spillway, and the march had come to a halt. In front of cruisers stood a phalanx of deputies with shotguns at port arms. And in front of the deputies stood Sheriff Buck Perkins himself, a ten-gallon Stetson tipped back on his head and a toothpick in his mouth. His weight was cocked onto his left hip, and his right hand rested on his waist just above his holstered pistol.

"I guess you folks gone just about far enough now," Sheriff Perkins drawled, the toothpick dancing up and down on his lower lip as he spoke.

"We have a permit for this march," Dr. Brown called across to him. Dr. Brown turned his head to Everett Essex and said, "Show him the paperwork."

Everett started forward with the documents they had assembled for the march. But Sheriff Perkins said, "Y'all needn't even bother me with any irrelevant pieces of paper."

"But we have a duly signed permit for this march on this day on this route," Dr. Brown said, taking the permit from Everett and stepping toward the sheriff. Dr. Brown usually dressed more formally, but today he wore an open-collared white shirt and gray slacks.

"Now, I told you not to be coming any further," Sheriff Perkins said. Behind him his deputies simultaneously cocked their pump-action shotguns.

Dr. Brown stopped where he was. "Surely, Sheriff," he said, raising a hand to shield his eyes from the morning sun, which was glinting off a police car into his face. "Surely we can discuss this. There must be some mistake."

"Ain't no mistake."

"But we have this permit." Dr. Brown extended his hand, holding the document toward the sheriff.

"That document don't give you automatic permission to cross this here bridge."

"It gives us permission to march along Airline Highway, U.S. Route 61, from the boundary of Jefferson Parish to the boundary of St. John Parish."

"I believe it might," the sheriff said. He took the toothpick from his mouth and spit over his right shoulder.

"Well then, I'm afraid I don't understand," Dr. Brown said.

"And they said you was the smart nigger," Sheriff Perkins replied. He laughed and his deputies laughed along with him. "Said you was a doctor of something or other."

"We obviously have permission to cross this bridge because it's part of Airline Highway."

"Well, now, you see, that's where you're wrong. 'Cause, technically speaking, this bridge ain't a part of nothing but itself. It joins up to Airline Highway on its either end. But it itself is a causeway cross a dangerous spillway, and it falls to my responsibility to determine whether it's safe to cross it or it ain't safe to cross it."

"Why wouldn't it be safe?"

"Well, now, I'm glad you asked that. See, I have reports that there's been dangerously rising river levels up north of us on the Mississippi and whatnot."

"Yes?" Dr. Brown said. Behind him the marchers fidgeted in the glare of the bright light. And across from him on the river side of the highway, cars slowed as they came off the south-bound span of the causeway to rubberneck at what was going on in the north-bound lane. Some drivers even pulled their cars off the highway to watch the proceedings until one of the sheriff's deputies crossed over, made them drive away and began to windmill the cars behind to keep on moving toward New Orleans.

"Might have to open the floodgates at any moment. Never know."

"But so what?" Dr. Brown said. "That's what the causeway is for. The water drains from the river *under* the highway into the lake."

"Under the *bridge*," Sheriff Perkins said. "Not the highway. Water drains under the *bridge*."

"Okay? So it drains under the bridge? So what?"

The sheriff grinned, showing his teeth all around the toothpick that was clamped between them. "So the bridge might not be safe. All that water rushing around those pilings. Anything could happen. This thing ain't never been opened before. We know the floodgates on the river work. But we don't know if the causeway can take it if we have to open them. See what I'm driving at?"

"I don't see at all what you're driving, sir," Dr. Brown said. "I notice that you haven't closed the south-bound span of the causeway. Cars have been passing us quite regularly in the south-bound lane all the while we've been talking."

"That's just it," the sheriff replied, licking his lips and using his tongue to move the toothpick from the left corner of his mouth to the right. "Only got cars on the south-bound span. We can clear cars off the span in ten minutes. Less. But you nigra pedestrians. Gonna take you people two hours to walk across this thing. That's too long. If they gotta open the floodgates, we might not be able to get you off in time. Can't take the risk. People tell me you're an awfully important colored fella. I wouldn't want anything to happen to you. So I think you best take my advice and just turn on around and head on back where you come from."

Dr. Brown returned to huddle with his advisors. The sheriff's story was preposterous, of course. The Mississippi River had never topped its levees since they'd been raised during the 1930s. And the river crested in the spring when the northern snow melt brought water down the Ohio and the Missouri, not in the summer. No one among the CSCL had heard a thing about rising water levels or the threat of a flood. This was just a pretext to stop the march.

"I say we march on," Robert Brown said. "We've got a permit. The law's on our side." Dr. Brown stared hard at his son, and Robert frowned and looked away.

Hodding Morris, who was on the march to handle any legal difficulties that might develop, reviewed the parade permit and then told the group, "The sheriff is full of it. We can get an injunction and make him move out of our way."

"Yeah, but how long is that going to take?" Robert Brown snapped.

"Robert," Dr. Brown said, "I want you to take up your position at the rear of the file."

Robert stared at his father and didn't budge. "This instant, young man. Move it."

As Robert walked away, Jeff said to Tommy, "You, too, buster."

"Aw, come on, Daddy," Tommy protested. "I didn't say anything."

"And now you have," Jeff said. "We've serious business to do. To the rear, march."

"Thing is, Robert's right," Jeff said as the boys moved away. "We can disband today. Hodding can get us an injunction. But how long's that going to take. A couple of days at the least?" He looked at Hodding who nodded. "So then we get the injunction, and we come back, and they cook up some other phony baloney to stop us. Maybe here. Maybe somewhere else. Whatever. They could keep us from getting to Baton Rouge before next Easter if we have to go to court for half a week for every mile we walk."

"How about this?" Everett Essex proposed. "We've only come a mile. What if we walk back to the airport, get on the phone, get some buses brought out to us and ride across the causeway. Man said he was only stopping pedestrians. Other side of the causeway we resume walking. We should still be able to reach Laplace by dark."

Everett's plan was quickly adopted, and Dr. Brown led the marchers curling around back toward Moisant Airport. The problem was that the deputies who had blocked the highway behind the marchers now wouldn't let them cross back into Jefferson Parish. The authorities in the adjoining parishes were obviously in collusion, and the marchers were now trapped on a stretch of concrete laid over a marsh.

Concerned that the march lacked a Jefferson permit, which might be used against them in news reports and court proceedings, Dr. Brown turned his marchers around again and led them back to the spillway bridge and a smiling Buck Perkins. There Dr. Brown pleaded with the sheriff to move his men aside and let the marchers pass peaceably, but, predictably, Perkins refused. In that light, the CSCL leadership gathered to consult one last time.

"We knew it could come to this somewhere," Dr. Brown told his associates. "We walk with God. And we have no choice but to walk on. This is what we'll do. Ten of us will walk forward to test the intentions of Sheriff Perkins and his deputies. Everyone else will stop where we are now. If the first of us are merely arrested, the rest should come forward and surrender to arrest as well. If there is violence perpetrated against our persons, those behind the first ten are immediately to sit and wait to be arrested."

Dr. Brown pointed out the nine he wanted to follow him. All were Negroes, and Jeff protested that he wasn't included. "It's about integration," he said. "And in this crowd, you can't have integration without including me and Preacher."

Dr. Brown smiled for a moment, like the sun breaking briefly through the clouds on an overcast day. But then his seriousness returned, and he asked which of the first ten would like to wait with the others. When none volunteered, he said, "Then there shall be twelve of us."

"An appropriate number, wouldn't you say," Jeff observed.

"Indeed," Dr. Brown replied. And then he asked the other eleven to join hands with him. "Our Father, which art in heaven," he prayed. "Hallowed be Thy name. Help us always to walk in the light of Thy divine guidance. Help us to be brave even though we are afraid. And help us to forgive these men who oppose us and may do us violence. Help us to remember that only by holding out the olive branch of forgiveness may we walk with Jesus at our side. In the name of your son, who died for our sins, amen."

"Amen," the others echoed.

They turned and began walking toward Sheriff Perkins and his deputies. And it was Jeff who first began to sing: "He's got the whole world, in his hands."

Immediately the others joined in: "He's got the whole world, in his hands."

And those who waited behind began to sing with them: "He's got the whole world, in his hands." Together they all began to clap in unison. And together they sang: "He's got the whole world in his hands."

The sheriff's deputies began to crowd in around them from either side. And still they sang: "He's got you and me, brother, in his hands." The sheriff's deputies began to jostle them so that they were forced into single file. And they sang on: "He's got you and me, brother, in his hands."

Then there was chaos. A gun butt was slammed down on the head of George Washington Brown and another between Everett Essex's shoulder blades. Jeff threw his hands up on top of his head to protect himself, and three fingers on his right hand were broken as a gun butt smashed him to the ground. A shotgun blast echoed out into the hollow of the spillway, and a flock of brown pelicans nesting in the sawgrass was startled into flight.

Sirens sounded from behind them on the highway. A gun butt crushed into the side of Preacher Martin's face, damaging optical muscles and leaving his vision impaired for life. And the twelve fell to the ground, where they were kicked, over and over again, by frenzied black boots.

And the singing stopped. And Robert Brown and Tommy Caldwell tried to rush to their fathers but were held back by their friends, three on each of them.

And the Jefferson Parish deputies, responding to the sound of the discharged shotgun, arrived with their pistols drawn, and the marchers thought they were about to be murdered. Their leaders cried for them to sit, and some did, but others panicked, bolted and ran. The police chased those who ran and beat them with nightsticks while other policemen waded into the crowd of those who sat and beat them as well.

And across the way, having circled to the river and through the spillway at surface level on River Road and back up to Airline Highway on the north side of the causeway and across the causeway on the south-bound span, a location crew from WDSU-TV captured it all on film.

This was hardly the last atrocity the state and nation would witness in the struggle for civil rights. More violence lay ahead in Philadelphia, Mississippi; in Selma and Birmingham, Alabama; in Harlem and Watts; on a motel balcony in Memphis; in the ballroom of the Ambassador Hotel in Los Angeles; and on the rostrum of a Baptist church in New Orleans. But this was the nation's first taste of Jim Crow's jackboot captured live and delivered into America's living rooms in time for supper, and its ugliness had a startling impact.

Buck Perkins tried to take a hard line. He charged Dr. Brown with assault and battery on a law enforcement officer and inciting to riot, and he charged the other eleven members of the CSCL vanguard with resisting arrest. But the people of Louisiana saw the footage of what had happened. They knew the truth, and the next morning, arriving by car and bus and taxicab and bicycle, abandoning their cars in a traffic jam that stretched four miles back from the St. Charles Parish line, more than forty thousand people descended on the Bonnet Carré Spillway. Realizing that crowd might be volatile if he tried to block it, Buck Perkins ordered his deputies off the bridge lest they be stormed, overrun and trampled.

Forty thousand people walked the seven miles across the Bonnet Carré causeway that day. And as they walked, they sang: "He's got you and me, brother, in his hands. He's got the whole world in his hands."

chapter thirteen

J EFF CALDWELL FIRST MET BILLYE MONROE on a bright, warm Sunday afternoon in September of 1941, at a coffee for new freshman girls. The coffee was given the second week of the fall semester by the dean of women at Valmont College, a Baptist school in the small central Louisiana town of Oakwood. Jeff and Billye were both seventeen, and they couldn't have been more different.

Billye was there in the student union Great Hall with the other new girls on campus. Sofas and chairs had been gathered from other parts of the union and arranged so that all one hundred six invitees could sit in a huge semicircle facing the dean. Valmont didn't allow fraternities or sororities and, of course, didn't hold school dances, so other than Sunday church service this was the first occasion for the young women to dress up. All of them wore smart fitted suits, small hats with ornamental veils, and white cotton gloves buttoned at the wrist.

Jeff was there because he was working. He was one of three boys the dean of women had employed to serve coffee and sweet rolls and to clean up afterwards. He had graduated first in his high-school class the previous June, and he'd won one of two Billy Sunday Scholarships for boys preparing for the Southern Baptist ministry. (The other freshman recipient was Ed Martin of Mer Rouge, whom the boys in the dorm had already started calling "Preacher.") The scholarship covered Jeff's tuition and dorm fees, which his family could never have paid. To cover his board, he worked in the campus cafeteria. In order to buy such items as tooth powder, shaving cream and shampoo, Jeff had lined up a job setting pins at the Alexandria bowling alley on Friday and Saturday nights. He was always looking out for additional jobs, such as the one at the welcoming coffee.

Billye, in contrast, was a middle-class girl, whose family was paying for her education. Her father, Prescott, was a prosperous pharmacist who operated his own drugstore in Shreveport. Her mother, Mabel, ran the front cash register, where she dispensed free advice to the female clientele about various beauty products. But even though Mabel worked the same long hours as her husband, from 9 A.M. to 6 P.M. six days a week, she still referred to herself as a housewife. And she always counseled Billye and her two other daughters that to succeed in life they would have to marry a professional man the way she had, a man, Mabel said, "who knows how to take care of a woman like your father does."

Billye was a smart young woman who had graduated fifth in her class at Byrd High School; only her B grades in math kept her from finishing first. She had studied diligently in high school, but her true ambitions, guided by her mother's attitudes and expectations, were social rather than academic. She dated the captain of the football team her senior year. She was elected homecoming queen and designated a "beauty" in the school yearbook. And she headed off to college without real career goals. She joked that the only degree she hoped to earn at Valmont was her MRS, and as far as she was concerned the sooner the better. "I just hope I can find the right man before I have to declare a major," Billye teasingly told her best friend, Pam Pendergast, as they were packing clothes into Billye's wooden steamer trunk.

"But what about Bobby?" Pam asked, referring to Bobby Polaski, star halfback and Billye's high-school steady.

"Bobby was for high school," Billye explained. "I'm talking about the man I'm going to marry. I haven't even met that man yet." Bobby's daddy was a mechanic, and Billye was sure that Bobby, who made C's in English and history, would be a mechanic, too. Billye liked Bobby Polaski. He was good looking and fun, and she liked the fact that together they were such a popular high-school couple. But she never considered herself to be in love with Bobby, never entertained any idea that they might get married some day. He was not the person she wanted to spend her life with. So Billye left Shreveport to go off to college with every intention of marrying someone else. A future doctor or lawyer, she figured.

Despite such seemingly worldly ambitions, Billye Monroe was neither a cocky nor calculating young woman. Nor, despite her expectations of honoring her mother's counsel to marry a professional man, was she genuinely mercenary in her attitudes. Her parents were comfortably middle class but hardly rich. Billye didn't hunger for wealth or status. She considered herself practical, but she longed to know love.

By the time of the dean's welcoming coffee, Jeff had already spotted Billye, although she had not yet noticed him. They had two classes together, Freshman English and Freshman Math, and he'd had his eye on her for twelve hours already. There were other attractive young women at Valmont, but Billye, Jeff thought, was special. She captivated him from the first moment he saw her when she walked into English class in her straight brown skirt and snug, striped cotton top, a stack of books clutched against her breasts like one might hold an infant. Jeff thought Billye looked like Carole Lombard, whom he'd seen in *Fools for Scandal* and *Mr. and Mrs. Smith*. Like Carole Lombard, Billye was glamorous in her fine and stylish clothes, her long legs sheathed in stockings, her soft brown hair curled into a pageboy, her creamy cheeks perky with a dash of rouge. No girls from New Peterstown dressed like Billye Monroe. Their clothes didn't outline their bodies the way hers did.

Billye passed so close to Jeff that first day he thought for a second they might actually touch, and he thrilled to the air that stirred over him as she walked by. He could smell the heady scent of her perfume. She moved down the aisle to his left to take a seat in the center of the room behind him, and Jeff had to will himself not to turn around to look at her. He presumed she must be rich, although this was not one of her attractions. If she was rich, he reasoned, she might well think herself too good for a dirt-poor boy like himself. And so, right from the beginning, a powerfully contradictory thing happened inside Jeff. Even as he found himself desiring this beautiful young woman, aching to know her and win her, at the same time he found himself resigned, should he ever get to be with her, to losing her because he wasn't good enough for her.

For the next two weeks, Jeff desperately tried to dream up some pretext for introducing himself to Billye. Should he claim he'd forgotten his homework assignment? No, he didn't want to make a bad impression. Should he ask her what she thought about some specific comment one of their teachers had made? That would seem transparently forward, wouldn't it? He had overheard her say to a friend that she was terrified of college algebra "because I can't even add two plus two and get four every time." Math came easily to him. Should he volunteer to help her with her homework? Something like that had possibilities, he guessed, but he mustn't make her feel insulted. And how did he get around the fact that whenever possible he eavesdropped on her conversations? Nothing was right yet; nothing was natural the way Jeff knew it had to be. So he waited—not patiently—but he waited.

Jeff didn't take the serving job at the dean's coffee with any idea that he might find a chance to talk to Billye Monroe. But when the opportunity presented itself, he seized it. He was all decked out in his cafeteria whites, starched white pants and white double-breasted jacket that buttoned up to the collar. He knew it was just a server's uniform, but he thought he looked good in it. He had admired the look in the mirror over his dorm-room sink before heading off to the union. Jeff and the two other boys working the event filled their silver trays with cups and saucers, a stack of white cloth napkins, a clatter of teaspoons, a silver bowl full of sugar cubes and a silver pitcher of milk. Then they filled each cup full of steaming black coffee from the urn they had wheeled in from the kitchen. The girls were seated around the Great Hall, and the boys' job was to serve them at their seats. When his tray was ready, Jeff moved briskly to a place in the room so that, in the natural course of things, he would serve Billye fourth.

As with the other girls, when Jeff came to Billye, he bent from the waist to lower his tray so that she could help herself. Billye took a napkin and placed it across the hem of her navy suit skirt and her stockinged knee, which was crossed over her other leg. As she selected her cup and saucer, Jeff said with as much casualness as he could manage in an opening he'd been mentally rehearsing since he'd seen her come into the room, "You're Billye Monroe, aren't you?"

"Why, yes I am," Billye said. She smiled broadly, her lips peeling back to reveal pink gums as well as straight, white teeth. She had a large mouth, he thought, and he imagined the sweetness of kissing her. His face was within inches of hers; he could smell her perfume again, and he felt a tingling in his groin from being so close.

"You're in my English class," Jeff said. "Math, too."

He saw her eyes wrinkle at the corners; he realized she was straining to place him, and he felt a needle prick of irritation. But then she smiled broadly again and said, "Sure, I know you. You're—"

"Jeff," Jeff said when she hesitated. "Jeff Caldwell."

"Of course," she said. "I know you, Jeff." She smiled again, not showing her teeth this time, and her green eyes flashed in a way he found deliriously exciting. With one hand she balanced her cup and saucer on her napkin, and with the other she reached for the pitcher of milk.

"You sit behind me in both classes," Jeff said. "I sit up front."

Billye knitted her brow and said, "Sure." She poured milk into her coffee, put the pitcher back on the tray and selected a spoon, which she placed into her cup and began to swirl.

"Sugar?" Jeff asked. "I guess you're supposed to use those tongs for the cubes," he added hurriedly, "but you can use your fingers if you want."

"No, thanks," she said, shaking her head slightly. "I don't use sugar."

"You watch your weight, I guess," Jeff commented.

Billye giggled. "You think I need to?"

"Oh, no," Jeff said, feeling himself flush. He was making an idiot of himself. He stepped to his right and bent down to offer his tray to the next girl, then turned his head to say something more to Billye. He wanted to extricate himself, to explain that he was trying to compliment her slim figure, not the opposite. But she had already turned to talk to the girl on the other side of her. Jeff turned back to the girl he was serving, hoping the heat he felt in his face didn't show. Billye and the other girl laughed out loud, and Jeff wondered if they were laughing at him.

When he saw Billye come through the door to English class the next morning, Jeff glued his eyes to the Walt Whitman poem they were going to discuss. But as she passed his chair, she said, "Hi Jeff," and he looked up, trying to appear startled. She smiled; her green eyes, wrinkling at the corners, were warm and inviting, like a shady stretch of grass on a late-spring day. The clock on the wall framed her head like a halo. It read 7:55, and Jeff willed it to stop so class wouldn't start.

"You don't think Dr. Rankin is gonna give us a pop quiz, do you?" Billye asked.

Jeff hesitated, then said, "Naw. I doubt it."

"I sure hope not," Billye said. She smiled again and moved on to her seat behind him. His heart raced, as if he were in the middle of a quarter-mile sprint. He was so in love with her that he didn't hear a word Dr. Rankin said about Walt Whitman.

In math class the next day, Jeff volunteered to go to the board to solve an equation and the teacher commended him for the clarity of his work. On his way back to his seat, he dared a glance in her direction, and she smiled in return, sending a thrill through his insides as if he'd been caressed. In English class on Wednesday, he answered several questions to nodding approval from Dr. Rankin. Each time he spoke, he thought of her behind him and wondered if she was impressed. After class, Jeff took his time closing his text and notebook so that Billye would pass by him on her way out. Then he quickly stood up and followed her; in the hall she shortened her stride and stepped to the side so that he came abreast of her.

"Say, Jeff," she said, "I gather you really understand this Over-Soul business?"

Jeff looked at her and shrugged as they fell into a leisurely pace down the hall. "Sure," he said. "I guess so. Don't you?"

"Well, I understand what Emerson is saying," she replied. "Or I think I do, anyway. But I guess it doesn't seem exactly Christian."

"I hadn't thought about it like that," Jeff said with a laugh. "Emerson is a classic figure in American literature." He hated himself for sounding so stiff.

"Well, I know that, silly," Billy said. "We read 'Self-Reliance' and 'Friendship' in high school. It's just that this isn't a Louisiana public school. It's a Baptist college."

"So?" Jeff said. "We're still supposed to get a regular education. The Bible says that Jonah was swallowed by a whale, but I'm betting the biology department doesn't try to teach us that a whale shuts off its digestive juices every time it swallows a human being."

"That's a good point," Billye said, laughing. "Still, I don't think Pastor Biltmore—he's the pastor of my church in Shreveport, that's where I'm from—I don't think he'd like this Over-Soul business at all. It doesn't seem to involve accepting Jesus Christ as your Lord and Savior."

Jeff laughed again, a little nervously now. He couldn't quite peg where this girl was coming from. "Are you that devout?" he asked.

"Well, I'm baptized," Billye said, "if that's what you mean."

"Of course," Jeff responded. They had just stepped through the doors to the outside, and he put his hand up to his forehead like a visor to protect his eyes from the shock of the bright sunlight. "I would guess most everybody who goes here has been baptized, wouldn't you?"

"I guess," Billye said.

"What I'm saying," Jeff said, "is that I think some people are just more flexible in their religious views than others. Some people think every word in the Bible is literally true—like Jonah and the whale—and other people think that some of the stuff in the Bible is just stories. You know, to teach a point, but not necessarily to be believed at face value."

"Okay?" Billye said. She was interested, but she did not quite grasp what he was driving at. She had only brought the whole business up to make conversation. He was a cute guy, and he seemed really smart, and he'd talked to her at the dean of women's coffee. She just wanted to be nice and not be thought stuck up.

"My point is that you and I may be Baptists, but that doesn't mean that Baptists agree on everything because they don't. That's why we have so many Baptist churches—because people disagree about this or that thing. It also doesn't mean we can only learn things from other Baptists. Emerson was at least a Christian. My Western Civ teacher is having us read Plato and Aristotle. And they weren't even Christians."

"Of course, they were born before Christ," Billye pointed out.

"True," Jeff said. "But you see my point."

"Yes," Billye said. "I do."

"So does that bother you?" Jeff asked. "That's what I meant by asking how devout you were?"

"Bother me?" Billye responded.

"That they're teaching us stuff that's not Baptist?"

"Of course not," Billye said. "A lot of my girlfriends back in Shreveport aren't Baptist."

"What are they?"

"Methodist. Presbyterian. Catholic."

"You have Catholic girlfriends?" Jeff asked.

"Yes. Plenty."

"Where I'm from—"

"Where are you from?" Billye asked.

"New Peterstown."

Billye wrinkled her brow.

"It's about forty miles from here," Jeff said. "You wouldn't have heard of it. It's out in the country. Anyway, people in New Peterstown don't think Catholics are even Christians."

"You believe that?" Billye said, shocked.

Jeff laughed. "No, what about you?"

"No!" Billye said.

"Good," Jeff said.

"Why good?" Billye asked.

"Because it's bad to judge like that," Jeff responded. "That's something in the Bible I do believe every word of, 'Judge not, that ye be not judged.'"

"Now you sound like the devout one. You sound like Pastor Biltmore, quoting the Bible and all."

"I am devout," Jeff said. "But in my own way. I don't know if I like sounding like your pastor or not. But I do want to be a pastor."

"You do?" Billye asked too quickly, showing her surprise.

"Yes," Jeff said. "Why? You sound surprised."

"Oh, well, I don't know," Billye said. "You're so good in math and everything. I thought you might want to be—I don't know—an engineer or something." Jeff frowned at such a notion. "And you're good in English, too, so I thought maybe you might want to be a lawyer."

"Is there something wrong with wanting to be a pastor?" Jeff asked her.

"No," she answered quickly. "Of course not."

After that neither of them knew what to say, and an awkwardness sprang up between them like a translucent screen. Finally, Billye said, "Well, I guess I need to go study." They headed off in different directions, Billye toward the freshman women's dorm and Jeff to the library. Jeff was at a loss as to what had happened. Who could ever tell what girls were thinking?

Billye smiled at him in math class on Thursday and again in English on Friday, and that emboldened Jeff to ask her out. He worked at the bowling alley on Friday and Saturday nights, so when he called her from the phone in the lobby of his dorm, he asked her if she would like to go to church with him on Sunday night and walk to the drugstore afterwards for a malt or a Coke. His disappointment was huge when she said she already had other plans. Did she just not want to go out with him? Why? Was it becaused he planned to become a pastor? Was she only interested in someone who wanted be an engineer or a lawyer?

Jeff slunk back to his dorm room where his roommate, Benny Calhoun, determined instantly what had happened, just from looking at Jeff's face. Jeff didn't like Benny much. They didn't have much in common, and though Benny came from a middle-class family, Jeff considered him coarse. Benny was a physical-education major from Lake Charles, a football player with a slight chip on his shoulder because he hadn't gotten the scholarship to LSU he thought he deserved. Jeff, in contrast, wasn't much of an athlete. He thought that athletics were overrated and most athletes accorded an importance they didn't deserve.

But Jeff and Benny weren't enemies, either. They talked, like all roommates. Jeff had told Benny about his infatuation with Billye Monroe, how pretty he thought she was, how classy and how smart. Although Jeff thought Benny was just a dumb jock with an unrefined fondness for making comments about excretory functions, Benny was plenty smart enough to put two and two together and come up with romantic disaster. And he was insensitive enough to give Jeff a hard time.

"What's eating your liver?" Benny asked when Jeff returned to the room with downcast eyes and a stricken face. Benny lay in the bottom bunk staring at Jeff over a copy of *Life* magazine.

"Nothing," Jeff said, slumping into the room's one easy chair.

Benny swung his legs over the side of the bed and sat up. "Oh yeah?" Benny said. "Your face looks long enough to wipe your shoes on without lifting your feet."

"Leave me alone," Jeff said.

"You asked that girl for a date, didn't you?" Benny said. "That Billye girl you been mooning about."

"No," Jeff said. "I most certainly didn't."

"Now aren't you ashamed of lying to your roomie? You planning on being a preacher and all."

"Leave me alone," Jeff said.

"I believe that Shreveport girl done shot you down, now didn't she?"

"You better shut up." Jeff said.

"Yeeeeeeeeeeeeeowwwwwwwwww," Benny said, making the sound of a diving airplane's grinding engines. "Shot your old country butt down like one of them RAF fighters. Yeeeeeeeeeeeeeowwwwwwww. Pquuuuwwwwwwwwwww. I seen it on the newsreel. Shreveport Blondie puts one right into the snout of old Jeff the Kraut Bomber. Mayday. Mayday."

"You're a rat, you know that, Benny?"

"Calling me names ain't going to get you into whatshername's panties, country boy."

"You're disgusting."

Benny's face abruptly shifted from taunting to somber. "Aw, come on, Jeff, take a joke, will you. You're not the first fella to get a thumbs down from a pretty girl. Won't be the last, either. And unless you get married to the next girl who goes out with you, she probably won't be the last girl who turns you down. You don't even know why, I bet."

"She said she had other plans."

"There," Benny said. "So why the tragedy? You asked her out too darn late. Girl as pretty as you say she is already has a date on Friday and Saturday when you don't ask them out until the Monday before."

"I asked her out for Sunday night," Jeff said miserably.

"Uh oh," Benny said, making a face of feigned disgust. "It's looks like a Mayday after all. Yeeeeeeeeeeowwwwwwwww. Pquuuuuuwwwww."

"Knock it off, will ya."

"Jeezums, you're a soft skin, aren't you? Where were you gonna take her on a Sunday night anyway? Shows even aren't open on Sundays."

"To church," Jeff said. "I asked her to go to church. That's why I think she said she had other plans. That, and because I don't think she's interested in somebody who's going to be a pastor."

"Maybe," Benny said.

"Yeah, probably. I guess that must be it," Jeff said.

"Maybe not, too," Benny said.

"What else?"

"Well, bubba. Something I kind of been meaning to talk to you about. Could maybe be the problem." Benny cast his eyes on the floor, then looked out the window at the shadows of pine trees wavering in the thin moonlight. "I know it's because you're always working and everything over in the cafeteria and in the bowling alley on weekends. But sometimes you get kinda ripe."

Jeff looked up at Benny to see what kind of prank he was starting on now. But Benny's face was devoid of his habitual smirk, and he looked away the instant they made eye contact.

"What are you talking about?" Jeff asked.

"You know," Benny said, shrugging.

"What the hell are you talking about?"

"You're kinda strong sometimes. Women don't like that. They want a man to smell fresh."

Jeff sat up in his chair and leaned forward. "What are you telling me, you turd?"

"Hey, man," Benny responded, looking Jeff full in the face. "Don't start putting that on me. I ain't the one smells like a mule half the time."

"You saying I stink? I take a shower just like everybody else. Three, four times a week. I like the showers they got here."

"Three, four times a week ain't enough, bubba. You gotta do it every day."

"Bull feathers," Jeff said.

"What's more," Benny said, recognizing Jeff's hurt and ignoring his hostility, "you gotta get yourself some underarm deodorant. I know you don't got none 'cause I've lived with you a month now and I ain't ever seen you put any on."

"What in the world are you talking about?" Jeff demanded.

"Underarm deodorant. It's not just for girls, if that's what you think."

"Just because I'm from the country," Jeff said, "doesn't mean I'm some rube you can just tell a bunch of bunk so you can make a fool of him."

"I ain't fooling with you."

"Right. And Hitler isn't the dictator of Germany."

Benny shook his head. He got up from the bed, tossed the magazine back on his pillow and walked to the door. Before walking out, he looked at Jeff, who didn't turn to meet his gaze. "You know your problem, Caldwell? Only truth you ever want to hear is the truth you already know."

Jeff was humiliated by the twin disasters of that Monday night. He didn't know if Billye had rejected him because of his professional ambitions or because he had body odor. Whatever it was, he conceded abject failure in his pursuit of Billye Monroe and hated himself for being the man that Billye Monroe didn't want.

Across the campus that night Billye was in an entirely different frame of mind. She was startled to learn that Jeff was studying for the ministry. In the life she imagined for herself after college, there was always marriage, and her husband was never a pastor. But that's not why she turned him down. She wasn't offended that he asked her to go to church. She and Bobby Polaski, who wasn't even Baptist, had gone to Sunday-night services lots of times during high school. Billye had told Jeff the truth. She had other plans for that Sunday night. She had agreed to go to church with another boy.

In the coming weeks Billye waited expectantly for Jeff to ask her out again. She liked him. He was nice looking and gentle, and the more she was in class with him, the more she became convinced that he was the smartest boy she had ever met.

But Jeff did not ask her out again. Billye was thoroughly puzzled by this. She made a point of greeting Jeff in class. But he left the classroom immediately after class, so Billye couldn't engage him in conversation the way she had before. After a time, she presumed he must have found another girl to date. She wondered who it was.

But Jeff didn't even attempt date to someone else. He withdrew into himself and began to make vague plans to transfer. To LSU maybe, or Mississippi College. Somewhere where the fact that he'd had body odor wasn't known. He studied hard, he showered every day and used the stick of Mennen he bought at the Rexall, and he kept to himself.

And then on December 7, the world changed. Japan bombed Pearl Harbor in Hawaii, and America was catapulted into war.

School let out for the Christmas holidays two weeks later, and Jeff returned to New Peterstown. His older brother Wayne was already in the Navy, so there was much talk of war and speculation about where Wayne would serve and what kind of action he would see. But mostly the talk around the table concerned the other Caldwell boys' patriotic responsibilities. Forgetting his own injuries in the Great War and his enduring anger at the government about his veteran's pension, Pruitt declared that Jeff had to join up immediately.

"Jeff's in college," Osby pointed out.

"So what?" Pruitt responded. "I ain't so keen on this college business to start with. Boy's always put on airs, and his being in college is making it worse. Anyway, college is a luxury this country can't afford in a time of war." Pruitt looked at Jeff directly. "I'll be expecting you to do your duty right after Christmas."

"Why, Jeff's got his exams to take after Christmas," Osby responded, astonished and alarmed. "And he won't even turn eighteen until February. There'll be time enough for him to decide what to do about the service once school is over next spring."

"Well, I done read in the paper," Pruitt argued, "where a boy can go at seventeen if he has signed permission from both his parents." They had finished eating a meal of collard greens, boiled ham and cornbread, and Pruitt pushed the dishes in front of him toward the center of the table.

"That he won't be getting," Osby said. "Both parents would include me, and I won't do it."

"You'll do it if I tell you to," Pruitt threatened. "You'll do it for your college-boy pet, and you'll do it for James the day he turns seventeen. I won't have one of my sons hiding behind your apron when there's a war on, when there's Japs and Germans to kill."

"I won't do it for either one," Osby said.

"The hell you won't," Pruitt said, rising from his chair, his voice loud and heated.

Osby picked up the carving knife she'd used to slice the ham. "I'd cut off my hands first," she said. Her voice was quiet, but she stared at her husband with an iron gaze. "I'd cut off my hands, my boys would stay home, and you wouldn't have anyone to fix your meals, clean your house and wash your clothes. And if you don't believe me, you just try and make me."

"I'll go when I'm eighteen, Daddy," James said. "You know I will. Just like Wayne. I'm sure the war will still be going on. It's just getting started now."

"Shut up, you chicken dirt," Pruitt said to James. Then he looked at Osby, who stared back at him unflinching. Suddenly his arm swept out and he knocked half the dishes off the table.

Osby squeezed the carving knife and brought it handle down flush against the table. "That doesn't change a dern thing, Pruitt Caldwell. Not one dern thing."

He muttered an unintelligible oath and strode from the room onto the back porch, slamming the screen door behind him.

But none of these theatrics really mattered. Jeff had already decided to enter the army as soon as he turned eighteen. Osby pleaded with him to seek the draft deferment available to ministers or at least to enter the service in the chaplaincy corps. She was sure the New Peterstown pastor, who had allowed Jeff to preach at the church twice already, would gladly arrange to have Jeff ordained. But Jeff would have none of it. He'd only had a single semester of college, and ordination ought to wait until he graduated from the seminary. Meanwhile, a war was on. His responsibility was clear. He and Preacher Martin had agreed they would enter the army together on the "buddy system."

Both of these young men took their Christianity seriously, and both felt significant conflict about serving as soldiers, possibly being called upon to kill an enemy. Jesus told His followers to love their enemies. He chided His disciple Simon Peter for trying to defend Him with physical force, and He forgave those who put him to death. In wrestling with their religious responsibility, Preacher and Jeff discussed whether their faith required that they apply for conscientious-objector status. But they were without models for such an action. In the end, they decided to respond to patriotic duty, to place themselves willingly in the same harm's way that their fellows did, and to pray fervently that God would relieve them of any requirement to take a human life. Both young men hoped that by serving together they could provide spiritual support for each other.

Jeff's week and a half at home that Christmas was the longest consecutive period of time he would spend there for the rest of his life. He studied for his exams, which would begin the week after he returned to campus. And he tried to stay out of Pruitt's way. But father and son got into it when Pruitt realized that Jeff was taking sponge baths every day. Jeff badly missed the hot showers in his college dormitory. Washing with a cold wash cloth while standing barefoot over a drain hole in the floor of the unheated wash shed was an unpleasant process. But he wasn't going to break his daily bathing routine just because the facilities at his parents' house were so uncomfortable. Three days before Jeff returned to college, Pruitt came into the wash shed to find Jeff clad only in his white boxers, rocking his bare feet from side to side on the cold floor, rubbing deodorant under his arms.

"What's that you're doing there?" Pruitt asked his son. "You're not turning pervert on us, now are you? I guess that's one way you could keep your chicken behind out of our war."

Jeff ignored his father's sarcasm. "I'm just putting on deodorant." He held the rectangular stick out at arm's length to show it to his father.

"Get that away from me," Pruitt said. "What is that sissy stuff any way?"

"Underarm deodorant," Jeff replied. "It keeps you from smelling bad."

"Won't keep me from smelling bad," Pruitt said. "I wouldn't rub none of that stuff up under my arms if you paid me to do it. That something they give you at college?"

"No, of course not. I had to buy it at the Rexall."

"And you spent good money on it?"

"They don't give it away for free."

Pruitt stepped close to his son and thrust out his chin. "You getting smart-mouthed with me, boy? I'll whip your college hiney before you can say jack rabbit."

Jeff snapped the lid on the deodorant and put it into his shaving kit. The rectangular leather bag was one of his treasured possessions, a gift Osby had purchased with her egg money when Jeff left for college.

"I don't want you wasting money on dumb stuff like that," Pruitt said as Jeff pulled a white T-shirt over his head.

"Wasn't your money," Jeff said.

"Yeah, well, I don't remember seeing you offer any up for all my food you been eating."

"How much you want?" Jeff asked.

"How much you got? Must be plenty if you got some to waste on stuff you smear into your underarm hair."

Jeff slipped on his trousers and sat down on an old chair to put on his shoes and socks. "I don't have a lot. But I got enough to give you some for what I ate, if you think that's fair."

"Of course, I think that's fair," Pruitt said. "You don't live here no more. I ain't getting no work out of you. I don't see no benefit to you whatsoever unless you pay me for your food."

"How about two dollars?" Jeff asked. He finished tying his shoes, stood up and pulled his wallet from the hip pocket of his pants.

"How about three," Pruitt said.

Jeff pulled two ones from his wallet, and then counted out another dollar in coins. Pruitt crammed it all into the front pocket of his overalls and left the wash shed without another word.

Three days later, Jeff returned to school. He took his exams, making all A's, but didn't register for the spring semester. He did, however, continue to live in the dorm. Under the special circumstances of the era, the college allowed young men waiting to enter the service to continue residing in their dorms on a week-to-week basis. As soon as exams were over, Jeff and Preacher went to the army recruiter in Alexandria and arranged to enlist on Preacher's birthday, exactly one week in February after Jeff's. The recruiting official promised they could serve together throughout the war on the buddy system. Despite this arrangement, Jeff received a draft notice ordering him to report to the induction center on his own birth date. They were not able to unsnarl this typical snafu, and Jeff and Preacher were separated for the entire war.

The day before he was to report for boot camp, Jeff ran into Billye Monroe en route to his dorm room from the library, where he had returned books. The day was sunny and crisp, with a steady north wind singing through the pine trees. Billye was wearing a straight wool skirt and a tight sweater, a bright red scarf around her neck.

"Hey, Jeff," she said when their paths crossed.

"Hi," Jeff responded, his voice flat, still nursing his embarrassment.

"I haven't seen you since last semester," she said. "Did you get your A in English?" Her long brown hair kept whipping across her face, and she smiled each time she had to reach up and pull her hair back.

"Yes," he said. "How did you do?"

"I got an A, too, if you can believe it. Got a C in math, though. Probably a gift, I guess. I never did know what was going on. I had hoped maybe I could get you to help me with math this semester. I'm really lost now."

"I would have," Jeff said, shrugging and feeling himself clumsy. "But—" He stopped abruptly, not knowing what else to say to her. The wind continued to whip her hair; she pulled it into a ponytail with the thumb and index finger of her right hand, causing her right breast to rise and flatten. Jeff looked away.

"But I hear you're off to the war pretty soon," Billye said.

"Yeah," Jeff replied. "How'd you hear that?"

"Oh, I asked around when you didn't show up in any of my classes this term."

"Yeah," Jeff said, wishing he knew how to talk to this girl who was being so nice to him.

"So how soon?" Billye said. "When are you off?"

"Tomorrow," Jeff said.

"Army?" she asked.

"Yep," he said. "Over hill, over dale." He wanted to shoot himself for saying that.

"Well, I hope you'll take care of yourself," Billye said. "We'll miss you."

"Thanks," Jeff said. He looked at her, and she smiled, and his heart melted, and in a swirl of tender feelings for her, he suddenly felt afraid. He was going off to war, and he might not come back to this well-manicured college awash in the fresh scent of pine where there was still so much to learn, to this place that was like a dream to him, a heavenly escape from the hellish environment he grew up in. He might not come back to this beautiful girl in her stylish clothes who was also like a dream to him. He imagined himself in a foxhole somewhere, stranded on a treeless plain, the pounding of huge guns ringing in his ears, the air stinging with the smell of sulfur. He imagined the whir of grinding engines and the crush of vegetation and stone under metal and the realization that he was stranded in the open with only the dirt of his own digging for protection and the enemy bearing down upon him in tanks. He imagined the panic of trying to outrun armor and the instant death of machine-gun bullets.

Jeff felt about to cry, not from fear, but from the love he felt for all he was about to leave behind, all he had found since he had left the hard red soil of his parents' plot of earth in New Peterstown. He was about to leave everything he had learned to love so quickly, and he might never return. Or he might return altered in some horrible way, crippled perhaps, or changed inside. His throat felt thick, and his lips trembled. He looked away from her; the wind gusted, and his eyes stung.

Billye could tell that Jeff was different from before, but it didn't occur to her that he was on the verge of weeping or that he might be afraid. She thought the war was terrifying, but apart from those slain at Pearl Harbor, the list of American dead had not yet grown long, had not yet included anyone she knew. She presumed his strong feelings arose from patriotism, and she understood the duty young men felt to leave their lives behind to fight this war. For she had such feelings herself.

"My girlfriend and I," Billye said, "Pam Pendergast, a girl I went to high school with back home in Shreveport, Pam and I are going to go to work for the USO. It's mostly volunteer, but they have a statewide office down in New Orleans. We're going to get jobs there."

"When?" Jeff said, curious at this revelation.

"Right after school is out. My family wants me to finish my freshman year."

"What kind of work are you going to do?"

"Secretarial stuff, probably," Billye said. "I'm a pretty good typist."

"And your parents don't mind?" Jeff asked. "Your dropping out of school?"

"They're concerned, I guess. But they understand. What with the war and all. I just want to help some way. I'll go back to college when the war's over. I promised them that." The wind stilled, and she dropped her hair back around her shoulders. She smiled. "So—I'll see you back here."

"Yeah," Jeff said. "I'll see you then."

"Could I ask you something?" Billye said.

"Sure," Jeff replied.

"Could I give you a hug? For luck, I mean?"

Jeff didn't answer, but he stepped forward. They put their arms around one another and squeezed each other hard. His lower jaw trembled, and he had to bite his lower lip to keep from crying.

"You take care of yourself," Billye whispered.

"You, too," Jeff said.

Then they headed off in opposite directions, Jeff mopping tears with the back of his hand. When she was perhaps a hundred yards away, Billye turned and waved. But Jeff didn't see her.

chapter fourteen

AYE WATSON HAD JUST UTTERED the astonishing words, "Or maybe I do," when she broke down and began sobbing. Before she could collect herself, Agent Mason slammed open the door and strode back into the motel room at the Fountainebleau.

"All right," Mason said. "I'm going to have to ask you folks to leave. I checked up on you at the *States-Tribune.* You aren't writing any story that concerns this girl, and I'm ordering you out of here. I don't like being lied to."

"Didn't know there was a federal statute against lying," Preacher said. "Betcha Lyndon don't know that or he might be packing his bags for Leavenworth as we speak."

"Don't test me, mister," Mason said.

"We have a right to visit with our friend," Glenda said. "And you can't hold Faye against her will." To Faye she said, "They can't make you stay here. We can get a lawyer to make them let you go."

"If you want us to protect you," Mason said to Faye, "then you're going to have to let us call the shots."

"I do feel better off here," Faye said to Glenda. "They're right that a lot of people out there might think I had something to do with this." She looked fleetingly at Preacher and Tommy before casting her eyes down on the floor. "I'm really tired now—"

"So that settles it," Mason said. "I'll be happy to escort you folks back to your car."

It appeared they had no recourse, so they rose to leave. At the door, Glenda said to Faye, "You have our phone number, honey. These men can't stop you from calling us if you want to." She looked at Mason before continuing. "Moreover, I have every intention of visiting with my friend whenever she wants to see me. Is that understood?"

Mason responded, "Okay, folks, let's move it. The young lady has indicated she's tired."

"You guys are a sorry bunch of peckerheads," Tommy said as he followed Glenda past Mason and out the door.

"You really don't want to mess with me, son," Mason replied. "You have no idea what I can do to you."

Tommy stopped and turned around. "I don't like being threatened, sir," he said. "I hope you realize you've just done so in front of three witnesses."

Mason stepped out onto the walkway, brushing Tommy's chest.

"Hey!" Tommy complained, furious at the obvious attempt at physical intimidation.

"Go away, hippie," Mason said.

Preacher stepped between them, circling his arm through Tommy's as if they were two Italian gents off for a stroll. "Let's be on our way, young buck," he said and began moving off so that Tommy either had to follow along or snatch himself rudely away. Tommy's feet shuffled on the concrete for a step or two, but he let himself be led away.

"The Bible addresses this situation, I think," Preacher said as they walked off. "There's a time to stand. And a time to be bland. Something like that. I may be paraphrasing somewhat."

Catching his breath from a rush of adrenaline, Tommy realized abruptly how much trouble he'd almost gotten into. He patted Preacher's arm.

"There's a time to rise up and a time to wise up," Preacher said. "I think maybe that's how that verse goes."

Back in the parking lot, Preacher, Glenda and Tommy talked for a while about what Faye may have been on the verge of saying before she broke down and Agent Mason barged in. "I can't imagine she really knows anything," Glenda said. "It must just be some intuition she got from Ben's behavior in the days before—"

Eventually, they decided to wait a bit and try to talk to Faye again.

"One thing you can count on." Preacher said. "If the cops thought she was involved in any way, they wouldn't let us have any access to her at all."

The next morning, six days after Ben Watson shot and killed Dr. Brown, Glenda and Tommy were at Charity Hospital sitting with Jeff when two doctors and a nurse came into the room and asked them to wait outside in the hall. Jeff was sleeping, but his condition had improved, and hopes were strong now that he would recover. The fluid build-up in his lungs was a cause for concern, but his other vital signs were encouraging.

Glenda went to the waiting room. But Tommy wanted to talk to the doctors, so he leaned up against the wall just outside the door; he could hear the sheet rustle as they pulled it down over Jeff's body and tape rip as they peeled away bandages to examine Jeff's wounds. After fifteen minutes the younger of the two doctors came into the hall to speak with Tommy.

"Are you Reverend Caldwell's son?" the doctor asked. He was half a foot shorter than Tommy, swarthy, pudgy and slightly damp looking. But there was a gentleness in his face.

"Yes, I am," Tommy said, extending his hand. "Tommy Caldwell."

"Michael Boudreau," the doctor said as they shook hands. "Second-year resident." He put his hands in the baggy pants of his white uniform and jiggled his keys. "So, how's he doing?"

"You tell me." Tommy said. Referring to Jeff's personal physician, he added, "Dr. Franklin told us yesterday he wasn't out of the woods but that signs were good. He's still sleeping a lot. And he's dopey sometimes when he's awake. Not raving or anything. But not clear, either."

"That's mostly to be expected," Dr. Boudreau said. "I'd say we're on the road to recovery, God willing, of course." He tucked his upper teeth down on his lower lip and made a sucking sound. Tommy felt an icicle of dread creep down his spine. "We're a little concerned about the sleeping, though. All in all, he ought to be more alert."

"What are you trying to tell me, doctor?"

"Nothing probably. Just trying to keep you informed. We're watching the situation. Gathering information." The nurse passed through the door beside them in a swish of starched white and was followed immediately by the older physician, Dr. Samuel Lowenstein, whom Tommy had met previously. He was a tall, thin, bespectacled white man who had let his graying curly hair grow out into a modest Afro. "I just explained to Tom here," Dr. Boudreau said to Dr. Lowenstein, "that we were a bit concerned about his dad's retarded alert responsiveness."

"Could it be the drugs?" Tommy asked. "Some kind of reaction to the pain medication?"

"Possibly," Dr. Lowenstein said.

"But not likely," Dr. Boudreau added.

"Has your father had any history of depression?" Dr. Lowenstein asked.

"No," Tommy said.

"No shock treatment?" Dr. Boudreau said. "No mood elevators?"

"Heavens, no," Tommy said. "I mean, Dad has had his blue moments like anybody. But never anything that required medical treatment."

The two doctors looked at each other. "Well," Dr. Boudreau said, "we were just speculating. Depression often manifests itself in this kind of thing."

Tommy laughed mirthlessly and said. "Dad has been shot by a man he'd worked with for years, and his friend was shot at his side. He probably *is* depressed. Wouldn't you be?"

"Of course," Dr. Boudreau said.

Tommy could have made a list of other reasons his father might be depressed. He lost his church. His wife divorced him. His second marriage failed after just two years. And then the trauma of the times. Martin Luther King was gone. Robert Kennedy was gone. The war raged on. Richard Nixon was resurgent. George Wallace was poised to carry the South in November. And now George Washington Brown.

"Anything else you might tell us?" Dr. Lowenstein asked.

Tommy shrugged. "Dad has had his problems. I'm a little worried about his drinking."

"He drinks daily?" Dr. Lowenstein inquired.

"Yes, I'd say he does."

"To inebriation?" Dr. Boudreau asked.

"Rarely." Tommy said. "Sometimes."

"His symptoms aren't inconsistent with alcohol withdrawal," Dr. Boudreau said. "Still, I doubt that's the source of our problem. But thanks. That might help."

"I have one other question," Dr. Lowenstein said. "Since the morning after the shooting, the police have been asking to talk to your father. Dr. Boudreau and Dr. Franklin and I have been holding them off, wanting to give your father proper time for recovery. Now that it's been nearly a week, they're becoming more insistent. And medically speaking, I don't know that we continue to have excuses to hold them at bay."

Tommy wrinkled his brow. "Gee whiz, they can't really talk to him until somebody has told him Dr. Brown didn't make it."

"He doesn't know?" Dr. Boudreau asked.

"He knows Dr. Brown was shot," Tommy said. "But I don't think he knows the rest. And I don't want the police telling him. I want a friend of his here when he's told. How long do I have?"

"I can probably hold them off until this afternoon," Dr. Lowenstein said.

"And you think he can handle this news?" Tommy asked.

"Medically speaking, yes," Dr. Lowenstein said, "It's possible that hearing the truth could even prove therapeutic. Some part of his depression, if that's what he's suffering from, could be triggered by dread: fearing to hear the worst. By facing it, perhaps he can move on."

When Tommy and Glenda woke Jeff, he wanted some juice, and Tommy went to fetch it. Glenda sat at his bedside as she often did, touching Jeff gently on the hand as she talked to him. When Tommy returned, he helped Jeff drink the juice, holding the glass and bringing the bent straw to his lips. Both Glenda and Tommy tried to draw Jeff into conversation. They told him about their visit with Faye, but that seemed to distress him, Faye no doubt invoking thoughts of Ben. Jeff drifted in and out of consciousness. Sometimes he babbled unintelligibly, unable, or perhaps unwilling, to focus. But when Preacher walked in, Jeff's mind seemed to clear.

"Look who's here." Jeff said, beaming. "My old partner in crime, Lefty Asshole."

Preacher chuckled and said, "You're about the only man I know's got enough assholes to have a left one. Course that's because you were always full of more shit than the rest of us. Needed more than one asshole to get it all out."

"Nice talk," Glenda said, laughing. "Exactly what seminary course taught all that?"

"Wasn't eschatology," Preacher said. "Though there was plenty of bullshit in that, too. So it must of been Introduction to Scatology. Required course as I remember."

Jeff laughed, and Preacher pulled a chair up to the foot of the bed and slapped lightly against the sheet over Jeff's legs. Jeff looked at Glenda and said, slurring his words a little, "Man's an outlaw, you know. Always called himself an outside agitator. Used to tell the reporters that was his occupation."

After a moment of awkward silence, Tommy asked, "How you feeling, Pop?"

"Fiiine," Jeff said, dragging out the word like an inebriated person.

Preacher grabbed hold of Jeff's toes and squeezed them through the cotton sheet. "We got some tough news for you, old soldier. You think you're up to it, or should we wait till you get more of your strength back?"

"What's the news?" Jeff said, wrinkling his brow. "I don't have cancer, do I?"

Tommy was startled by that response. "Dad," he said. "Do you know where you are?"

Jeff looked around as if sizing up his surroundings. "This is the Monteleone, isn't it?" he said, referring to the elegant old French Quarter hotel.

Tommy could hear Glenda suck in a bite of breath. "Do you recollect what happened at the church during the rally last Sunday night?" Tommy inquired.

Jeff looked around at Tommy with wide red eyes. "Of course, I do, you ninny."

"This isn't the Monteleone Hotel, Dad," Tommy said.

"Ain't the Jung neither," Preacher said, "though it might smell about as bad."

Jeff smiled broadly, looking at his old pal. "Goddammit, I know it's Charity Hospital. People keep asking me if I know where I am, like I was shot in my thick skull, not in the chest."

"Well, Jeff, why did you ask if you had cancer?" Glenda wondered.

Jeff looked at her and rolled his lips in between his teeth. "Joke," he said. "I was making a goddamn joke, but nobody thinks I'm funny anymore. Except Preacher. He's the only one in the bunch of you with a sense of humor."

"Jeff," Preacher said, squeezing Jeff's toes again. His voice dropped low and soft, and Tommy thought of Jesus raising his hand to still the tempest raging across the Sea of Galilee.

"God love you, brother," Preacher said amidst the stillness. "G.W. didn't make it."

Jeff's face sagged; it was as if he instantly aged five years. His eyes darted around the room, as if he were a man in desperate flight, cornered and looking for an escape route. Finally, Jeff looked at Preacher, breathed deeply and said, "Gone, huh?"

"I'm afraid so, bubba," Preacher said.

Jeff's eyes fell on the expanse of white covering him up to his armpits, and he tugged the sheet at his waist into pleats between his fingers. "Yeah, well," he said. "It's what I figured."

"I'm sorry, Dad," Tommy said.

"You two old troublemakers went back a long way," Preacher said.

"Long way," Jeff repeated. "They got another one, now. By all rights they should have got me, too. Not sure I don't wish they had."

"Now, don't be talking like that, Jeff," Glenda said. "You don't mean that."

"Well, I mean it," Preacher interjected.

Jeff looked at him and tilted his head. "You wish they got you?" he said.

"Hell, no, I don't wish they got me," Preacher said. "Why would I want to get shot? From the looks of you, it hurts to get shot. I mean you."

"I did get shot," Jeff said.

"I can pretty well tell that, bubba," Preacher said. "I wish he'd gone ahead and killed you too; then I wouldn't have to waste my morning jabbering with your lazy ass lying in the bed feeling sorry for yourself."

Jeff started chuckling. "You rotten bastard." Then he was coughing, laughing and groaning all at once. "Ow, you lousy peckerwood. You're making me laugh till I rip myself open."

"Just doing the Lord's undertaking," Preacher said. "You up there in the bed wishing to die, so I'm just rousting myself like the servant I am, trying to tickle you to death."

"Stop it," Jeff said, pressing his hands down over his bandages. "It's not funny, dammit." But he kept on laughing.

Jeff's mood of hilarity did not last long after Preacher left. Glenda went home to rest, and as Tommy watched, the depression edged back into Jeff's face like a pot filling with water from an open tap. "Do you want to talk about what happened?" Tommy asked, thinking that talking might be a way to relieve Jeff's sorrow.

"What's there to talk about?" Jeff replied, his eyes not leaving the sheet across his chest.

"Well, there's a question I'd like to ask you," Tommy said. Jeff didn't respond or even look up to meet his son's eyes. "When Preacher was here," Tommy went on, "you said about Dr. Brown that *they* got another one. What *they* were you talking about?"

"Klan," Jeff said. "Who else? Klan bastards. Killed Medgar, that's for sure. And those sweet children in Birmingham. Haven't proved it yet, but they will. Klan was behind Martin, too. Different Klan, maybe, with Martin. Big Klan. Big-money Klan. But they've always been there, wearing banker's suits and getting the rednecks in white sheets to do their bidding. That's the way it was with Martin, you mark my words."

Tommy touched Jeff's knee through the sheet. "Dad, are you telling me that you think the Klan had something to do with shooting you and Dr. Brown?"

"Who else?" Jeff said. He looked away and waved his hand dismissively.

"Dad," Tommy said gently. "Don't you remember who shot you?"

"You," Jeff said staring at the wall.

"What?" Tommy said, startled. "Me?"

"Not you," Jeff said, correcting himself as if irritated that Tommy didn't understand what he meant. "Who?"

"You don't remember?" Tommy asked.

"How could I remember?" Jeff said. "I wasn't there."

Tommy was alarmed by this exchange and tried to reassure himself that Jeff was just tired. "Dad," Tommy tried again. "Ben Watson shot you and killed Dr. Brown. Do you remember that? Are you trying to tell me you think Ben had something to do with the Klan?"

Jeff looked up at the ceiling, letting his eyelids fall open abnormally wide. "Man is a fragile vessel," he said. "Short of life should he live long. G.W. was my friend. And now he's gone. The flesh is weak. Guns are strong."

Jeff looked past where Tommy was sitting near the end of the bed and stared at the wall behind his son. "George Washington Brown," he continued. "Old bastard was kind of full of himself, you know. Or that's not it exactly. He wasn't a vain man. Just very formal. Determined always to appear dignified. And he had this sense that dignity proceeded from formality. Not at all an uncommon approach among educated black men of our generation. Very precise in the way he said things. At least that's the way he was around white folks. He was a little looser with his black buddies, I think. Still, even they mostly addressed him as Reverend Brown, and then Dr. Brown, never even as George. Lord, how we had to tweak him to get him comfortable with our calling him G.W. He came to like it, though, after a time. Refer to himself that way. Call you up on the phone, say 'G.W. here' when you answered."

Tommy made no further attempt to quiz Jeff about Ben Watson and his possible connection to the Ku Klux Klan. Instead, Tommy asked about Jeff's first meetings and involvement with Dr. Brown, and Jeff told him stories Tommy had heard before but liked hearing again. Tommy was comforted by the stories, by the richness that swelled into Jeff's voice, and the pleasure Jeff took in recalling the alliance he and Dr. Brown had made when they were young. Jeff talked until he fell asleep, and Tommy was sorry when the stories ended.

Later that afternoon, police investigators showed up—two New Orleans police detectives accompanied by an FBI agent. All three men were white; all wore dark suits. The New Orleans policemen asked the first questions while the federal agent listened attentively and took notes in a flip-top, black notebook. An officer named Detective Lipinski started the questioning, and Jeff was notably muted in his responses. All the buoyancy he'd shown with Preacher had now disappeared.

"Do you recall the events of last Sunday evening?" Detective Lipinski asked. He was a short, ill-kempt man with thinning black hair. "Do you recall the shooting?"

"Yes," Jeff said.

"And you recall who shot you and Dr. George Washington Brown?"

"Yes."

"You knew the assailant?"

Jeff didn't answer immediately, but finally he said, "Yes, I did."

"And you can name him?" Detective Lipinski asked.

Jeff's eyes darted from one to the next of the three men questioning him. "Yes," he said.

"Will you state his name for the record?" The detective's forehead shone, its oiliness no doubt aggravated by his habit of touching the back of his wrist to his hairline.

Jeff sucked in a deep, seemingly peevish breath. "No," he said.

The two detectives looked at each other, obviously surprised by this answer. "You know the identity of the shooter, but you're refusing to name him. Is that what you're telling us?"

"My recollection could be wrong," Jeff responded. "It could have been a bad dream."

"Sir," Detective Lipinski said, "You and your associate Dr. George Washington Brown were shot by a man named Ben Watson. Do you recollect that fact?"

"I used to call him Tick Tock, I believe."

"And do you recall—" Detective Lipinski began.

"Let me ask you a question," Jeff interrupted. "Ben Watson is dead, isn't he? He blew his brains out, didn't he? What's this all about?"

"Do you know why Ben Watson might want to shoot Dr. Brown?" Lipinski asked.

Jeff lay silent for a long time. "No," he said, finally. "I have no idea. I guess he must have just gone crazy."

"Do you know if he was a member of the Communist Party?" the FBI agent asked. Paul Smythe, pronounced to rhyme with "scythe." His lean physique, crewcut, dark-rimmed glasses and prominent nose gave him the appearance of a hawk. Jeff winced at this ridiculous question and placed a hand flat on the bandages over his wound.

"Sir?" Smythe prompted.

Jeff looked at him with one eye closed. "What's the matter with you people? You've tried to stick us with the commie label for years. But no, Ben Watson was not a member of the Communist Party. And even if he had been, that would not have made him one iota more likely to try to kill me."

"You have said that you thought *they* had shot Dr. Brown and yourself," Smythe said. "You implied that Ben Watson belonged to the same *they* who killed other national figures. Do you have information which could point to Ben Watson's involvement in such a conspiracy?"

The oddness of this question didn't immediately dawn on Tommy, but it evidently occurred to Jeff instantly. "When did I make such a statement?" Jeff asked. "I don't remember making any such statement." But he had, of course, that very morning.

"Witnesses have given evidence of your having made such a statement," Smythe said.

"Who?" Jeff asked.

"I'm afraid I'm not at liberty to say," Smythe responded.

"Tell them they were mistaken," Jeff said.

"They were not mistaken," Smythe rejoined.

Jeff settled back against his pillow and closed his eyes. "Go away," he said softly.

"Are you not willing to cooperate in this investigation?" Detective Lipinski asked.

"Tommy," Jeff said to his son, his eyes still closed, "the bastards have bugged the room. Maybe in the telephone. Maybe in the lamp. Hell, maybe at the end of the catheter tube.

Maybe they're listening to me from the inside."

Tommy stared hard at the three lawmen. Lipinski and his partner both looked away, but Smythe stared back. "I hope you have the proper authority for any device you've installed in this room," Tommy said. "You can bet our attorneys will—"

"Shut up," Smythe ordered.

"Hey," Tommy said, "you can't talk to me like that."

"You want to stay in this room," Smythe said, "you better do what—"

Jeff raised his hand, and Smythe stopped. "What's this all about?" Jeff asked. His voice seemed tiny and far away. "What do you guys want?"

"We're trying to understand what motivated Ben Watson to murder George Washington Brown," Detective Lipinski said.

"We'd think you'd want to help us," Smythe added.

"I do," Jeff said. "But I can't."

chapter fifteen

H E NEITHER PLANNED NOR INITIALLY REALIZED IT, but Jeff Caldwell changed his life when he delivered his Christmas sermon in 1963. It was Christmas Eve, and the service was held at 5:30 so that families could go on to other festivities. Billye and the women of the church had decorated for the season. Potted red poinsettias sat against the sides of each pew in the two center aisles and in a row across the front of the rostrum. Spruce garlands framed the baptismal font and draped the backs of the pulpit chairs and the ends of each of pew. Cranberry-scented white candles burned in candelabra in the church's four corners. The whole sanctuary smelled of evergreen and spice.

The congregants sang "Silent Night," "O Little Town of Bethlehem" and "O Come All Ye Faithful." The children of the church acted out the nativity scene. Then Jeff rose to speak. As he walked from his chair to the pulpit, he took his sermon notes from the inside pocket of his suit coat. He smoothed the typed pages and reached into the breast pocket of his coat for the reading glasses which corrected his farsightedness. Peering through the half-lensed spectacles, he stood silent for an uncomfortably long moment. Tommy and Danielle wondered if he had brought the wrong notes. Billye worried that Jeff had suffered something more serious than a concussion on the Bonnet Carré Spillway bridge.

Finally, Jeff removed his glasses, looked up again and uncharacteristically said, "Let us pray." As heads bowed in front of him, he said, "Oh God, maker of all things, designer of all life, You call us to You especially in this season of the birth of your son, Jesus. Let us hear your call. Let it become clear to us what it is we must do. And let us pledge ourselves this night to do it in the new year which is before us. Give us courage, God. Give us the courage of righteousness. We ask these things in the name of Jesus whom You sent into the world to shine His light upon us and whom You bade lay down His life so that we might be free. Amen."

Jeff looked up again and stood silent once more before he began, "We live in times of sweeping changes. We gather together but one sad month since our president was slain, but even in our mourning, we believe that God is with us. In the lifetimes of all but the children among us, we have fought and won a great war against aggression and tyranny. And we have felt that God was on our side. We have presided over a miraculous rebuilding of the countries of our defeated enemies, who are now our allies. And we have done this in the confidence that God was on our side. Today we enjoy a time of peace and unparalleled prosperity. There may be clouds on the horizon, but the sun shines upon us. And we continue to believe that God is on our side."

Jeff paused and licked his lips. "Well, I tell you, my beloved brethren, I believe that God has placed a great test before us. And His almighty allegiance depends on how well we do. We are like Abraham, asked to sacrifice Isaac, like Noah, asked to build a vast ark to the derision of his neighbors. We are like Job, asked to love God in the face of changes to our lives we did not expect and cannot fully understand."

Jeff looked out into the congregation with shining eyes. "This is a season of bounty," he continued. "We feast in this season, savoring the riches of the earth. And we give in this season, savoring the riches of the spirit. And as the Apostle Paul reminds us in the Book of Acts, chapter twenty, verse thirty-five, Jesus has said it is more blessed to give than receive."

Jeff breathed deeply and smiled broadly. "We live amid such bounty. We enjoy so many blessings in this great country: the blessings of freedom and opportunity, the blessings of material comfort. These are the blessings we have all received, every one of us in this room. And now we must share them with those who have not yet received such incredible blessings."

Jeff lowered his voice to a stage whisper. "We are obliged, yes obliged, to share these blessings with our brothers who have them not. Yes, we are obliged." And almost shouting, he said, "OBLIGED BY JESUS."

As he often did when he preached, Jeff left the pulpit to stalk the rostrum like a pacer who walks to sort through a problem, often speaking sideways rather than directly to his listeners. "I am struck by the oddity of how we behave in this country. We prepare CARE packages by the hundreds of thousands and transport them to the deprived people of Africa. This is certainly an example of sharing our blessings. And the members of this church give generously to the Foreign Mission Board that supports the work of our brave missionaries who spread the gospel to the people of Nigeria and Kenya and Ethiopia and all along the wide, languid waters of the Congo. This is certainly an example of sharing our profound spiritual blessings."

Suddenly Jeff stopped and faced forward, "And yet we allow our Negro brothers and sisters in our own country to go hungry and remain ill-educated. We allow them to wander in the trackless desert of hopelessness. How can this be? How *CAN* this be?"

Jeff returned to the pulpit now, slipping on his glasses and shuffling the pages of his notes as he continued to speak. "But maybe that is the wrong question. Maybe that is an irrelevant question. Or maybe that is a question of relevance only to historians who want to understand the past. For in the future we can behave this way no longer. We cannot. We can *not*. And I'll tell you why. Or better yet, I'll tell you two reasons why."

Jeff smiled and bit lightly for just a moment at the right corner of his lower lip. "First, we must begin to share our blessings of freedom and opportunity with our Negro brothers because we cannot afford to do otherwise. That's right, *we* cannot afford to do otherwise. Because it would be counter to our own self-interest. Yes, our *own* self-interest. Think about that for a second. I spoke earlier about clouds on the horizon of our unparalleled prosperity. I think we all know what those clouds are. They are the harbingers of distant thunder, of lightning bolts of oppression and godlessness that burst into the heavens from behind the iron and bamboo curtains. We enjoy a time of peace. But it is an uneasy peace. We have devised weapons capable of obliterating any enemy that would dare to rise against us, but our enemies possess the same weapons, so we find ourselves in a standoff. We fight our enemy not with machine-gun bullets and lobbed mortar shells and saturation bombs from our B-52s, not with the weapons that defeated Hitler and Mussolini and Hirohito. No. We fight this so-called Cold War with the very principles on which our nation was founded. Khrushchev says that the Soviets will bury us. He says that communism is the path to liberty. But we know better. We *know* better. And now we must *show* better. After nearly two hundred years we must finally provide, in the words of our Pledge of Allegiance, liberty and justice FOR ALL."

Jeff slipped his glasses on again for just a second, then yanked them back off and stared solemnly at the congregation. "That's one reason. And it's a good one. Self-interest. To protect our way of life from the Soviets and the Chinese and their minions, we must make sure that our enemies can point to no categorical failings in our system. That's an excellent reason."

Jeff lowered his voice again for a sentence before resuming in a normal tone, "But I'll give you a better one. The first reason protects our way of life. The second reason protects our way of *afterlife*. Jesus has made his demands upon us abundantly clear. We are to love our neighbors as ourselves. We are to take up our crosses and follow Him, for none otherwise cometh unto the Father. We must share our bounty with our Negro brothers and sisters precisely because Jesus demands it of us. He *demands* it of us. And we defy the wishes of our Lord and Savior only at the cost of our immortal souls, only at the price of damnation, only at the expense of eternal separation from the face of almighty God."

Jeff raised his hand to the center of his forehead and for a moment shaded his eyes with his palm. "And so in closing, I propose that the membership of this church make a gift to the community in which we live. A gift of an invitation to men and women of whatever race, to come and join our membership, to come and join us in worshiping Jesus who taught us to pray, our Father Who art in heaven—"

After the service, on the way home in the family's Rambler station wagon, with Tommy at the wheel and Jeff in the front passenger seat, Billye and Danielle in the back, Jeff asked what everybody thought of his sermon. He often did this, elicited comments and led a discussion about what he'd said and how well it had been received. Tommy responded, "Great, Dad. Good points all the way."

"It was fantastic, Daddy," Danielle said. "I wouldn't mind having Negro girls in my Sunday School class. I'd make friends with them."

Billye, however, didn't offer a comment, and after a moment, Jeff sat up straighter in his seat. Tommy glanced over at his father and watched Jeff's face light up as the car passed under a street lamp and then fall back into shadow. After a half a minute or so, Jeff twisted a bit to the left and asked, "What did you think, Billye?"

"I just wish you could have waited a week or two," Billye said from the dark of the back.

Jeff faced forward again. "Oh?" he said. "Really? Why would you wish that?"

Billye didn't respond immediately. "It was just a thought," she said finally. "It doesn't matter, I guess."

Jeff licked his lips. "Of course it matters," he said.

"No, it doesn't," Billye said. "Forget it, honey. Really."

"Well, I don't think I can forget it," he replied. "That may be the most important sermon I've ever preached. Here I've been working for civil rights for over a decade, and I pastor an all-white church. How hypocritical is that?"

"It's not hypocritical, Jeff. It's—"

"Of course, it's hypocritical," Jeff interrupted. "How could it be anything else?"

The ride from the church was little over a mile, and Tommy was already pulling into the driveway. "Let's not talk about this," Billye said. "Okay?"

"But I think we need to hash this out," Jeff said.

"No, really," Billye said as she got out of the car. "Let's just go in and eat so we can have Christmas. We can talk about this tomorrow or some other time."

Tommy and Danielle glanced at each other apprehensively as they got out of the car.

Inside, Billye directed Tommy to put a white table cloth on the dining room table and to set out the silverware while she and Danielle prepared a meal of turkey, cornbread dressing, green beans, brown-and-serve dinner rolls and sweet potatoes.

Normally, Jeff would have sat in the living room and read the newspaper or a magazine, but tonight he lingered in the kitchen. "Billye," he said, "I really think I'm going to have to insist your telling me what you found so objectionable about my sermon."

"Please, honey," Billye said. "Don't make a scene. It's Christmas."

"I'm not making a scene. I'm trying to have a discussion. Kids? Am I making a scene?" He looked at his daughter. "Danielle, am I making a scene?"

"I don't know, Daddy," she said. "I don't even know what a scene is."

"I really am sorry, Jeff," Billye said. "Your sermon was wonderful, as always. If I apologize, can we just let it drop?"

"No," Jeff said.

"All right. If I explain what I meant, can we eat our dinner and then have Christmas?"

"That's all I'm asking," Jeff said.

"What I meant was, I wish you could have let the people in the church have their Christmas. It's the holidays. It's a time for families. A time to be happy. I just wish—"

"And how many Negroes do you think are happy tonight?" Jeff snapped.

"Lots of them," Billye said with edge in her voice. "Those who are with their families, having a meal and looking forward to opening their presents."

"That's just it, Billye," Jeff said. "They don't have any presents to open. Most of them don't."

"Jeff," she said. "I know—I know probably better than anyone else how much your civil-rights work means to you. I know how much you crave justice for the Negroes. And you're right—of course you're right—to lead our church to accept Negro members."

"But?" Jeff interjected when she paused.

"But—" she continued. "Well, there is no but, really. It's just that I didn't think that the Christmas sermon was the time to do it. People don't want to think about hard things right now. Can you blame them?"

"Yes, I can blame them. Negroes have been waiting to be treated decently for 350 years. They shouldn't have to wait even one day longer."

Billye wiped her hands on her apron. "You know, Jeff, people in our church admire you. Most of them, anyway. They look up to you. You shouldn't always look down on them."

Although the family often opened their presents on Christmas Eve, they decided to wait until Christmas morning that year. When Danielle and Tommy went to bed, they could hear their parents still talking behind the closed door of their bedroom. After Danielle had turned out her light, Tommy crept out of his room and stood quietly outside his parents' room. "I don't think we've resolved this," Tommy heard his father say.

"But we have," Billye said. "I've taken it all back. I've apologized. What more can I do?"

"You're just saying that because you want to go to sleep."

"No, really, I'm not."

"Paul says in his letter to the Ephesians, 'Let not the sun go down upon your anger.' I've always tried to live by that. You know I have."

"How well I know it," Billye said.

"See," Jeff said. "Now that's sarcasm, sarcasm that can only be born of anger. So we haven't got it worked out, have we?"

"I'm just tired, Jeff. I'm exhausted. I wasn't being sarcastic. I was joking."

"You're so tired, you'd say anything just to get me to let you go to sleep."

"Yes, I would. Tell me what you want me to say, and I'll say it."

"But that's no good, don't you see? You have to mean what you tell me."

"I do mean it, Jeff. I'm so sorry. I was wrong. I wish I'd never said a thing."

The next morning as they opened their presents, Billye's face was drawn with fatigue; dark circles under her eyes made her whole face look gray. She tried to be cheerful, but her children could tell it was a strain. Jeff sat in his easy chair and said little until he got up and went to his study and returned with an unwrapped department-store box, which he handed to Billye. "I almost forgot," he said. "Sorry it's not wrapped."

"Thanks, honey," Billye said and opened the box. Inside was a lavender negligee, low cut and diaphanous. "I don't guess I can model this in front of the kids," she said, sniffling. She got up from her spot on the sofa and stepped over to her husband. They kissed quickly on the lips, and then laid their cheeks together. Jeff cupped his hand around the back off Billye's head and held her against him until she laughed and protested, "Let me go, silly."

Before Wednesday-night prayer meeting in the first week of January, 1964, Jeff met with his board of deacons to draw up a plan for implementing the invitation he'd proposed in his Christmas sermon. He wanted the deacons to draft a statement which could then be considered by the entire congregation at the next church business meeting. Jeff and the deacons met around the two long tables in the adult men's Sunday School room.

"I'd like to be among the first to address this issue," Jesse Kardowski said just after Jeff

gave the board his directions. Kardowski was the father of Tommy's classmate Earl
Kardowski, the fleet and shifty halfback on the McDonogh football team. Jesse Kardowski
was a thin, wiry man in his early fifties, slick bald on top with a fringe of gray. He earned
his living as an internal auditor for the New Orleans office of Shell Oil.

"I want to go on record as being totally opposed to what you're proposing," Kardowski
said. "You're going too far now. The members of this church have tolerated all your so-
called civil-rights activities for years. But this is too much. This is *my* church. I've been
coming to this church all my adult life, since it was just a First Baptist mission and this whole
area was just a ridge into the swamp. I've tithed to this church for thirty-two years. And
even though you've been our pastor for a long time now, I think this church is more mine
than yours. I was here when this building was built."

Jeff leaned forward on his elbows and started to speak but thought better of it and
sat back.

"Now, Jesse," chairman of the deacons Farley Smithson said, "this church doesn't
belong to you any more than it belongs to me, and I've been here as long as you." Tall,
thin and silver-haired, Smithson owned a prosperous men's clothing store a half-block
off Canal on Camp Street. He had a salesman's smooth manner and considered himself
good with people.

"Not quite as long," Kardowski said. "I remember when you joined the church."

"This church doesn't belong to any person," Associate Pastor Quentin Lloyd said. "It
belongs to God. Let's all keep that in mind."

"Here's my point," Kardowski said. "We have this church. And the Negroes have their
churches. We're here to worship God, not make statements about politics, about integration
and civil rights and whatnot. Why would a Negro even want to come to this church? Just
to make trouble is about the only reason I can think of. In which case, why would we want
to let such a person become a member?"

Some of the men at the table nodded, and Jeff's heart sank. They obviously hadn't been
listening to a word he said from the pulpit.

"Actually, Pastor," Farley Smithson said, "I've been thinking about what you said in your
Christmas sermon. And I've been thinking about your desire for a policy statement since
you asked me to call this meeting."

"I'm glad someone has," Jeff said and smiled broadly. He intended this remark as a kind
of joke, a way to lighten things up. But it came off sour, and no one laughed.

"Anyway," Farley said, "I came over to the church and asked Naylynn to give me our
current policy on membership. Just as I suspected, it makes no mention of race whatsoever.

It just says that we accept new members on the basis of profession of faith and baptism, or on the basis of a membership transfer letter from another Southern Baptist congregation."

"Yes?" Jeff said. "I'm not sure I'm following you."

"Well," Farley explained, "as it happens, all our members are white and—"

"And always have been white," Jesse Kardowski interjected.

Farley smiled patiently and continued, "And always have been white. But there's nothing in our constitution that says all the members have to be white."

"We had a Mexican family who were members once," Woody Harkins said, whether to be helpful or just to add information was unclear. "Some of y'all remember them. Right after the war. Hernandez family. He worked off shore for Mobil."

"I think the Hernandezes were Puerto Rican," Sonny Jenkins said.

"And we've got a dago right here on the board of deacons," Sal Licotti said, getting the laugh he intended.

"Sal Licotti is as close to a Negro as I want coming to my church," Jesse Kardowski said, laughing along with everybody else. "And I wouldn't want him if it weren't for his beautiful wife who is only Eye-talian by marriage." An uncomfortable silence followed the laughter.

Finally, Jeff said, "I still don't think I quite see what you're driving at, Farley."

"Well," Farley responded. "It seems to me that we don't really have to do anything at all. We don't have to change anything since our constitution doesn't preclude a Negro member now."

"That's remarkable," Quentin Lloyd said. "You'll probably be amazed to know I had exactly the same thought on the drive over here this evening."

Jeff looked daggers at Lloyd, but the associate pastor didn't meet his eyes. Lloyd was a big man, a former Chinese Bandit on Paul Dietzel's 1958 national champion LSU football team. Jeff liked Lloyd's youthful enthusiasm and had initially been swayed by Lloyd's barrage of flattery. After a time, though, Jeff had noticed that Lloyd flattered almost everyone. He followed Tommy's athletic feats in the newspaper, for instance, and was forever telling Jeff what a great kid Tommy was. He always called Tommy "Tiger," which Tommy detested.

"So you're proposing that we just do nothing whatsoever," Jeff said to Farley, not attempting to disguise his testiness.

"I'm saying I don't think we *need* to do anything, Pastor," Farley replied.

"Well, that's just not acceptable," Jeff said.

Farley drummed his fingers on the table and said, "Okay. Maybe you should share with us your concerns, and then we can try to address them."

"I want this congregation to make clear to our city's Negro community that we believe it our Christian responsibility to open our fellowship to people of whatever race."

"What do you want us to do, Pastor?" Jesse Kardowski snapped. "Put up a big sign that says, 'Negroes welcome here'?"

"I would think the cross on the steeple of this church is just such a sign," Jeff retorted.

"Pastor," Farley said in a slow, calm voice, "in light of what you desire, I propose that the other deacons and I try to draft a statement that we feel, if not unanimously—" He looked at Jesse Kardowski and then continued, "—then by consensus is something we could recommend to the church. We'll report back to you, say, in two weeks?"

Before the meeting two weeks later, Jeff read Farley's policy draft with a sense of frustration, dismay and anger. The statement proposed a membership committee that would interview any Negro who might apply for membership in the church and make a recommendation to the whole congregation as to whether the applicant should be accepted or rejected. Jeff began the meeting with his deacons by waving the document at them and announcing, "Gentlemen, this will not do."

"I told you he wouldn't accept it," Jesse Kardowski said to no one in particular.

"We worked hard on this, Pastor," Farley said. "And it has our unanimous support."

Jeff put his head in his hands and wiped his palms down over his eyes and cheeks. "Don't you men see what is wrong here?" He looked around the room at faces that registered confusion, hurt and indignation. "Don't you see how insulting this is? This is the opposite of the kind of message I want our church to send. How do we treat white people who apply for membership? Think about that. We sing the invitational hymn. And anyone who wants to join the church comes forward. They state to the pastor whether they are seeking membership by profession of faith or by transfer. And then we take a vote. And that's it. And no one is ever rejected. But now you men want to establish an entirely different policy for Negroes. Forgive me, gentlemen, but what is wrong with you people?"

"I'll tell you what's wrong with me," Jesse Kardowski said. "I'm sick and tired of you harping on and on about the Negroes. None of whom with any sense want to come to this church in the first place."

"Pastor," Farley said, "I would urge you to believe that this policy was prepared in good faith. But listening to your objections, I can see how we have indeed erred by creating two pathways to church membership, one for white, one for Negro." Farley looked around the room at his fellow deacons before continuing, "If I may speak for the board, I'd like to explain to the pastor the nature of our thinking."

The other deacons nodded their assent, except for Jesse Kardowski, who made clucking noises and refused to meet Farley's eyes.

"Several of our number," Farley said, addressing Jeff, "voiced concerns that a Negro or some group of Negroes might try to join our church, not truly to share our fellowship, but simply to further some political objective. That, of course, would not be an acceptable reason for seeking membership. And that's what might conceivably be different about the application of a Negro. A white person could not possess such a motive. Hence our desire to have a membership committee interview any Negro applicant for the purpose of determining his true motives."

"I am so ashamed," Jeff said. He shook his head. He was so angry he was afraid he was going to begin weeping. "I am so ashamed."

"You think we haven't listened to you, Pastor," Sal Licotti said. "But we have. A lot of us really have. And we've prayed about this. I know I have. You've asked us to think about something a different way than we've thought about it our whole lives. And we're trying. This statement we've proposed really represents that. We're not saying we wouldn't accept a Negro member. Only that we want to be sure the Negro really wants to worship with us and nothing more than that. If that's what it means to be a Christian, I'm ready to go to church with a Negro. I think most of us are. That probably wouldn't be true at most Southern Baptist churches, but I think it's true of the membership of Gentilly Boulevard. It's certainly true of the lay leadership."

Jeff abruptly stood up. "I am so disappointed," he said. "I don't think I can listen to this any longer."

"Please sit down," Farley said. "I would like to offer an amendment to our proposal. Perhaps we can solve this problem a different way and one which will prove satisfactory to you."

Jeff sat back down. "What if," Farley continued, "we create the membership committee as proposed and require all applicants to go before it, whatever their race, white as well as Negro."

Farley thought that Pastor Caldwell would accept this plan. It seemed the perfect solution. He was shocked when Jeff stood up again, walked to the doorway where he stopped and said, "I can't believe you men don't see what I'm driving at. I want us to reach out to the Negro community, and we can't do that by creating a membership process that's different from the one at every other Baptist church. I am so distressed about this that, frankly, I don't know if I can continue as your pastor. I am going to leave you to deliberate about this without me."

There was a stunned silence after Jeff left the room. No one knew what to say. Pastor Caldwell had always been a principled man, and that was why his congregation admired him. Even if they didn't agree with him on lots of things, they believed he was trying to do the right thing. Heretofore, however, he had reserved the exhibition of his principles for his sermons and his civil-rights activity outside the church. His sudden determination to exert his will with direct regard to the church itself left the deacons astonished, hurt and not a little angry.

During the following week, Jeff worried about this impasse more than he would have imagined. He did not tell Billye what was going on. He figured the deacons would break down and give in to his wisdom on this matter and that someday soon Gentilly Boulevard would be able to accept Negro members. Jeff prayed about this matter a great deal. He had no doubt that he was right, and he believed that God would stand with him as He always had. God had spared him at the Battle of the Bulge, on the Freedom Ride in the dark Alabama countryside and at the mouth of the Bonnet Carré Spillway bridge. He was chosen. He knew this, and he was humbled by it. But he bore a heavy burden never to turn away. It was his duty now to lead his congregation to become the first integrated Southern Baptist church anywhere in Louisiana. So he didn't pray that God show him the way. For he knew the way. He prayed that God would help him forgive his deacons for resisting his leadership.

Jeff was correct in much that he presumed during the week he waited after giving the deacons his ultimatum. Gentilly Boulevard Baptist would indeed become the first integrated Southern Baptist church anywhere in Louisiana. But it would not become so under Jeff Caldwell's leadership. For when Jeff met with his deacons the following Wednesday evening, they had not agreed to adopt a membership policy in accordance with his will. They had, instead, voted to adopt the membership policy as amended by Farley Smithson during the previous meeting. They had, furthermore, voted to accept Jeff's resignation.

"We take this action with a great deal of regret," Farley said at the meeting, speaking on behalf of the other deacons. "We know how involved you are in this issue. And we know how genuine your feelings are. But we need to move at our own pace. And we need to free you to move at yours. We wish you well. We are sure you will find meaningful ways to continue your service on this matter in other places. And we will pray for you and hope that you will pray for us as well." Smithson went on to say the deacons would propose to the congregation that Jeff be carried on salary until the end of June or until he secured other employment. The Caldwell family could remain in the parsonage until that time.

Jeff felt as if he'd been kicked in the stomach by a mule. He was barely able to breathe, unable to respond. When Smithson finished speaking and dismissed the meeting, Jeff remained in his chair at the head of the table without moving. Most of the deacons hung their heads and left the room quietly. But several came up to where Jeff was sitting. They wanted to shake his hand. Sal Licotti squeezed Jeff's shoulder as he said, "I want you to know how much your ministry has meant to me, Pastor. I think I've become a better man because of you."

Farley Smithson lingered to the last. After Sal left, Farley shut the door to the Sunday School room and sat down with Jeff. "I know this comes as a shock to you, Pastor. And I know that in the days to come, as you face the uncertainties that lie ahead, you may contemplate trying to fight this thing before the whole congregation. I hope you won't do that. It wouldn't be a good thing for the church."

Jeff actually hadn't yet thought of fighting. But Farley talked calmly on and explained the hurtful things that might happen if Jeff tried to resist the deacons' decision. And Jeff saw that he was right.

After a time, Jeff barely heard the words Farley said to him. When Farley left the room, Jeff contemplated what to do next. Quentin Lloyd conducted the Wednesday-night prayer service, but Jeff always attended if he was in town. Instead of going to prayer meeting, when he finally stirred from the Sunday School room, without even stopping in the office for his suit coat, Jeff walked straight out to his beige Rambler station wagon and drove to the Black Orchid cocktail lounge about ten blocks from the church.

Inside, there was no overhead lighting. A row of booths against the wall was lit only by flickering red candles on each table. Three patrons sat at the bar, which was lit only so the bartender could see what he was doing. All had cigarettes going, but the permeating smell of smoke in the low-ceilinged room was obviously the product of many years of business. Jeff stood in the doorway a moment, blinking until his eyes adjusted, and then hesitantly sat down in the second booth from the door. After a moment, the bartender called over to him, "We don't have table service. What can I get you?"

"Oh," Jeff said. He rose and walked over to the bar.

"So what'll it be?" the bartender asked again.

"Uh, whiskey," Jeff said.

"Bourbon?"

"Do you have Jack Daniels?" Jeff inquired.

The bartender frowned. "I think we can probably handle that," he said.

"Jack Daniels then," Jeff said. He and Preacher Martin sometimes drank Jack Daniels when they were out of town together, always in a motel room to avoid being seen by someone Jeff knew among all the teetotaling Baptists in the world. Preacher would buy a bottle in a liquor store, and they'd have what Preacher liked to call "a toddy." Jeff thought about calling Preacher now. But he wasn't yet ready to tell anybody what had happened. He was embarrassed. How could he have miscalculated the situation so badly?

The bartender poured Jeff a drink, and Jeff returned to his booth where he sipped on it and tried to figure out what to do next. He'd been at Gentilly Boulevard Baptist Church for nearly ten years. Now he was going to have to move his family. That wouldn't affect Tommy much, Jeff guessed. Tommy would graduate in June and could move into a Tulane dorm. But Danielle was just going into ninth grade and couldn't remember living anywhere else.

Jeff ordered a second Jack Daniels. When he got his third, he bought a pack of Kents, too. He never had done much drinking—a few times when he was in the service, a couple now and then with Preacher for the shared feeling that they were above the silly taboos of their denomination. But Jeff had been a serious smoker as a young man, and he'd enjoyed it, preferring it vastly to the tobacco his father and brothers chewed. He had quit when Billye was pregnant with Danielle and his smoking aggravated her morning sickness. He missed it sometimes. But lots of Baptists thought smoking was almost as bad as drinking, and he noticed that it was not a habit practiced by pastors at the really prestigious churches.

Sitting over his third whiskey, Jeff loosened his tie and unbuttoned the top button of his white shirt. Then he lit up his smoke. The first one tasted awful. The second was better. The third tasted good. Jeff didn't go home until after midnight, seven glasses of Jack Daniels and a half pack of Kents later. He wasn't drunk, he didn't think. But he could feel the effects of the booze, so he drove home slowly, both hands on the steering wheel, carefully thinking his way through every turn.

His family met him at the front door. Billye threw her arms around his neck saying, "My god, Jeff, where have you been? I've been just about to call the police. You've had us worried sick."

Danielle hugged him from the side and said, "Pee yew, Daddy, you smell like an old ashtray."

"Jeff?" Billye said, pulling her head back and looking up at him. "Jeff, you've been drinking."

Jeff didn't say anything, and Billye stepped away a bit, still keeping her hands on his chest. Tommy sensed something horrible was happening. He looked at his father, whose shirttail was hanging out in the back, and then at his mother, whose face seemed to flash an inventory of possible responses to his father's condition.

Billye took her husband by the hand. "Come in here and sit down, Jeff. We need to talk. All of us need to talk."

Jeff allowed himself to be led to his easy chair, where he sat down and folded his hands in his lap.

"I know what happened at the deacons' meeting today," Billye said. "When you didn't show up at prayer meeting, I asked Farley if he knew where you were. He told me that you'd tendered your resignation. But Quentin said it was more complicated than that."

Jeff started to explain his understanding of what had happened, but he kept slurring his words and shaking his head. Finally, he said, "I don't feel well. I ought to go to bed."

"Danielle, go put on a pot of coffee," Billye ordered. "Honey, we need to talk. We have to decide what we're going to do."

"No!" Jeff said, standing up unsteadily. "I have to go to bed." He took a step and almost lost his balance.

"You ought to be ashamed," Billye said. "Letting your children see you like this."

Jeff made it to the hall door and steadied himself by grabbing the door frame. "Go ahead," he said. "Turn against me. I knew you would." He looked drunkenly at Tommy and then at Danielle, who was coming out of the kitchen. "I knew you all would," he said. "For it is written in the book of Job that all would be lost, all riches, all reputation, even beloved wife and children. All. All lost."

Jeff and Billye were already at the breakfast table when Tommy came down the next morning. Billye had made eggs, bacon and pancakes—highly unusual for a school day when breakfast fare usually consisted of cereal and milk or toast and hot chocolate.

"No," Billye said to Jeff as Tommy walked into the kitchen. "No. We've got to fight."

"How can I fight?" Jeff said. "I told them I would resign if they wouldn't design a racially integrated membership policy, and they wouldn't do it. They accepted my resignation."

"The deacons can't accept your resignation," Billye argued. "That's a matter for the whole congregation. We're not gonna just walk away from a life we've built. The deacons can recommend what they will. But we'll take this before the whole congregation, and we'll win."

When Tommy arrived home from basketball practice that night, he went into the kitchen to find his mother tight-lipped in the process of making dinner. She barely greeted him and seemed to punctuate every gesture with a little more force than necessary, setting each pot down with a little bang, opening a drawer with a snap, causing a clatter of metal as she searched for a utensil.

"Where's Dad?" Tommy inquired.

"I don't know," Billye replied. "Go wash up for dinner."

Tommy laughed. "What are you talking about, Mom. I just took a shower after practice."

"Well, set the table then," she said.

While Tommy was in the dining room laying out silverware, napkins and side dishes, Danielle came in and said to him, "There's something very weird going on here."

"No shit, Sherlock," Tommy said. "Our father's lost his job. Pretty soon they'll be repossessing all your forty-fives and my collection of used Converse high-tops."

"Stop it. This is serious," Danielle said and started to cry.

Immediately, Tommy took his sister in his arms. "Hey, Dani, I'm sorry," he said.

Crying into his shirt, she said, "I'm scared, Tommy. What's going to happen to us? Daddy's gone crazy or something. He's not here again, and Mommie doesn't know where he is."

"It's going to be okay," Tommy said and kissed the top of his sister's head. "Come on, Dani. This happens to people. Fathers lose their jobs sometimes. But the world doesn't end."

"That's easy for you to say. You're about to go off to college. And you have a scholarship. But I haven't even started high school yet. We're going to have to move out of our house. What if we have to move out of town? I won't go. I'll come and live with you at your dorm."

Tommy knew that was impossible, but he smiled and said, "Sure, baby, sure. No matter what else happens, you're my sis, and I'll look out for you. Even after I'm married." He kissed the top of her head again. "Probably for sure after I'm married because you'll start being an old maid around then. Ugly as you are, nobody will ever want to marry you."

"Oh, stop it," Danielle said, sniffling, looking up into her brother's face. She wore her long blond hair pulled off her face with a headband. Her straight white teeth were accentuated by gorgeous dimples when she smiled. She was quite beautiful, and she knew it.

"Nobody will want to marry you," Tommy repeated. "So you'll have to come and live with me and my wife. We'll let you be our maid."

"You rat," Danielle said. She smiled and hammered at Tommy's chest with her fists.

"You two come in here and fix your plates," Billye called out.

Tommy and Danielle broke apart and went into the kitchen where Tommy asked,

"Aren't we waiting for Dad?"

"No," Billye said.

Danielle looked at Tommy who said, "Why not? He didn't go out of town, did he?"

"I don't know," Billye said, and then she collapsed into tears too, bending at the waist as if she'd been struck a blow in the belly, finally resting her elbows against her knees and sobbing. Danielle began crying again as she and Tommy rushed over to their mother.

"Oh, Jesus," Tommy said.

"Mommie," Danielle said. "Stop it, Mommie. Please stop it. Please."

Tommy helped his sister and his mother into the dining room, then went back into the kitchen and poured them glasses of iced tea. When he returned, Danielle was kneeling beside Billye, her head on Billye's lap. When he was seated Tommy said, "Mom, you need to tell us what's going on."

Billye blotted at her eyes with her napkin and took a swallow of tea. She started to speak, but her voice caught in her throat, and she swallowed hard.

"We're going to fight this thing, right?" Tommy said. "I heard you talking with Dad this morning, and you're absolutely right. The deacons can't accept Dad's resignation if he withdraws it. We can take this to a business meeting of the whole church where we'd win. Wouldn't we?"

Billye shook her head in a tight motion side to side, almost as if she was shivering. She swallowed hard again. "Your father isn't going to fight."

"Then we'll fight for him," Tommy said. "You and me and Danielle."

Billye shook her head in that shivering motion again. "He wouldn't let us," she said. "But it doesn't matter. We wouldn't win anyway."

"I don't believe that," Tommy said.

"I talked to Farley today," Billye said. "I thought for sure he'd help us. But he won't. He'll oppose us. And if he opposes us, we don't have a chance."

"Well, we'll organize a boycott or something. They're firing Dad because of his civil-rights work. We'll keep them from having church at all. Dr. Brown will get all the Negroes in town to hold a demonstration."

"Tommy," Billye said, "You know that won't happen. Your father would never put Dr. Brown in that kind of position."

She was right, of course. But at barely eighteen years old, Tommy looked at life through the eyes of an athletic competitor. He didn't know how to accept defeat.

"Well, then, fuck 'em," Tommy said. "Fuck 'em all. Fuck every one of 'em."

Billye glared at her son. "Thomas Peter Caldwell," she said. "I absolutely won't have language like that in this house. You get out of your chair and come over here this minute."

"I'm sorry, Mom," Tommy said.

"Over here, right now," Billye commanded.

Tommy stood up and walked around the table to his mother who looked up at him and slapped his face. He drew back in shock, his hand against his cheek.

"Stop it now," Danielle wailed. "Stop it, stop it, stop it."

"We will not be reduced to white trash because of this," Billye said. "We will retain our civility and our dignity if we haven't another thing in this world."

Jeff did not come home at all that night. But he did call the next morning to tell Billye that he was all right. He wouldn't tell her where he was, however, only that he'd gone away somewhere to think. He wouldn't say when he was coming home, either. But he promised to call every morning.

In his absence, Billye tried to keep her family to its usual routine. On Friday and Saturday nights, she and Danielle went to watch Tommy play basketball, but the results only further blackened the family's spirits. Tommy had a subpar game Friday, including a turned ankle, and a poor one Saturday that contributed to an upset loss.

Tommy's poor weekend performances on the basketball court put him in a particularly sour mood on Sunday morning when Billye woke him for church. "I'm not going to church," he told his mother as he walked into the kitchen still wearing his pajamas. "Why would I want to sit and worship with people who are putting us out of our home?"

Billye was dressed in black stockings and high heels, a straight black linen skirt, a white blouse and a matching black jacket. It was an outfit she'd worn lots of times before, but now she looked as if she were going to a funeral.

"Go get dressed, Tommy," Billye said in a soft voice. "We're going to church, and I don't want to argue with you about it."

"I don't understand," Tommy said. "I don't understand why you'd even want to go."

"I want to go because it's my church."

"Well, it's not *my* church. Not anymore."

"Go get dressed, Tommy. You have to trust me. It's the right thing." Billye looked at her son's frowning, angry face. "Do it for me. Okay?"

Tommy didn't say anything else. He returned to his room and dressed in his suit and a thin red tie. In a small act of defiance, though, he put on a pair of black Converse high-tops instead of his dress loafers. Fortunately for Tommy, Billye was too distracted to notice, for she would have insisted that he change.

Usually they sat separately, Danielle and Tommy with friends their own age, Billye by herself or with one of the deacons' wives. Today they sat together, the children on either side of their mother, in the second pew from the back in the center section. On the rostrum Quentin Lloyd sat in the chair Jeff usually occupied. Farley Smithson sat in the chair usually filled by the associate pastor. Tommy began to seethe as soon as he saw him.

After the hymns and a choral number, Smithson approached the pulpit with an unsmiling demeanor. "I have sad news to impart," he announced. "This past Wednesday night, before a meeting of the board of your deacons, Pastor Caldwell announced his resignation from his ministry here at Gentilly Boulevard Baptist Church."

There was little reaction from the congregation. Obviously, the word had spread from the deacons and their wives to other members of the church. Tommy knew it was unreasonable, but he felt betrayed that not a single soul leaped up and demanded to know how this could have happened.

"Pastor Caldwell has served this church since 1954," Smithson continued. "And we will always remember him with great fondness. He departs to concentrate his ministerial activities in the area of racial relations, which, as you all know, has been of great concern to him for many years. Pastor Caldwell could not be with us today. But Mrs. Caldwell and Tommy and Danielle are here, and I know you will all want to join with me in wishing them Godspeed."

Tommy wanted to leap up and scream at Smithson and every other dirty traitor in the whole church. He wanted to call them bigots and cowards and worse. He wanted to curse and spit and stomp out never to return. But he felt his mother's hand reach up to his arms which were folded across his chest. She already held Danielle's hand with her left; now she took Tommy's hand into her right. The three of them sat there holding hands while Quentin Lloyd preached a sermon titled, "The Changing of the Guard." And all the while Tommy sat silent as he knew his mother desired, all the while he sat with her to show the congregation the face of untarnished dignity and stoical pride that she desired, he berated himself for lacking the courage to make a truly nasty scene.

No one came forward during the invitational hymn, and while the congregation sang the last verse, Quentin Lloyd walked to the rear of the church so as to greet parishioners as they departed. Before the benediction, however, Farley Smithson moved to the pulpit again and said, "I neglected to announce earlier that Reverend Lloyd has agreed to serve us as interim pastor while the board of deacons prepares its nominees for a pulpit search committee. We ask God's blessings for Reverend Lloyd during this time of transition."

From the back of the church, Quentin called on Jesse Kardowski to give the benediction. As Jesse launched into a long-winded prayer, Tommy saw Jesse's son Earl staring at him from the right side of the church. The two young men nodded at each other almost imperceptibly.

Then Tommy felt his mother poke him gently and whisper, "Let's slip on out now."

Tommy immediately stepped out into the aisle, let his mother and sister pass and then followed them quickly into the vestibule where Quentin Lloyd was standing by the door. He shook first Danielle's hand and then said to Billye, "I am praying for you." Next Quentin took Tommy's hand and said, "Hang in there, Tiger. I know this business cost you about ten last night, but you'll be right back on your game. Just wait and see."

Afterwards, Tommy reflected that had Quentin not said something about basketball, he might have just gone on home. As it was, it took a moment for Quentin's words to sink in. He just nodded as the associate pastor spoke to him and then followed quickly after his mother and sister, who were hurrying down the steps so as to get away from the church before they had to face any of the emerging parishioners. By the time he reached the car, however, Tommy was a furnace of barely controlled rage.

"Drive home without me," he told his mother

"What?" Billye asked. "What for?"

"I'm all ticked off about everything," he said. " It'll do me good to walk home."

"You want me to walk with you, Tommy?" Danielle asked. "I don't mind."

"No," Tommy said.

"I'm going to have lunch on the table by one o'clock," Billye said. "You be home by then, or I'm going to be upset."

Tommy started down Gentilly Boulevard in the direction of home, but as soon as Billye drove out of sight, he turned around and walked back to the church where he paused across the street to watch the crowd of Sunday worshipers visit on the plaza, no doubt buzzing about his father's sudden resignation. When the crowd finally began to dwindle, he crossed the street, grunted greetings to the few lingering church members who spoke to him, and jogged up the curved, annatto steps and into the vestibule where Quentin Lloyd was still talking to a handful of parishioners. Jesse Kardowski, his wife and their son Earl were among them.

When the Kardowskis departed, Quentin stepped over to Tommy and extended his big paw, which Tommy accepted automatically. As Quentin knocked against Tommy's wrist with the Bible he held in his left hand, the strength of his grip reminded Tommy what a big man he was. At age twenty-seven he was hardly as fit as he'd been on the field at LSU's

Tiger Stadium, but he was still obviously strong. No doubt to ingratiate himself, he'd adopted a stooped posture that de-emphasized his size, but at two hundred forty pounds, he weighed seventy pounds more than Tommy.

"I know this has to be a hard time for you and your family, Tiger."

"Don't call me, Tiger," Tommy said.

Quentin hung on to Tommy's hand and began to pat with the Bible at Tommy's elbow. "Okay. All right," he said, chuckling a little. "I'm a Tiger man myself, so I always use that word as a compliment. Now that the Greenies have you sewn up over at Tulane, I won't call you 'Tiger' anymore. Star like yourself, I guess you can be called about anything you want. Am I right?"

"Shut up," Tommy said.

"Excuse me," Quentin said, dropping Tommy's hand and rocking back on his heels.

"Let me ask you something, Mr. Lloyd," Tommy said. "Did you help do this to my dad?"

"What are you talking about?" Lloyd said. "Of course not. There's not a man in this world I admire more than your father."

"Yeah?" Tommy said. "Then what are you doing agreeing to be the interim pastor. Why didn't you resign in protest?"

"In protest of what, son? Your father resigned. What is there to protest?"

"Don't give me that malarkey. You and I both know—"

"I think you better remember where you are, young man. I won't tolerate the use of coarse language in God's house."

"What?" Tommy said. "Malarkey? That isn't even a bad word, asshole."

Quentin turned and laid the Bible he'd been holding on the table just inside the door. "I'm not going to tell you this but once, buster. You best be walking out of here before I forget I'm a man of peace."

Tommy snarled, "Piece of shit is more like it."

"I'll snap your punk ass like a twig," Quentin said, lunging forward. But as he reached out for Tommy with both hands, his leather shoes slipped on the hard terrazzo floor of the vestibule. Reacting with a point guard's quickness, his rubber-soled shoes assuring his footing, Tommy stepped slightly to his left and broke Quentin's nose with a right-hand punch that knocked the associate pastor to his knees. Tommy stood over him, both fists still clenched.

"Try to get up, Mr. Lloyd," Tommy said, "and I'm gonna stomp you something bad."

Quentin looked up at him but said nothing, and Tommy left the church.

Tommy kept to himself all afternoon. After supper he took three aspirin tablets and went to his room. He was in bed when Farley Smithson called and told Billye what Tommy had done. Farley said it might be best if the family didn't come back to the church for a while. He was going to take the liberty during the next week of packing up Jeff's things in the office. He'd call when he was finished and have them dropped by the parsonage.

When she got off the phone, Billye came into Tommy's bedroom. He pretended to be asleep. She sat on the side of the bed and touched his face with her hand. He blinked, then opened his eyes.

"Did you hurt yourself when you beat up Quentin after church?" she asked. "Farley Smithson just phoned and told me what happened."

"My hand hurts," Tommy admitted. "And my wrist some. But I didn't break anything." Billye sat silent for a bit, stroking her son's face and then his chest. "Are they going to arrest me?" Tommy asked, his voice quavering despite his effort not to sound upset.

"No, baby," she said. "They're going to let it go. But you know you were wrong, I hope. And how lucky not to get in serious trouble."

Tommy didn't answer. He did know he was wrong, and he was ashamed, but he didn't feel lucky at all.

"I want you to promise me something," Billye said, looking away from him. "Will you? I want you to promise me that this is the end of it. Will you promise me that now?"

"But it isn't the end of it, Mom. Dad's been screwed. We don't even know where he is."

"He'll come home. He's trying to figure out what to do, and then he'll do it."

"We'll do it with him," Tommy said.

"Of course we will," Billye said. She looked at her son solemnly and patted his leg. She didn't confess to him the complex nature of her feelings, how her anger at the church was mixed with anger at her husband. She didn't tell Tommy how she'd resented having a part-time husband for most of her marriage, how violated she felt at Jeff's righteous stubbornness having now turned her world upside down. Instead, she said, "As much as possible, honey, I want you to avoid thinking about this. I want you to enjoy the rest of your senior year. It's such a special time. I don't want you to miss it. Leave this at home every morning when you go to school."

But Tommy couldn't leave it at home. It was already at school waiting for him.

Monday afternoon in the school gym locker room, while he was getting ready for basketball practice, Earl Kardowski stopped in front of Tommy's cubicle in the team cage while Tommy was lacing up his sneakers. Tommy had smeared his sore left ankle with a powerful deep-heating liniment called Atomic Balm, and the skin on his lower leg was already starting to tingle. He knew from past experience that it would start burning as soon as he worked up a sweat and would be so tender to the touch by the end of practice that he'd try to keep it out of hot water while he showered.

"Hey, Caldwell," Earl said, "I know what you did at church yesterday, you chickenshit."

Tommy looked up and said, "Get away from me, Kardowski."

"I ought to kick your yellow-belly ass."

Tommy stood up and tried to brush past, but Earl chested him, and when Tommy tried to forearm him away, Earl grabbed Tommy's green practice jersey with two hands and slammed Tommy into a row of steel lockers, bruising his upper back on a combination lock. The two boys were separated by teammates before any punches were thrown.

"You guys know what our nigger-loving star player did yesterday?" Earl yelled, twisting in the arms of Clint Carter, who held him in a full nelson. Dedicated weightlifting had made Earl strong and thick-chested, but he was no match for Clint. Earl was only five seven, one eighty-five. Clint was six five, two twenty. "This guy sucker-punched a minister," Earl said. "Fucking broke the preacher's nose."

"I didn't sucker-punch him," Tommy protested. He was being held by Sidney Detweiler, but he wasn't struggling, so Sidney released him.

"You better fucking let go of me, Carter," Earl said, "or I'm going to kick your ass, too."

"Yeah," Clint laughed, pulling Earl up onto his toes. "You and what army?"

"Hey, fuck you, man," Earl said.

Out of Sidney's grip, Tommy winced as he rotated his shoulders. "You okay?" Clint asked.

"Yeah, I'm all right," Tommy replied. He bent down and touched his toes to stretch his back.

"What's this all about?" Sidney asked. He was Earl's best friend, but he had better sense.

Tommy answered this question by addressing Clint, who had been his best friend since third grade. "Bastards fired my dad. Kardowski's old man was probably part of it."

"Fuck you, Caldwell," Earl said. "Your nigger-loving old man up and quit, and that's all there is to it. Good riddance to him."

Tommy rushed toward Earl, but he was caught and pulled away by Sidney.

"See what I'm telling you," Earl said. "Chickenshit sucker-punched Pastor Lloyd just like he was gonna do to me."

Tommy practically went limp in Sidney's arms, Sidney let him go again, and Tommy sat down on one of the locker-room benches. "I didn't sucker-punch him," Tommy said. "Lloyd's a goddamn traitor, and I told him so. He got pissed off and came after me."

"Your story, Caldwell," Earl said. "Lloyd played defense at LSU, man. He'd eat you like cheese on a cracker."

Coach George King came into the locker room and asked what was going on. Clint let Earl go, but nobody said anything until Sidney Detweiler finally said, "Nothing, Coach. Just having a little discussion. Nothing to it."

Coach King looked at Tommy, who was the only boy sitting down. "That right, Caldwell?" he asked.

"That's right, Coach," Tommy said. "Nothing going on. Nothing at all."

Coach King turned his attention to Earl, whom he'd seen in Clint's wrestler's grip. "You messing up again, Kardowski?" he asked.

"Hey," Earl complained. "Why do I always get blamed?"

Coach King replied, "'Cause you're usually guilty, son."

Then Coach King said to everybody, "Center court, forty-five seconds. Let's hit it. You guys can't beat Chalmette, Jesuit's gonna make you look like the girls' team." He left the locker room and everybody hurried to finish dressing for practice.

"Ain't that typical," Earl said. "Caldwell beats up a minister. They let him walk. And I get my ass in a sling for calling him on it."

Tommy stood up and jogged past him without answering. When he hit the tunnel just outside the locker room, he sprinted all the way out to the floor.

Behind him, as the other boys walked out to practice, Clint said to Earl in a low voice, "You got any bright ideas about being the agent of some kind of payback on Tommy, you're gonna answer to me, Kardowski. You try to undercut him, I'm gonna break your leg. You try to elbow him, I'm gonna tear your arm off and you'll have to carry the ball at McNeese next year with one hand. You get my gist? I don't want to see you even guarding him tight."

Earl and Tommy had played in the same football backfield from eighth through twelfth grade, and it seemed to Earl that Tommy always got more credit than he deserved and Earl got less. And then there was all the nigger shit Tommy was into, recruiting guys from the team to go on marches with that communist George Washington Brown. He knew that Clint and Tommy had been playing pickup games with the niggers over in the Calliope Projects, too. That was against the law or something, he thought. Or ought to be anyway.

Sometimes Earl thought he could smell the nigger in Tommy's basketball clothes. But what did he care? He didn't give a shit about basketball anyway. Pussy game. Took a pussy like Caldwell to be any good at it. Pussy quarterback who could play a whole football game without getting his jersey dirty.

Look at Caldwell's whole pussy basketball routine. Always the same on game day, superstitious prick. First, he took off his clothes and hung them on his cubicle pegs, all except his skivvies, which he didn't take off. Put a clean pair of underpants for after the game up on a peg with his street clothes. Then he put on his jersey. In jersey, skivvies and bare feet he'd pad out to the training room to get taped. Had bad ankles. Got taped even when he didn't need to. He was nursing a turn now. Coating himself good in Atomic Balm. That's what gave Earl the idea. Caldwell would be full of that menthol smell, and he wouldn't notice.

Game night against Jesuit, Earl got dressed first and did his dirty work while Tommy was in the training room. Sat down on the bench in front of Tommy's cubicle as if he was just retying his shoes. Made the switch in a flash. Only person saw anything was Sidney. Earl winked at him. Sidney didn't know what was up. Earl wasn't telling him, either. Once it was done, Earl stood up and stretched. Touched his toes. Jogged in place. What was that all about? It was a joke, him pretending to want to get loose. Game like this against Jesuit, he had about as much chance of seeing floor time as he had of dunking the ball this lifetime.

Tommy came out, both ankles wrapped in white athletic tape, the left one stained red from the Atomic Balm. Earl was back in front of his own cubicle now. Tommy pulled on his socks first, twisting them back and forth till he got them some way he liked, then his shoes. Then he pulled on his jock. Yep, over his fucking skivvies. What kind of sissy shit was that? Stepped into his shorts, carefully tucking his jersey inside. Then his warm-ups. How soon was it going to hit him? Earl couldn't fucking wait.

On the way down the tunnel, just when they began to pick up the crowd noise from the gym floor, Sidney sidled up to Tommy and said, "I think I saw Earl messing with your stuff while you were getting wrapped. I don't know what he was up to. Nothing, I hope, with a game this big on the line."

Tommy had no idea what Sidney was talking about. But halfway through warm-ups he could begin to feel the sensation, first just an unusual warmth in his crotch. Then his entire groin was on fire.

Tommy ran over to Coach King and said, "I gotta go back to the locker room. I'll be right back."

"You sick, kid?" Coach King asked.

But Tommy had already run off the court. In the locker room he stripped out of his warm-up pants, pulled off his shorts and yanked down his jock and underpants. That's what Sidney was trying to tell him: goddamn Earl Kardowski had rubbed Atomic Balm into his jock. His testicles and penis were on fire. He ran to the sink in the bathroom and washed himself as best he could. He didn't have any time. He could hear the horn sounding. They would be announcing the starting lineups in a matter of seconds.

Tommy dried himself off with paper towels from the dispenser and ran back to his cubicle. Maybe this wasn't going to be so bad. He'd wear his practice jock, but now his clean pair of skivvies was gone. Kardowski had stolen his underwear. This was unbelievable. He always wore a pair of briefs under his jock. Tommy grabbed his dirty jock and pulled it on as quickly as he could. Still a little damp. He could live with that. Damn if he couldn't still feel the heat. He put his shorts back on, tucked in his shirt, carried his warm-up pants over his arm as he sprinted back up the tunnel to the floor.

Somehow Tommy managed to ignore the scalding sensation in his crotch when the ball was in play. But he nearly sank to his knees with pain at the quarter break and every time-out. He found himself bouncing on his toes, almost jumping up and down at every dead ball. But he didn't know what else to do. He'd already washed himself. Maybe he ought to go wash some more. But he wasn't going to miss this game because of Earl Kardowski.

As soon as the horn sounded to end the half, Tommy bolted down the tunnel and back to the bathroom where he once again stripped out of his shorts and jock to wash himself. He was in such pain he wasn't sure whether the washing was even giving him any relief. Even the cold water felt hot when he splashed it between his legs. He wiped himself off with paper towels and was just about to put his jock and shorts back on when Clint Carter came into the bathroom.

"What's wrong, T.C.?" Clint asked. "You sick? Hasn't affected your jumper."

"Bastard Kardowski smeared my jock with Atomic Balm. My balls are on fire, man."

"Jesus," Clint said. "Little shit scalded your balls. He could have made you sterile or something. I'm gonna snap that half-pint fucker like a piece of dry spaghetti."

"Save it up," Tommy said. "Prick would like nothing better than to cost us this game." Tommy reached down to step into his jock again, but when he did, he saw it was a MacGregor. All Tommy's jocks were Bikes. That's how the bastard had done it. He'd switched Tommy's out for his own, which he'd smeared with Atomic Balm ahead of time. That meant this jock was loaded with the stuff, too. Tommy quickly peeled it off. "You got an extra jock?" he asked Clint.

Clint snorted. "Hey, I love you like a brother, but a man doesn't share his jocks."

"I'm serious, man. I can't put this one back on. It might bake my balls all the way off."

Clint said he had a dirty one in his cubicle, and Tommy allowed that it would have to do. Later, they would laugh about the incident and refer to themselves as the Strap Siblings. But the burning in Tommy's groin persisted through the second half and for a couple of days after the game. He probably should have seen a doctor. But Tommy never even told his parents what Earl did to him that night, for the whole incident embarrassed him deeply. However much pain the stunt caused him physically, it caused him more psychically, that someone he had known for so long could hate him enough to do such a thing. By never talking about it with anyone but Clint, it was as if he could erase the event from his own history.

chapter sixteen

FROM THE TIME JEFF AND BILLYE walked away from each other at Valmont in April of 1942, they wrote to each other almost every day. Billye kept him informed when she moved to New Orleans to work for the USO after the spring term ended in early June. She and her childhood friend Pam Pendergast got jobs as secretaries and rented a small apartment together on Camp Street, half a block upriver from Washington Avenue. They commuted to their office on Lafayette Square via the Magazine Street streetcar. Every Wednesday and Saturday they served as hostesses for the USO social functions.

Jeff finished boot camp at Fort Sam Houston near San Antonio in May and was sent to a training school for radio operators at Fort Rucker in Alabama, graduating in the last week of June. From there he was sent to Fort Gordon near Augusta, Georgia, for still additional training. Finally, he was ordered to New Orleans where he bivouacked at Jackson Barracks for four days before he shipped out for England on the USS *Benjamin Harrison*.

While in New Orleans, Jeff was at liberty. He and Billye agreed excitedly to meet at the servicemen's dance she was hosting on his first night in town. At seven o'clock, Jeff walked into a Jung Hotel ballroom strung with red, white and blue streamers. Billye was standing at the punch bowl, and she looked gorgeous. She wore the green strapless gown she had worn to her high-school prom. Her brown hair hung to her shoulders in soft curls. Her cheeks glowed with a hint of rouge, and the dark red lipstick she was wearing made her teeth sparkle in contrast.

Jeff took a place at the end of the line and inched forward, his eyes glued to Billye the whole time. Huge casement windows were cranked open, although the thick summer air that wafted inside didn't do much to cool things down. The eighteen-foot ceilings helped a bit, as did the forest of ceiling fans that swirled overhead. The room was abuzz with chatter, but the spirit of frivolity seemed a desperate gesture to hold the reality of the war at bay.

Billye didn't see Jeff until she was about to hand him a cup of punch, and then she almost dropped it. Her reaction to seeing him was even stronger than she had thought it would be. He was staggeringly handsome in his uniform, ramrod straight, brass buttons polished to a gleam. She wanted to run around the table to hug him. Billye handed Jeff his punch and smiled widely. "Look at you," she said.

"I'd rather look at you," he responded. They both stood there awkwardly, neither knowing what to say next. The soldier in line behind Jeff cleared his throat.

Billye giggled. "I guess we're holding up the line," she said as Jeff stepped to the side. "But don't you go away."

She poured a cup of punch for the next soldier who took it and passed close enough to Jeff to whisper, "Looks like you're gonna get lucky." Jeff flushed crimson and didn't reply as the man walked away.

Eventually, the line at the punch bowl dwindled away, and Billye and Jeff were able to sit and talk. She asked about his training and what his responsibilities would be in England. They talked of school and people they knew, but the conversation was strained. They really did not know each other that well.

At 7:30 the band started up, an all-Negro swing band that filled the ballroom with dance music. It was hard to talk then, but they leaned their heads close together to exchange snippets of conversation. Jeff could smell Billye's perfume, the faint scent of flowers, and he felt delirious being so near her.

They sat through several jitterbug numbers as the floor swirled with dancers. Then the band leader stated his pleasure at being invited to play for the fine men in uniform who were serving their country in this hour of crisis. Jeff heard all of this but paid attention to none of it. He was thinking of Billye Monroe and how much she stirred him. He wanted to take her into his arms, but as he sat beside her, he couldn't think of a thing to say to her.

When the band swung into a slow number, Billye leaned over to Jeff and said, "Do you like to dance?"

What could he say? He had grown up in a tiny Baptist community where dancing was considered a sin. The fact that he didn't share that notion didn't matter. He squirmed in his chair a long moment before responding. Finally, he admitted, "I don't know how."

"What?" Billye said. "You must know how to slow dance anyway. How to box step."

"No, I don't," Jeff said. "You know, Baptists don't believe in dancing."

"Bull feathers," Billye said, laughing. "Most of the kids I went to school with—" Suddenly she stopped, her eyes wide. "You really don't believe in dancing? Because you're going to be a minister?"

"No," Jeff said, shaking his head rapidly. "That's not it. I just don't know how."

"Well, I can teach you," Billye said. "Come on."

She stood up, grabbed him by the hand and led him to a corner of the dance floor where there was some space. "It's easy," she said once she had fixed their arms on each other properly. "You just start off with your left foot and then make a box." She backed away from him, pulling him along with her. But rather than gliding, he lurched and stumbled. She giggled, and he felt his cheeks grow hot with embarrassment. "Don't be a scaredy cat," she said. "I'm not going to bite you. Come on, let's try it again."

This time it went a bit better, and after two more slow dances, Jeff had mastered enough of the basics to be able to move around a little. Billye praised him extravagantly, but he felt awkward and foolish. When the band played another jitterbug, he begged off trying to learn that too, and they returned to their seats. Almost immediately, another soldier asked Billye for a dance, and Jeff sat by himself feeling stupid. Better to look foolish, he chided himself, than to let Billye go off with someone else. His relief was enormous when Billye returned to the chair next to his after dancing with the other man.

"Boy," she said, fanning her face and neck with her hand, "you forget how much exercise you get from dancing the jitterbug." She looked at Jeff. "Sure you don't want to try? I don't want to be the only one here sweating like some old plow mule."

"I don't guess I better," Jeff said. And once again he detested his cowardice when Billye was dragged off by still another soldier. This time she stayed on the dance floor for three consecutive songs and went to the punch table before returning to sit next to Jeff.

"Hi, stranger," she said. Jeff answered her by smiling and raising his eyebrows. Billye sipped from her cup of punch and then touched the cup to her forehead. "Want some?" She extended the half-full cup toward him. There was a little smudge of lipstick around the rim.

Jeff shrugged. "Thanks," he said, taking the cup and deliberately putting his lips directly over the lipstick smudge. The act felt delicious, but sinful, like kissing her without her knowing it. Billye took the cup back, drank from it again and set it on the floor at her feet. As she bent forward, Jeff was able to look down her low-cut gown. He really wasn't able to see that much more of her bosom than the dress itself revealed, but the indecency of sneaking a look made him tingle.

Using a napkin, Billye began to mop gently at her brow all around the hairline. Then she lifted her hair to the top of her head and touched the napkin to the sides and back of her neck. "My momma told me it would be hotter than Hades in New Orleans, but I thought she was just saying that to talk me out of coming down here."

"New Orleans does have a reputation for being hot," Jeff said, inflecting his voice slightly. Billye giggled and began to fan herself again. She moved her hand away from her face and began to wave it up and down over the crease of her bosom, a gesture Jeff thought wildly erotic. Her nose was shining. He watched a rivulet of perspiration run from the hollow of her neck down toward her sternum.

"I'm afraid that draft mule hasn't got a thing on me now," Billye said. Jeff wrinkled his brow. "In the sweat department, I mean. 'Course my mama would dust my bottom for ever admitting to sweating. She taught me better. Horses, mules and colored people sweat. Men perspire. Ladies glow. Have you ever heard that?" She laughed. "I'm glowing so much right now that if you wrung me out over the river it might cause the levees to break."

Jeff laughed. "Billye Monroe, I wonder if there's a single thing you'd be afraid to say."

She looked at him, laughing in surprise. "What did I say? I didn't say anything indecent."

"No, no, no," Jeff responded. "You're just so frank."

"Well, I feel like a frank," she said, eyes gleaming, "a hot dog frank on a hot griddle. Sizzle, sizzle, juice running out every which a way."

Jeff laughed out loud but blushed as he did so.

The band started a slow number, and Billye said, "Hey, soldier, they're playing our song."

When the USO dance ended at 9:30, Jeff asked if he could see Billye home. She didn't want him to go to all that trouble since Jackson Barracks lay in the opposite direction. "I have to catch the St. Charles Avenue streetcar," she said. "You could walk me there."

They strolled down Canal Street under a gray night sky. The temperature had dropped only slightly, and the air felt thick and sodden, like a cloud of wet cotton. "I am absolutely wringing wet," Billye said as they walked along. "I'm a lucky girl that you'd even agree to dance with me without blotting me off. I swear I always thought it was hot in Shreveport. But there's never a time back home when it's like this. I feel like a used mop."

Jeff laughed and shook his head. He was warm too, but this muggy heat was nothing compared to the scorch of the midday sun he'd worked under for much of his life. Still, he thought her complaining was funny, and he suspected that his laughter only encouraged her to complain all the more. "If I was any hotter," Billye said, "you could rent me out as a stove."

A streetcar was just making its one-block arc onto Canal when they reached Baronne Street, so they ended up waiting a quarter hour for the next one, not that either minded. Jeff asked if he could see her again, and they agreed to meet the next night and go to a movie.

When Billye saw the next streetcar coming, she put her arms up around Jeff's neck and laid her face against the brass buttons on his tunic. Pleased but surprised, he circled his hands at the small of her back and pulled her against him. "I'm going to pray for you every night," she said. "Pray for you to come through this old war safe and sound." As Jeff squeezed her to him, Billye turned her head up, and her eyes glinted in the yellow light of a street lamp.

He ran his right hand up under her hair, which shone in the light, and up her neck, which was indeed damp from all her dancing. The dampness of her neck excited and touched him, made him feel hungry for her and made him feel her vulnerability and her fragility. When he kissed her, it was the most wonderful kiss he had ever experienced. She tasted of fruit punch and lipstick, and her lips were soft and succulent; he wanted the kiss to last forever. But the streetcar rattled to a stop, and they broke apart. Billye laughed a little, touched his face and said, "Jeepers, soldier, I think I'll remember that for a while."

"I'll remember it forever," Jeff said. She turned and scrambled onto the streetcar and was gone in a screech of wheels on rails. Jeff stood and watched it roll away until it became just a dot of yellow light that swung counterclockwise and disappeared at Lee Circle.

After she finished work the next afternoon Jeff and Billye met under the clock at D.H. Holmes department store on Canal Street. They walked into the French Quarter to eat the *plat du jour* at Tujague's and then strolled back to the Loew's on Canal where they saw John Ford's *How Green Was My Valley*. When it was time for Billye to go home, Jeff insisted on accompanying her. At her apartment, she invited him upstairs for a cup of coffee. Billye's roommate excused herself almost immediately.

Billye made coffee, and they drank it sitting next to each other on the small sofa. The living room had no overhead light and was lit by two shaded lamps. They talked about the movie, which both had found profoundly moving. Suddenly, without transition, they began to kiss, madly, like starving people gorging on a discovered cache of food. When Jeff touched her breast through her clothes, Billye moaned and kissed him more fiercely. She didn't protest when he unbuttoned her blouse and touched her underneath her clothes. But she pushed his hand away, however, when he tried to put it under her pleated skirt. When he cupped his hand between her legs on the outside of her clothes, she writhed at first, but finally she pushed his hand away from there, too. When he tried to put it back, she said "No" and abruptly stood up.

Jeff didn't know what to do. He was so aroused he was panting. Billye was breathing hard, too. Her face was flushed and glowed almost orange in the yellow light of the lamp. She always looked so smart, and now she was a rumpled mess. Her slip was twisted and showed through her blouse, which was pulled out of her skirt and unbuttoned half way down.

"I'm sorry," Jeff said.

Billye licked her lips and tucked in the tail of her blouse. "Maybe I should get some more coffee," she said. "Would you like some more coffee?"

"No," Jeff said. "I ought to go. I don't want to keep your roommate awake."

Billye didn't say anything, so Jeff stood up and put on his overseas cap. At the door he said, "Really, I am sorry. I shouldn't let myself get carried away."

Billye didn't look at his face, but she reached out a hand and laid it flat against his chest. "Don't be sorry, honey," she said, slipping her fingers under the lapel of his jacket. "I'm not sorry. It's just that—" She looked up into his eyes. "I'm not the kind of girl who—"

"I'm sorry," Jeff said.

Billye squeezed his lapel in her fist, pulled him toward her and rose on her tiptoes to kiss him gently. Her lips were cool and moist, and he tingled as she let the kiss linger lightly. "You go on before we're both sorry," she said.

"Can I see you tomorrow?"

"You better," she said.

As Jeff walked away, feeling at once elated and remiss, he ruminated on the fact that she had never rebuttoned her blouse.

It was 10:30, and Jeff felt too jangly to return to the barracks. So he rode the streetcar back down to the Quarter where he planned to walk off his nervous energy. He fell in with a group of four soldiers he knew casually from the barracks and followed them into a bar where for the first time in his life he drank alcohol. Jeff knew that Southern Baptist preachers were supposed to be teetotalers, but he didn't really think that drinking was sinful in and of itself. Even if it was, he reasoned, he was going off to war; like all the other men in uniform, he deserved a little leniency.

After a couple of drinks, the servicemen hit the strip clubs on Bourbon Street, filling themselves with the wonders of female flesh. Eventually, one soldier proposed that they go to a place called the Black Lantern a few blocks away in Treme. The Black Lantern had table service and a jazz band, but there was no doubt that it was a house of prostitution where all the working girls were Negroes. As soon as the men were seated, the hostess asked if they wanted company, and when one soldier said, "Yes, indeedy," they were immediately joined by light-skinned women wearing slit skirts and flimsy blouses with no underwear. Jeff did feel that this was a sin, but he made no move to leave.

Jeff's girl identified herself as Dixie, and she ordered something called a "champagne cocktail" which cost Jeff $1.50. Jeff estimated Dixie's age to be thirty. She was slim but full-breasted, and in the dim light she seemed pretty. She got down to business fast, her hand keeping time to the music on Jeff's knee. Pretty soon she'd moved to his thigh. When the music stopped, she let her fingers stray to his crotch. "I just came here to talk," he told her.

"This ain't a place for talking, honey," Dixie responded, laughing deep in her throat. She snuggled close to him, took his earlobe wetly in her mouth, then whispered, "I just know you want some of this brown sugar before you go off to war."

"Really, I just want to talk," Jeff said.

"You can talk all you want upstairs," she whispered. "Say whatever you want. I like it."

"I just want to sit here and have a drink," Jeff said. "I'll gladly buy you another."

"I got money to earn, sweetie. Don't make what I need sipping soda water." When Jeff didn't respond, Dixie snickered, "Cat got your tongue, soldier? Pussy could get your other tongue."

"How much does it cost to go upstairs?" Jeff said abruptly, his voice cold.

"Now we're talking," Dixie said. "Ten dollars hand, come and go. Twelve-fifty head, same. Fifteen dollars regular, long as it takes, slow and sweet."

"I'll take regular," Jeff said.

"Straight chocolate cream," she said. "Just the way I like it. With a cherry on top."

They went upstairs, with Dixie leading the way. He watched the swing of her behind as she lifted each leg to rise a step, and he found himself aroused. At the top of the stairs, they walked past a burly man who sat scowling with his arms folded across his chest in a straight-backed wooden chair. Dixie greeted him as Big Toby, and he answered her only with a grunt. In the room, Dixie directed Jeff to sit on the edge of the double bed. She stood in front of him before an unpainted gray-wood table on which were set a bowl and a pitcher, a lamp and a few other objects, including a porcelain Jesus, his arms raised like wings.

"I got to collect before we start," Dixie said. "House rules." Jeff handed her a ten and a five, and to his considerable discomfort she tucked the bills under the Christ figurine. "This Jesus ain't mine. Just goes with the room. But I like him. Unlike most men I know, he ain't cheated me once." She laughed heartily, and as she moved toward the head of the bed, she undid a clasp and pulled her skirt away like a matador whipping his cape in front of a bull. When she noticed Jeff contemplating the figurine she said, "Soldier boy, you gonna pray or fuck? Both four letter words, I guess. But one of them pays off a lot more reliably." Jeff turned to her. She was naked from the waist down, standing there brazenly with her legs planted wide apart.

She nodded toward the table. "Service usually keeps you boys pretty clean. But wash yourself up in there."

Looking at the bowl and pitcher, Jeff thought of the Negro girl Leila he had been with before. She had been so shy. Is this what she'd grown up to be?

Abruptly, he stood up. "This isn't such a good idea," he said. "I'm just going to go."

"What?" Dixie said, genuinely surprised. "Hey, come on. Get your pussy before you go off to war."

"No, I don't think so," Jeff said. "I don't want to do this anymore."

"Big Toby out there ain't gonna let you have your money back."

"That's okay." Jeff started toward the door. "You keep it. It's my gift to you."

Dixie snorted. "Don't go congratulating yourself for doing me any favors, soldier boy. Long as I been off the floor, I earned this money. Gift, my ass."

Jeff stopped at the door. "I'm sorry. I shouldn't even be here. I shouldn't have come."

"Honey, you didn't," Dixie said.

Her howls of laughter followed him down the stairs. Jeff thought of Leila again; he thought of what men did to women who sold their bodies to survive. The world was a wretched place, he thought, and he was its collaborator.

Edgy and depressed, Jeff wandered back to Bourbon Street, stopped in the first bar he found, ordered two shots of bourbon and knocked them straight back, one after the other. Then, in a series of bars, he proceeded to get drunk. At first the sensation was pleasant, and he felt an absurd optimism about his circumstances. But he kept drinking shots until he became dizzy. Sometime after midnight, he found himself with a paper cup of beer in one hand and his other arm hooked around a light pole, muttering questions at passersby. His mouth felt dry, but the beer he kept pouring into it did nothing to slake his thirst.

"Working for the mayor of New Orleans tonight, soldier?" he heard a voice say, and he swung around to see a blue-uniformed police officer regarding him. Jeff nodded suddenly. "Helping out our city by holding up that light pole?" the officer said. He was in his fifties, with a soft face that was smiling and pleasant. He wore his police hat pushed back on his head. Jeff squinted at him, and a nimbus seemed to form over the officer's head.

"You talking to me?" Jeff said.

The policeman laughed quietly. "Looky here, my man," he said. "You look an awful lot like a candidate for the MPs. You wouldn't want to get caught up in one of their dragnets, now would you?"

"Nooooo!" Jeff said. "Nosiree, I wouldn't."

The officer smiled. "You think you can put one foot in front of another?"

Jeff let go of the light pole and stood up straight. He attempted to click his heels together and salute but lurched forward and stumbled into the arms of the policeman who grabbed him in a chest-to-chest embrace.

"Whoa there," the policeman said. "Throw your right arm around my shoulders and let's take a walk."

He steered Jeff to the kitchen of a seafood restaurant and got him a cup of coffee, then started Jeff walking again toward the river. At Decatur, the ripe smell of the Jax brewery was so strong that Jeff stopped to vomit into the gutter. They turned downriver and found an open-air church service being held under the shelter of the French Market roof. A woman sat at a wheeled piano and played "Shall We Gather at the River" for a congregation of about fifteen men, more than half of whom were in uniform; several, like Jeff, were obviously drunk. A dark-haired man in a suit stood in front of the gathering with a hymnal and waved his arm to lead the singing.

The policeman guided Jeff to a folding chair and sat next to him for a moment. "I'm gonna leave you here now," he said. "I have to go back to my beat. Somebody here will see that you get back to your barracks."

"This is like a church," Jeff said.

The officer smiled again. "You take care, soldier."

"Maybe I ought not to go to church when I'm drunk," Jeff said.

"Or maybe that's just when you should go," the policeman said.

The next morning, although monumentally hung over, Jeff called Billye and told her he would like to take her to her favorite restaurant; they agreed to meet at Galatoire's when she got off work at 5:30. In the late morning he did some shopping and returned to the barracks for an afternoon nap. He still had a headache when he set off to meet Billye. On the way, he bought six red roses from a street vendor—and a yellow carnation boutonniere for himself.

Inside the bright atmosphere of Galatoire's, Jeff and Billye were shown to a table against the mirrors. When a waiter in a tuxedo asked for their drink orders, Billye requested iced tea. Jeff hesitated a moment and then ordered a Jack Daniels and Coke. Hair of the dog, his bunkmates had told him.

"I see you've learned to take a drink in the service," Billye said.

Jeff shrugged. "Don't you ever have a cocktail?"

"Why, no," she said. "I'm a good Baptist teetotaler."

Jeff sighed. "Eventually I'll be one too. Not many Baptist preachers last too long if their congregations catch them with a glass of whiskey."

"That doesn't bother you?" Billye asked. "Wanting to be a preacher in a religion that believes something you don't."

"It's not the religion that believes it. It's the people. And if they want to believe it, that's okay, I guess. I'm certainly not saying people *ought* to drink. But Baptists are awfully screwy about this. The Bible doesn't say Jesus turned water into R.C. Cola."

Billye laughed. Jeff could be funny. And she liked the way he had strong feelings about things. "You know," she said, "Pastor Biltmore told our youth group that when the Bible said Jesus drank wine, what it meant was just Welch's Grape Juice, like we have at the Lord's Supper. All the kids made fun of him, called him Pastor Guiltmore."

"That's what happens when you tell people lies," Jeff said, not smiling. "You make them cynical."

The waiter returned with their drinks, and Billye suggested menu selections. Her recommendations were good, but Jeff was less interested in the food than she wanted him to be. Still, he was pleased that she seemed to enjoy herself so much. Over coffee, he took her hand. She smiled at the intimacy of this gesture of holding hands on the top of a table in a crowded restaurant. He had an intensity that she found very attractive.

"Billye, I want you to know something about myself that you wouldn't have any way of knowing." He grimaced with the effort of telling her, which she found endearing. She squeezed his hand.

"I'm going to make something of myself. I come from poor people. Uneducated and unsophisticated people. But I'm going to make something of myself. I'm going to do something worthwhile. I don't know how or exactly what, but I am. I know it. I'm going to come back from this war and do something important."

Billye squeezed his hand again. "I know you're going to do exactly what you say."

Jeff reached into the inside pocket of his uniform jacket and wrapped his hand around a small square box. He moved the bread plate aside and set the box between them. "Will you marry me?" he asked.

Billye gasped. "Oh Jeff, honey. I wasn't expecting this. I don't know what to say."

"Say yes." He opened the box and nudged it toward her. Inside was an engagement ring with a tiny white diamond that glinted almost blue under the restaurant's bright lights.

"This is beautiful, Jeff. This is so sweet of you."

"Does that mean yes?"

Billye laughed. "Oh, gosh," she said. "I'm just so taken aback."

"I love you, Billye Monroe," Jeff said. "I've loved you since I first saw you walk into English class. I have to go overseas two days from now. I'd sure like to go as your husband."

Billye's mind raced. This was all so sudden. And such a big step. So permanent. And yet, she cared for this boy in a special way. And she didn't want to hurt his feelings. She looked at him and smiled. "Yes," she said. "Yes, Jeff Caldwell, I will marry you."

He looked so sheepish, but smiled so broadly her heart melted, and she felt a rush of love for him. She got up and walked around the table and kissed him for such a long time that people in the restaurant took notice. When she stopped, they all clapped, and though she blushed doing so, Billye turned to the other diners and bowed, causing them to clap all the harder.

Jeff wanted to find someone who would marry them that very night, but Billye insisted that they wait until the next afternoon. The wedding was performed by a municipal court judge, with Billye's roommate the only attendant. Jeff wore his uniform, and Billye wore the suit she'd worn to the dean's reception. Pam bought Billye a small bouquet of flowers to hold during the ceremony. They exchanged simple gold bands they'd bought that morning. They were both so nervous they stumbled over their vows and had to repeat them.

The newlyweds spent their wedding night at the Monteleone Hotel. Billye had bought a sheer black nightgown that morning at Maison Blanche; she put it on in the bathroom after bathing. "Man, oh man," Jeff said, when she came out, and she was thrilled at the earnestness of his clumsy compliment.

"Are you done?" he asked, smiling, almost breathless. He was sitting on the bed in his undershirt. He had taken off his shoes and socks, but not his trousers. "I mean, should I go bathe, or do you need to get back in there?"

Billye laughed, although why she couldn't exactly say. "No, honey, I'm finished," she said.

When Jeff came out of the bathroom, he had put on a thin cotton robe. Billye had turned off the overhead light and lit red candles. She waited for him in the bed with a sheet pulled up over her. She stared at him frankly as he slipped off the robe and slid into the bed next to her. She had taken off her gown and was completely naked.

Billye twisted on her left side and touched his face. "Hello, my handsome husband," she said. She slid her hand down his chest to grasp his erection, feeling him jump as she did so. "What are you thinking about?" she asked, giggling.

"Oh, nothing," he said, his voice sounding reedy.

"I'll bet you're thinking about something," she said. Suddenly she whipped the sheet off him like an artist removing the shroud from a marble statue.

"What are you doing," he squeaked, covering himself with his hands.

"I want to look, how about it. I haven't ever seen a naked man before."

"Billye, you're embarrassing me."

Billye whistled. "Man, do I like the looks of this."

"Could you just put the sheet back over me."

"But this is my first time," she said. "I'm not done yet."

She knelt on the bed beside him and kissed the center of his chest, then his neck, then his chin. He rolled on top of her. She winced as he entered her, but she was very wet.

"Not so fast, Speedy Alka-Seltzer," she said.

chapter seventeen

I T WAS NATURAL FOR Jeff Caldwell to be obsessed by the Ku Klux Klan, which had been a presence in his life since he was a child. The night he, his father and his father's friends blew up the road-construction equipment, that had been Klan work. They didn't wear sheets. But it was Klan work all the same. And it was one of sundry elements in his past that haunted Jeff and made him feel that he had to do an awful lot of good to make amends.

The Klan had plagued Jeff's work since he first became involved with George Washington Brown in the early 1950s. The visible Klan showed itself in bed sheets and burning crosses. The invisible Klan corrupted police officers, cowed public officials and committed cowardly murders of the brave and the innocent. The hooded face of the visible Klan was but a boil on the surface of the skin, below which lay a cancer—the terrifying, widespread willingness of Southern white society to tolerate Klan atrocities rather than embrace men of different color as their human brothers. This willingness manifested itself in three ways. One part was pure racist, if largely silent, agreement with what the Klan was willing to say out loud. Another was indifference. If black men and activists suffered, most white people weren't either one. The third part was fear. The multitude of whites were intimidated, forced by fear of retribution into tolerating acts of violence they themselves would never commit or even privately condone. But publicly they held their tongues. To speak out was to be noticed.

Jeff had spoken out for a long time, of course. In the early 1950s, he dared assume that the Klan would not harm white men, particularly not white ministers who spoke out in the name of the teachings of Jesus. Jeff was probably naive even then. Certainly by the 1960s he no longer believed such nonsense. The Klan tried to beat him to death on the Freedom Ride. White civil-rights workers were murdered in 1964 and 1965, including Viola Liuzzo, a white woman. Children were killed by a Birmingham bomb. These acts chilled Jeff to his marrow, and he lived in fear that the Klan might hurt his own family.

That's what made so astonishing Jeff's decision in 1967 to undertake a very public ministry to the members and leadership of the Klan. This mission was born in the context of a troublesome splintering in the civil-rights movement. And like many of Jeff's more daring public actions over the years, it originated in the mind of Preacher Martin.

As young blacks grew impatient with the civil disobedience practiced by Martin Luther King and George Washington Brown, as they rallied to militant cries of "black power," they became suspicious of men like Jeff Caldwell playing central roles in a movement that ought to belong to Negroes alone. They didn't even like the word *Negro* anymore. Preacher's responding idea was to take the movement into the white community. The germ of this notion was planted when Preacher was commissioned by the *Atlantic Monthly* to write an article on the "religious precepts of the Ku Klux Klan." The Klan had always identified itself as a Christian organization. How did they manage to marry the teachings of Jesus with their unashamed willingness to employ violence against people they opposed? That was a question Preacher posed to Shane Rollings, the Grand Imperial Dragon of the Confederate Union of Klans, who was then the nation's most visible Klansman.

Preacher met with Rollings in Jackson, Mississippi, and came away feeling for the first time in his life that he understood how Neville Chamberlain could have so misread the diabolical nature of Adolf Hitler. Rollings was an articulate if uneducated man. He ran his own road-construction business. He was smart enough that he'd learned how to bid a job with uncanny accuracy, even though he'd never graduated from high school. And though he was hardly a rich man, he had become quite comfortable, owning a Cadillac and a four-bedroom house in the north Jackson suburb of Glen Acres. This was quite an accomplishment, he assured Preacher, for a dirt-poor kid who'd grown up chopping cotton on his daddy's tenant farm in the Delta.

Rollings was soft-spoken and understated. In his "aw shucks" manner, he protested repeatedly that reports of Klan violence were greatly exaggerated. He had done his homework, and he made references to Preacher's writings by title and theme. He knew that Preacher played the guitar and liked to sing. When the interview was over, Rollings asked Preacher to lead a hootenanny for his bodyguards, employees and family members.

Maybe he didn't think Preacher would do it, but Preacher took a guitar and led them in singing "Michael Rowed the Boat Ashore," "Where Have All the Flowers Gone?" and such hymns as "The Old Rugged Cross," "Just As I Am" and "Love Lifted Me."

Everybody was fresh scrubbed and exceedingly polite, and they sang along with as much earnestness and apparent conviction as movement volunteers. Preacher found the experience oddly moving and therefore disturbing. He dared wonder if Shane Rollings could be converted. He doubted it; he judged Rollings' seeming reasonableness a calculated pretense. But if Rollings couldn't be converted, maybe his followers could. Thus began an impossible dream.

At first, Jeff deemed Preacher's fascination with the Klan and Shane Rollings dangerously quixotic. But Preacher kept quoting Jesus's command to "love our enemies" and Paul's direction that "if your enemy is hungry, feed him; if he is thirsty, give him drink." Gradually, Jeff began to toy with the idea of reaching out to the Klan in some public way. Perhaps their children could be influenced by civil-rights leaders willing to treat them as human beings rather than vermin. Then, in the summer of 1967, Shane Rollings went to jail for income-tax invasion. The feds charged that he had diverted Klan money to enhance his own lifestyle without reporting it as income.

At Preacher's urging, acting on Jesus's specific command in Matthew 25 that "Inasmuch as ye have done it unto the least of these, my brethren, ye have done it unto me," Jeff decided to make a publicized visit to Shane Rollings in prison. At first, many of Jeff's movement associates opposed the idea. The Klan had shed too much blood.

But Dr. Brown understood the message Jeff wanted to deliver, not necessarily to Rollings himself, but to Rollings's followers, namely that all those who had been fighting for civil rights in the name of Christian brotherhood really took the teachings of Jesus seriously, really did believe in the brotherhood of *all* men.

Despite Dr. Brown's endorsement, however, many remained offended by the initiative. The junior staff members, who were not consulted, thought that Jeff had lost his mind. Tommy Caldwell felt that way. So did Ben and Faye Watson. They had seen the ugly, menacing faces of the Klan at too many rallies. They had been jostled and spit on too often. Faye had been called "nigger bitch" too often and recalled too vividly a Klansman's sneering desire to rape her with his axe handle before he chopped off her arms and legs and pissed into her face.

But the junior staff wouldn't have persuaded Jeff to change his mind had he consulted them. He had a message to send to Klansmen and Klan sympathizers, and he had decided he could best deliver it by visiting Rollings at the federal prison in Huntsville, Alabama. Rollings, who had never been directly connected to any act of violence and was not considered a flight risk, was housed in the prison's medium-security wing. He had served without incident three months of what would turn out to be an eighteen-month term. Jeff met with Rollings in a large, open room during visiting period. They sat on either side of a painted redwood picnic table. Preacher sat next to Jeff and took notes on the meeting for a magazine article.

Rollings was a big man of Irish parentage. He was nearly six-three, thick-boned and wide-hipped, but angular, not fleshy. He was thirty-seven that summer. With his toothy smile, shock of red hair and freckles, he reminded Jeff of Howdy Doody.

"I'm sorry to find you in here," Jeff began.

"Aw, I'd think you'd be glad a man of my reputation was locked away," Rollings said.

"I wish that no man ever had to be imprisoned," Jeff said.

"Okay," Rollings said. "Let's not quibble." He smiled. "I couldn't outwrangle you anyway. You preachers know how to put things." He nodded toward Preacher Martin. "This one sure does. I think he's 'bout turned half my family into nigger-lovers just because he can sing like an angel and tell funny stories."

"How is your family?" Jeff asked.

"They're doing all right, Reverend," Rollings responded. "Thanks for asking."

"You have how many children, Mr. Rollings?" Jeff inquired.

"I have three children. All girls. Jennifer will go to Southern Miss in the fall. Jeanine will be a junior in high school. Jane Anne will be in the eighth grade."

"You started young," Jeff said.

"Married at eighteen. First baby at nineteen."

"How are your finances?"

"We've taken a beating," Rollings said. "Fighting a court case is expensive as hell. Pardon me, expensive as all get out."

"You don't have to apologize about swearing," Jeff said. "I was a sergeant back in the big war. I've heard my share of salty language."

"As a matter of fact," Preacher said, "quite a bit from your brothers in the Klan."

Jeff darted a glance at his colleague.

"I know," Rollings said. "I've asked the boys to watch their mouths when ladies and children are around. But they get carried away. I'll keep on 'em about it, I promise you. When they let me out of this here cage, that is."

"May I ask you, Mr. Rollings," Jeff said in a quiet, mild tone, "how you can state a concern for polite behavior and all the while countenance the kind of mayhem you have promoted and the murder you have condoned?"

Rollings smiled as if rueful and shook his head. "Now your buddy here," he said, indicating Preacher with a thumb, "asked me something similar. And I tried to explain to him that every time there's violence, the newspapers and the TV says it was the Klan that done it. But there's lots of angry people out there."

"But you do approve of violence?"

"I think violence begets violence. Ain't that in the Bible?"

"Something like that, yes," Jeff said.

"Well, I take note of the fact that when they forced the niggers into Little Rock High the National Guardsmen was carrying M-1s on their shoulders, not giant sticks of licorice. Same thing when they backed George Wallace out of the doorway down in Tuscaloosa."

"It's true the guardsmen were armed," Jeff responded. "But they didn't shoot anybody."

"Man wields a gun to make me do something, he's at least threatening to shoot me."

"But surely you can't equate using soldiers to enforce the peace with shooting people in cold blood or blowing up children in a church?"

"I don't equate it."

There was a short silence. Jeff waited for Rollings to continue. When he didn't, Jeff glanced at Preacher and then said to Rollings, "Meaning?"

"Meaning nothing, I guess. I don't know nothing about any of that stuff."

"But surely you know that it was Klansmen who did it."

"No, I don't, sir. That ain't been proved. And I don't know a thing about it."

"Well, do you approve of it?"

"I don't approve of killing. The Bible says it's wrong right in the Ten Commandments. But at the same time, I think a man's got a right to defend himself." Jeff started to respond, but Rollings cut him off, "You said you were a sergeant in the big war. Drafted?"

"Volunteered."

"I figured you for the kind of man who would have volunteered. Did you see any action?"

"I ran a supply unit," Jeff said. "France and Belgium, Germany."

"So you didn't get into much of the hot stuff."

"Just once. Battle of the Bulge. They pushed our lines back on us."

"Did you fight?" Rollings asked.

"Yes, I did. I had no choice."

"You fought for your country."

"I think at the time I fought for the men around me. The men I served with."

"See," Rollings said, smiling as if sheepish. "We're not so different. You're a clergymen. You know better than I do that the Bible says thou shalt not kill. But there comes times when you don't have any choice. It don't make it right. But no choice is no choice."

"So you do condone what your fellow Klansmen have done," Jeff said.

"I wish you wouldn't say that. The Constitution says you're innocent till you're proven guilty. And that ain't happened."

"But you condone the violence," Jeff persisted.

"Naw, I don't condone it. But I try not to judge it. People are fighting for their way of life."

"Mr. Rollings," Jeff said, "you're fighting for a way of life where one group of men gets to trample on the rights of another group. You're an intelligent man. You can't believe that's right."

"I got no desire to trample on any man's rights. And no man has a right to trample on mine. I don't want my children going to school with niggers, and the federal government and folks like you are trying to make them. Instead of trying to do that, why don't the government round up all the niggers and send them back to Africa? That's the way to make this problem go away."

"But really, Mr. Rollings!" Jeff said. "You know such a thing is impossible."

"I certainly do not," Rollings said. "They say we're gonna put a man on the moon in the next couple of years, and if we can do that, we can certainly send the niggers back where they came from. And without killing or hurting none of them, either."

They talked on for a while. Rollings never raised his voice or ranted. He was polite and smiled often. But he had an answer for every point Jeff tried to make, and Jeff knew beyond question that Rollings would never succumb to the forces of logical discourse. Before he left, Jeff asked Rollings if there was anything he needed. Rollings thanked him and said no.

"Is there something we might do for your family while you're incarcerated?" Jeff asked.

"Naw," Rollings said. "I guess not. They'll be okay. The Tri Kaps are looking out for them."

"Tri Kaps?"

"My fraternity brothers," Rollings said without irony. "Kappa Kappa Kappa."

Jeff stood to leave, and Preacher took a photograph of him shaking hands with the Klansman.

"I hope you'll come back to see me again?"

"Then I will," Jeff said.

"You know," Rollings said, "maybe there is something you could do for me and my family. You could pray for us. Will you do that?"

"Yes," Jeff said. "I will."

As he left the prison, he reflected that praying for Shane Rollings and all his Tri Kappa brothers was probably his best hope for changing their tormented hearts.

Two weeks before Dr. Brown was killed, Shane Rollings was brought up on new charges. The avowed Klansman who was apprehended only moments after killing Pastor

Cletus Moore when he blew up the Mount Holly Baptist Church in Mobile, Alabama, stated to police that he had acted on direct orders from Grand Imperial Dragon Rollings himself. Rollings denied the allegations, and investigators were unable to establish that the bomber and Rollings had ever had contact. But then Rollings denied the Klan's hand in any violence whatsoever.

When Tommy Caldwell arrived home on the night he witnessed his father's hospital meeting with New Orleans police officers and the FBI agent, Glenda had a meal of spaghetti and meat sauce, salad and hot bread prepared and ready for the table. Tommy was surprised because they normally prepared meals together.

"Hey, what's this?" he asked as he passed into the dining room and saw Glenda at the kitchen counter. She had on shorts and a T-shirt covered by a blue denim apron down to her knees.

"It's a sumptuous repast," she said, turning to him. "I just want to do right by my man." Tommy looked around as if she might be talking to somebody else. "Okay," he said, looking back at her. "Who are you, and what did you do with the real Glenda Russell?"

She stood on tiptoe and kissed him on the nose, her thick middle bumping into him.

"Glenda Caldwell," she said. "You always forget that I'm an old married woman now."

"Yeah?" Tommy said, circling his hands around Glenda's waist and pulling her against him. "How'd you get somebody to marry you? Get yourself knocked up?"

Glenda locked her arms around Tommy and laid her head flat against his chest. "You're an ugly piece of white trailer trash, Thomas Peter Caldwell. You don't deserve a loyal wife like me. I may be knocked up, but I'm an excellent cook and bottle washer."

"We don't wash our bottles, liar. And if you're an excellent cook, it's a trait you developed today while I was still at the hospital."

"I guess I'll just eat all the spaghetti myself, smartass. I'm eating for two, you know."

"I don't think we have to go that far," Tommy said. "Upon second thought, you are an excellent cook. It's one of your hidden talents."

Without letting go of him with her left arm, she leaned back and hammered on his shoulder with her open right hand. "You're asking for it, buster," she said.

"You're beautiful when you're angry," Tommy said.

"No, I'm not. I'm not beautiful. I'm a fat ugly pig."

"Stop it. We've already agreed. For a fat ugly pig, you're exceedingly beautiful."

She pinched him in the soft flesh of his lower back, and he yelped.

Tommy carried the food to the table, and they sat down to eat. Tommy tasted a bite of the spaghetti and said, "Why, I believe you are an excellent cook, after all. This is delicious, and I'm not able to steal any of the credit. Why did you go to all this trouble by yourself? Aside from its being your duty, of course."

"I knew you'd be tired from being at the hospital all day."

"Thinking of me," Tommy said. "What did I ever do to deserve you?"

"Nothing, I don't think."

Tommy nodded. "I knew it was either something or nothing. One of the two."

As they ate, Tommy told Glenda about Jeff's suspicions that the FBI had bugged his hospital room. "You think there's anything to that?" she asked.

Tommy shrugged. "FBI bastards certainly aren't our friends. Hoover's a bigot who bugged Dr. Brown. So, yeah, there could be something to it. Or it could be Dad is paranoid. Waxing paranoid seems pretty reasonable for someone who was just shot by a man he's known and trusted for years."

"Hard to argue with that," Tommy agreed.

After dinner, Glenda sat at the kitchen table while Tommy washed the dishes. "You think Dad's going to make it?" he asked.

"Of course," Glenda said. "He's improved every day. Why? Don't you?"

"Yeah. I guess. He's just so vague sometimes. It's not that he raves exactly. But sometimes I don't know what he's talking about. It's as if he's gone somewhere else and only drops back in when you really demand it. Like that 'Do I have cancer' business. What was that all about?"

"He said he was joking."

"Yeah," Tommy said. "Maybe. But it seemed like he was out of it and then claimed to be joking as a way of covering up. He used to do the same sort of thing when he was really hitting the sauce after he and my mother split up. He'd be almost blind drunk, and he'd say something stupid, and when Danielle or I would comment on it, he'd claim to be joking."

"Jeff had a drinking problem?" Glenda said. "I mean, I know he's no teetotaler, but—"

Tommy shrugged. "From the time he lost his job at Gentilly Boulevard until he married Naylynn, a period of over a year, he had a big problem. When Dr. Brown created a position for him at CSCL headquarters that summer, he told Dad he couldn't come in with liquor on his breath. So Dad cleaned up his act during working hours. But he still got wasted every night."

"I never would have guessed that," Glenda said. "Jeff always seemed so, I don't know, certain about things, I guess." Tommy didn't say anything. "Wouldn't you agree with that?"

"I don't know. I've seen things you haven't seen. Dad was always a driven guy."

"Hmmm?" Glenda said. "Driven? I'd choose a word more like committed. Or principled. Anyway, maybe if he seemed vague today, it was because of the pain medication."

"Probably that's it," Tommy said.

"You should try not to worry," Glenda said.

Tommy was already in bed reading the current issue of *Newsweek* when Glenda came to bed wearing only the blousy top to her shorty pajamas. In the last couple of weeks, she had grown uncomfortable in the bottoms. The elastic bit around her swelling middle. The queen-sized mattress was on box springs sitting on the floor, and as she squatted down to get under the sheet, she said, "We're going to have to get a bed soon, or one day I'm not going to be able to leverage myself up off this floor. I'll get in bed one night and just stay there until I have the baby."

Tommy laughed and promised they'd get a bed that weekend. They talked awhile about schedules for the next day, and then they made love. The fact that she was pregnant made him feel so tender toward her he sometimes thought he might cry. Afterwards, they lay next to each other in the dark, and Tommy continued to stroke the flat of his hand back and forth across her taut middle. Stroking her, Tommy said, "Dad said something strange to me today. Said he thought the Klan was involved in the shooting."

"Well, then, he is out of it," Glenda said.

"Yeah," Tommy said. "It's what I thought at first, too."

Even though the room was completely dark, Glenda rolled over on her side to face Tommy. "What?" she said. "Ben Watson was married to a Negro, for Christsake. He may have been a little uptight. And he obviously went off his rocker. But he was no secret Klan operative. You and I knew him too well for that. He was a true believer."

"Yeah," Tommy said. "I'm just turning ideas around. But here's what I've been thinking. Ben couldn't understand what Dad was doing, making those prison visits to Shane Rollings. It really offended him."

"It offended you, too. And you certainly didn't murder Dr. Brown and shoot your father."

"Well, I don't understand it. You're the only one of the younger staff who thinks it's okay."

"I think it makes a statement about Christian charity," Glenda said. "A daring one, too."

"All right," Tommy said. "I don't want to debate that anymore right now. Dad's Klan grandstanding has offended me, and I didn't shoot him because of it. But I'm married to you, not Faye. I haven't liked it, but I'm not married to a black person. See what I'm saying? How much more offensive is it if the person you love more than anything in the world is a Negro and your boss is holding well-publicized meetings with the country's most famous Klansman?"

"You're saying that Ben fired those shots to kill Jeff and not Dr. Brown?"

"Well," Tommy said, "yes, I guess that is what I'm saying. That's the scenario I'm playing around with, anyway. At first glance it seems far-fetched. But at least it's a reason. We haven't been able to come up with anything else at all. Before Ben started shooting, he said, 'I know what you did.' Everybody thought he meant something Dr. Brown did—or something Ben *thought* Dr. Brown did. But what if he meant something Dad did—consorted with the Klan. Gave the hand of fellowship to Shane Rollings. Maybe Faye complained about that to Ben. Maybe Ben thought he could only prove his worthiness to be married to a black woman by—"

Tommy shrugged. "Perhaps that's why Faye said maybe she knew why Ben did what he did. Maybe that's why she got so upset and wouldn't talk to us anymore."

"I don't know," Glenda said.

"No," Tommy said. "I guess not. But remember, Faye's father was the former pastor at Mount Holly Baptist in Mobile. It could have been her father the Klan killed when they blew the church up. That would upset anyone. We know it upset her. She talked about it a lot. What if it upset Ben enough that he decided to shoot Dad for consorting with the enemy?"

"And then Dr. Brown was killed by accident?"

"That's the theory," Tommy said.

"I don't know," Glenda said. "It has a kind of logic, I guess."

"It would also explain why the FBI has been all over Faye like gravy on rice. In fact, since Dad thinks the FBI is bugging him for some reason, maybe they're somehow behind the whole goddamned thing. Maybe they were feeding Ben some kind of noise. Maybe they got him riled or helped get him riled. What if the FBI told Ben something like Dad knew in advance that Shane Rollings ordered the Mobile church bombing but wasn't coming forward? Would that push a guy like Ben Watson over the edge?"

"Tommy, stop it," Glenda said. "You're getting crazy."

"Thanks a lot."

"Listen to what you're proposing, honey. Hoover hated Dr. Brown, not your father."

"I'm sure he hates Jeff Caldwell, too."

"Okay," Glenda conceded. "You're right. Hoover probably hates Jeff, too. But you'll have to admit that he surely hated Dr. Brown more."

"Okay," Tommy said. "Of course, you're right about that."

"So if the FBI was going to set up an assassin, the target would have to be Dr. Brown."

"And look who's dead," Tommy said defensively. He was just spinning theories in the dark. He already saw how Glenda was demolishing this particular FBI angle.

"But according to your Klan theory, Ben would only be after Jeff. The FBI couldn't have known Dr. Brown was going to get in the line of fire."

"All right. All right," Tommy said. "But I still think we may be onto something with the Klan stuff."

Glenda stroked Tommy's bare chest, soothing him. "Will you be mad if I say something?"

"What," Tommy said, already irritated.

"I don't think I believe any of it," Glenda said.

"Well, what do you believe?"

"I'm not sure that worrying ourselves about this is what we ought to do."

"Don't you want to know what happened?"

"I suppose," Glenda said. "Though it's obviously not going to change anything. It's not going to bring Dr. Brown back to life. But if I believe anything, it's that we probably won't ever know why Ben did what he did."

"Well, I want to know," Tommy said.

"I know you do, baby."

"Will you go back to see Faye with me tomorrow?"

"I guess," Glenda said. "You want to ask her about this Klan business?"

"Yes," Tommy said.

"She may not want to tell you. If you're right, she really may not want to tell you."

"She almost told us the last time we saw her."

"She almost told us *something* the last time we saw her. We don't know what."

The next morning, Tommy called Preacher Martin and asked him to go back with them to see Faye again. Then he expounded upon his Klan theory. "What do you think?" he asked Preacher.

"Bubba," Preacher said. "I don't know what I think. And, frankly, I hope you're wrong."

"Why?" Tommy asked.

"Two reasons," Preacher said. "One good, one not good. The not good one is purely selfish. It was me suggested your Daddy get hooked up with Shane Rollings. I sure hope that hasn't come around and got G.W. murdered."

"And the better reason?"

"I hope that little black girl, who has already lost her husband in this horrible mess, doesn't have herself to blame."

"Well, I obviously wouldn't want that to be true either," Tommy said.

"So I hope you're wrong," Preacher said.

And it turned out he was.

In the late morning of a typically sultry summer New Orleans day, Glenda, Tommy and Preacher went again to the Fontainebleau. It was so humid Tommy's shirt was sticking to him by the time he climbed out of his Volkswagen. As before, two FBI agents were stationed outside Faye's room. They were no more friendly than before, but eventually the visitors were admitted. Faye's appearance and demeanor suggested a profound depression. A tray of room-service food had been picked at and abandoned. Two uneaten fried eggs glistened in a pool of cold grease. Faye's hair was matted on one side where she'd lain on it and not bothered to brush it afterwards. Her shapeless dress was wrinkled, as if she'd slept in it.

Glenda made small talk for a while. And then, as gently as he could, Tommy asked Faye about any possible Klan connection to Ben's becoming an assassin. Faye said there wasn't one. And then she told them exactly why her husband had shot Jeff Caldwell and killed George Washington Brown.

"Because I was sleeping with him," Faye said.

chapter eighteen

THE DIRTY SECRET of the civil-rights movement was George Washington Brown's promiscuity. It was both his Achilles' heel and an emblem of his complicated humanity. After 1963 when he became one of J. Edgar Hoover's dark obsessions, he was followed, spied upon and bugged until the day of his death. During that time, the FBI amassed a huge file documenting Dr. Brown's infidelities. He seldom spent a single night on the road without a bedtime companion. His sexual appetite and personal charisma were such that women practically stood in line to sleep with him. Housewives, working women, college girls, black, white, Asian, American Indian, yes, sometimes more than one at a time. He could, and so he did.

At a rally or during a speech, Dr. Brown would spot an attractive woman who seemed to be listening to him with particularly rapt attention. Afterwards, he'd have one of his young lieutenants invite her to visit with him. "Cutting the calves," they called it. Dr. Brown would take the woman into a private room somewhere, the pastor's study, a Sunday School room, a meeting room at a convention hall, and talk quietly with her about the movement. Would she like to accompany him and some others to a place where they could unwind a little? She seldom said no. On the rare occasion that she got as far as Dr. Brown's hotel suite only to indicate she didn't want to sleep with him, he apologized profusely, savaged himself as weak and begged her to pray for him. But this seldom happened.

Dr. Brown's ceaseless sexual activity made J. Edgar Hoover almost insane with anger. His rages against Dr. Brown were legend at FBI headquarters. His routine epithet for Dr. Brown was "the big cheese nigger pervert." It infuriated Hoover that Dr. Brown could get beautiful white college coeds to give him oral sex.

Once, after listening to Dr. Brown in the throes of sexual ecstasy with a white woman, as if in parody of Nikita Khrushchev, Hoover took off his shoe and pounded the tape machine to pieces, hurling across the room what he could not otherwise destroy. Hoover swore a vendetta against Dr. Brown. "I will see that hypocrite unveiled and shamed for the animal he is," Hoover would declare to any agency employee he might encounter when he was overseeing reports about Dr. Brown's latest sexual conquests.

As early as 1964, Hoover began to send Dr. Brown anonymous letters. The first one said, "We know what you do every time you spend a night outside the city of New Orleans." Another said, "A man as filthy as you should be ashamed to present himself as a leader of an entire race of people. Resign or be revealed." A third said, "Resign lest we be forced to reveal to your wife what goes on behind the closed doors of your motel room."

Subsequently, Hoover sent Dr. Brown letters purporting to be from women with whom he'd had relations. These letters claimed that Dr. Brown had impregnated the writer, or given her a sexual disease, or caused her to divorce. Each claimed that Dr. Brown had ruined the writer's life and demanded that he retire from his civil-rights leadership as penance. Later still, Hoover sent letters of the same type to Annette Brown, demanding that she use her influence to get her husband to withdraw as head of the CSCL. Annette took these letters to her husband and told him she understood how viciously hard it was for him to lead the life for which he had been chosen.

Ultimately, Hoover resorted to sending Annette Brown a notorious tape recording of her husband with two white college girls. On it Dr. Brown could be heard praising the girls'"pretty little pink pussies" and rhapsodizing about how much he liked to "stretch your ruby-red lips" and "fill each of your pretty round mouths with my long black cock." The sex talk between Dr. Brown and his partners was not all that different from the kind of exchanges sexually active people often have with their partners. But few people have their bedroom conversations recorded. The male voice on the tape was unmistakably that of Dr. Brown, but Annette Brown assumed it was an impostor. She was sophisticated enough to presume that her husband had not always been faithful. But she knew he loved her and their children, and she knew that, aside from his work, his family was the center of his life. Had she known the details of Dr. Brown's sexual activity, she would have been hurt, but she did not seek to learn the details. If he took pleasure in the arms of another when she was not with him, she did not want to know.

From the Garden of Eden forward, it would seem that the end of man is to know, to follow the trail of knowledge wherever it leads. And generally man presumes that knowing is superior to not knowing. Certainly, the trail of knowledge can lead to vaccines against smallpox and polio. It can lead to airplanes and space travel. It can lead to refrigeration and air conditioning. But it can also lead to nuclear bombs, ICBMs, Nazi medical experiments and bacteriological weapons. Not all knowledge is good. Sometimes the absence of knowledge is superior. Sometimes choosing not to know is an act of benevolence, an act of wisdom. And Annette Brown understood this as most people do not.

Viewed in historical perspective, George Washington Brown's habitual sexual infidelity provided at once his worst moments and, ironically, some of his finest. For the sake of his family and his enduring reputation, how much better it would have been had he adhered to the moral presumptions of his day and profession. But he did not control himself, and thus he hurt some of those who admired him. After his death, when the truth was forced upon them, he hurt his family. And yet, it is a measure of Dr. Brown's astonishing courage that he never cracked under Hoover's assault. He absolutely did not want to be found out as a philanderer. Had Hoover succeeded in making Dr. Brown's infidelities public knowledge during his lifetime, Dr. Brown would have suffered mightily in the humiliation. But he never contemplated surrendering to Hoover's blackmail. And Hoover could not take his information directly to the press because all of it had been gathered through illegally planted listening devices and wiretaps.

The hurt Dr. Brown's indiscretions inflicted on those who cared about him was greater than he ever came to understand. He was like a tightrope walker who knows what he does is dangerous, knows that he can fall and be killed, but knows that fact only abstractly because he never, ever, expects to fall. But those Dr. Brown hurt did not include the countless number of women with whom he slept. Each remembered her dalliance with Dr. Brown as a special treasure she would carry in her heart forever. Some deluded themselves into thinking that they were among a tiny, select few. Others recognized and accepted the truth that there were many besides themselves. But none had regrets. And this was hardly because Dr. Brown was such a spectacular lover, for as Preacher Martin said in summary about the sexual act in all its variations, "There are so many different ways to get there, but arriving is always just about the same." So it wasn't the sex itself these women treasured, but the intimacy, the fleeting closeness each enjoyed with a man of such greatness. And whatever his failings, George Washington Brown had surpassing greatness in him.

But he did hurt some of his admirers who came to know his weakness of the flesh. Among them was Tommy Caldwell. Tommy would always regard his discovery of Dr. Brown's infidelity as the day the world changed for him, the day a certain cynicism entered his life, never to depart.

It happened in the summer of 1964, the summer after Tommy graduated from high school, the summer of the Mississippi voter-registration drive, during a year that was already the most tumultuous of Tommy's young life—the year his parents separated and divorced.

Tommy told himself that as a grown man about to enter college, he could hardly be affected by the fact that the acrimony between his parents had become so horrible they couldn't live together any more. He told himself that the problems between his parents were *their* problems, not *his*. He told himself he could love them equally, separate and apart, the same way he loved them together. But he knew that everything he told himself was a lie.

Tommy couldn't love them equally, separate and apart, the same way he loved them together. Apart, he didn't love either one of them as well. For though he tried not to, he judged them. He judged his father for being first so stubborn and then so weak. Tommy was an athlete, and he judged his father in an athlete's terms, for being unable to handle defeat.

Jeff's sudden reliance on the balm of alcohol disgusted Tommy, not because he felt that drinking was inherently evil, but because Jeff nursed his wounds with bottles of Jack Daniels in such a morose and, to Tommy's mind, cowardly way. Since civil-rights work was always Jeff's first calling anyway, Tommy hardly minded that Jeff accepted a full-time position with the CSCL after his messy departure from Gentilly Boulevard Baptist Church. But Tommy hated the fact that Jeff didn't fight for his pastorate.

Nonetheless, disappointed as Tommy was in Jeff, he was even angrier with his mother, for the separation and subsequent divorce were her doing. She wouldn't tolerate Jeff's drinking, and she couldn't abide his relentless characterization of himself as Job, whom God was testing by taking away all that he cared about. Tommy realized that Jeff became, for a time, practically intolerable, but still he blamed his mother because she gave up. When the family moved out of the parsonage in April, she took a three-bedroom apartment uptown and began to support herself on the meager salary she earned as a general-education-degree tutor at the city's home for unwed mothers.

In the aftermath of the separation, Tommy sought out Dr. Brown for counseling. The two families had known each other for so long, and Tommy's admiration of the man was so great he wanted Dr. Brown's guidance. At the time, Dr. Brown was preparing the voting-rights crusade, but it never occurred to Tommy what a strange request it was to ask such an important man for pastoral counseling of the most personal kind. Years later, when he reflected on his tunnel vision during that period, he recalled with embarrassment and awe the two occasions on which he met with Dr. Brown in the pastoral study at the Dryades Avenue Baptist Church. For Tommy, Dr. Brown's greatness stemmed not just from his masterful oratory and his boundless courage, but from his ability to remember that in the sea of troubled humanity in need of vast programs to address their problems, there are individuals who need a sympathetic ear and a comforting hand.

That was why Tommy, already vulnerable from witnessing the failings of his parents, became so distressed to discover those of his great hero. It happened on an early July morning in Jackson, Mississippi, at the Westchester Arms, a Negro hotel where the CSCL had established its campaign headquarters for a mass voting–rights demonstration at the state capitol. The white volunteers and staff were staying at the Wayside Inn, a white motel about fifteen minutes away. Tommy shared a room with his father.

Two days before the demonstration, Ben Watson, Robert Brown and Tommy were assigned to build placards with other volunteers, including Faye Robinson, Ben's girlfriend from Mobile, and Glenda Russell, a Kansas City, Missouri, girl who had just finished her sophomore year at Valparaiso University.

Jeff, Tommy and Ben ate breakfast in the Wayside Inn coffee shop. Glenda, Karen Ashe, a Valparaiso classmate, and another young white girl sat at the next table. After breakfast, the young women went straight to a Negro church to build signs and mimeograph flyers while Ben and Tommy set off to pick up Robert in Ben's green-and-white Ford Falcon. Ben pulled up at the front door to the Westchester Arms, and Tommy hopped out.

In the lobby, the tall, thin young Negro desk clerk eyed Tommy warily when Tommy asked him to ring up Robert's room. The clerk studied his ledger for a second and then said, "His room ain't one with a phone."

"Well, what's his room number then?"

"I'm not supposed to be giving that out," the clerk said. "To strangers," he added. Tommy figured he qualified as a stranger by virtue of being white.

"I'm supposed to pick him up," Tommy explained, figuring that the clerk didn't want to be responsible for letting a Klan terrorist into the hotel. "We have to go get supplies for the demonstration."

Tommy was dressed in Bermuda shorts, a red Banlon shirt and a pair of Weejun loafers without socks. He was white, but he didn't look dangerous. Finally the clerk informed him that Robert was in Room 521. The elevator wasn't working, so Tommy jogged up the four flights of stairs, actually glad for the exercise. He'd stayed out late with Ben and Robert the night before so he wouldn't have to watch his father swill Jack Daniels in the motel room. As a result, he hadn't gotten up early to run the five miles he liked to do each morning. Tommy knocked on the door to Robert's room several times but got no answer. Maybe Robert was already downstairs. Tommy was just about to jog back down to the lobby when Faye Robinson came out of Room 523, and he asked her if she knew Robert's whereabouts.

"Try the CSCL suite," Faye said. "411. Got coffee and doughnuts in there."

"Gotcha," Tommy said, flashing her the okay sign with his thumb and forefinger curled into a circle. "Knowing Robert, he could smell those doughnuts from up here. Thanks."

Tommy spun away and bounded down the stairs two at a time. The door to 411 was cracked open, and he pushed his way in without knocking. And that's when it happened. He entered the living room of the suite just as a door to one of the bedrooms opened and a young Xavier University girl came out, a purse over one shoulder and a hand down the front of her black dress, obviously adjusting her undergarments. She had fine, mocha-colored skin and a spray of freckles across her pretty face. Tommy had met her when they were campaigning down in McComb. He didn't remember her name—Dolores maybe—but he remembered that she was pre-med. Preoccupied with her clothing, the girl failed to see that Tommy had come in. She was halfway across the room when she finally looked up to find him staring at her.

"Hi," she said and giggled as she walked quickly past him.

"Hi," Tommy said and was just about to ask where Robert was when he heard a voice from the room she had just left.

"Honey, close that door," the unmistakable voice of George Washington Brown said. When he got no answer, Dr. Brown came to the door to close it himself. He was dressed only in a pair of white boxer shorts and an unbuttoned long-sleeve white dress shirt.

Later in life, Tommy looked back on himself as an eighteen-year-old just out of high school and was amazed that he could ever have been so naive, could ever have believed that men actually were the people they pretended to be. He was not a completely inexperienced kid. He was technically a virgin; he and his high-school girlfriend Tammy Bailey had never had intercourse. But they had petted to orgasm—his orgasm, anyway; so Tommy wasn't a prude. But he did actually believe that most husbands and wives were faithful to each other and that only sinful people committed adultery.

For two days, Tommy carried the knowledge of what he'd seen around inside him. Finally, on the night before the demonstration, as they were getting ready for bed, he told his father that he wanted to return to New Orleans first thing in the morning.

"What are you talking about?" Jeff asked. He'd had a couple of beers with dinner, and he was on his second Jack Daniels.

Jeff took a sip of his drink and said, "G.W.'s gonna make one of his vintage speeches, and we're gonna kick some cracker butt in the morning. Man, you don't want to miss that. We're gonna fill the street in front of the capitol with ten thousand Negroes and enough white liberals like you and me to add a dash of salt to the pepper. Yes, sir. We're gonna scare the petticoats off the Mississippi belles and make all those segregation-now-and-forever legislators wet their britches wondering what would happen if we rushed the place."

"Maybe you're going to do all that, but I'm not," Tommy said.

"What's got your skivvies twisted, son?" Jeff said. "You been wearing a long face around here for two days. You've gotta take some pleasure in what we do. We're doing good, boy. Most folks, they spend their lives just marking time. But we're actually doing good. Savor it." Jeff lifted his glass out toward Tommy as if he was making a toast.

"I'm sick of watching you booze it up every night," Tommy said. "This room smells like a bar."

The color drained out of Jeff's face. Tommy had never spoken to him like that before. Jeff put his glass down on the night table and sat on the bed facing his son. Tommy had stripped down to his jockey shorts and dropped to the floor to do pushups.

Tommy finished doing his exercises and flopped on his bed. Jeff waited until Tommy's breathing returned to normal then said, "What's bothering you, Tommy?"

"Nothing," Tommy replied.

"Well, obviously something is bothering you. You come in here tonight and tell me you want to go home before the demonstration we've been working on for ten days."

"I just want to go home," Tommy said.

"Go after the demonstration."

"I want to go first thing in the morning."

"Well, son, I don't even know if there's a bus first thing in the morning."

"I'll hitch then."

"Tommy, you've got responsibilities. We're counting on you to marshal. You've always helped out before. You're good. You're young and strong, and it's important to have some white faces out there. Make it plain that whites want this, too."

"Yeah," Tommy said.

"What's the problem? You got girl trouble back home? I think you ought to check out that Glenda Russell. She's a dish."

"She's two years older than me."

"Why is that a problem?"

"I'm going steady, Dad. Remember?"

"What's that? Going steady. You're not married, right?"

Tommy sat up in bed and stared hard at his father. "Well, some people are married. Am I right? And marriage ought to mean something. Going steady means something to me. It means giving your word."

"Tommy, I'm sorry about what happened between me and your mother. I'll always—"

"I'm not talking about you and Mom. And I don't *want* to talk about you and Mom. I'm talking about Dr. Brown."

Jeff picked up his glass of whiskey but then set it back down. "What do you mean, you're talking about Dr. Brown?"

"I saw him," Tommy said. "I saw him with that Xavier girl. That new pretty girl. Dolores or something. She's young enough to be his daughter."

"Tommy," Jeff said, shaking his head, his voice low, his eyes on his feet.

"Did you know about this, Dad?"

Jeff shook his head again. "I didn't know about Dolores, no."

"What?" Tommy said. He leapt to his feet, towering over his father who sat bent over, his head in his hands, his elbows on his knees. "What do you mean you didn't know about *Dolores*? Have there been others? Is that what you're telling me? That he's done this before?"

Jeff looked up at his son. "You're young and idealistic. You don't understand."

"What don't I understand? That adultery isn't really a sin? That there are really only nine commandments?"

"You don't understand that men are weak. That even great men have feet of clay. I don't claim to be a great man myself. But as my son, you know that I have feet of clay." Jeff nodded toward his glass of whiskey on the night stand. "You've pointed out one of mine tonight. G. W. doesn't drink. Maybe he should."

"Exodus 20 doesn't say 'Thou shalt not drink.'"

"This has been a horrible year," Jeff said solemnly. "You've had a lot of shocks. And I'm sure you're angry at me as much as you are at G. W."

"Right," Tommy said. He got up and walked around the beds toward the bathroom. "I'd only be as angry at you if I found out you had cheated on Mom."

Tommy stepped into the bathroom, turned on the water in the sink and washed his hands vigorously. When he came back, drying his hands on a white towel, he said, "You and mom had problems. But you were faithful to each other. Right?" He lay back down on his bed, folded two pillows under his head and stared at the ceiling.

"You know, I presume, that I've had sexual relations with Naylynn. Your mother and I are still married until the end of this month. So I guess that makes me an adulterer, too."

"You've had sex with Naylynn since you were separated from Mother, right?"

"Yes, I presumed you knew that."

"I knew it," Tommy said. "But you weren't with Mother anymore. And Mother gave you no hope of reconciling."

"That's right," Jeff said quickly. "And Naylynn and I will marry after the divorce. But I hope you know she won't ever replace your mother."

Tommy sat back up and put his feet beside his father's in the space between the two beds. "And that's why, even when things were going bad, you wouldn't have cheated on her, and she wouldn't have cheated on you."

Jeff looked up at his son with sad, hooded eyes. "No, I wouldn't," he said. "I wouldn't."

"See, that's what matters. Loyalty. I can even admire your loyalty to Dr. Brown right now. But I don't want you to make excuses for him. He's a hypocrite, and all the while he holds himself up to be our leader."

"That's something else you don't understand. He doesn't hold himself up to be our leader. *We* hold him up as our leader. We ask so much of him, and he gives us everything he's got. If we would let him, if his conscience would let him, if God would let him, he would step aside and fall on his knees in gratitude."

"Don't talk like that about God," Tommy snarled. "It's disgusting. He talks about God's call, and he makes a mockery of it. He asks us to march in Christian brotherhood. And all the time he's fucking the Christian sisters."

Tommy's use of the word *fucking* crackled through the air like an electric charge. Tommy heard foul language as often as any male his age, but he seldom used it himself. And he had never used it in front of his father. He half expected his father to slap him. Years later, he would wonder if that's not what he really wanted: righteous indignation, a return to order, a reassertion of adult authority.

But Jeff did something Tommy didn't expect. Jeff tried to teach Tommy a lesson. "I presume you're trying to shock me. Saying the word *fucking* like that. Would it surprise you to know that I know such words too? Fuck, shit, cock, dick, prick, pussy, cunt. I know all those words." Jeff smiled wryly, not looking at his son. "They teach them to you in the Army if you didn't know them before." He looked back at Tommy now. "Not one of those is the dirtiest word in the English language, son. Not one of them. The dirtiest word in the English language is *nigger*. That's the most vile. You really want to shock me? Say that word and mean it." Jeff's gaze locked into Tommy's until Tommy looked away.

"I would never say that word," Tommy said softly.

"You wouldn't even say that word about Dr. Brown, your fallen hero, whom you've discovered to be a sinner? In your disappointment, wouldn't you say it about him?"

"Of course not," Tommy said.

"No," Jeff said. "You wouldn't. Angry as you are at him, ashamed as you are of me for drinking and divorcing, I know you wouldn't. I've taught you too well. And that's what you will come to see with time. The teacher is never faithful to the lesson, but that doesn't make the lesson any less true."

As he lay in bed that night, worrying with unwanted knowledge and contemplating his father's response, Tommy decided that Jeff was right: the struggle for civil rights was bigger and more important than the morality of any one person. So Tommy stayed and participated in the demonstration the next day, and he stayed on as a movement volunteer.

Tommy's group of young people worked and traveled together for the entire summer. As a college graduate and the oldest, Ben Watson was put in charge. The others in the group were Ben's girlfriend and future wife Faye Robinson, also a college grad; the two Valparaiso white girls, Glenda Russell and Karen Ashe, both going into their junior year; and the two youngest—Tommy, who was just out of high school, and Robert Brown, a high-school senior.

It was thrilling for these young people to see the gratitude in people's eyes when they helped register them to vote, particularly the old people who had assumed that voting was a privilege they would never enjoy.

Because money was scarce, the young volunteers stayed in the homes of local Negro leaders—often ministers, but more common folks, too. Robert and Tommy always tried to stay together. Tommy found Robert's presence a comfort, a bridge across the racial divide. The people with whom they stayed were gracious and generous, often giving up their own beds so the boys would not have to sleep on the floor. Still, however polite they were, Tommy felt a certain reserve and formality in their dealings with him, a certain wariness no doubt born of inexperience in relating to white people. Having Robert there made it easier on both Tommy and his hosts.

Ben Watson normally stayed somewhere else. Tommy always wondered how he fared. Ben was uneasy with people he knew well; how uncomfortable he must have felt with strangers from another region, class and race. After a time, Ben and Faye began to stay with the same families—obviously not sleeping in the same bed as Tommy and Robert often did, but at least under the same roof. Tommy assumed that arrangement made things easier for Ben.

Every morning by 6:15, before the heat of the day became too suffocating, Tommy and Robert got up and ran. On dusty roads through the flat flood plains of rich black soil in the Delta or up and down the gully-scarred red clay hills in the northwest, or along the brown and gray sand beaches of the Gulf Coast, they ran together—partners, compatriots and friends—stride for stride, gasp for gasp, grunting out a conversation as they kept themselves in shape. As they ran along the dusty lanes and blacktopped highways, they drew stares from the drivers of passing vehicles—stares of wonder from Negroes, stares of hostility from whites—these two young runners, one black, the other white, bare except for shorts, socks and shoes, their torsos glistening with perspiration, their T-shirts tucked into the waistbands of their shorts and flapping behind them like battle flags.

That voting-rights summer of 1964 was a paradoxical time. Especially after their colleagues James Chaney, Andrew Goodman and Mickey Schwerner disappeared from Philadelphia, it was a scary time. But for Tommy Caldwell it was also a time of escape. His family was in such disarray that he was glad to be away. It was a time of serious commitment. All the volunteers felt they were participating in something of historic importance. But for all that, it was also a time of fun. Whenever possible, the six team members got together. Ben Watson and Faye Robinson both played guitar. Gradually the team divided into couples, Faye and Ben, Tommy and Glenda, Robert and Karen Ashe. They sang folk songs and hymns. They made out. Tommy and Robert felt like studs because they were with college girls, older girls from the North who sprinkled their conversation with the occasional salty word, a practice Tommy found positively titillating.

Tommy didn't plan to be unfaithful to his high-school steady, Tammy Bailey, who was waiting for him back in New Orleans. He was attracted to Glenda immediately, but she was older, and from the way she talked and rolled her eyes and made off-color remarks, he assumed she was "experienced." She had a way of sticking her tongue in the corner of her mouth when she said something sarcastic that Tommy found both alluring and intimidating. But as the summer wore on after the Jackson demonstration in June, Tommy and Glenda worked together so closely they became friends. After a day of canvassing, they liked to hang out together.

Their romance started with a touch, and it was Glenda who initiated it. The six teammates piled into Ben's car late one afternoon and went for an after-work picnic in the Tombigbee National Forest. They built a campfire and roasted weenies on straightened coat hangers. They ate, and then they sang "Blowin' in the Wind" and other folk songs. When Ben played "Amazing Grace," everybody let Faye sing it alone. She had a beautiful alto voice, and Tommy was moved every time he heard her sing it. While Faye sang, Glenda took Tommy's hand, pulled it into her lap and interlaced their fingers. Tommy might have interpreted this gesture as sisterly, but he didn't. He squeezed Glenda's hand as if it were a lifeline, and she squeezed back.

On the drive back to the little burg of Louisville where the six of them were staying with three different families, Glenda sat on Tommy's lap in the back seat, his arm circling her waist so that he could feel the flatness of her stomach. This chaste but intimate physical contact aroused him, and he desperately hoped she wouldn't notice. She sat up straight, facing away from him, but every time Ben rounded a curve or hit a bump, she fell back against him, and he would breathe in her scent, a mixture of wood smoke from their campfire, the shampoo she used, and an aroma that was purely her own. For the rest of his life Tommy couldn't smell wood smoke without thinking of Glenda and the first night of their love.

When they dropped off Glenda and Karen, Tommy had to climb out of the little two-door car to let Karen out. The sky was clear, and the moon was so bright it illuminated the yard and porch as if with a silver spotlight. Tommy followed Karen and Glenda up on the porch of the tidy but unpainted wood house where the girls had been staying for the last five days. It was not yet ten o'clock, but the house was dark. Karen pulled the screen door open quietly, handed it to Glenda, and slipped through the front door on tiptoe.

Holding the screen door open with her left hand, Glenda turned toward the yard. "Tommy?" she said, lifting her face up to his.

He stood there without speaking, and as she smiled, he could see orbs of ivory in her dark green eyes. She rose on her toes, pulled Tommy to her with her free hand, then kissed him lightly and quickly on the lips. "Good night," she said.

Then she did that teasing thing with her tongue in the corner of her mouth. Tommy put both his arms around her and kissed her full on the mouth, which she opened as she kissed back. As she let go of the screen door to put both arms around him, it slammed with a crack like a gun shot. They jumped apart and whirled around as if under attack.

Karen rushed out of the house whispering in indignation, "What is the matter with you two? Are you trying to torment these people for letting us stay with them?"

When Tommy and Glenda realized what had happened, they started to giggle, biting their lips trying to remain quiet. In the car Ben, Faye and Robert guffawed. Karen cupped her hands around her mouth and whispered out to the car as loudly as she could, "Hey, you guys, shut the dickens up." But the three in the car laughed even louder.

When lights came on inside the house, the laughter grew louder still. Glenda stepped to the edge of the porch and raised her middle finger to the sky. The lady of the house poked her head out to ask if anything was wrong, and Karen began to apologize profusely, following her back into the house.

Tommy backed away, sheepish that he had caused such a commotion, but Glenda reached out, grabbed his belt, pulled him to her and kissed him again. The people in the car howled. Finally, they broke apart. Tommy returned to the car where his friends seemed to think they had seen the comedy of the year. Glenda stood in the moonlight on the porch, shooting them the bird with both hands, pistoning her arms back and forth like ack-ack guns.

Tommy would not end that summer the technical virgin he had been at the beginning. He borrowed Ben's Falcon one night to take Glenda to a movie, and afterwards, they consummated their love in the back seat. Thereafter, they sneaked away whenever they could, and the frantic, hurried, often cramped sex they had together was wonderful.

With time, the specific details of these acts of coupling faded into a happy erotic blur. But that first night—singing around the campfire and the ride back with Glenda on his lap, their first kiss on the porch—that night was etched in Tommy's memory forever. He could summon its every detail for the rest of his life.

The CSCL suspended the voting-rights campaign for the week around July 4 so that everybody could take a break. Many volunteers went home to be with their families. Glenda and Karen caught a Greyhound bus to Biloxi to lie on the beach. Jeff picked up Tommy and Robert and drove them to New Orleans.

Once they were back in the city, Jeff convinced Billye that the whole family should get together for an Independence Day cookout. Tommy was skeptical. When he was growing up, his family had done back-yard barbecuing perhaps three times. Moreover, Tommy could never remember his family celebrating the Fourth of July, ever.

But Jeff made a big pitch. They were still a family. They still loved each other, even if he and Billye couldn't live together anymore. Finally, against her better instincts, Billye relented. But she warned Jeff that she remained determined to go through with the divorce.

As planned, Jeff arrived at Billye's apartment with a new hibachi about four o'clock, but he hadn't thought to bring charcoal or lighter fluid. Tommy volunteered to run to the drugstore, and Danielle went along for the ride. When they returned, Billye and Jeff were sitting on lawn chairs in the back yard of the complex. Jeff was perched on the front edge of his folding chair; it had tipped forward off its back legs and looked about to collapse. Billye was crying.

"Mommie!" Danielle yelped. She dashed across the yard and knelt at her mother's side.

Tommy set the bag of supplies down on the card table Billye had set up in the yard. Underneath it was an ice chest with bottles of Coke and Barq's. The day was miserably hot, without a whisper of breeze; the scraggly hackberry tree in the corner of the yard provided only mottled shade.

"What's going on?" Tommy asked.

Jeff stood up. "Your mother and I have been talking," he said.

"Yeah?" Tommy said. "About what?"

Billye sniffled. "About nothing," she said. "We haven't been talking about anything."

"Yes, we have," Jeff said. "And I might as well bring it up in front of the whole family."

"We haven't been talking, Jeff," Billye said. "You have."

"Okay," Jeff said. "I've been talking. And I think we ought to tell the kids what I've been talking about. Okay? Is that all right with everybody?"

Nobody said anything.

Finally, Jeff said, "Your mom and I have been talking about getting back together."

"*You've* been talking about that, Jeff," Billye said. "I haven't."

"So let's ask the kids," Jeff said. "Wouldn't you two kids like to see your mom and me try to work things out?"

Neither Tommy nor Danielle said anything. Things had been horrible since the day Jeff lost his job. But, yes, of course, both children wanted their parents to get back together.

"Come on now, kids," Jeff implored. "You gotta help me out here. Your mom thinks things are better for you two if we don't get back together because all we do is fight. You gotta tell her you think we can all live together without fighting. She'll listen to you. But she won't listen to me anymore."

Nobody said anything. Jeff broke down and began sobbing. "Goddamn it, kids, you've got to help me."

Danielle started crying, too. As she had done with Billye, she knelt at Jeff's side and said, "Don't cry, Daddy. Please don't cry."

Jeff put his hand on Danielle's shoulder to leverage himself out of his chair. He stepped to Billye's chair, knelt in the grass in front of her and bent forward so that his head was at the level of her calves. He took the hem of her long, loose summer dress, touched it to his face and wet it with his tears. "I'm begging you, baby. In front of my children, I'm begging you. Don't do this to me. You've punished me enough now. Don't do this to me anymore."

Billye reached out and touched him gently on the top of his head, but she didn't say anything.

Jeff looked up expectantly and said, "Billye, honey?"

And Billye said, "I'm sorry, Jeff, but—"

"No!" Jeff cried. He began to slap at Billye's hand with both of his, wheeling his hands over the top of his head one after the other like someone trying to wave away a hornet. "No! No! No!"

Tommy stood up and stepped over to his father. "Stop it, Dad. Stand up and stop humiliating yourself."

Tommy reached down and slipped a hand under his father's arm, trying to lift Jeff to his feet. But Jeff turned the helicopter slaps on Tommy. "No! No! No!" he said.

Tommy waited until Jeff stopped slapping the air, then lifted him to his feet. "Dad—" Tommy said.

But Jeff cut him off, saying, "Naked came I out of my mother's womb, and naked shall I return hither: the Lord gave, and the Lord hath taken away; blessed be the name of the Lord."

chapter nineteen

J EFF CALDWELL WAS TRAINED in the infantry. He was farsighted, and this perhaps helped his performance as a marksman. He was trained in close-quarters combat, so he knew how to shred an enemy's guts with a bayonet thrust, how to slice a man's throat open with a knife and how to stab through the ribs into the heart or from behind into the kidneys. He was even trained in how to fight without a weapon, to use his hands to crush a windpipe or snap a neck. But as he learned all these things, he prayed fervently that he'd never have to take a life.

Trained after boot camp as a radio operator, Jeff was sent to England, where he was put in charge of training other radio operators. He was promoted to corporal, then to sergeant. He was scheduled to go ashore at Utah Beach on D-Day, but he broke his index finger playing catch. Thereafter, he was reassigned to a supply unit that finally went into France after the liberation of Cherbourg. If he couldn't handle a rifle, he was told, he could certainly handle a clipboard. In the still segregated and racist armed services of the time, all the members of Jeff's company were Negroes except for officers and sergeants. Since the Negroes were kept at the rear and judged unreliable under fire, they were treated with contempt by the front-line soldiers.

Still, they did their duty. Jeff and his men followed Patton's Third Army across France and into Germany. The hours were long. The work was hard. The food was bad. Baths were infrequent. Accommodations were nonexistent. And as the offensive bogged down in the late fall of 1944, the ground was cold. But the fighting was always in front of them. Jeff and his men were vital to the war effort, but aside from the occasional German sniper cut off from his lines, they were in greater danger from food poisoning than from Nazi weapons.

Jeff knew that Hitler could only be defeated by force of arms, but he felt that God had taken special notice of his desire to serve without having to take a life. Then, in December, the lead troops were pushed back right on top of Jeff's supply unit. In the Battle of the Bulge, Jeff's company of loaders, haulers and drivers were suddenly forced to become warriors.

The Germans had advanced more than fifty miles when Jeff and his men were ordered to dig in near the town of Bastogne which, they were told, had to be held. The German infantry fought furiously for control of this crucial crossroads village. Jeff's company B was posted in a forested area to the east of town. Over a period of thirty-six hours their position was attacked three times; each time they held. His men fought well, and Jeff's desire not to take a life was denied.

As the Germans began to withdraw, Jeff's platoon was ordered to advance down the road toward Bonn. It was Christmas Eve, and it was bitter cold. Fresh snow covered the ground; a thick, cold mist obscured their vision and soaked through their uniforms. They were miserable, and they were scared. Company B was not battle-hardened like the veterans of the front; its men had not developed the numbing fatalism of the soldiers they supplied. Jeff and his men were twitchy as they moved down a road lined with trees. They flinched at the sound of a snapping twig or rustling branch. The first German they killed that day was not even armed; he was trying to surrender. He came at them out of the mist like a ghost, and they opened up on him immediately. He was sixteen years old.

A ravine ran down the west side of the road; the six-foot-wide stream that cut through its bottom was frozen over. As they walked, the land on the east side rose gradually until it was a ridge about thirty feet high. The men kept their eyes peeled left and right, but there was no sign of the enemy. Just over a kilometer from town, they approached a cluster of common-walled, two-story houses. Three houses backed up to the ravine on the west side; two snugged up to the ridge on the east. Had they been seasoned troops, had their lieutenant not been one of OCS's ninety-day wonders, they might have circled down into the ravine behind the houses; at the very least, they would have sent only one man between the houses to check them out. Instead, thinking the Germans were again in retreat, they marched into a withering crossfire. The Germans had posted machine-gun teams on the top floor of the second house on either side of the road. Each M-50 controlled the entire road except for the space directly below it, and that space was controlled by the gun opposite.

Lieutenant Martin Bivens was shot in the face and killed instantly. He was twenty-three years old. Like Jeff, he had wanted to go back to college at the end of the war. Billy Mason, hit in the throat, choked to death on his own blood. He was nineteen and wanted to be a movie actor. Eighteen-year-old Terrence Jones was hit in the femoral artery and bled to death within three minutes. His daddy had a good job on the line at Chrysler, and Terrence had figured to work beside him after the war. They were the three men up front. Jeff was walking in the middle of the platoon, about even with the front door of the first house when the firing started. He crashed into the house on the west side of the road and was followed in immediately by Rodney Miller and Bernie Adams. Radioman Adams was hit twice in the back coming in; one round blew his heart apart. He fell face-down in the doorway, and two more rounds tore off his right foot. Jeff and Private Miller dragged his body into the house, but he was already gone. Adams had wanted to drive a milk truck for the one dairy company in Birmingham that hired Negroes. He was twenty years old.

Nelson Bennett, Francis Dixon and Lionel Russell managed to get into the house opposite. Tony Garrett crashed in behind them but took a slug in the shoulder that left his left arm useless. In the road behind this group, Fred Bofinger and Marlon Long were cut down before they could get to cover. Easygoing Fred Bofinger had played the harmonica and mostly faced the world with a wide smile. He was twenty. Marlon Long, nineteen, was Fred's best friend. He had a daughter who was born about the time his platoon turned north and east from Avranche. Behind them James Vaughn and Hector Ortega got to cover behind the house where Jeff and Rodney Miller took refuge inside. Vaughn tried to return fire but drew it before he could get a shot off. The bullet missed him but slammed into the house's wood frame right beside his head and sent a splinter the size of a grown man's thumb into his right eyeball. Terrified, Ortega began running back the way they had come and was brought down by a shot through the back of his head. It blew off his nose, lip and upper teeth as it exited. Ortega was from St. Petersburg, Florida, and had hoped to own a fishing boat. He was nineteen.

Once Jeff had Adams's body in the house, he stripped off the radio and feverishly called for help. "Mayday, mayday," he screamed. "We've been ambushed. Need assistance. Now."

"Who is this?" the radio squawked back.

"Caldwell," Jeff yelled. "Baker Company. Third platoon. We're under heavy fire. We need immediate assistance."

"Just a second," the voice said, and the radio fell silent. Just then the two M-50s fell quiet, and Jeff was afraid that the Germans would come down to the street to grenade them.

"Help me! I'm blind!" James Vaughn screamed.

"Set up by the front door and cover the street," Jeff told Private Miller. Miller moved across the mouth of the door and the M-50 opened up again, slamming shells into the house with the impact of bricks.

"Where the hell are you?" Jeff screamed into the radio.

"Baker Company?" the voice box squawked. "You guys are a supply unit."

"Goddamn it, we're pinned down out Bonn Road, one click, maybe one point five."

"Says here you're a nigger unit," the radio voice said. "Noncombatants."

"Jesus Christ, you son-of-a-bitch," Jeff screamed. "We're on patrol, and we're pinned down. We need immediate assistance."

"Where's your lieutenant?" the radio blared.

"Dead. Half the squad is dead."

"How many you lost?"

"I don't know, you asshole, but we're going to lose everybody if you don't get reinforcements out here, right now."

"See what I can do. And if I was your black ass, I'd stop calling me names."

"I'm not black, you nitwit," Jeff yelled into the radio. "I'm a white sergeant."

Jeff turned to Rodney Miller, who was staring at him with wide blank eyes.

"Thanks for making sure they know we got a live white guy out here with us," Miller said.

"Count the men off, Private," Jeff ordered.

"Baker Three!" Private Miller called out the doorway. "Count off! One's down."

"Two," Nelson Bennett yelled.

Miller knew that Bivens was down. He waited for four. When it didn't come, he said, "Shit," and yelled "Five" for Jeff.

"Six," Francis Dixon yelled.

"Seven," Bennett yelled for Tony Garrett, who had fainted.

There was no eight, nine, or ten, and after waiting for them, Rodney Miller said, "Sweet baby Jesus," and yelled out, "Eleven."

After another short wait, Lionel Russell yelled out, "Thirteen."

No one called fourteen, but James Vaughn did scream, "Help me! I'm blind!"

"Who's hit in the face?" Miller yelled.

"I think it's Vaughn," Nelson Bennett yelled back.

And the M-50s opened up again.

Miller said to Jeff, "Counting you and me, Sarge, we got seven left, one hurt bad—can't see. We got to figure out a way to get those nests before they figure out how shot up we are."

"We can't even get out the door," Jeff said. "We've got to try to control the road, keep 'em from getting a grenade on us and wait for reinforcements."

Jeff relocated so he could watch the road back toward Bastogne in case the Germans tried to circle around. "Bennett," Jeff yelled across the way. "Control the road in both directions. I've radioed for backup. Anybody hit?"

"Garrett," Nelson Bennett yelled back.

"Bad?" Jeff yelled.

"Ain't good," Bennett replied.

"Jesus," Jeff said.

He looked at Miller, who started to say something but thought better of it.

"May goddamn day," Jeff yelled into the radio. "Can you confirm relief or not?"

"Read you, Baker Three," the radio said. "Artillery notified, spotter en route as we speak."

"No, you asshole," Jeff screamed. "No, no, no. We're right on top of them. You can't take them out without taking us out."

"Then get the hell out of there, Baker Three," the radio said. "You got three-four minutes, maybe five, till black thunder."

"Oh, Jesus Christ," Jeff said. "They're going to kill us."

"Probably didn't believe you was white," Rodney Miller said. "Shore don't give a shit about any of us. Not such as they'd risk a white soldier to save us."

"You were right. We're going to have to take out the nests," Jeff said. "Here's the plan: You're going to have to pop out and lay as much fire across from us as you can. I'm right behind you, and I take five strides and put a grenade through the second-floor window on this side."

"Never work," Private Miller said. "Maybe five-percent chance you could pull that off. You're shot for sure; me too, probably."

"Five percent is better than what we're going to have in here. Now let's do it, soldier."

"I do the grenade," Private Miller said. "You lay down the fire."

"You're a better marksman than I am," Jeff said.

"I'm also taller, stronger and a helluva lot faster."

"Jesus, all right," Jeff said. "Switch sides with me."

They changed sides of the doorway. Private Miller was now a step and a half closer to the enemy. Jeff hoisted his M-1 to his shoulder. He looked at Rodney Miller, who crossed himself. Jeff wasn't Catholic, but he crossed himself, too.

"God bless you, Private. We go on three."

"God bless us both," Rodney Miller said.

Jeff counted them down and jumped out of the house, firing as he moved, squeezing round after round, as fast as he could pull the trigger, into the open window one house over and one story up. Rodney was out so fast behind him it was as if they were a single person dividing in half. As Jeff kept moving directly across the street to draw fire away from Rodney, he took one round in his left calf, all flesh, and another across his right knee—a scratch really, although it nicked the patella. The ploy worked and gave Rodney the time he needed; he traveled the distance to the second house in fewer than four full strides and launched a grenade like a Clyde Lovelett running hook. It sailed through the window like a basketball shot passing through the hoop without drawing iron. It actually hit the seventeen-year-old from Munich in the face an instant before it blew off his head and killed the two other young men with him.

But then Rodney's luck ran out. The M-50 across the way swung back on him. One round blew off his left arm; another punched a hole through his back and out his chest. Rodney Miller had been a star forward on his high school basketball team. He had hoped he might get a college scholarship after the war. But on December 24, 1944, his speed, grace, coordination and courage condemned him to die.

Jeff kept running straight across the road and made it into the house with the rest of his unit. He didn't even have to order the next response. With the west-side gunners silenced, Nelson crept up under the east-side nest without being seen and put two grenades through the window, one immediately after the other. The grenades killed the man on the M-50 and the rifleman at his side. But a third German had anticipated what was coming and was already in the first-floor hall; as the grenades exploded above him, he burst into the road and shot Nelson Bennett through the chest. Jeff put a bullet through his forehead an instant later. The German boy was only fifteen. Nelson Bennett had played the trumpet and loved Louis Armstrong. He was twenty.

"We've got to get out of here right now," Jeff said to Francis Dixon and Lionel Russell, who were in the doorway of the first house on the east side. "Incoming in ninety seconds, maybe less."

"We can't leave Tony," Lionel said.

"Get him and move it," Jeff said. "Fast."

Francis and Lionel got Tony Garrett between them and dragged him into the road as Jeff checked James Vaughn. The entire right side of Vaughn's face was covered in blood. The huge wooden splinter he'd pulled out of his eye was gripped tightly in his hand. He was dead. Vaughn had worked alongside his father, shining shoes in a Minden, Louisiana, barbershop. At twenty-three, he was the oldest man in the unit.

As Francis and Lionel came out with Tony, the first round sailed over their heads and blew a crater in the ridge face fifty yards beyond the last house. Francis and Lionel tried to run, a practical impossibility with Tony unconscious between them. Jeff ran back to them and grabbed Tony by the back of his belt to lift his feet off the ground. The three of them ran together, carrying their comrade like an illegal flying wedge in football.

They headed across the road and toward the ravine at a point distant enough to afford them protection. The second round dropped into the very center of the east-side row houses, which collapsed as if they'd been built of playing cards. Fifteen seconds later the west-side houses exploded and slid into the ravine. A spinning piece of shrapnel sliced through Lionel Russell's jugular vein. He lived only long enough to slap his free hand to his neck and say, "Shit."

Lionel Russell's family were sharecroppers near the Sabine River town of Newton, Texas. He was nineteen years old. He probably could have saved himself had he not gone back for Tony Garrett, who no doubt would have been grateful had he made it. But he didn't. He died of shock not long after Francis and Jeff got him to a medical unit in Bastogne. Tony was from Louisville, Kentucky, and had wanted to be a high-school teacher. He was twenty-two.

Like Jeff Caldwell, Francis Dixon managed to get home from the war. He went to Chicago rather than back home to Birmingham and got a meat-packing job with Hormel. The work was unpleasant, but the pay was good. Francis suffered badly from depression, however, and began to drink. In the early 1950s he spent twenty-seven months in a V.A. mental hospital. Francis received no medal for his service in World War II. He and Jeff never saw each other again after the day of the Bonn Road Battle, but Jeff nominated Francis for the Bronze Star. The review board ruled that such a distinguished battle honor was unwarranted. Francis died in 1955 of a heart attack; he was thirty-three.

Jeff nominated Rodney Miller for the Medal of Honor. The review board ruled that Jeff's account of Miller's heroism was not adequately substantiated. They dismissed Francis Dixon's corroboration as "a colored soldier's natural desire to enhance the achievement of a member of his own race."

Jeff was still walking when he arrived back in Bastogne, but it took seventeen stitches to close the bloody wound to his left calf. The wound to his knee, it turned out, was worse. Bone fragments from the top of the patella had slipped into the joint. He was sent to the rear and eventually to England for surgery. Although his recovery was technically considered one hundred percent, the knee would bother him periodically for the rest of his life. But it bothered him more that God had not answered his fervent prayers that he be spared the experience he had on Christmas Eve, six weeks short of his twenty-first birthday.

Like a great many men of his generation, Jeff Caldwell returned from his service in World War II a man in a hurry. He was already twenty-one years old, and he had only a single semester of college rather than the degree he would otherwise have had. The semester was already underway in September of 1945 when he resumed his studies at Valmont.

Billye arrived in Oakwood within the week. Their reunion took place in the student-union cafeteria, where she waited for him after his Saturday-morning class. She stood up when he came in, and for a moment they froze, each uncertain what to do next.

Jeff had not seen her in more than three years. She was more beautiful even than he remembered. But she wasn't a girl any longer, he thought as he looked at her. She had a look of sophistication now that he didn't recall. She had lived in the city for three years and had experiences that he had missed out on. He could never have those years back; he could never share those years with her.

Finally, Billye stepped toward him, threw her arms around him and kissed him.

"I missed you so much," Jeff whispered, his lips against her neck. He squeezed her so hard she had trouble breathing. He buried his face in her hair; she smelled like lilacs. Although it had been ten months since he'd left the battlefield in Belgium, it was only now that the war really seemed over.

The rest of that afternoon and that night over dinner, Jeff and Billye tried to get reacquainted. "I'm going to work so hard," Jeff assured her as they sat over Cokes. "I've always worked hard, and I'm going to work harder yet. I'm going to get straight A's, and I'm going to get a scholarship to the seminary in New Orleans, and when I finish, I'm going to get a good church. And I'm going to be able to have some things that I never had growing up. I'm going to be able to provide you the kinds of things you're used to."

Billye urged him not think in those terms, not to think of her as a burden or as someone who needed special things. They would be fine—better than fine, because she fully intended to work herself when she finished college. Her mother had always worked, and so would she. She'd like to be an architect, maybe, and architects made good money.

Jeff protested that he wasn't making himself clear. "It's not about things, not about possessions, although I intend for us to be comfortable. I want to make a difference. That's what I'm trying to express. A difference for myself and you, sure, but a bigger difference, a much bigger difference. Do you understand?"

"I don't know," Billye said.

"I think this world is going to change," Jeff said. "It needs to change, and I think it's going to. What we did over there, what we did since Pearl Harbor, it seems incredible. But we did it. It was horrible. Don't get me wrong. It was unspeakable. But all around the entire globe, we changed things. We saved things. We proved something—to the world, and to ourselves too."

Billye had no idea what he was talking about, but she was fascinated by his urgency and conviction. "Now we have to change the things that are wrong here," Jeff continued. "Poverty, ignorance, certain people being treated differently from others. I'm going to play a role in that."

At dinner, Billye showed Jeff three albums of photographs she had taken of sites around New Orleans. He told her he liked them, but he didn't really understand her purpose in taking them. The photographs weren't of people she knew and often weren't pictures of people at all but of buildings or boats on the river. He asked her about the snapshot of a grizzled, gray-skinned man standing beside a scale and holding up a fish the size of a man's forearm. The man smiled broadly at the camera showing his missing teeth.

"That's the guy I bought fresh fish from in the French Market," she explained.

The fond way Billye talked about her photographs worried Jeff. Maybe she had grown too enamored of the life she'd made for herself in New Orleans to settle easily into the very different life they were embarking on together. She told Jeff about all the things she had made for her apartment, the slip covers on the two wing chairs she had bought at a rummage sale, the curtains on her windows, the mantel clock she had bought on Magazine Street and repaired and refinished herself.

That night they went to see Humphrey Bogart and Lauren Bacall in *To Have and Have Not*. Jeff told Billye that she looked like Bacall, only prettier. They spent the night at the Faraway Arms. They had had only one night together before the war, and they were as shy with each other as newlyweds, which basically they were. They undressed and bathed separately, and Jeff shaved and doused himself with aftershave. Then they made love, too hurriedly, but with great mutual need. Afterward as Jeff lay on his back, Billye sat up with the sheet tucked under her arms. Gently she reached out and touched the scar on his knee.

"This is where?" she asked.

He shrugged.

She bent forward and kissed the scar. "I'm so glad you're safe," she said.

Too soon, they ran out of things to say. To end an uncomfortable silence, Billye asked, "What are you thinking about, my handsome war-hero husband?"

"I guess I was thinking about biology."

"Well, I like that," Billye said, laughing. "I guess I've been thinking about biology, too."

"What?" Jeff said. "What are you laughing about? I've got a test on Wednesday. I thought maybe I ought to be studying."

Billye laughed again. "Well, let's start studying," she said. She slowly folded the sheet down to reveal her right breast. "For instance, Mr. Caldwell. Could you identify this? Or this?" She rubbed a thumb across her nipple, causing it to stiffen.

"What are you doing?" Jeff said. His face flushed with embarrassment, which Billye found endearing. She kissed him softly, lingeringly, her upper body coming completely out from under the covers, her right breast flattening against his chest.

"I'm trying to help you with your biology," Billye said, giggling. "So far you haven't gotten a single answer right." She cupped her breast and lifted it. "This is a breast," she said, "though men have other naughty names for it. And this—"

"Billye—" Jeff said.

"Maybe we should switch to some questions about the male anatomy," she interrupted. "For instance, what do you call this?" She touched him, and he was hard again. Immediately he rolled over on her again. She cupped the back of his neck and spoke to him softly as he thrust into her. "Slow down, baby," she said. "This time let's make it last a little while."

Jeff gasped as he stopped and looked into her face with a helplessness that touched her. Afterward, as they lay cuddled together, Jeff felt uncomfortable and vaguely discontented. Billye seemed to know things he didn't.

The next morning, just as Jeff began to stir awake, Billye rolled against him and flipped her thigh over his and began to rock herself against his hip. "Hey," he said, "what are you doing? It's Sunday morning."

She purred and kept rocking against him. "So?" she said, her movements unceasing.

"We have to go to church."

"We have plenty of time." She took him in hand.

"That's not the point," Jeff gasped.

"What is the point?" Billye asked. She crawled on top of him and put him inside her.

"This is Sunday," he said, his words coming out in pants.

"Oh?" she said, speaking to him with her eyes closed, her hand helping herself. "Somewhere in the Bible it says, 'Thou shalt not have intercourse on Sundays'?"

"Don't talk like—" Jeff started to say, but then he put his hands on her buttocks as she raised and lowered herself until she shuddered and fell forward on top of him. Jeff didn't know what to make of this woman he had married. He thought she was indescribably wonderful, but she didn't act like a wife.

As they were getting ready for church, Billye witnessed something puzzling. She came into the bathroom where Jeff had just finished shaving his face to find him daubing his shaving brush soap under his arms. "What are you doing?" she asked.

"Shaving under your arms?"

"Yes," he replied. He raised his arm and put his left hand on top of his head and began to draw the double-bladed Gillette through the soap in his armpit. She could hear the blade scrape against stubble just as when she shaved herself.

"I didn't realize men shaved under their arms," Billye said. "My father never did. I don't think any of the guys I went to high school did either."

Jeff continued to scrape under his left arm, flinging the soap into the sink and running the razor under the flowing tap after each stroke. "I didn't shave under my arms in high school either," he said. "But, of course, I also didn't use underarm deodorant. An army buddy taught me to do this in England. Mark Schwain. A very refined fellow from a wealthy family in Connecticut. Thank God the world is becoming a more civilized place. Women smell like you do, and men will start to smell better."

Jeff turned to look at Billye, who was staring at him with a peculiar look on her face. "That's among the changes I was talking about," he explained.

"But not one of the more important ones," Billye laughed.

On Monday, Billye began looking for a job. She needed to find work immediately so they could afford to rent an apartment. Billye volunteered to call and ask her father for help, but Jeff wouldn't even consider it. "I'll not have your family think their son-in-law is a deadbeat," he said.

When Billye had failed to find anything by midweek, Jeff borrowed a car on Thursday evening and drove Billye to his family's home in New Peterstown, about forty minutes away. She didn't like this, particularly since the Caldwell home had no telephone; their arrival would be unannounced. But she had no alternative to suggest. Jeff was adamant that they not spend any more money on a hotel room when they had no income. Staying with his family would be fine, he said. His relatives sometimes moved in for months at a stretch.

Jeff had warned Billye that his family's house was "primitive," but she was still unprepared for what she found. The wood-frame house was unpainted, with a rusted tin roof, patched here and there with tar. A porch swept across the front and around both sides, although it had been closed in with screens on the right side and was used for sleeping during the warm months. The dirt front yard, shaded by two huge live oaks, had patches of green and black mold. Billye presumed that the mold, or some condition of the gray clay soil, was what made it stink, but she soon learned that it stank because the Caldwell men urinated off the porch at night rather than trek down the path to the privies behind the house.

Osby came out on the front porch when she heard the car pull up. The sun was down, and the light was draining off to the west. The family home had gotten electricity in 1939, and lights had already been turned on inside. The porch, though, was still lit with kerosene lanterns that hung from hooks screwed into the rafters. Osby squinted into the twilight out beyond the fence and fetched a match from her apron pocket to light a lantern.

"It's me, Mama," Jeff called out. "Me and Billye."

"It is *I*, son," Osby called back. "A college man ought to know that. It is *I*."

"Mama's a strict grammarian," Jeff said to Billye as they walked through the yard.

"It is I, Mama," Jeff said with a chuckle as he started up the steps to the porch. "Billye and I. Is that better?"

"It would be better if you'd remember it on your own," Osby said. Jeff gave his mother a hug, and the two of them touched cheeks.

"This is Billye," Jeff said. "My wife."

Osby stared at Billye without smiling. "Nice to meet you, daughter," she said. Billye stepped forward, intending to hug her mother-in-law, but Osby turned back toward the front door. "The night chill is coming on. Come on inside, and I'll put another log on the fire." Osby pulled a straight-backed, unpainted wooden chair across the floor and placed it between two others already facing the fire. "Y'all go on and sit down. I'll go fix some coffee."

"Oh, don't go to any trouble," Billye said. "I'm fine, really."

Osby looked at her again without smiling. "Our dishes are clean," Osby said. "I'm sure Jeff has told you that we don't have running water, but our well is deep, and the water is boiled before I pour it over the grounds."

Billye flushed, and Jeff said, "Billye's just not much of a coffee drinker, Mama. But I'd like a cup if you've already got some made."

Osby seemed to Jeff to have grown more somber now that her children were all gone. The youngest, Franklin, had left just this fall with a scholarship to LSU; like Jeff and Vivien, he had been class valedictorian. Always thin, Osby now looked skeletal, as if she were drying out from the inside. She went into the kitchen and returned with two cups of steaming coffee. She and Jeff made identical loud slurping sounds as they tried to drink without scalding their mouths. There was no conversation whatsoever.

"Where's Daddy?" Jeff asked finally.

"He's over at Ralph's playing dominoes," Osby said. "Be back directly if they don't get into the homemade. If they do, then he might not come back tonight at all. You know how that goes."

After another lengthy silence, Osby said, "You staying the night?" Jeff indicated that they were. "I figured so when you got here so late. I'll put sheets on the bed in Vivien's room."

"Oh, I can do that," Billye said. "I don't want you to go to any trouble."

"Wouldn't hear of it," Osby said. "A guest in my house is treated like a guest."

After a time, Pruitt came in. "Come in and meet your new daughter," Osby said without really looking at her husband. He wore denim overalls and long johns and smelled of cigarette smoke and sweat. He didn't appear to have shaved in a day or two; his face was bristly with white stubble.

"Daddy, this is my wife, Billye," Jeff said.

Pruitt's face cracked into a lopsided grin and showed his tobacco-stained teeth. "Aren't you a pretty picture," he said. "Stand on up here and let's get acquainted."

Billye stood up, and Pruitt wrapped her in a bear hug. She patted his back until he finally let her go. Another straight-backed chair was pulled into the semicircle, and the four of them sat together, staring at the fire, talking only sporadically. Pruitt chewed tobacco and spit the juice into a Libby's green-peas can.

Shortly before nine o'clock, Jeff went to the car and got their suitcases, and Osby got up to put sheets on the bed in the little bedroom Pruitt had built when Vivien was twelve. The room was unheated, but the bed was piled high with quilts, all handmade by Osby.

When Jeff and Billye were situated in Vivien's room, Osby said to her son, "You better show her where the lantern is on the back porch and then take her back to the women's toilet." Osby squatted down, slid a covered bowl out from under the bed and craned her neck up to Billye. "Slop jar is for the middle of the night." She stood back up, wiped her hands down the front of her apron and nudged the bowl back under the bed with her foot. "I'm sure you haven't ever had to use one of these, but it's the best we have, so it'll have to do."

Not knowing what to say, Billye shrugged.

"Come on, honey," Jeff said, "I'll show you the way to the outhouse."

On the back porch Jeff took down the two kerosene lanterns. He lit them and handed one to Billye. They walked through the back yard, around the wash shed, past the hen house and through a stand of pine trees. Jeff held the lantern low to show Billye the packed dirt of the trail.

"You can see where you're going just by following this path," he said. After a moment he added, "You know, when I was growing up, we considered ourselves better off than a lot of folks because we had enough land to get our outhouses a good distance back away from the house. Also, we have two, one for women and one for men." They had come to a spot where the trail forked at forty-five degrees. Jeff pointed off to the right. "Yours is down that way."

Billye really didn't need to go, but she headed on down the dirt path another twenty yards or so. She certainly wasn't going to use the chamber pot. The smell of the privy was overpowering from ten feet away. She tried to breathe as little as possible. Inside there was a hook to hold her lantern and a board with two uncovered holes side by side. She lowered her underpants, clutched her skirt up in a fist and hovered over a hole to urinate without actually sitting down. To make matters worse, there was no toilet paper, only a stack of old newspapers. Billye had a packet of tissue in her purse, but she hadn't brought it with her. This would take getting used to.

Jeff was waiting for her at the fork in the trail when she returned. "I told you this was primitive," he said and grinned.

Billye wanted to cry, but she bit her lip in the dark. This was what she had chosen for herself. She wouldn't be defeated when she had only just begun her life with this man. When they got back to the rear porch, Billye asked where she could wash, and Jeff led her over to the oaken bucket, dipper and washing bowl, beside which sat a cake of white soap, covered with swirls of dried lather. He poured two dippers of water into the bowl and got her a fresh towel from the shelf to the right.

"I mean where can I wash privately," Billye said through tight lips.

"It's okay," Jeff said. "Everybody washes here." Then suddenly he understood what she meant. "You want to bathe at this time of night? We'd keep Mama and Daddy up heating water."

"I can use cold water," Billye said. "But I do want to wash privately."

Jeff took her down to the wash shed and left her there to perform her cold ablutions. She hadn't uttered a word of complaint, but he was worried that she thought she was too good for the stark accommodations. On the other hand, *he* thought she was too good for them, too.

Jeff was already in bed when Billye entered Vivien's room. Washing had chilled her, and she shivered as she undressed, especially when she removed her shoes to stand on the cold floor. Billye was putting on her black nightgown when Jeff said, "I don't think you ought to wear that, do you?"

"Why not?" she said. "It's my nicest thing. Don't you like the way I look in it?" She turned to Jeff, knowing that he could see her breasts and pubic hair through the diaphanous material.

He licked his lips. "I don't want Mama to see you in something like that," he replied. "It isn't really decent."

"But you like it?" Billye said, in a small voice.

"Of course, I like it, honey. It's just so—"

Billye pulled the gown over her head, ran across the floor and flung herself into bed naked. Jeff was wearing an undershirt and a pair of boxers. She hugged herself up against him.

"Now don't start that," Jeff said.

"I need your body heat," Billye said. "I'm freezing."

"Right," Jeff said. "I give you some of my so-called body heat and pretty soon you'll be wanting something else."

"So?" Billye protested. "We're newlyweds."

"Yes, and the walls in this house are paper thin. And I've already learned that you can't control yourself. Besides, I need to talk to you."

Billye spun away and lay on her back. "What?" she said with a mock pout.

"I think I'm going to have to leave you here tomorrow."

Billye rolled up on her side. She hadn't anticipated this at all. "Why?" she asked.

"I don't know if I can get the car again. Probably not, in fact. If you come in with me, we'll just have to pay two bus fares to get back out here tomorrow night."

"I don't know, Jeff. Your mom doesn't seem to like me very much."

"Nonsense. She's just worried that you're not used to the conditions here."

Billye *wasn't* used to the conditions, but she didn't say so. They talked awhile longer and fell asleep without making love. Jeff got up at sunrise and drove back to Valmont for Friday classes. Billye struggled awake awhile later, intimidated by the cold room and the fact that her husband had left her with virtual strangers. When she finally got out of bed, the floor felt like ice.

She hurried into her clothes, rushed into the living room where a fire was roaring and tried to warm herself by rubbing her hands briskly up and down her arms. Eventually, reluctantly, she made the dreaded trip to the outhouse. But she had been sitting there in cold misery for only a minute or so when Osby opened the door to the privy and walked in. Billye was shocked and embarrassed.

"I thought I saw you heading out here," Osby said. "I wanted to bring you this." From the pocket of her apron she produced a roll of white toilet paper and handed it to Billye. "We have to make do with torn up newspapers ourselves, but I like to keep a store-bought roll around in case we have a proper guest like you in the house." Billye accepted the toilet paper without comment and set it down beside her. Then Osby lifted her dress, sat down beside Billye and emptied her bowels noisily.

When Jeff returned that night, he told Billye that he thought she should stay with his parents until Christmas; he would come to stay with her on weekends. But Billye agreed to stay only through that weekend. Jeff tried persistently to change her mind, but in a tense, whispered conversation on Sunday night, she told him flatly that she was either getting on a bus the next morning with him or going back to New Orleans; he could choose.

Jeff Caldwell never stopped loving Billye Monroe, not then when she refused to bow to his wishes, not two decades later when she divorced him, not for years afterward. He was never prepared for the strength of her personality, never comfortable with the fact that she did not automatically embrace his ideas. But she remained in his mind the most beautiful woman he'd ever seen. Having her consent to be his wife, having her share his bed, having her with him through the changes in his life always seemed a blessing that he never deserved.

chapter twenty

JEFF CALDWELL WAS SCHEDULED TO MARRY Naylynn Jensen on October 11, 1964. When the board of deacons forced Jeff to resign that spring, Naylynn showed her loyalty by resigning in protest as secretary at Gentilly Boulevard Baptist Church. Jeff's marriage to Billye collapsed shortly thereafter, and Naylynn stepped in to pick up the pieces. She was subsequently hired as a secretary at CSCL headquarters.

On the Friday night before the Sunday wedding, Jeff's friend Preacher Martin took him out for a drink at the Black Orchid. Seating themselves at a booth, they ordered their drinks and talked about the voting rights campaign of the previous summer and about the movement's next steps.

Eventually, just after their fourth round arrived, Preacher brought up the real reason he wanted to get together. "Your Miss Naylynn really knows how to fill out a skirt and blouse," Preacher said.

Jeff looked at his friend over his drink. He knew Preacher well enough to realize that this wasn't just an idle comment. "I'll take that as a compliment," he said.

"You can take it however the hell you want," Preacher said. "But the compliment was to her and not to you."

Jeff laughed.

Preacher lit up an unfiltered Lucky Strike. "Them big titties of hers all real or part foam rubber?"

Jeff felt a bit as if he'd been slapped, but he laughed again. "Let's not be talking dirty about the woman I'm about to marry," he said.

"Oh, come on, let's," Preacher replied. "Here I been stuck with boring old Nell Leigh through seventeen years, I kind of get a vicarious thrill out of thinking a man my age is dipping his wick into some ripe young stuff like Naylynn Jensen. I do presume that you've been firing that low hard one into her strike zone even though you aren't properly hitched yet."

"What's got into you?" Jeff said. "You don't talk like this."

"Probably just the whiskey." Preacher picked up his glass, clinked it off Jeff's and took a swallow. "Nothing provides an excuse like whiskey. But really, brother, don't hold out on me. I mean, let's face it, Nell Leigh is forty going on ninety-five."

"Stop it," Jeff said. "Nell Leigh is as attractive as she ever was."

Preacher took a big drag on his cigarette and then crushed it out. "So if you don't mind my asking, I bet Miss Naylynn is a hot piece, isn't she? Man, she's had eyes for you since she saw what a big cheese you were during the integration crisis. Nothing gets a good girl as worked up as a righteous man."

"If you don't quit this, I'm going to leave," Jeff said.

Preacher took out his pack of Luckies, shook it once and offered it to Jeff, who waved it away. "You and me go back a long ways, bubba; am I right?"

"Of course," Jeff said. "You're my oldest friend."

"So you believe I love you?"

Jeff nodded.

"You're damn straight I love you, old soldier," Preacher said. "That's why we have to talk honestly here before it's too late." Preacher lit a fresh cigarette. He took a deep drag and blew out a plume of smoke that couldn't be seen in the haze of the dark bar. "You sure you don't want a cigarette? You don't smoke some of these I'm going to smoke all of them by myself."

Jeff took a cigarette but stuck it behind his ear instead of lighting it.

"You're marrying Naylynn, so that means you love her?"

"Yes, it does," Jeff said.

"Well, here's the question: You love her with your heart or with your dick?"

"You know, you're about the only person on earth I'd let talk to me like this."

"I know that," Preacher said. "Answer my question."

"She's saved my life these last few months."

"See, you're not answering my question. Way I have it figured, she's saved your life these last few months by worshiping you when you were bad off."

"I love her with my heart, Preacher."

Preacher wiped his hand down across his face and sighed loudly. "I'm praying that's the truth," he said. "But I'm not going to let my prayers deter me. I'm going to ask you, brother to brother, not to marry this girl no matter how lonely you are and how good she is in the sack."

"The wedding is less than two days from now," Jeff said. "I can hardly call it off. I don't want to, but even if I did, can you imagine how hurt Naylynn would be?"

Preacher nodded solemnly and looked at his friend with sad eyes. "I can," he said. "And

I'm praying for myself for advocating something so cruel."

"So why are you doing it?"

"We've already established that, asshole. Because I love you. Because you're my comrade in arms and because I'm a son-of-a-bitch hypocrite who will suffer extra punishment in the afterlife for ever referring to myself as a Christian. Because I don't know that girl well enough to ache for her. Because I think I know what's right for you. And she isn't."

"Why would you say that?"

"Because you're married to Billye Monroe, you dumb fucking shit."

"But I'm not married to Billye," Jeff said. "You *know* that. We're divorced."

"The Bible doesn't recognize divorce. It's contrary to God's will and Jesus's teaching."

Jeff laughed. "Man, it's funny hearing you set up shop with the fundamentalists."

"Then you haven't been listening to me all these years. I am a goddamn motherfucking cocksucking bum-humping fundamentalist."

"You're some kind of nut. That's for sure."

"Guilty," Preacher said. "I'm a nut you've got to listen to before it's too late."

"Preacher, old friend," Jeff said. "The Bible may disapprove of divorce. But in the State of Louisiana, I'm divorced no matter what the Bible says. And that's the way Billye wants it."

"It's not the way she wants it."

"Who says?"

Preacher slapped his hand on the table for emphasis. "I say."

"She said something to you?"

"No, she didn't. I know because I know."

"How do you know?"

"I know because God called me into his service and gave me divine insight, made me into a booze-swilling, snake-handling, faith-healing know-it-all. I know because I know."

"You don't know," Jeff said.

"You're a stubborn, stupid moron."

Preacher got up from the table and returned with a bottle of Jack Daniels. He sat down and poured two fingers into his glass.

"You switching to my brand?" Jeff said.

"Only because I can't afford two bottles," Preacher said. He lit up another Lucky Strike. "Man, I hate drinking in bars."

"Too expensive?"

"Too smoky," Preacher said. They drank another round and when they got up to leave, Preacher said. "You'll think about what we talked about tonight? About you and Naylynn?"

"No, I won't," Jeff said.

"Yes," Preacher said. "You will."

Late the next afternoon Preacher stopped in unannounced to see Billye, who greeted him with a hug. He let her fix him some coffee but came right to the point as they sat in the living room and balanced cups and saucers on their knees.

"If you don't do something to stop him, your husband is going to make the mistake of his life," Preacher said.

Billye's face tightened, and her full lips straightened into a thin line. She took a sip of coffee and stared into the cup. "If this is why you came over today, you're wasting your time."

"It's *my* time," Preacher said. "Who better to waste it than me?"

Billye laughed. "You know, it's too bad Jeff never had your sense of humor. He might have done better if he had. He could have used a number of your traits, in fact."

Preacher rubbed his hand across his balding pate. "I would have traded him a fistful of my traits for his head of hair."

Billye stared out the window. "Nobody ever said Jeff wasn't a handsome man. Least of all me. He's always had the girls after him. Now he's older, but they're the same age."

"I don't remember that he was such a hot potato when we were all together at Valmont back in the Paleozoic Age."

"Ah, but you should have heard the girls in the freshman women's dorm."

"So you thought he was a catch?"

Billye smiled sadly and nodded.

"Then don't let him get away. It's not too late, I swear it. One word from you and he'll call that wedding off tomorrow."

Billye looked out the window and smiled again, as if remembering something pleasant. "You're a good man, Preacher Martin. Jeff is lucky to have a friend like you. I am, too."

"Then you'll do it?" Preacher said, the words bursting out of him like a hiccup. "You'll call him and try to work things out?"

"No," Billye said, shaking her head. "No, I won't."

"But he's your husband," Preacher said.

"He's not my husband, Preacher. We're divorced."

"That piece of paper from the State of Louisiana is just writing. It doesn't mean a thing. Jeff's a stupid horse's ass, and he's about to ruin the rest of his life. But he is your husband."

Billye closed her eyes and shook her head. "No," she said. "No, he's not. He's been sleeping with that girl. He's her husband now."

"They aren't husband and wife, girl," Preacher said. "And they won't ever be, no matter what they and George Washington Brown say in that service tomorrow. They don't have history together like you and Jeff. They don't have children. What they have is born not of love the way you and Jeff knew love, but of need, the need to be admired and the need to possess the object of admiration. This is unhealthiness, and it will produce heartache greater than any Naylynn will know if you make Jeff stop before it's too late."

"Jeff says he loves her," Billye said. "He told me that. His lips to my ears."

"Oh, Jesus fucking Christ," Preacher said. He didn't know that exchange had taken place. No doubt in trying to make Billye jealous, Jeff had only hardened her determination.

"Do you want me to try to stop the wedding even though he loves her?"

"Yes," Preacher said. "We aren't talking about love here. We're talking about temptation of the flesh and nothing more. We're talking about something rooted so deeply in Jeff's character that neither you nor I will ever entirely understand it. We're talking about a longing that is the source of both his strength and his weakness, the source of his decency and his courage and his astonishing blind stupid optimism and also the source of his self-destructiveness."

"I'm tired, Preacher. That's what it comes down to."

"You have to listen to me, Billye. It's temptation of the flesh. Nothing more."

"And you have to listen to me. I'm just plain worn out."

Tommy Caldwell knew the temptations of the flesh. In the summer before his freshman year at Tulane, he was unfaithful to his long-time sweetheart, Tammy Bailey. Tommy and Tammy had begun dating in junior high and going steady when he was a sophomore in high school and she was a freshman.

Tommy felt unfaithful from the moment he allowed Glenda Russell's hand to slip into his as they listened to Ben Watson and Faye Robinson play guitar and sing folk songs in a Mississippi national park. In fact, he had felt unfaithful even before that. From the moment he met Glenda early in that freedom summer of 1964, he had thought she was so dazzling that he deliberately never mentioned Tammy in Glenda's presence.

Later, when they came to know one another, Glenda asked if he didn't have a girlfriend "back home," and he told her there was "nobody special." Tommy felt guilty about such denials, but he tried to justify them as minor and harmless betrayals. But then he held Glenda's hand and kissed her, and he let her tell him she thought she was falling in love with him. Guilt loomed so large in his eighteen-year-old mind that he didn't immediately confess his love for her, even though he knew he was falling in love with her, too. And he didn't because he still loved Tammy Bailey, the girl "back home" who Glenda thought didn't exist.

During the week of July 4, when the voting-rights volunteers took a respite and Glenda went to Biloxi with her schoolmate Karen Ashe, Tommy went home to New Orleans, where he told Tammy Bailey he loved her and had sex with her eleven times in nine days. That made him feel even worse, because every moment he was with Tammy, he felt guilty about deceiving Glenda, with whom he felt himself now to be in love.

Tommy still loved Tammy, he told himself. He'd always loved her and always would. But they were growing apart. She was his childhood sweetheart; his adult love was Glenda. As soon as vacation was over, Tommy rushed back to Mississippi and began to have intercourse with Glenda Russell in the back seat of Ben Watson's car.

But as the summer wore on, Glenda began to complain that she felt uncomfortable about having sex with a man who was afraid to say he loved her. Tommy tried to defend himself by saying he just wasn't a person who talked very easily about his feelings. But then Glenda rightly began to complain about that, too, and began to wonder aloud if perhaps the problem was Tommy's youth. He was barely out of high school. Perhaps their two-year age difference was greater than she'd initially realized. Finally Tommy told Glenda the truth: that he was madly in love with her, that he didn't think he'd ever been in love with anyone before, that only since he'd known her did he begin to get a glimmer of what love actually was. They made a pact to be faithful to each other though they would have to separate at the end of August.

But when the summer ended, Tommy went home and made love with Tammy Bailey the very first night he was back in New Orleans—three times in a twelve-hour period, twice that first night and once the next morning. She was so bubbly and so pretty, and she smelled so good. He'd never stopped caring about her, and she was so glad to see him, he just couldn't help himself. The night was an erotic splendor and a total disaster.

Tommy was going to tell her about Glenda. He had to tell her. He planned to tell her that very first night. But he had to find the right opening, an opportunity to be gentle and to explain his regret and his conviction that it was for the best and his desire that they always think well of each other. But Tammy had made plans of her own. She had planned their reunion down to the last detail, and he found himself trapped in her preparations with no avenue for polite escape. Or so he told himself.

They went to a movie. Tommy had planned to tell her after the movie, when he took her for a hamburger and root beer at a drive-in on Elysian Fields. But Tammy said that Carol Durham, her best friend, was having some people over for pizza and she'd promised to come by after the movie.

When they got to the Durham house, it was dark. "I'm sure they're here," Tammy said, clambering out of the car and almost running up to the house. "They're probably having a make-out party and have all the lights off so people can fool around a little bit."

There was about to be a make-out party with a whole lot of fooling around, all right. But it was going to be a party of two. The Durhams were on vacation, and Carol had given Tammy her key so she and Tommy could do something they'd never done before—make love in an actual bed, naked, instead of just hastily rearranging their clothing in a parked car, jumping with fright every time another car's headlights swept by.

Tammy had told her parents that she was staying overnight with another girlfriend. She could spend the night with him, an experience Tommy had never had with Tammy or Glenda. He and Glenda had talked about getting a motel room the whole of their Mississippi August, but they never had the time or the money.

So despite his pact with Glenda, the first woman Tommy would spend the night with would be the one with whom he was no longer in love.

Tammy swept into the Durham house with a deliciously rapturous giggle, instantly peeled off her T-shirt and bra, threw her arms around his neck and stuck her tongue into his mouth. She had gone to so much trouble. How could Tommy possibly tell her no?

He couldn't tell her no that night or the next morning or for two painful weeks thereafter. His conscience ate at him like a swarm of termites. Finally, he did the right thing. He took her to a movie, and then to a drive-in for a hamburger, and while she was eating, he told her. He told her he still loved her but "only as a friend," which he hoped they could remain for the rest of their lives. He told her he wasn't right for her and that they "should see other people," that they should see what it was like "playing the field for once" after going steady for so many years.

Tammy wasn't fooled for a second. "There's someone else," she said. "You met someone this summer in Mississippi. You talked about her when you were home for the Fourth. A college girl from up north somewhere. Villanova or something. You talked about how smart she was. But you said she was too old for you and that you were just friends. And now you want to be just friends with me."

"That's not how it is," Tommy lied.

Tammy opened the passenger-side car door and threw up into the parking lot. Then she began to cry. She didn't stop crying for three hours. She wouldn't let him take her home, even though she was out past her curfew. Tommy, too, was miserable. He couldn't comfort her, because he'd just broken up with her. Every time he tried to take her into his arms, she screeched, "Don't touch me!" When she did finally let him take her home, it was she who grabbed him and kissed him with an open mouth tasting of vomit. "Oh, Tommy," she said, squeezing him, her face muffled against his chest, "I will love you forever."

In subsequent days she would call him at his Tulane dorm "just to talk" and end up crying inconsolably. Twice she asked him to meet her "as a friend," and he agreed, but when they got together, she spent the whole time crying. So he decided the best thing for her was to cut off all contact, to drop the pretense that they could remain friends after having been boyfriend and girlfriend for so long. When he told her over the phone one night that he thought it best they not see each other or even talk to each other again, she begged him, pitifully begged him, not to hang up because she would never hear his voice again. Tommy talked to her until she finally let him go. He pledged never to get himself in such a circumstance again, never again to hurt someone like he hurt Tammy Bailey.

But he did, of course, because human beings do not learn their lessons easily or, sometimes, at all.

Tommy and Glenda maintained a long-distance relationship for two years until Glenda graduated from Valparaiso. They wrote letters, and they talked on the phone. They spent their Thanksgiving, Christmas and spring-break holidays together. And during the summer of 1965 they worked together on a CSCL program on the south side of Chicago, one of the movement's first ventures out of the South and into the large urban Negro communities in the North.

After Glenda graduated in the spring of 1966, she moved to New Orleans to work at movement headquarters. Her specific assignment was to work as Jeff Caldwell's advance assistant, setting up his appearances and supervising the details of his travel, schedule and out-of-town accommodations. This involved some travel for her as well.

Glenda took a small apartment close to Tulane. Tommy continued to live in the dorm, where his fees and meal plan were covered by his basketball scholarship, but he spent many nights at Glenda's apartment. They planned to marry after he graduated.

For the most part, their relationship was everything Tommy could have wanted. Glenda was smart, pretty and committed to the kinds of social issues Tommy had been raised to believe were the determinative measures of a person's character. But they had their difficult times. Tommy thought Glenda was out of town too much. She thought he was too obsessed with basketball; he spent an hour or more a day in extra practice, before and after the daily team practices. An English major, he also spent a lot of time studying and doing library research for papers. He had less time for Glenda than she'd expected when she moved to New Orleans to be near him.

But their occasional squabbles did not affect their commitment to each other, and they often speculated about what course their lives would take after Tommy's graduation and their marriage. Tommy hoped to earn a Ph.D. in American literature, with a concentration in modern Southern writers. But the war in Vietnam was an increasing concern, particularly as 1966 gave way to 1967.

At first it seemed that Tommy might have to enter the service, but the closer he got to graduation, the more adamantly opposed to the war he became. Eventually he decided that he would seek conscientious-objector status; if it was denied he would go to jail.

In the summer of 1967 Tommy attended the National Student Association's annual congress in Washington, D.C., where his opposition to the war was solidified after he listened to presentations by Tom Hayden of the Students for a Democratic Society and Congressman Allard K. Lowenstein of New York. That congress also proved to be the occasion of his once again surrendering to the temptations of the flesh. This time, he knew, it was more serious, for he and Glenda were engaged and planning to marry in less than a year.

Tommy's undoing was his old girlfriend, whom he had not seen or talked to in three years. By the summer of 1967 Tammy had finished two years at the University of North Carolina. Tommy thought she had changed almost completely. She was more mature and more serious—no longer a girl concerned with dance steps and the right outfit for a party, but a young woman interested in ideas and dedicated to her studies. She even looked different. Instead of the short, bouncy flip she'd worn in high school, Tammy now wore her blond hair long and straight and pulled back off her face with a leather headband. Instead of the Villager skirts and sweater vests she'd worn in high school, she now dressed in miniskirts and floppy, knee-high black boots. She looked scrumptious, Tommy thought, when he saw her from across the main ballroom of the congress. But he had no intention of approaching her. He assumed that she wouldn't want to see him. He was wrong.

Tammy asked him to join her and some other delegates who were going out for pizza. She'd love to catch up. What was wrong with that, Tommy reasoned. They ate pizza and drank pitchers of draft beer with six other college students. Tammy and Tommy sat and talked at one end of the table, Tammy smoking Winstons from a red and gold pack she carried in its own little snap purse. She had picked up the habit at college and said she'd adopted it "just for now." She had decided to major in physical and cultural anthropology and was going on an archaeological dig in Peru the following summer. She had transformed her cheerleader's enthusiasm into academic zeal and vocal opposition to the war. She had also decided that monogamy was sexist (the first time he ever heard this term), another of male society's devices for controlling and debasing women.

"So you believe in free love?" Tommy asked, invoking a catch phrase of the day.

"I don't believe in slogans," she responded. "Free love is a male fantasy where the guy gets all the chicks he wants. I believe in free choices. Men and women involved with each other as equals, sexually and in every other way."

Tommy wasn't sure that he understood her distinction, but he nodded in feigned thoughtfulness as if he did.

"That's one thing that was really good about our relationship," Tammy told him, pouring herself a third glass of beer. "We were just kids. We didn't even know what we were doing when we first got started. But it was always equal, I think. I wanted you as much as you wanted me. I never felt coerced by you or used in any way. I learned a lot from you, and I hope you learned stuff about women from me. I always thought you respected me. And that meant a lot."

"Then you've forgiven me?" Tommy said. "For breaking up with you?"

Tammy tilted her head and smiled, crinkling her eyes at the corners. She lit a fresh cigarette and blew the smoke upwards and off to the side. "No way, Jose," she said. "I haven't forgiven you. Not now and not ever. You broke my heart, you asshole."

Tommy was taken aback. Their conversation had been so natural and friendly. "I'm sorry, Tammy," he said. "I really am so sorry."

"Yeah, yeah, yeah," she said. "And the Pope's a Baptist."

"What can I say?" Tommy asked.

"You can't say a thing, you jerk. You did it. I lived with it. And I got over it. Or I got over you, anyway. What choice did I have? But that doesn't mean it didn't happen or that I won't always have that particular scar. Of course, it's like you said when you were trying to use bullshit as anesthetic—it's allowed me to play the field. I'm not sorry about that, if you know what I mean."

Tommy wasn't sure he did know what she meant; he presumed she was trying to be sexually suggestive. She was probably just needling him to see if he'd say ouch.

When he didn't respond, Tammy said, "So you still seeing old whatshername. Or did you throw me over for a passing fancy?"

"Her name's Glenda," Tommy said. "Glenda Russell."

"She's the one, huh? Way I figure it, she must be something if you chose her over me."

Tommy shrugged, feeling awkward that the conversation had taken this turn. He didn't want to hurt Tammy's feelings by dwelling on the fact that he'd chosen someone else.

"She must be an old lady by now, huh?"

"She's out of college," Tommy said, " if that's what you mean."

"Yeah, well, lucky her. Out of school and still got you." Tammy smiled and took a drag on her cigarette. When they left the pizza restaurant, Tommy intended to go back to his own hotel, but Tammy and her crowd urged him to go with them.

"Tammy's got some dynamite weed," a fellow named Ted said.

So Tommy tagged along with the North Carolina crowd. They stopped in at a liquor store, bought a couple of bottles of cheap Chianti in little wicker baskets and went to Tammy's room.

Tommy didn't usually drink much, so he was a little high from the beer. But he liked smoking marijuana, liked the sensation the drug created of watching yourself from another place. He had a momentary concern about going to Tammy's hotel room, but he put it out of his mind. What could possibly happen in a room full of other students? Even if Tammy regarded herself as sexually liberated, she probably wasn't into orgies. Or so Tommy rationalized his decision to go along.

They sat around on the floor of the hotel room and passed around joints and the bottles of wine until one by one the other students got sleepy and left. Tommy knew he should leave, too, but he didn't. The exact sequence of events would remain forever hazy in his dope-altered mind. But everybody was gone, and he was lying on the floor with his eyes closed. Then Tammy was standing over him, a leg on either side of his chest.

"Hey," she said.

His eyes swam open to look up at her. She was like the Colossus at Rhodes, rising above him in her knee-high boots, short black skirt and tight, sleeveless yellow T-shirt. Without consciously deciding to, he twisted his head, trying to see under her skirt.

From high above him, Tammy grinned. "Yes, I am wearing panties. I'm not trying to flash you, old beau."

Tommy flushed and diverted his eyes. He was wider awake now, but completely trashed. He sat up abruptly, his face rising right into her crotch.

"Hey," she said. "That's a little forward, isn't it?" She laughed, and pushed his forehead away with the heel of her hand.

Tommy fell back groaning, "I wasn't, Tammy. Really I wasn't."

"Yeah, yeah, yeah," she said. "And you didn't break up with me, either. Here I thought you wanted to be a linguist, and it ends up you want to be a cunnilinguist."

Tommy was too dazed to laugh.

"Hey, that was funny, Caldwell. You used to have a sense of humor. What'd that old lady do to you to make you so serious? Linguist, cunnilinguist, don't you get it?"

All of a sudden he did get it, and it seemed the most hilarious thing he'd ever heard. He began to laugh hysterically, so hard he began to gasp for breath.

Tammy knelt down beside him and touched his face. "Hey, Mr. Automatic, you're stoned out of your gourd, aren't you?"

That seemed funny, too, and launched Tommy into another gale of helpless laughter. "Goodness," Tammy said. "You're a mess. You know, you're gonna have to sleep here tonight."

"Uh-uh," Tommy said but then collapsed again into laughter.

"Uh-huh," Tammy said. "I'm not walking you back to your hotel, and I'm not letting you try to find it on your own. You might end up in another country."

"I am not," Tommy said, giggling.

"You are, too," Tammy said. "But don't get any ideas."

"I want some more dope," Tommy said.

"Yeah, well, wanting and getting are two different things, as you've helped me understand."

"I can't have any more?" Tommy said.

"No, you've had plenty."

"I've got to go home," Tommy said.

"Yeah, yeah, yeah. We've already covered that," Tammy said.

"You won't let me?"

"No."

"Where am I gonna sleep?"

"Well, you can sleep in the bed. But I'm warning you not to get any ideas."

"Ideas about what?"

"Jesus," Tammy said. She stood up and helped him to his feet. "Come on, Gunner," she said. "Come on over here and lie down."

Tommy lay down on the bed, and Tammy unbuttoned his shirt and then unbuckled his belt and unzipped his jeans.

"That's just to make you comfortable." She made no attempt to remove his clothes. "You can get undressed if you want, but I'm really serious about telling you not to get any ideas."

Tommy fell asleep while she showered. He woke up when she returned to the bedroom wearing a robe and smelling of soap and hot water.

"You still here?" she said.

"I'll go," he mumbled.

"Yeah, yeah," she said. She sat on the bed and pulled off his loafers and socks. "Now you want to take off your shirt and jeans or not?"

"Okay," Tommy said.

"I'll take that for a yes." She helped him out of his shirt, and he arched his back so she could slip off his jeans. She pulled the spread and sheet out from under him, covered him, then went to her side of the bed and sat down, facing away. "You're pretty fucked up, huh?" she said.

"I guess so," Tommy said. "I don't do *this* too often."

"You certainly don't do this too often," she said.

"Yeah," he responded.

"All right," she said. "I'm going to get into bed next to you now. Okay?"

"Okay."

"And you're not going to get any ideas, am I right?"

"Okay," Tommy said.

Tammy took off her robe and slipped naked into bed beside him. They lay still for a second before Tommy turned and kissed her. And she rolled down his briefs. And they were lost. As he entered her, she cradled her hand around the back of his head and whispered into his ear, "You fucking bastard. I've missed you so much."

Tommy woke up early the next morning with Tammy still sleeping beside him. He crept out of bed and dressed; he thought about sneaking out without waking her. But then he thought better of that. He sat in a chair by the window, which overlooked an air shaft, and waited for her to wake. After a half hour, she stirred and, with her eyes still closed, threw an arm onto his empty side of bed. She shuddered and rubbed her eyes with the heel of her hand. Finally, she opened her eyes and saw him. "You're still here," she said, her voice flat.

"Yes," he said.

"I have a headache," she said.

Tommy stood up. "Can I get you something?"

"Sure," she said. "I have aspirin in my case in the bathroom."

Tommy went into the bathroom and brought back two aspirins and a plastic glass of tap water. Tammy sat up, and the sheet fell away, revealing her breasts. She didn't bother to cover herself, and Tommy looked away. "It was great seeing you again," he said.

"Thanks," she said. "Me, too."

After an awkward silence, Tommy said. "I better get going."

"Yeah," she said. She brushed her hair off her face and then pulled the sheet up to cover herself, clutching it with a fist at the base of her throat.

"I waited until you woke up. I didn't want to just take off without saying goodbye."

"Yeah," she said.

"I hope we can be friends now."

Tammy brought the glass to her lips and looked at Tommy over the rim. Her eyes were red from last night's drinking and smoking. She tilted her head back and drained the water.

"Yeah, yeah, yeah," she said.

After sleeping with Tammy, Tommy tried to console himself with a long series of arguments. Yes, he was engaged, but he wasn't married. It would be different if he was actually married. He had been both drunk and stoned and so was not in control of himself. He'd had sex with Tammy so many times in the past, it didn't really matter that he did it with her one more time. Sleeping with Tammy was a different order of infidelity to Glenda than sleeping with someone else would have been. It was Tammy's fault. She got him high. She wouldn't let him go home. She put him in her bed and took off his clothes and got into bed next to him naked smelling—smelling so utterly like herself. She seduced him plain and simple.

There were other arguments as well, but every one, Tommy knew, was an outright lie.

After their night together, Tammy began to write to Tommy at his Tulane dorm. Not wanting her to feel used, he wrote back. Tammy's letters did not exhibit the kind of hysteria she had shown after their breakup in high school. Some were merely newsy; others rummaged through ideas she was wrestling with in her school work. But she did occasionally reflect on their long relationship and the meaning of their recent night together, trying to assess whether it was a positive or negative thing. Tommy kept writing her because he felt she was dealing with matters in a mature fashion and because he still had tender feelings for her and always would. She called him when she came home for Christmas break and wanted to get together for a drink. He agreed and invited Glenda to accompany him to meet Tammy at Pat O'Brien's in the French Quarter. Glenda chose not to go, but she did not try to keep Tommy from going. The visit went well, and Tommy hoped they might actually become friends the way he wanted them to be.

Tommy erred in not telling Glenda that he and Tammy had been writing each other.

He didn't tell her because of guilt. And his failure to mention the correspondence made Glenda first curious, then puzzled, then suspicious, when she found Tammy's letters on Christmas Eve. Glenda had decided to surprise Tommy with a new double-breasted blazer. While Tommy was out Christmas shopping, she asked the resident counselor at the athletic dorm to let her into Tommy's room to hang the new jacket in his closet. She was delighted to think of his surprise when he returned to his room to find it. But while she was in his room, she found the rubber-band-bound bundle of Tammy's letters on top of Tommy's desk. He had preserved them in their envelopes, and the return address spoke to Glenda like a whisper from Iago.

Glenda picked them up, ruffled them with her thumb and put them back down. Why had Tommy never mentioned getting all these letters from his old girlfriend? She picked them up again and smelled the whole package. They weren't perfumed; that was good. No doubt just two old acquaintances staying in touch. She put them down and turned to leave. But then she turned back and picked up the stack of envelopes again. She looked at the postmark of the one on top. Earlier this month. She peeled back envelope after envelope. They'd all been written this fall. Was Tommy writing to this girl? He'd just seen her ten days ago. Was something going on between them? Of course not. They didn't even live in the same city. And Tommy had asked Glenda to go with him when he met Tammy for a drink.

Glenda started to put the letters back down. Instead, she sat on the bed and read them, one after another, in horror. The repeated phrases "after our night together in August," "just after our fling in D.C.," "when we had our one-night-stand as 'adults'" stabbed into Glenda's heart like an ice pick.

Glenda took the letters and the new sports coat with her when she left. She gave both of them to Tommy when he came to pick her up that night. They had planned to go to Billye's house for Christmas dinner, but Glenda didn't go. She explained how she had found the letters. Tommy tried to argue that she had no right to read them. Glenda conceded that point, but said it didn't make any difference because she had read them and now she knew. And though she wanted to, she couldn't unknow. She knew, and she would always know. And she couldn't stand knowing and there was no way to stop knowing. That was the incontrovertible problem. And now she couldn't marry Tommy.

This was when Tommy learned something important about justice. Justice, if it is true justice, is by definition fair. But even true justice isn't always right. Glenda's action was just. It was fair. Tommy had been unfaithful and was therefore unworthy of her. But Glenda's action was not right. His action was wrong. He deserved punishment. But her response was not right either, because there is something that is more important than justice, something that transcends the demand for justice, something that sets aside the balance of justice. In that moment, for the first time, Tommy really understood the different emphases of the Old and New Testaments. Justice is what we want for wrongs done to us. Old Testament. Not displaced but transformed in the New Testament. The sacrifice of Jesus offers us the mercy and forgiveness we crave for the wrongs we have done to others.

Glenda didn't go to Christmas dinner with Tommy that night, and she refused to see him for nearly three months. She hung up when he called her, closed the door in his face when he went to her apartment, sent his letters back unopened. But he persisted, for that was his way. Finally, in March, she began to accept his phone calls. She was seeing someone else, she said. And Tommy thought he might die.

He had other serious concerns as well. He was nearing the end of his senior year, and he was 1-A. He'd already passed his draft physical. His application for conscientious-objector status had been denied, and what awaited him that summer was a Hobson's choice of unacceptable alternatives: surrender to the draft and fight a war he felt morally reprehensible, flee to Canada never to return or go to jail.

Tommy's only respite from these considerable worries was basketball, which he infused with greater energy and devotion than ever before. It was his refuge, his passion. And he knew the end was near. He'd made second team All Southeast as both a sophomore and a junior, and he would probably make first team this year. But his playing days were drawing to a close. He was good, but his skills would not take him to the next level, and he knew it. He would be a college English professor, never an NBA point guard.

Then the game that had been his refuge and his passion became his salvation as well. It happened at the Tulane gym against Georgia in the last game of the season. On a drive to the basket, Tommy came down on the foot of a Bulldog forward who was trying to take a charge. The crowd in the tiny gym was roaring, but Tommy could swear he heard the ligaments in his left ankle tear with a series of sickening clicks. He was hurt so badly he couldn't even shoot his free throw. Five months later he was excused from the draft as physically unfit.

Billye wanted Tommy to proceed directly to graduate school. She and her new husband would help defray whatever expenses he could not cover through fellowships and assistantships. But Jeff argued that, if Tommy was sincere in his application as a conscientious objector, he ought to do some kind of alternative service even though the government couldn't require it. When Billye learned of Jeff's stance, she was so furious she called to argue with her ex-husband. Why should Tommy put his life on hold to meet some idealistic standard? He could go to graduate school, get on with his life and continue to do volunteer civil-rights work just as he always had.

Jeff listened to Billye's arguments pleasantly and politely and promised that he wouldn't pressure Tommy or push his view any further. He would not agree, however, to tell Tommy that he'd been wrong. In the end, to Billye's dismay and frustration, Tommy sided with his father and accepted a position as a CSCL staffer. Graduate school could wait.

Tommy's ruptured ankle, excruciatingly painful though it was, had another important benefit as well. As he was helped up by teammates, the first person who rose to give him an ovation was Glenda Russell, a worried frown wrinkling her brow as she pounded her hands together frantically. If Glenda was still coming to his basketball games, then she wasn't as closed to reconciling as she had pretended. That gave Tommy the hope he needed to continue pursuing her, which he did with the kind of relentlessness he brought to any endeavor that really mattered to him. Late in March she finally agreed to see him, not for "dates" but for "talks." Tommy's doggedness finally won her over. He just wouldn't stop telling her that he was sorry and that he loved her. But if Tommy's perseverance contributed to winning Glenda over, that's not why she ultimately married him in May as they had always planned. She married him because, even knowing what she did, even knowing that she would always know it, she loved him still.

Given Tommy Caldwell's personal experiences in yielding to temptation, one would have expected him to be better prepared for the news Faye Watson delivered in her motel room seven days after the shooting of Jeff Caldwell and the murder of George Washington Brown. "I was sleeping with him," Faye said, and Tommy felt as if he'd been shot himself.

The revelation was horrible. And yet, of course, he knew. He knew Dr. Brown had his liaisons. He'd known it for years. Short of the actual sex itself, he'd even witnessed it. It was Dr. Brown's weakness, Jeff Caldwell had explained to Tommy. It was proof of his humanity.

But Tommy's mind demanded distinctions. There was wrong, and there was greater wrong. It was wrong for Dr. Brown to cheat so wantonly on his wife Annette, who had stood by him for so long and at such great sacrifice. It was wrong for him to cheat on Annette with a long series of college-girl volunteers. But if the young women were willing to be used in that way, which Tommy gathered they were, at least the wrong done was confined to Annette. For all Tommy knew, she might long ago have made a forced peace with her husband's wandering eye.

It was a greater wrong, Tommy reasoned, for Dr. Brown to have conducted his many brief affairs with married women. With married women the wrong extended beyond Annette to include the cuckolded husbands.

But it was a greater wrong still, Tommy felt, for Dr. Brown to sleep with Faye Watson. Faye was Ben Watson's wife, and Ben was as dedicated a movement soldier as had ever worked for the CSCL. Ben idolized Dr. Brown. Ben would have died for Dr. Brown. In sleeping with Faye, Dr. Brown snatched away from Ben Watson the two things in the world that mattered most to him, his beloved wife and his cherished hero. Tommy felt crushed by the weight of what he knew and wished that he didn't know.

"I was sleeping with him," Faye said, and Tommy felt his knees go weak as Faye collapsed into a spasm of crying.

"Oh, no," Glenda said, throwing her arms around Faye, hugging Faye close to her swollen belly.

Even Preacher was rocked. "May God forgive us all," he said.

Suddenly Tommy was angry—angry at Faye. "Why did you do it, Faye?" he demanded. She responded only by twisting her face away and crying more loudly.

"Why did you do it, Faye?" Tommy asked again, without concealing his contempt and his anger. "Don't you know how much Ben loved you?"

"Leave her alone," Glenda said. "Can't you see she already blames herself?"

Tommy ignored her. "I want to know why you'd sleep with Dr. Brown when you knew how much Ben loved both of you."

Faye sat up and looked at Tommy now. "No," she said. "I mean, yes, I did sleep with Dr. Brown. But that was years ago—before Ben and I got together. Ben never knew about that. Or, at least, I don't think he did."

She began to cry again.

"I was sleeping with your father. That's what Ben knew."

So what Tommy thought he knew, he didn't. Truth is elusive. It remains the same but constantly shifts its shape. Truth exists outside of us, and we should be wary of anyone who claims to know it for certain—anyone, including ourselves. What Tommy thought he knew, he didn't, and what he now knew in its place was unthinkable: George Washington Brown hadn't died for his own sins but for those of his friend. He hadn't died for a black man's lust but for a white man's. That's what Tommy knew now.

And even now he didn't know it all.

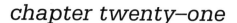

chapter twenty–one

AFTER FAYE WATSON CONFESSED HER AFFAIR with Jeff Caldwell, Tommy and Glenda waited with dread for the story to break in the national press. They were so appalled by Jeff's actions that they barely cared about the embarrassment the revelation would cause for him. But the affair was so sordid, they feared it would cast the entire movement in a squalid light. Weeks went by, however, and the story never broke. Jeff left the hospital, went through a year of severe alcohol abuse and finally righted himself enough to land a church in Elgin, Illinois.

With the FBI bird-dogging Faye, it seemed inevitable that she would eventually tell them what she had revealed to Tommy, Glenda and Preacher—and indeed she did. But the FBI never went public with the story.

Documents secured under the Freedom of Information Act in 1993 reveal why. Ben Watson did not catch Faye and Jeff on his own. The FBI caught them. The agency had installed cameras in a hotel room, intending to catch Dr. Brown *in flagrante delicto*. But they snared Jeff and Faye instead.

Hoover wanted to embarrass Dr. Brown and was willing to do so by embarrassing Dr. Brown's top white lieutenant. So the agency gave the photographs of Jeff and Faye to Ben and tragedy ensued. Afterwards, the FBI's desire to hide its role in the matter had the ironic and unintentional consequence of protecting Jeff Caldwell, too.

Instead of being exposed to public condemnation, Jeff was exiled to the lonely desert of self-recrimination. He gradually recovered from the physical wounds he suffered at the antiwar rally in 1968, but the psychic damage he suffered on the night he lost his friend and comrade, the man he most admired, healed slowly and incompletely. He never returned to his work with the CSCL, and as a result, he gradually slipped from his place on the American political and cultural stage.

After George Washington Brown's death, the civil-rights movement fractured and lost its momentum. Eventually, the war in Vietnam ended. Reporters who had covered Jeff Caldwell moved on to other events or became press officers for the political candidates of the Me Generation.

Jeff's broken marriages made it difficult for him to find employment in the church of his rearing, but the more liberal and forgiving United Church of Christ accepted him into its fold and allowed him to earn a living for the remaining two decades of his life. He first served as pastor of a small church in Elgin, Illinois. In 1972 he returned to New Orleans as pastor of the affluent St. Charles Avenue Congregationalist Church, where he remained until his death. Financially at least, he was comfortable at the St. Charles Church, which paid him a generous salary and provided a lovely four-bedroom parsonage on tony Newcomb Boulevard, where he lived for seventeen years, first with his third wife Francine, whom he married in 1970. In 1985, Jeff and Francine divorced. Three months later he married again, and he lived with his fourth wife Muffin until his death in 1989.

Tommy Caldwell went to his father's hospital room the night of Faye Watson's revelation and found Jeff watching an episode of *Gunsmoke*.

"Got some interesting news today," Tommy announced. Jeff didn't take his eyes off the television set. "Glenda and I had another visit with Faye Watson. Preacher, too. Want to know what she told us?"

"She told you something?" Jeff turned to Tommy, his eyes hollow like someone coming off a heroin binge.

"Oh, yeah," Tommy said. "She told us something. Want to hear about it?"

"No," Jeff said.

"Yeah, I bet you don't," Tommy said.

"She shouldn't have said anything," Jeff said. "It doesn't do anybody any good."

"I can see how you would say that. It doesn't do you any good, that's for sure. But maybe she needed to get it off her chest. Maybe she needed to face up to her own culpability in the deaths of Dr. Brown and her husband."

Jeff squinted, as if staring at something in the distance. "How did Ben know?" he asked. "We were very careful."

"What does it matter, you bastard?"

Jeff seemed not to hear his son, not to notice that he was being cursed. His eyes darted back and forth as he tried to solve the riddle of how Ben had known Faye was sleeping with his boss.

Jeff looked at Tommy. "She must have told him," he said. "But why? Is that how he found out?"

"WHO CARES?!" Tommy exploded, and Jeff blinked rapidly, startled by the violence of his son's reaction. "WHO THE FUCK CARES, YOU SON-OF-A-BITCH?" Tommy lowered his voice and spoke through gritted teeth. "How does it feel to have done what you did, Jeff?"

It was the first time in his life that Tommy had addressed his father by his first name. He would do so the rest of his life.

A nurse stuck her head in the doorway and looked around for a second with a puzzled expression. When she walked away, Tommy said, "How does it feel to know that your inability to control your goddamn dick has left two people dead? George Washington Brown took bullets meant for *you*. Your friend. The man who bailed you out when you couldn't handle losing your job. The great George Washington Brown. He's gone, and you're still here. How do you live with that? You might as well have pulled the trigger yourself. You couldn't control yourself, and you created a monster. Dr. Jeff Frankenstein. How do you live with the fact that you broke the spirit of decent, idealistic Ben Watson who won't even enjoy anonymity in death, whose memory now will live forever in infamy as Dr. Brown's murderer? Ben believed in you and followed you and looked up to you. You humiliated him. How could you do that?"

"I wasn't thinking of him," Jeff said.

"Yeah, I guess you weren't," Tommy snarled.

"You don't understand."

"No, I sure as hell do not."

"He was impotent," Jeff said.

"What?" Tommy said, sucking in his breath.

"He was impotent and I—"

Suddenly Tommy's face was up in Jeff's, his nose just inches from his father's. "ARE YOU REALLY TRYING TO DEFEND YOURSELF AS JUST TRYING TO SATISFY A POOR LITTLE WIFE WHOSE MOUSE HUSBAND COULDN'T GET IT UP?"

"No, no, no, I was just—"

"SHUT UP. YOU SHUT UP YOU WORTHLESS FUCK."

The nurse returned. "What's going on?" she asked.

"Nothing," Tommy said.

"I'm going to have to—"

"You're not going to have to nothing," Tommy said, walking past her. "I was just leaving."

Glenda seemed physically sickened by Faye's revelation. The situation nauseated Tommy as well. He had lived in the world. He knew about infidelity—his own, Dr. Brown's. But his father's transgression seemed so indifferent to possible consequences, so blindly selfish, that it was of a different sort altogether. Tommy recognized that his father was suffering from profound depression. His guilt about Dr. Brown's death was no doubt considerable. But even when Tommy confronted him at the hospital, Jeff seemed unable to express any compassion for Ben Watson—the man he had cuckolded, the man he had driven to murder. Tommy found that despicable.

When Tommy returned from the hospital, he found Glenda lying on her side in their darkened bedroom, her legs curled up and her hands tucked around her distended abdomen. Tommy sat beside her and rested a hand on her hip. "You okay?" he asked.

"I don't feel too well," she said.

"Because of today?"

"I guess," she said. "Probably. Maybe I'm just sick to my stomach."

Tommy took a deep breath and sighed. "I feel sick to my stomach, too. And I know it's because of what Faye told us."

"What did Jeff say?"

"Nothing. Bastard said nothing at all."

"Nothing?"

"Said Ben was impotent. Fucking asshole. As if that explained things."

"That must have been how it started," Glenda said.

"What?" Tommy said.

"Jeff and Faye. Faye told me that Ben was impotent."

"You knew? Why didn't you ever tell me? I don't seem to know a goddamn thing."

"Faye told me in confidence. She particularly didn't want you or Robert or any of the other men to know. You can understand that."

Tommy shrugged in response.

"I told her it was probably performance anxiety," Glenda said. "Sensitive guy like Ben. May have had all kinds of screwed up notions about sex. Sex and sin, you know. I recommended marriage counseling and suggested they talk to Jeff. I thought maybe he could help Ben realize that sex was not innately sinful."

"He cured the problem all right. Faye got all the therapy she needed."

"I don't think I will ever be able to relate to him again," Glenda said.

"That makes two of us," Tommy replied. "I just wonder who is going to relate to him once the world knows what he did?"

The world, of course, did not learn what Jeff Caldwell did. But if public light did not fall on Jeff's role in the assassination of George Washington Brown, Tommy's sister Danielle shined a private light on aspects of their father's behavior to which Tommy had been perhaps willfully blind. When Tommy drove Danielle to the airport for her return flight to Chicago, he confided to her the story of Jeff's involvement with Faye Watson. Danielle asked bitterly why Tommy seemed so surprised. As they waited for her plane in a flight lounge, she told her brother why she and Jeff had become estranged.

"He was doing Naylynn," Danielle said.

"After he and Mother broke up," Tommy said.

"Before," Danielle said.

"Before he and Mother broke up? He was doing Naylynn *before?*"

"You betcha," Danielle replied

"I don't believe it," Tommy said. "Dad has gotten himself completely fucked up these last few years. But he wasn't doing Naylynn when he and Mom were still together. After they separated, yes, but not when they were still together. That I don't believe."

"Believe it," Danielle said.

"Honey," Tommy said. He reached across the table and laid his hand atop his sister's. "You're just saying that because you're so loyal to Mom. She probably believes it because Dad ended up marrying Naylynn so soon. And that's understandable enough. But I don't think anything was going on."

Danielle sandwiched Tommy's hand between both of hers. "You know, big brother, you are surely the straightest arrow in God's entire quiver."

"What the hell's that supposed to mean? I'm not so straight."

"Sure you are. You're a believer. You believed in Dr. Brown, and you believed in Dad. I don't believe in anything anymore. But I *know* some things. And I know Dad was fucking Naylynn."

"How do you know?"

"Because I was his beard. The son-of-a-bitch. I was thirteen years old, and I was the apple of his eye, the pretty little blonde who loved her daddy and thought he was the greatest man in the world—greater even than Dr. Brown. He told me he needed me to keep a little secret between just me and him. He would tell Mommie he was taking me shopping or to help him run errands, and then he would drop me off at the movies by myself or give me money for a soda and a magazine at the K&B. And he would go over and knock off a piece of Naylynn, and then he'd come back and get me. It was our little secret, our secret from Mommie that we'd ever been apart. Think about how low that is. Bastard used his own daughter as cover for fucking his secretary."

"I don't know what was going on," Tommy argued, "but I'm not convinced he was necessarily fucking Naylynn. There's low and then there's low."

"Whenever he came back to pick me up, he reeked of her perfume."

"Still," Tommy said.

"You don't want to believe this, do you? Even after what Faye told you, you want to believe that some part of the fairy tale world you lived in—of righteous causes and athletic triumphs and a hero dad—was really true."

Tommy pulled his hand away from his sister's, but she grabbed it and pulled it back across the table. "Mommie thinks he was unfaithful to her for years. She didn't want to believe it, of course, so she tried to ignore her suspicions. And she never had proof until Farley Smithson said they'd been seen together at the church."

"Jesus," Tommy said.

"Why do you think Mommie suddenly decided not to fight for Dad's pastorate?"

"I can't stand this," Tommy said.

Danielle stroked his hand. "I know you can't."

"Why didn't you ever tell me?"

"At first because I was duped. I was Daddy's confidante, and I was keeping our secret. Later because I was ashamed. Later still because Mommie asked me not to."

"Why would Mother want to protect Dad?"

"Oh, Tommy," Danielle said. "It wasn't Daddy she wanted to protect. It was you."

Tommy believed everything his sister told him: all the details of her experience and the logic of her conclusions. But Danielle did not know for certain that their father had been unfaithful to their mother, and Tommy stubbornly chose to believe that he had not.

For still, Tommy did not know it all.

Tommy and Jeff had little contact for years after the night of their hospital-room confrontation in September of 1968. Until the publication of Tommy's Ph.D. dissertation in 1980, they saw each other only once, in the summer of 1969, and it was a horrible experience.

When Jeff got out of the hospital, Tommy resigned his position with the CSCL and entered the Tulane graduate program in English in the spring semester. In January, Glenda gave birth to their daughter, Shannon, who had Glenda's fair skin and brown hair and Tommy's eyes and nose. As Shannon grew, Glenda and Tommy thought she resembled Danielle more than any other member of their families; they liked that because Danielle was beautiful and dearly loved by both of them.

The sad 1969 incident happened on July 4 and recalled the Independence Day family gathering five years earlier when Jeff had broken down in his failed attempt to dissuade

Billye from divorcing him. Danielle was home from college, and the family had gathered for a cookout at the Uptown home Billye shared with her second husband. Tommy had never severed his relationship with his mother, but things had been cool between them from the time of the divorce until Tommy belatedly understood how self-sacrificing his mother had been.

Jeff was at the bottom that summer. Preacher Martin made several efforts to get Tommy to visit Jeff, but Tommy wouldn't do it. Preacher said Jeff wanted to see his granddaughter. Tommy told him no, more than once, expecting each time to be admonished by his old friend. But Preacher never uttered a critical word, saying always, "I understand. Maybe some other time."

Jeff's desire to see Shannon precipitated the depressing scene that developed about 10 P.M. on July 4. He had assumed that they would all be with Billye on a holiday, and he was parked in front of her house when Tommy and Glenda came out on the front porch to go home.

When Jeff saw them, he got out of the car and started toward the house. Glenda, who was holding the baby in her arms, saw him first. "Isn't that your father?" she said to Tommy, who was talking to his mother and sister in the doorway. Jeff waved, then tripped on a tree-root-raised slab of cracked sidewalk. He didn't fall, but his arms windmilled around first one way and then the other as he fought to gain his balance. It was apparent that he was drunk.

"Oh, good lord," Billye said. "Tommy, go help him before he hurts himself."

Tommy started down the steps. Behind him Danielle said, "I'll go, too. He might listen to me."

"You bring the baby on back inside," Billye said to Glenda.

"Hello, son," Jeff said, smiling at Tommy as if he saw him every day. He stuck out his hand, and Tommy delayed a mean moment before shaking it.

"And look who's here," Jeff said breathily. "Danielle."

"Why wouldn't I be here?" Danielle said. "I live here."

"Of course," Jeff said.

"What do you want, Jeff?" Tommy said. He seemed to tower over his father, who seemed shrunken and soft.

"I thought you might give me a peek at my granddaughter," Jeff said.

"Tonight's not such a good time," Tommy said.

"Why, didn't I just see her up there on the porch?" Jeff said. "I'd just like to see her, give her a little kiss, that's all."

"Another time would be better," Tommy said.

"Daddy," Danielle said, "why don't you go on back home? I promise that Tommy and I will bring Shannon by some time when you haven't had so much to drink."

Jeff's lip curled. "No, you won't," he sneered.

"Go on home, Jeff," Tommy said.

"No!" Jeff said. "I came here to see my granddaughter. Now I am your father, and you will do as I say."

Tommy laughed contemptuously. Jeff tried to go around Tommy toward the steps, and Tommy put out his arm to block him. Jeff ran into Tommy's arm, and his equilibrium was so unsteady he reeled backwards and sat down hard on the sidewalk.

"Oh, Jesus," Tommy said.

"I want to see Glenda," Jeff said. "Glenda wouldn't bruise me around like this."

"No one's bruising you around," Danielle said. "You're drunk. You can barely stand up."

"Glenda doesn't want to see you," Tommy said. "And she sure doesn't want Shannon to see her grandfather drunk on his ass."

Tommy knelt beside Jeff and placed a shoulder under one of his father's arms. "Help me get him up," Tommy said to Danielle.

"God, he stinks of whiskey," Danielle said.

When they had Jeff back on his feet, Tommy said to him, "Give me your keys. I'm going to drive you home."

"I want to talk to Billye," Jeff said. "She won't allow our two children to manhandle me."

"Daddy, it's late," Danielle said. "You're making a scene. Give Tommy your keys so he can take you home."

"I will not do it!" Jeff yelled.

"Danielle," Tommy said, "see if we can turn him around and get him into his car before someone calls the police."

"I *want* someone to call the police," Jeff said. But he allowed them to steer him back to the street.

"Now, give me your keys, Jeff," Tommy said.

"Where's your mother?" Jeff demanded.

"She's inside," Danielle said.

"Inside?" Jeff said, as if the idea hadn't occurred to him before.

"Where are your keys, Daddy?" Danielle said. "Are they in your pants pocket?"

Danielle stuck her hand into the front pocket of her father's pants, and Jeff twisted away from her saying, "Stop that!"

"I'm just trying to get your keys," Danielle said. She could hear them jingling and persisted in trying to get her hand deep enough into Jeff's pocket to fish them out.

Jeff slapped her, hard, right across the face. "I told you to stop that," he said and slapped her again before she could draw out of range.

Tommy was enraged. He rammed his left forearm up under Jeff's chin, grabbed hold of his father's shirt with his right hand, and slammed him up against the car.

"I could snap you like a dried twig, you pathetic bastard," Tommy said, his face just inches from his father's.

"Don't hurt him, Tommy," Danielle said. "He's drunk."

Tommy kept Jeff pinned against the car, his fist twined in Jeff's shirt front, his forearm across his father's throat. "The son of a bitch slapped you," Tommy said to his sister.

"I'm okay," she replied.

"I ought to bust you up," Tommy said to Jeff. "You stinking drunk."

Jeff's eyes seemed to clear slightly, and he stared hard at his son. "Ought to have a drink yourself sometime, Tommy. Then maybe you wouldn't be such a self-righteous jerk."

That's when Tommy slapped him the first time. Jeff made no effort to resist, but he said, "Look at the son I raised to believe in nonviolence. You make me so proud."

"I'm going to teach you a lesson," Tommy said. "Remember when I was eight and Danielle was four and she grabbed a crayon I was using and I smacked her? Remember that, Dad? And you took me into your bedroom and you punched me on the arm. Remember that?"

"Let the day perish wherein I was born, and the night in which it was said, there is a man child conceived."

"Shut up," Tommy said, and he slapped his father's face again.

"Tommy, stop it," Danielle said.

"I'm teaching him a lesson," Tommy said to Danielle without looking at her. To Jeff he said, "And after you punched me the first time, you asked me if I liked it and I told you no, so you punched me again, in my shoulder, hard enough to knock me down on my fanny. Remember that, Dad? You said if I hit people littler than me then bigger people had a right to hit me. Remember? I remember, Dad. It was a good lesson."

He slapped his father again.

"Tommy, don't!" Danielle said.

Tommy ignored her and spoke only to Jeff. "See, like a lot of things with you, you're real good at teaching the lesson, but not so good at learning it."

"I was disciplining her," Jeff said, slurring the word *disciplining*. "I'm her father. I told her to stop."

Tommy slapped him again.

"Well, now I'm disciplining you," Tommy said. "And here's the lesson. Don't ever come around us again, or I will hit you some more. Do you understand me?"

"For the thing which I greatly feared is come upon me," Jeff said, "and that which I was afraid of is come unto me."

"Danielle, come get his keys out of his pocket before I crush his larynx so I never have to listen to his self-pitying bullshit ever again."

When Danielle had the keys, Tommy directed her to open the back door, and he maneuvered Jeff onto the back seat.

"Lie down," Tommy ordered. "And don't make me have to tell you twice." Jeff lay down, and Tommy closed the door.

"Are you okay?" Tommy asked Danielle.

She touched her face. "It stings a little. But I'll be all right."

"Bastard hit you hard enough to leave a bruise."

"It's okay, Tommy. It's the summer. I don't have to see anybody. If it leaves a bruise, I'll just stay inside until it goes away." She handed Tommy Jeff's car keys. "Drive him home. I'll take Mommie's car and bring you back."

That night Tommy dreamed about fighting with his father. But in the dream, he threw punches, not slaps, and in the dream he knocked his father down. When Jeff was down, Tommy beat him as he lay on the ground, curled into a ball, his arms wrapped around his head. Tommy stood over his father and demanded that Jeff get up and fight, but Jeff remained curled in a ball. And Tommy began to cry and to slap his father's arms in a frenzy, demanding over and over, "Get up and fight. Get up and fight, you quitter. Get up and fight."

This dream would return two and three times a week for the next twenty years.

It was not inevitable, perhaps, but as time went along, scientific developments made it increasingly likely that he would come to know. He might not have known so soon. Perhaps if all things had fallen into place just so, perhaps if he had been extraordinarily lucky, he might have escaped the knowledge altogether. But Tommy's life—which had always seemed so lucky, which gave him strength and athletic prowess, which gave him a good upbringing, he believed, in spite of what happened to his family later on, which kept him out of the war he detested without his having to leave the country or go to jail, which gave him a beautiful daughter and a wife who forgave him when she might have justifiably walked away, which seemed packed with good fortune beyond his fair share—Tommy's life turned unthinkable, the day he came to know it all.

Once he knew it all, he realized that knowing it changed everything, erased all previous knowledge, made all things previously true, false and all things previously false, true. Once he knew it all, he understood that heretofore he had known nothing whatsoever.

All was construct. All was imposed. The calendar said it was October, 1971. A definite fixed time. But he was like a man lost in space. Time has no meaning across the vastness of the universe where past, present and future are inextricably intertwined. What was up? What was down? All was weightlessness. There was nothing to hold on to and nothing to push off from. There was a flash of pain, and an understanding of the kindness of death, the release that death proffers like a cup of nepenthe, the sweet draught that erases the cruel agony of knowing what ought never be known. A flash of unbearable pain. An understanding of God's benevolence in making men mortal. Then numbness.

Tommy felt he had no choice but to put his life away, to abandon it completely. He did not prepare. He did not pack. He did not say goodbye. He simply went. He asked his question. He got his answer, and he went away. It was 7 P.M. when he got into his ancient black Volkswagen and drove out of the city. He had no destination clearly in mind. Movement was the key. In movement there was not renewed life but the faint affirmation of existence. Tommy tried not to think, but only to drive. Perhaps he would visit with Danielle, now in her last year at Northwestern. Perhaps he would look up his old high-school teammate Clint Carter, who had just started practicing law in San Francisco. But probably not. What were relatives and friends in a universe where two plus two equaled three and five simultaneously but never equaled four?

Tommy drove north on U.S. Highway 61, using Interstate 55 wherever it was finished. He listened to the National League championship playoff game between the Giants and the Pirates on New Orleans station WWL, which he was able to pick up all the way to Jackson, Mississippi. When the game was over, he switched stations repeatedly as they faded out, one after another, strong and clear for a few miles, then fuzzy and intermittent, then gone, an emblem of his life. He stopped for gas. He bought large cups of coffee in Styrofoam cups every couple of hours. He drove on through the night. The speed limit was seventy miles per hour on I-55 and on the four-lane stretches of U.S. 61. But his car wouldn't go over sixty-two unless he drafted behind an eighteen-wheeler, when he could get it up to eighty.

The sun was up by the time he reached the outskirts of Memphis. He should have been exhausted. But he didn't feel tired. Drained maybe, vacant, but not sleepy. He took I-55 out of Memphis into Arkansas and then switched back and forth on U.S. 61 when he had to. By 3 P.M. he was in St. Louis.

He stopped at a diner for three fried eggs and more coffee. From St. Louis he continued north on Route 66 toward Chicago and hit the twenty-four-hour mark of his journey in Joliet. He could have made it on to Evanston in another ninety minutes. But he couldn't think of what he would say to Danielle or what he would ask of her. So he turned west on Interstate 80 where the trucks were plentiful and the drafting was good. He found WWL again, arcing from Louisiana out to the Great Plains, and listened as the Pirates denied Willie Mays a last trip to the series as a Giant. God was not in heaven, and all was wrong with the world.

He was in Des Moines by midnight and in the middle of Nebraska by dawn. By noon he was in Cheyenne, Wyoming. The floor of his car was littered with coffee cups and wrappers from Snickers and Payday candy bars. He felt nauseated and unclean. But he drove on, heading west, a neo-pioneer who sought not the promised land of the American dream, and not escape which was unavailing. He put more gas and snacks on his gasoline credit cards, and he crossed into Utah as he completed his second day.

Tommy certainly felt the fatigue now. His system was a wreck of caffeine and sugar. But he pushed on, through Salt Lake City, across the salt flats and into the high Nevada desert. Around midnight he stopped for gas in Winnemucca. The attendant was a woman of about fifty, her skin leathery from too much sun, her eyes crinkled from too many cigarettes. Her hair was steel gray and had been permed. Her name plate said "Doreen."

Doreen rang up Tommy's purchases and took note of his bloodshot eyes and his agitated manner. "How many hours you been on the road, cowboy?" she asked.

Tommy was dressed in jeans, T-shirt and denim jacket. But he didn't think he looked like a cowboy. He'd let his hair grow since he graduated from college and wore it pulled back in a ponytail. He looked like a hippie or a vagrant.

Tommy shrugged in answer to Doreen. "Too long," he said finally as he signed his credit slip. "Not long enough."

"You get some rest," Doreen called as he walked back to his car. The Volkswagen didn't catch immediately when he turned the key. He had to try three times and stomp on the accelerator, flooding the car with gasoline fumes, adding to his nausea. But then he was off again, out into the most barren part of the American landscape other than Death Valley.

It was 3:30 A.M. when he broke down. He was drafting behind a United moving van when he started losing speed. At first he thought the big truck was simply pulling away, but then his speed fell below sixty-two and he realized he had lost all power. He pulled into the emergency lane at the right side of the highway and coasted to a stop. He wasn't out of gas, and his battery was strong, but the car wouldn't start. Any other time he would have been frightened, broken down in the middle of nowhere. But now he was too numb to care. Maybe a sudden storm would roar down out of Canada. He'd heard of such things happening in the fall. Maybe he'd freeze to death. Maybe that would be the respite he'd driven all this way to find.

Still, he did what he could. What else was there to do, but what he could? He didn't know any more about car engines than how to check and change the oil. But he'd learned that Volkswagens sometimes responded to random acts of banging about on the motor. So he got out and opened the engine cover in the back of the car and tapped everything he could reach. But it didn't work, and there was nothing else he could do. He needed to sleep, anyway; maybe while he slept, the Highway Patrol would come along and find him. He climbed into the front passenger's seat, reclined the back and slept for an hour, until he awoke from the cold. There was a picnic blanket he and Glenda kept in the baggage compartment behind the back seat. He wrapped up in it and slept again until 7 A.M.

He had no choice but to flag down help. But that proved more easily decided than achieved. Traffic was light, mostly tractor-trailers. Four and five minutes went by between passing vehicles. Tommy stood by the road and waved at each passing car and truck. The passenger cars moved into the left lane and sped past him, their drivers staring straight ahead as if he didn't exist. The eighteen-wheelers sounded their air horns sometimes and roared past him in a gale blast that stung his eyes and rocked his Volkswagen as if it were a child's toy. Eventually, he waved a white handkerchief as a sign of distress.

The trucks continued to thunder by, but after a few minutes, a Rambler station wagon, like the one Jeff drove, slowed down as it approached him in the left lane. A family of four was inside, mother and father up front, a boy and a girl, both under ten, in the back. They were clearly frightened at the prospect of trying to help. The car didn't stop, didn't even pull over into the right-hand lane. But it slowed enough that Tommy was able to run alongside, where the wife had cracked her window perhaps three inches, to ask for help.

The wife turned and said something to the husband, and the station wagon jumped ahead and drove a hundred yards farther down the highway before it braked suddenly and swerved right all the way into the emergency lane. The husband got out and walked back toward Tommy. He was in his mid-thirties, medium height and stocky. He had black-rimmed glasses and wore his hair in a flattop. He might have been a military man, Tommy thought, although he wasn't in uniform. The man stopped ten yards away and spread his legs to the width of his shoulders. "You broke down, you say?"

"Yes, I did." Tommy grabbed the bottom of his jacket on either side, spread it open and then wrapped it around himself. He was cold, but his purpose was to show the man that he wasn't carrying any weapons stuck in his belt.

"What's the problem?"

"Don't know. I just lost power. Now it won't start. I don't know anything about car motors. What about you?"

"Not really," the man said. "I could maybe push you, you know, to jump start it."

Tommy got behind the wheel, and the man backed his station wagon slowly along the emergency lane until he swerved out onto the highway and got behind Tommy's car. The Rambler pushed the Volkswagen up to a speed of thirty-five and then backed off. The Beetle bucked, coughed and sputtered but never caught. They tried it two more times with no success. Both cars pulled back into the emergency lane. Tommy and the man got out to talk.

"I don't know what more I can do," the man said.

"Yeah," Tommy said. "Thanks. It usually works, a jump start."

The man bit on his lip. Tommy could see that the man was wrestling with another proposal, but Tommy couldn't imagine what. A ride into the next town, perhaps—but Tommy bet the man would prove skittish about letting a stranger into his car.

The man blew out a breath. "I guess I could push you on up to Fernley."

"How far's that?" Tommy asked.

"About thirty miles. We couldn't do more than about forty, I don't think." He thumbed toward the Rambler. "Only got a four in there. Course, your bug is light and all."

The Rambler pushed Tommy thirty miles farther west to the dry little town of Fernley, Nevada, and left him at a gas station. Tommy thanked the man profusely, and they shook hands. But the man never smiled, and they never exchanged names.

At first the gas-station mechanic refused even to look at Tommy's car because he didn't "have no metric tools for these foreign jobs." But eventually he agreed to poke around under the engine cover. He discovered the problem immediately—a cracked distributor cap. The station didn't have any parts. Tommy would have to go into Reno to get what the mechanic needed. How would Tommy get there? How the hell should the mechanic know? Tommy walked from the gas station back up the ramp to the interstate. He would thumb it, he guessed. Thirty-five miles. If he got a ride right off, he could be there inside an hour. Find an auto-parts store and buy a distributor cap. Thumb it back.

That's what he told Vince Woods, the black man who picked Tommy up in his new

Toyota Corona. But Vince thought the plan was flawed. Vince was an accountant, and he and his wife Veronica were moving from Chicago for a new job in San Francisco. He was a man with a big wide smile and no hesitation about expressing himself. Tommy had tried to get into the back seat when the Toyota pulled over for him, but Veronica had insisted Tommy ride up front because he was so tall.

Vince slapped Tommy on the knee. "What if the Fernley mechanic is wrong that it's a cracked distributor cap?" Vince pointed out. "You buy what he says and hitch back out there and it doesn't work. Then what? You already said the man doesn't have any metric tools, though that's damn hard to believe in this day and age. Maybe he just wants to gouge you. Hold you up legally. See what I'm saying?"

Tommy nodded. But what alternative did he have?

"We need another plan," Vince said and proceeded to formulate one. "Okay, I think I've got it. We get into Reno and call the Automobile Association. Use their towing service to get your car hauled in. Reno has a VW place, they should be able to fix you right up, whatever's wrong."

"But that'll cost me a couple hundred bucks, I bet," Tommy said. "Just for the tow, I mean. And I haven't got the bread."

"Not if you're a Triple A member," Vince said.

"Yeah, but I'm not," Tommy said.

"Yeah, but I am," Vince said and cackled as if he'd told a joke. Tommy wrinkled his brow, not understanding what Vince was proposing. "See, it's easy, man. I call Triple A and tell 'em I was driving my Volkswagen out this way and broke down in Fernley. Simple as that."

"And that'll work?" Tommy said.

"Won't work if we don't try it. Triple A doesn't know what kind of car I drive. Had a Pontiac Grand Prix till Veronica got pregnant and we decided we were required to be sensible. Now I've got this Corona." He grinned. "Check that. Now I've got this Volkswagen."

"But how did you get into Reno?" Tommy asked.

"You were nice enough to drive me. Me and my pregnant wife. In your new Toyota."

The only wrinkle in Vince's plan was that Triple A required that he ride in the tow truck back to Fernley. Tommy couldn't believe he agreed to do it, but he did. So Tommy sat in a coffee shop for nearly two hours while a garrulous black stranger did him an unsolicited act of kindness. While Vince was gone, he left Tommy in charge of both his wife and his new car. When Vince returned, Tommy asked if he could buy the Woodses a meal or something, but Vince said, "Nah, we've got to beat our moving van to San Francisco or the movers are liable to put our furniture in all the wrong rooms."

"But you have to let me do something for you," Tommy said.

"All right, I will," Vince said. "You're a Southern boy, am I right?"

"Yes," Tommy said. "New Orleans."

"I could tell by the accent," Vince said and smiled again. "Might not have picked you up but for your long hair. Heard you talk, might have dropped you right back off. Can't help myself. I get emotional sometimes. But I can tell you're a good guy."

"How can you tell that?" Tommy said. "All I've done is let you do me favors."

"Yeah, well now I'm gonna let you do me one," Vince said.

"Anything," Tommy said.

"Next time you see a black guy broke down on the highway, you stop and help him."

Vince and Veronica dropped Tommy off at the Rest Well motel five blocks from the Volkswagen dealership and drove out of his life to get on with theirs. Tommy got a room, took a shower, lay down on the double bed with a towel wrapped around his waist and began to cry. It was only the second time he had cried since he was eight years old.

What had precipitated Tommy's journey from New Orleans to Reno was a visit he made to his doctor on the morning of his departure. For two and a half years, Tommy and Glenda had been trying to have a second child. Their lack of success had led them to have their fertility checked. Glenda's doctor said she was fine. Tommy's doctor, on the other hand, told him he wasn't. "No problem with your semen level," the doctor said, "quantity, acidity and so forth. But you aren't producing live sperm." Tommy asked if this was a temporary condition. "No, it's not," the doctor said. "I'm sorry. But this happens."

"How?" Tommy wondered.

"Oh, any number of ways. Mumps. Trauma of some kind. Extremely high fever."

"I haven't had any of that," Tommy said.

"And ways we haven't figured out yet," the doctor said.

Tommy nodded glumly. "Glenda and I have enjoyed our little daughter so much. We just wanted to give her a brother or a sister."

"Then you've already adopted?" the doctor said.

"Oh, no," Tommy said. "Shannon is our natural child."

The doctor studied his lab report for some time. "How old did you say your daughter was?" he asked finally.

"She'll be three in January."

The doctor cleared his throat. "I don't know how to tell you this, Mr. Caldwell," he said, "but I would say from the few dead sperm appearing in your ejaculate that you haven't been capable of fathering a child for five years or longer, though I would say that there was a time you were fertile, in your teens."

"You're telling me that Shannon isn't my natural daughter?" Tommy said.

"Well, medicine is an imprecise science, Mr. Caldwell, but given what our research indicates, yes, that's what I'm telling you."

Tommy left the fertility clinic and went home, where he talked with Glenda at the square table in the kitchen. They could hear Shannon playing in her bedroom, two rooms away.

"The doctor says I'm infertile," Tommy told her.

"Oh, no," Glenda said. "Oh, Tommy, I'm so sorry. For both of us. And for Shannon. You know how she wants a baby brother or sister to take care of."

"The doctor said we could adopt," Tommy said.

"Then he thinks it's permanent?"

"He thinks so. Yes."

"How did this happen?"

"Well, he doesn't know. But I wonder if it didn't happen when I was scalded with Atomic Balm in high school."

"But Tommy—" Glenda said, and then her face sagged and her mouth fell open. "But Shannon—"

"Shannon isn't mine."

Glenda turned her face away. "Oh, Jesus," she said. "Oh, good Jesus."

"Who?" Tommy said.

"I didn't know," Glenda said. "You have to always believe me, I didn't know."

"Who?" Tommy said.

"I'm not going to say. It won't do any good to say. It could only do harm. Shannon is *your* daughter. You raised her. You love her. That's all that matters."

"My daughter?" Tommy said, his eyes vacant like those of a mannequin. He reached into his pants pocket, brought out his wallet, selected two photos and laid them side by side, one of Shannon, one of Danielle. "My daughter is my younger sister."

Tommy had figured this out although he hadn't wanted to. And even as he laid the photos next to one another, he wanted to be disproven. He wanted Glenda to maintain fervently that the man she was seeing during the time of their break-up in the winter and spring of 1968 was someone other than Jeff. He wanted her to deny that she'd ever had sexual relations with his father. But Glenda just looked at him and twisted her head slowly from side to side. And her blinking, huge, lovely brown eyes filled with tears and overflowed in twin rivulets down the prominent cheekbones that Tommy so liked to brush with his own face.

And then he knew it all.

chapter twenty–two

WHEN TOMMY CALDWELL AROSE in Reno, Nevada, on an October morning in 1971, he walked to a discount outlet near the Rest Well Motel. He bought two pairs of jeans, three blue T-shirts and six pairs of jockey shorts and went back to the motel to change before checking out. Then he got his car from the Volkswagen dealership and continued west on I-80. He drove more slowly now and stopped drafting behind eighteen-wheelers, content to putter along in the right lane at fifty-five to sixty miles per hour. He crossed the Bay Bridge into San Francisco in the early afternoon and drove north to the Golden Gate Bridge, then down into the quaint little village of Sausalito where he sat in the No Name Bar for a long time over an Irish coffee.

Then Tommy called his friend Clint Carter, whom he had not seen in three years. Clint took off work early, and they went to an Italian restaurant for poached salmon and pasta. They drank a bottle of Chianti, and as they ate, Tommy told Clint what had happened. Clint listened without comment, for he understood that was what Tommy wanted. When they finished eating, they went to Clint's apartment on Powell Street, where Tommy spent the night on a hide-a-bed in the living room.

The next morning Clint urged Tommy to stay longer, but Tommy told him he wanted to drive the Pacific Coast Highway. When Tommy left, Clint hugged him and held on to him for a full minute without saying anything. Tommy would never tell another soul what had happened—not his sister, not his mother, not Preacher Martin, not Shannon, no one. He didn't want them to know. For if they did not know, then it was not true. He had always assumed that truth is found in knowledge, but Tommy now knew that there was a different, sometimes superior, truth that lay in the absence of knowledge: the truth of innocence.

Tommy drove south from San Francisco and spent a night at Carmel, then drove along the towering bluffs over the Pacific on State Highway 1 and spent another night at San Luis Obispo. The next day he drove on into Los Angeles and rented a room for a week in Santa Monica. Each morning he went to UCLA and walked around the campus. Each afternoon he went to the beach and, despite the season, lay on the sand with his shirt off. On the seventh day, he went into the water. It was warmer than he expected but cold enough to take his breath away.

The next morning Tommy headed eastward on Interstate 10. He stayed in Tucson the first night, El Paso the second and San Antonio the third. He arrived back in New Orleans at 7 P.M., exactly seventeen days after he departed. He did not go home to the bungalow he and Glenda rented, but instead booked a room at the Wigwam Motel on Airline Highway. The next day he went to Tulane, withdrew from all his courses and resigned from the university. The day after that he reserved a U-Haul truck for December first. Only then did he go home.

Glenda was in the kitchen at the stove as Tommy let himself in the front door of the blue shotgun cottage. She turned and started toward him, wiping her hands on the denim apron she wore over a long-sleeved blue cotton dress. But before she had taken two steps in his direction, Shannon scooted around her legs and ran toward him, squealing, "Daddy! Daddy home!"

Tommy squatted down, and Shannon threw her arms around his neck. "I missed you," she said. "I missed you, Daddy." She kissed him wetly on the cheek.

He held her away from him to look in her face and brushed the bangs of her fine sandy hair off her forehead, making her blink and wiggle in his arms. "I missed you, too, sugar," he said.

Glenda came to stand over them and rested a hand on top of Shannon's head.

Tommy pulled the little girl against his chest and squeezed her to him. "I missed you, baby, more than you will ever know."

"Miss Mommie, too?" Shannon said.

Tommy stood up and looked at his wife as Shannon backed up against her mother's legs and pulled the long apron over her face.

"Miss Mommie, too," Shannon repeated, this time as a command rather than a question.

"Yes," Tommy said. "I missed Mommie, too."

As Tommy ate dinner with his family that night, he and Glenda restricted their conversation to matters concerning the meal. Tommy put Shannon to bed and lay on her bed reading Dr. Seuss stories until she fell asleep.

Glenda showered while Tommy was with Shannon, and Tommy showered afterwards. Glenda was in bed when Tommy came out of the bathroom. When he slipped into bed beside her, she turned off the light. They lay next to each other without talking, long enough for their eyes to adjust to the darkness and the light of the unsleeping city to seep inside.

Finally, Tommy said, "I've decided to move to Los Angeles."

"I see," Glenda said.

"I've rented a truck for December first."

"Okay," Glenda said.

"I would like for you and Shannon to go with me."

"Okay," Glenda said.

"That won't give you much time," Tommy said.

"Time enough," Glenda said.

And that was all. They lay there the rest of the night, still not touching, neither one sleeping, both trying to lie still so as not to disturb the other. The next morning they rose and began to pack. They spent Thanksgiving with Billye and Dennis and Danielle, who flew in from Chicago. Tommy told his mother and sister of his plans. They pressed him to explain why, but he would say only that he and Glenda had talked it over and decided it was what they wanted to do. On December first they left; Glenda and Shannon were in the Volkswagen and Tommy followed in the U-Haul truck. In Los Angeles they started over.

Tommy and Glenda never talked about her affair with Jeff in the winter and spring of 1968 after she broke her engagement to Tommy. It was like a bullet lodged close to a beating heart. The surgery required to take it out was too dangerous, too apt to result in sudden death. The best course was to let the body heal around it and go on with life. If good fortune prevailed, with time almost all normal function could be resumed. But the bullet, of course, would always be there.

Although they never talked about it, Tommy thought about it a lot, especially at the beginning. A part of him actually understood. The part that had watched his father stir crowds for years understood how attractive Jeff could be, bright, good looking, charismatic and full of genuinely righteous zeal. The young women flocked to George Washington Brown, and almost as many were drawn to Jeff Caldwell. They were like rock stars with a higher purpose.

At first Tommy proceeded from will rather than instinct, from logic rather than emotion. He decided that however ill-advised Glenda's involvement with Jeff had been, she had indeed chosen him over Jeff. And however deeply scarred he was, he determined that living without his family was worse than living with them. So he decided to forgive Glenda. The forgiveness didn't happen over night. It didn't happen when they first arrived in Los Angeles, and it didn't happen immediately thereafter as Tommy began graduate study in

American history. It didn't happen all at once. When it happened Tommy could never exactly say.

They stayed together, but they did not live the life they would have if Tommy had not cheated on Glenda and if Glenda had not become pregnant by Jeff. Their lives were greatly different, Tommy reckoned, more muted, less unguarded, much more deeply pessimistic.

And yet, gains were made as they almost always are when suffering is endured. Glenda got a master's degree in social work and began a clinical practice counseling battered and troubled women. Tommy developed a special interest in American Indians, a product, he presumed, of identifying with the victims of relentless injustice. Shannon grew up healthy and happy and beautiful, never quite understanding why she sensed in both her parents a core of sadness.

Life is full of ironies, of course. For as Shannon grew, Tommy's love for her seemed to expand like the boundaries of the universe. Today it was infinite. Tomorrow it was greater still. And yet Shannon was a daughter he could never have fathered. On the one hand, Tommy did not even try to forgive Jeff, whom he blamed in a way he didn't blame Glenda. But on the other hand, he loved Shannon, who was his father's child. Tommy knew that irony. And he willfully put it out of his mind.

In 1977 Tommy received his Ph.D. in American history and Glenda got her MSW. They moved to Indiana, where Tommy taught at Glenda's alma mater, Valparaiso University. *Midnight of the Savage,* Tommy's book on King Philip's War, was published in 1980. Arguing that the brutal New England war in 1776 and 1777 was the result of an attempt by the Puritan settlers to exterminate an entire Algonquin tribe, the book won prizes from the *New England Review* and the *William and Mary Quarterly* and resulted in a number of invitations to speak, including at Tulane.

Jeff and his wife Francine, whom Tommy had never met, came to Tommy's talk. Tommy and Jeff had not seen each other in more than a decade. After the talk, the Tulane History Department hosted a reception for Tommy. Jeff came through the receiving line carrying five copies of Tommy's book. Francine trailed him with five more.

"Presents," Jeff explained as he asked Tommy to sign them.

Jeff introduced Francine as Tommy wrote his name on a succession of title pages.

"It's a fine piece of work, son," Jeff said.

"He's read it three times already," Francine said. She laughed high in the back of her throat. "I think he's got it memorized."

"I think this is an important contribution," Jeff said, shaking a copy of the book like a fan. "If I might be afforded the privilege of saying so, I'm very proud of what you've done."

"Thank you," Tommy said.

"You ought to come by the house while you're in town," Francine said as they moved away.

"I'll try," Tommy said.

Two days later, Tommy did visit with his father for a strained hour. No ugliness emerged, but the meeting was as formal as if they were strangers. Tommy actually wondered if Jeff might begin addressing him as "Dr. Caldwell."

A new beginning had been established, however, and in the following years Tommy began to spend more time in New Orleans. In the late 1970s, in an amnesty program initiated by President Jimmy Carter, Robert Brown emerged from years in hiding and sought a role in public life. In 1981 Robert ran for the city council in a mixed-race district and brought Tommy in as a consultant to help him "understand the white issues." Robert lost that race, but Tommy was again a consultant when Robert won a seat in the state legislature a year later. In an era of rapidly changing demographics, when black urban politicians discovered the pleasures of black-majority districts and the temptations of strict color appeal, Robert stood out in hearkening back to his father's rhetoric about "black and white together." And Tommy was proud to lend his assistance.

During each of those many consulting visits home, Tommy made a point of spending at least one afternoon or evening with Jeff. Their visits remained uncomfortable. Jeff was presumably ignorant of Tommy's greatest grievance against him, and Tommy was certainly never going to let Jeff know what it was. But Jeff knew there were grievances enough. Tommy could tell by the shiftiness of Jeff's eyes whenever they met that he felt the lash of Tommy's disapproval when they were together. But they were civil. They talked about Reaganomics and affirmative action and other social and political issues of the day. They agreed on almost everything, but they communicated with each other very little.

Still, with the wound in Tommy's heart anesthetized by the passage of years, with insight derived from his own suffering, Tommy understood something about Jeff's behavior after his divorce from Billye. Tommy understood the desperation born of the emptiness that follows losing the thing that matters to you most. However imperfect he was, Jeff loved Billye. However much he had put her second to his career, however much he always thought himself unworthy of her, she mattered most. And he was never the same after he lost her.

Tommy knew this. And knowing it might have healed him. But knowledge is different from truth, for the former resides in the intellect and the latter in the spirit. And knowledge is Janus-faced; it can obscure as easily as enlighten. And only the truth can set you free.

Jeff's health declined rapidly after his fourth marriage, to Muffin. It was as if the last of his younger women finally succeeded in wearing him out. He became increasingly frail, and his rigorous intellect began to lose its edge. In the autumn of 1989 he suffered a devastating stroke, which left him disabled physically for a while and barely in control of his mental faculties. Although he did recover his ability to function, he survived for only about six months.

Tommy was with Jeff at the end. He, Danielle and Billye took turns sitting with Jeff and attending to his needs, fetching things he could not reach, helping him eat and drink. Usually they sat with him separately, in rotation with Muffin.

But sometimes Tommy and Danielle sat with him together. Tommy marveled at the way Danielle interacted with Jeff. She kept her hands on him constantly, twining her fingers with his, touching his hand, rubbing his arm, brushing her fingers against his cheek, pushing his hair back off his face. Tommy knew well of Danielle's enduring hostility toward Jeff, and Tommy knew that at least in some measure these gestures of deep filial devotion were pure theater, a loving show for a dying man, a performance for an audience of one. But Tommy knew, too, that Danielle's actions were something more. While part of her detested her father, another, equally strong part wanted even now to break through to him, to love him actually with all the fervency that her actions seemed to reflect.

And so, Tommy knew, Danielle felt a profundity of emotion for Jeff that Tommy could only envy. Although he didn't anymore, Tommy had hated Jeff for a long time. Watching Danielle with Jeff, Tommy ached to feel the emotions that she exhibited, however much her exhibition was orchestrated rather than genuine. Tommy's relationship with his father had always been formal, more mentor-student than parent-child, and that formality persisted into Jeff's last days. When they were away from the hospital, Tommy could let himself cry in his sister's arms, but he became stiff in his father's presence. Tommy wanted to love his father, although he did not particularly want to love the man who *was* his father. At the very least Tommy wished that he, too, could touch Jeff and speak words of love, however insincerely, could offer Jeff comfort in his waning days. Tommy wished he could let Jeff die feeling forgiven, even if Tommy's heart had yet to yield to the peace forgiveness can bring. To that end Tommy resolved to follow the model of his sister as best he could. He knew he could not pull it off the way Danielle did, but he resolved to act like the devoted son he had once been. The approach of death humbled him; it frightened him with its inevitability and its finality.

On the last night of Jeff's life, Tommy sat with him and recounted stories from his childhood and Jeff's youth. Jeff listened with his eyes closed, occasionally grunting in recognition of the events Tommy related. When the time came to leave, Tommy asked Jeff if there was anything else he could do for him, and Jeff asked for some cold water. Tommy went to the visitor's lounge for a cup of ice, brought it back and filled it with water and brought the straw to Jeff's lips. Jeff took the cup and held it; as he sucked at the straw, his gaunt face and hollow eyes and round sucking mouth reminded Tommy of Edvard Munch's *The Scream*. And Tommy bent and kissed his father's forehead, a gesture he had never before made, and he said in a whisper, "I love you, Dad. You were my hero, and I've always loved you so."

How desperately Tommy wanted this to be true. How urgently he wanted to be the kind of son who loved his father. So he bent and kissed his father's forehead and whispered, "I love you, Dad." And he did it before it was too late. And even as he did it, he knew that he did it not for Jeff, but for himself. And perhaps Jeff knew that too.

In Tommy's memory, Jeff had never told Tommy that he loved him: a Southern male thing, no doubt, emotion concealed far sooner than revealed. Jeff's hearing had been bad before his stroke and was worse afterwards; perhaps he simply did not hear. He continued sucking on his straw until he had drained the water and ice rattled in the cup. Then he looked at Tommy with watery eyes and said, whether in response to Tommy's whisper or to Tommy's bringing him the water, Tommy did not know, "Thanks, son."

And Tommy felt his throat thicken.

Tommy accepted the cup of ice, set it on the night stand, took off his father's glasses, folded them and laid them where Jeff could reach them. Jeff closed his eyes, and Tommy adjusted the lamp shade so that light no longer fell across his father's face. Tommy gathered his own belongings to make his way from the room.

When he reached the doorway, he thought he heard Jeff say in the faintest whisper, "I love you, Tommy. You are my son."

But when Tommy turned, his father's eyes were closed and his shallow breath was steady as if he were already asleep.

And Tommy never saw his father alive again.

Because Tommy was never certain of his father's last words to him, he chose to make another memory the benediction for his father's story. Slightly more than a year before Jeff's stroke, in the summer of 1988, Tommy attended New Orleans ceremonies commemorating the twentieth anniversary of George Washington Brown's assassination. A statue of Brown had been commissioned and was to be unveiled in the grassy neutral ground of Jefferson Davis Parkway at the intersection of Bienville Street.

Tommy flew into New Orleans and stayed with his mother as usual. On the night before the ceremony, he got a call from Preacher Martin, who asked Tommy to meet him for a drink at the Columns Hotel on St. Charles Avenue. When Tommy arrived, Preacher was sitting at a table on the porch, smoking a Camel Light with the filter broken off. Preacher was dressed as he had for years, in jeans, a polo shirt, a sports jacket and a blue Chicago Cubs baseball cap.

"What in the hell are you doing out here on the porch, old-timer?" Tommy asked. "Have you gotten too old to remember it's the middle of August?"

"I see you've gone soft up there in the North, Professor," Preacher said. "Man can't take the heat, ought to stay out of the South."

Tommy laughed. "I think the expression goes, if you can't take the heat, you ought to stay out of Harry Truman's kitchen."

"What did Harry Truman know? He was an irascible old bastard, and I don't like him even if he has become fashionable."

"Come on," Tommy said, "Let's go inside where it's cool."

"Naw," Preacher said. "Smoky as hell in there."

Tommy laughed. "You're a lunatic," he said.

"Thank you very much," Preacher said. "Now go in there and get yourself something to drink and bring me back a Johnny Red and water."

"You seen your old man yet?" Preacher asked when Tommy returned.

"Not yet."

Preacher took a sip of his drink, staring at Tommy the whole time. "But you're planning to," he said.

"I always do," Tommy replied. Preacher looked at him without saying anything. "In the last few years," Tommy added.

"You seen him this year?"

"I haven't been in town since Christmas, and he wasn't here. He and Muffin were on some cruise down to Cancun."

Preacher snapped the filter off another cigarette and lit it. "Old Jeff's not doing so well. Doesn't have good health habits like me."

Tommy smiled. He wished this man had been his father instead of Jeff. "Muffin sends us newsy little letters all the time, and she hasn't mentioned anything. What's the problem?"

"Old age," Preacher said.

"He's only sixty-four. That's not so old anymore. Besides, he's the same age as you. And despite your good health habits, you don't look in such bad shape."

"I just hide it better than he does. Besides, the man has had all these young wives. He kept getting older; his wives stayed the same age. They're probably fucking him to death."

"Yeah, well, my father's fondness for younger women is kind of a sore subject with me."

Preacher's eyes were glassy, and his hand shook as he brought the cocktail glass to his lips. He was getting old, too.

"Let me ask you something, Preacher. What is it about all the ministers of your generation couldn't keep their peckers in their pants?"

"Pussy'll make you do crazy things," Preacher said.

Ignoring him, Tommy said, "Dr. Brown, my father, Dr. King, slimeballs like Jimmy Swaggart and Jim Bakker. All adulterers. They think the ten commandments had an exception for preachers?"

"See, you ask me questions, and you don't listen to what I tell you. Old Testament is full of it. Good men, good pussy, bad combination."

"Yeah, well, why not you? I never heard a single rumor about you."

"You never heard it because I was too ugly to get any. Scrawny little bastard. My army pack weighed more than I did. Went bald when I was twenty-four."

"So you never cheated on Nell Leigh?"

"Only with my hand," Preacher said and chortled.

"God, I love you," Tommy said, laughing.

"Well, I love you, too, bubba. And that's why I'm trying to get you to do the right thing about your old man. You gotta remember there's lots worse things in life than extracurricular tail."

Tommy stared unsmiling at Preacher.

"Okay, you son-of-a-bitch. Your father fucked up. Big time. I don't defend it. He shouldn'ta done it. Neither shoulda G.W. nor any of the rest of 'em. But the fact is that they did, and there you have it. Do you wipe out everything else they did because of it?"

"G.W. was wiped out because of what my father did," Tommy snapped.

Preacher took a swallow of his drink and wiped his mouth with the back of his hand. "One way to look at it, I don't doubt."

"What other way is there?" Tommy said wearily.

"Might reflect that a maniac came up stalking G.W. with a gun and old Jeff went out to take the bullet. Didn't succeed, but that's what he did."

"That wasn't what happened, and you know it."

"Ben wasn't aiming to shoot G.W., I reckon, but who knew that at the time. Not even your old man, I figure. And I know what I saw. I saw a man waving a gun and screaming, and I saw Jeff Caldwell put himself between that man and his friend. What was understood and when, I guess Jeff will confide to his Maker someday. And at some level, it doesn't matter. Ben Watson knew what he did before. I know what Jeff Caldwell did that day."

Tommy didn't say anything in response, and Preacher reached out and squeezed Tommy's forearm.

The next morning before the commemoration, Preacher picked up Tommy at Billye's and drove him over to the Congregationalist parsonage. It had been a full year since Tommy had seen Jeff, and Tommy was shocked at his father's physical decline. Jeff used a cane now, and he looked so unsteady coming across the porch that Tommy jumped out of the car to help him down the front steps.

At the ceremony there were speeches by Everett Essex, Robert Brown, the mayor and Preacher, among others. Jeff had been invited to speak but had declined. It was a hot day, and the event was scheduled at noon so that people could attend on their lunch hour. But the turnout was poor. Twenty years had gone by, and Tommy knew there were kids in college who had never heard of George Washington Brown. Halfway through the speeches Jeff began to teeter. Afraid his father was going to faint from the heat, Tommy helped him to a concrete bench. At the end of the ceremony, however, Jeff insisted on getting up to join in as the crowd sang "We Shall Overcome."

Just as they had in the days of the movement, the crowd locked arms and swayed as they sang. Jeff squatted painfully to lay his cane on the ground in front of him, and when he stood, he and Tommy and Preacher and Robert and Everett and a line of others wrapped their arms around the shoulders of the person next to them and sang, Tommy and Jeff next to each other, father and son together, arm in arm, united, lifting their voices as one in their revered anthem of protest.

Fredrick Barton

Fredrick Barton is the author of the novels *Courting Pandemonium, Black and White on the Rocks* (originally published as *With Extreme Prejudice), and The El Cholo Feeling Passes.* Mr. Barton is also author (with composer Jay Weigel) of the jazz opera *Ash Wednesday.* He has written on film since 1980 for the New Orleans weekly *Gambit* and since 1989 for *The Cresset,* a national review of literature, the arts and public affairs. Mr. Barton's many writing awards include a Louisiana Division of the Arts Prize in Literature; the Alex Waller Memorial Award, the New Orleans Press Club's highest honor for print journalism; the Stephen T. Victory Award, the Louisiana Bar Association's prize for feature writing; the New Orleans Press Club's annual first prize in criticism on 11 occasions; and the William Faulkner Prize in fiction, awarded to *A House Divided.* Mr. Barton was educated at Valparaiso University, UCLA and the University of Iowa. He has taught at the University of New Orleans since 1979 and now serves as Dean of the College of Liberal Arts.